SO-AWD-065

# MURDER IN CONTAINMENT

*A Doyle and Acton Mystery*

Anne Cleeland

**ARTEMIS**
—PRESS—

Copyright © 2016 Anne Cleeland
All rights reserved.

ISBN: 0692774424
ISBN 13: 9780692774427

*For Justice Moore, who is truly honorable; and for all others like her.*

# 1

"Stand by."

Detective Sergeant Kathleen Doyle listened to Williams's voice in her earpiece, and held her breath; the suspect was approaching. It was cold, and as she crouched behind the unmarked police vehicle, she crossed her arms and huddled into the side of the car, her ears on the stretch. The nervous anticipation was not helping the uncertain state of her stomach.

"Stand by. DCI Drake at the ready."

Thankfully, there'd been two days in a row without rain, so it wasn't overly damp. Chief Inspector Acton hadn't wanted her anywhere near this particular trap and seizure, but she'd pitched a hormonally-induced fit, and he'd finally agreed to put her on the perimeter, as long as she swore on all the holy relics that she'd not stir a step. Over-protective knocker, she thought crossly; there was little that could go wrong with this particular suspect, and she'd certainly earned the right to be present when he was arrested. She watched her breath form a cloud on the vehicle, and then leaned in to press the side of her face against the cold surface, which seemed to relieve her nausea.

With some regret, she pulled away, because she was worried that the perspiration on her skin would make her stick to the car. Ignominious, is what it would be, to have to ask the arresting officers to peel her off the vehicle. She mouthed the word, "ignominious," and watched another cloud appear on the cold surface. Doyle was attempting to improve her vocabulary again, and that was a ten-pound word, if she did say so herself.

"Suspect approaches; stand by."

Letting out a careful breath, Doyle gathered her feet beneath her, slowly, so as not to allow her boots to scrape the pavement. With any luck, she wouldn't get sick alongside the curb and ruin everything. Mind over matter, she assured herself; best not to think about it.

Straining to listen in the silence, she waited to hear the footsteps that should be approaching on the street. Acton's team was stationed at their posts, well-hidden so as not to give the suspect any hint that he was enjoying his last few moments of freedom. The area around the park was as deserted as could be anticipated at this time of year, at this time of night, and in this area of London.

"DCI Drake to go."

Acton would be at the operational command post behind an enclosure wall, along with DI Williams, who was relaying his orders, and DCI Drake, who was to be used as the bait for this particular trap. Moving carefully to peer over the hood of her vehicle, Doyle saw Drake step forward and loiter at the edge of the sidewalk. He wore an overcoat that concealed a bullet-proof Kevlar vest, and no one observing him would imagine he was deliberately exposing himself to a killer; his posture was relaxed, his attitude slightly impatient. Drake had courage—you had to give him that; this killer's m.o. was a single shot to the back of the head, which was impossible to completely protect against. They were counting on the fact that the suspect didn't know that he'd been twigged, and therefore wouldn't shoot immediately, but would walk along with Drake, and then attempt to shoot him unawares. Hopefully before he could accomplish this aim, he would be taken down and arrested—easy to imagine the fuss Professional Standards would make, if this operation resulted in Drake's getting himself murdered.

"Stand by. On my signal."

Her gaze fixed on Drake, Doyle flexed her fingers in her gloves, and took a deep, careful breath. She was pregnant, and the only reason Acton, her husband, allowed her to be present was because she'd solved this thorny case, and therefore deserved to be. He also knew she wanted to speak to the killer because they were friends of sorts; as a compromise, he'd agreed that she could approach, once the cuffs were on.

The suspect was not your usual villain. Kevin Maguire was a newspaper reporter who was dying of cancer and—faced with his own mortality—had developed a fit of remorse with respect to murderers he'd unwittingly aided, in his career as a reporter. When Doyle realized that a serial killer was serving out vigilante justice, she'd painstakingly solved the case, although there hadn't been enough evidence to prosecute Maguire—that whole presumption-of-innocence thing was often a sticky wicket.

Even without evidence, she was certain that he was the killer, and so she'd confronted him to request that he stop killing people. He'd politely declined, explaining that he'd one more murder to do, and despite her best efforts, she could not talk him round. However, she'd left their meeting with the impression that the last victim was someone she knew, and so she'd put together a search criteria, trying to tie people she knew with Maguire's newspaper articles from the past. Even though it was like trying to find the proverbial needle in the haystack, as a result of her research, she concluded that Chief Inspector Drake might be a target, and so he was duly warned. When Maguire did indeed call to meet with Drake, this trap and seizure was quickly set up.

There—Doyle could hear approaching footsteps, coming from across the way, and she watched as the suspect came into view. Drake stood calmly by, his hands in his coat pockets. "Maguire?" the DCI asked in a genial tone. "Is that you?"

Small wonder he doesn't recognize him, thought Doyle. Maguire—formerly stout and rumpled in the best reporter tradition—was now positively cadaverous.

"Chief Inspector," the suspect replied in a thready voice. "Thank you so much for meeting with me; I hope it is not too inconvenient."

They turned to walk away from her, and Doyle could no longer make out the words. She knew the reporter had lured Drake to this deserted place by promising information that had to be delivered away from potential eavesdroppers—just the kind of thing most appealing to a detective, and most likely to get him out late, on a cold night. Any moment now; she held her breath, and waited.

"Go, go, go," said the voice in her ear. Drake shouted, and Doyle sprang up like a hound to the horn, unable to control her reaction, and banging her knee in her haste. She watched Drake easily overpower the weakened Maguire, as three other PCs closed in to bring the suspect to the ground.

"Suspect in custody. Stand down."

Since she'd promised Acton she would stay back until Maguire was cuffed, Doyle waited until Williams began reading the caution before approaching the group on the park's pathway. Acton was giving direction to the PCs and the evidence crew, whilst Drake calmly brushed the leaves off his overcoat, as though baiting a killer was nothing out of the ordinary.

The suspect also stood rather calmly— considering that his situation was now very bleak indeed—and fixed his hollow gaze on Doyle, as she came forward.

"Ah," he said, with a faint smile. "*Cherchez la femme.*"

Doyle wasn't certain was this meant, but soberly assessed him. "I wish you'd put an end to it, my friend. Now you'll be numberin' your days in prison, and with your own lurid story in the press."

"You warned me," the man agreed in a mild tone. "I should have listened."

This last remark, interestingly enough, was not true. Doyle had a gift for reading people—inherited, perhaps, from some distant Irish ancestor—and she could usually recognize when lies were being told. With a slight frown, she watched as the officers heeded Acton's signal to escort the suspect to the police vehicle. So—it appeared that Maguire had indeed listened to her, when she'd tried to warn him off, but for some reason he'd gone ahead and tried to murder Drake anyway.

As the PCs loaded Maguire into the back of the unmarked, Acton approached to pull her coat more firmly around her. "Williams will take him in for booking, so that I may take you home."

"I'm not feelin' so well," Doyle admitted, wishing she could go back and press her face against the cold car, again.

"I know."

Of course he did. She'd been minding her own business, working homicides with the famed Chief Inspector Acton, when he'd unexpectedly proposed marriage—unexpectedly being a nice way to say that she'd been completely blindsided. She'd known that he was brilliant and reclusive; what she hadn't known was that he suffered from an obsessive condition that featured her as its object. Because she wasn't sure how to handle such a situation, she'd decided that the better part of valor was to marry the man, and then work out what to do later. She'd no regrets, despite the occasional crisis—well, more than occasional, truth to tell, but hopefully tapering off. This one, for instance, had ended very satisfactorily, even though there was still a niggling loose end.

"Well done," said her husband quietly. "It was a good catch; you probably saved Drake's life."

"A life worth savin', knock wood."

This was the niggling loose end; Maguire's pattern had been to kill a suspect from an earlier cold case who'd been acquitted, based on Maguire's sympathetic newspaper coverage—but whom later events had shown was guilty, all along. For each of these victims, there was always a second, more recent murder. Doyle had found an old Maguire article in the archives about Drake, who'd been a Detective Sergeant at the time a civilian had been accidently killed. A pawn broker had reported a burglary, but apparently mistook Drake for the suspect. In the ensuing altercation, Drake had wrestled the man's weapon away, but in the process had accidentally shot and killed the pawn broker. The security video—grainy analog at the time—did not seem to show any wrongdoing by the detective, only a tragic case of mistaken identity. For once, Maguire's article had been on the side of the police, so that instead of showcasing the bereft widow, and reminding the public of other instances of police misconduct, he'd argued that an officer shouldn't be second-guessed, when confronted with such a dangerous situation.

However, since Maguire had indeed contacted Drake all these years later—and had planned to kill him—it raised an uncomfortable truth; it meant Maguire believed that Drake's shooting of the pawn broker in the old case was, in fact, intentional. Despite discreet inquiries, Doyle could not discover why this would be; Drake did not have a reputation for being quick to fire, and there'd been no other reports of excessive force in his personnel file. The handsome DCI had a reputation as a ladies' man, but other than that, he'd been an exemplary detective, with an eye to scaling the CID hierarchy.

It all made little sense, and Doyle was eager to ask some pointed questions of Maguire, now that the reporter was in custody. Acton seemed disinclined to pursue it—no doubt because Drake was a fellow DCI—but it didn't fit Maguire's profile to try to murder someone who was not, in fact, a killer. It would be a bit tricky, because Maguire's official interrogation would be recorded, but Doyle hoped she could arrange for a private moment to ask him why he thought Drake got away with murder, in that long-ago case.

A forensic photographer with the Scene of Crime Officers was asked to take photographs of Maguire's weapon as it was tagged-and-bagged, and Doyle noted that the photographer wasn't the blonde woman who usually worked on Acton's cases. Teasing, she asked him, "Where's your SOCO, Michael? Have you thrown her over, poor thing?" Acton was handsome and titled, which meant he had many admirers—not that he paid any attention. One of these was the female photographer who was only too happy to serve on any case under his supervision.

He didn't deem the question worthy of a reply, and instead took her elbow. "Let's take you home."

Doyle teetered on the edge of asking if she could ride in the unmarked police vehicle with Maguire, but decided she'd best not press her luck with Acton, and besides, she didn't want to be sick in front of everyone, and the odds were beginning to favor such a humiliating occurrence. Tomorrow she'd find an opportunity to meet with the suspect, once he'd had a few hours to stare at the bleak cell walls, contemplating his fate.

Their footsteps echoing in the now-quiet night, Doyle accompanied Acton over to the Range Rover. "Will you take the interrogation?" The Maguire case was a delicate situation, and Acton was usually called upon when the Met was probing into matters delicate. Scotland Yard would not be covered in glory by the revelation that murderers from prior cases had been allowed to go free, and even though it had been largely the press's fault, the press was unlikely to publicize this unhappy fact.

Acton was a favorite with the public, who considered him above reproach, in part because he held a title. For reasons that were unclear, the public loved its aristocracy. The illustrious chief inspector was often enlisted to handle any public relations problems that cropped up—indeed, he was already hip-deep in some mysterious case involving the Home Office, that was being kept very quiet. There was the Wexton Prison corruption case, too—quite the plateful, and the last needful thing was for the public to read about yet another situation where the justice system did not seem to be so very just, after all.

"We may need to call in someone from another jurisdiction."

Doyle nodded. Since the crime involved one of their own, it was probably more appropriate that the matter be handed over to someone not on staff at the Met, so as to avoid the appearance of impropriety. Unfortunately, this case had all the makings of a public relations nightmare: a serial killer, past murderers let go, and a cloud of suspicion hanging over a DCI. The case against Maguire was straightforward, of course—save for the niggling question about his motive for Drake's murder. Perhaps Maguire would agree to negotiate a plea, so that the CID could keep the more lurid details under wraps, and away from the papers.

After seeing her settled in the car, Acton pulled out into the street, adjusting the heater as he drove. "Are you hungry? Should we pick up a fruit pie, on the way?"

"No," Doyle replied shortly, as she didn't even want to think about eating. "And can you turn off the heat? I'll be needin' some cold air on my face, or I won't be answerable for the consequences."

He glanced over at her, worried. "Shall I roll the windows down?"

"Faith, I don't *know*, Michael." She immediately regretted her tone, and sighed in apology, as she leaned her head back on the leather headrest. "I'm sorry. I'm that sick of bein' sick."

"Hang on; we'll be home in short order."

Thankfully, the streets were quiet, and there wasn't much traffic, as he navigated his way toward their flat in Kensington. His mobile pinged, and after noting the caller's ID, he took the call. "Acton." He listened, then made an impatient sound. "Send him to the morgue, then. I'll need a full report."

After ringing off, he announced quietly, "Maguire's dead. Williams said he died in the car on the way to booking—some sort of seizure."

"Mother a' *mercy*." Doyle stared at him for a moment. "Have them check his hands and fingers for trace—he wasn't wearin' gloves, and he may have taken somethin'."

"Right," nodded Acton, as he rang the call-back to Williams.

Doyle rolled down her window, and took some deep breaths, trying to steady her stomach. Maguire hadn't much longer to live, and may have had something on hand, just in case suicide seemed the best option. She knew exactly how he felt, as she reached for one of the plastic bags she kept in the dashboard compartment for just this sort of occasion, and retched miserably into it—she couldn't even do a decent job of retching, being as she hadn't eaten much this day.

Her husband stroked her back in sympathy. "Not much more of this, I think; the nausea should be tapering off, soon." Acton had bought a medical treatise about pregnancy, and regularly studied its contents, comparing her progress.

"There'll be nothin' left of me soon."

"On the contrary; I would say there's definitely more of you, lately."

"Not the nicest thing to say, Michael." She was cross and tired.

"Nonsense. You are utterly beautiful."

With a mighty effort, she mustered up a smile, and leaned back to close her eyes. "I'm sorry I'm such a crackin' trial."

Her husband reached over and gently placed his palm on the slight bump of her abdomen. "Mary, you must stop plaguing your poor mother." Acton had decided the baby was a girl, and he'd further decided to name her after Doyle's late mother.

"You'll not fool her with your tone, Michael—she knows she's got you well under her thumb."

His hand wandered up to her breasts, which were more in evidence lately. "I'd like to have her mother under my thumb."

"Michael," she laughed, scandalized. "Not in front of the baby."

# 2

Once back at the flat, Reynolds took one look at Doyle, and insisted she be put to bed with a heating pad. The servant then prepared warm milk with dry toast points, and hovered with a critical eye while Acton coaxed her into eating them. Reynolds remarked to no one in particular that it was quite a long day for a lady in her condition, and Acton was immediately defensive, explaining that Doyle had insisted she attend the trap and seizure because she'd broken the case.

Doyle intervened to quieten everyone down, before her head started aching again. "I couldn't miss it, Reynolds; please don't blister Acton." She then told Reynolds about Maguire's unexpected death en route to his booking. "He may have done himself in, poor man."

But the servant was unmoved. "A good riddance," he declared as he cleared her plate away. "And it spares the rest of us from having to hear him made into a sympathetic figure by the press."

Doyle reluctantly fingered her cup; she was supposed to be drinking milk, but wondered if anyone would notice if she poured it into the Sèvres vase, on the sly. "It's a hard one you are, Reynolds. I felt sorry for him, myself; tryin' to find a way to ease his guilt."

But Reynolds only sniffed. "I'm afraid I haven't much sympathy for murderers, madam."

She sighed, and took another sip. "Then save your sympathy for the Met; it doesn't help public relations, to have the suspects dyin' in custody, willy-nilly. There'll be a *massive* review."

Reynolds knew upon which side his bread was buttered, and affected outrage. "Surely law enforcement cannot be blamed, madam, if the man was in ill health."

"There will be a review," Doyle assured the servant with deep regret. "A death in custody is always a black mark."

"I cannot imagine the public will muster any outrage," Reynolds insisted as he brushed up the last of the crumbs. "Instead, it's good riddance to bad rubbish."

"It's a hard one you are, Reynolds," Doyle repeated, rather wishing everyone would stop talking so that she could rest her poor head. "Life cannot be held so cheaply."

Reynolds assessed her with an expert eye. "That being said, perhaps we can make an attempt at chicken broth."

"Perhaps," said Doyle doubtfully. "Let me have a lie-down, first."

The men folk quietly withdrew, and Doyle lay in bed, clutching the heating pad and watching them move about the kitchen, as Reynolds served Acton his dinner. Thinking of nothing in particular, she dozed off, listening to the men's voices. Later, she awakened when Acton lifted the covers to join her in bed, moving carefully so as not to wake her. Remembering his earlier comment in the car, she moved toward him, receptive. Her libido had receded somewhat during the past months, but she was nevertheless willing to please him. He held her against him, however, and whispered that she should rest; it had been a long day. Happy to comply, she drifted back in to sleep, with Acton rhythmically stroking her arms, as was his habit.

Later that night, Doyle had another one of her dreams. Once again, she was in a room, watching as a man around her own age methodically barricaded the door, lifting heavy objects to pile against it, his back to her so that she could not see his face. There was danger on the other side, and she stood in uncertainty, wondering what she should do to help. The dream was extraordinarily vivid; even as she dreamed, she acknowledged to herself that it was a dream, and marveled that it didn't seem like a dream.

She awoke as she always did; suddenly, and with a start. She decided not to wake Acton this time; he needed his sleep as much as she did, and truly, it wasn't a nightmare—not the kind where you try to call out, but can't. Strange that she kept dreaming of danger; Acton probably would say it was a subconscious fear of childbirth, or some such—although why the young man was present wasn't clear. She wasn't certain, but she had the impression he was DI Williams. Silly, pregnant knocker, she chided herself; dreaming of Williams—it must be your hormones, running amok.

As though she'd conjured him up by the thought, Williams called her the next morning, after she'd settled in at work. "Hey."

"Hey yourself; what's up? Anyone else dyin' in custody?" She paused, and then added so as to tease him, "Sir." Since he was now a Detective Inspector, he outranked her.

"Not so funny, Kath. And here I was calling to offer contraband."

Leaning back, she smiled into the mobile. "You should be ashamed of yourself, Thomas; it's like a drug dealer, you are."

"Is that a no?"

"Heavens, no. When and where?"

"The deli?"

"It's rainin'," she pointed out, her gaze moving to the far windows.

"I'd rather not talk on the premises."

This was of interest, and so she slowly sat upright. "All right; I'll meet you there in ten."

"Do you have an umbrella?"

"Indeed I do," she replied, annoyed. Honestly; the men in her life treated her like she was a baby, just because she had forgotten an umbrella, once or twice in the past. "See you there."

After buttoning her coat, and duly hoisting her umbrella, she walked over to the deli, located down the street from headquarters. Doyle had been trying to give up coffee during her pregnancy—her only vice, truly—but would share a small cup with Williams on the sly once in a while. How much could it hurt? People had been drinking coffee since the dawn of time—she was certain her mother didn't stop drinking coffee whilst pregnant. Suddenly, she thought of her strange dreams, and it gave her pause for a moment. No connection, she decided resolutely, and carried on.

Once inside, she shook out her umbrella, and spotted Williams at a table away from the windows. He could be counted as her best friend, although there were those occasions when she had to keep him firmly at arm's length, because he carried a torch for her, did DI Williams. It was one of the hazards of being an emotional tuning fork, so to speak; you were aware of secret longings that were better kept secret. And as Williams was Acton's henchman, this made things a bit complicated—despite his sterling reputation, Doyle was aware that Acton was involved in some unsavory doings that couldn't withstand the light of day.  He was a vigilante in his own right, and her main goal in life—aside from trying to eat something, once in a while—was to try to keep her wayward husband on the straight and narrow path. For example, she was certain he kept a cache of illegal guns in the safe at their flat, and that he was involved in selling black market weapons. Williams was Acton's aider and abettor, but she truly couldn't fault him for it—it would be the pot versus the kettle, as she was an aider and abettor, herself. And despite his warm feelings for her, Williams behaved himself, and had been shown to be solidly in her corner, time and again.

She nearly snatched the coffee cup from his hand, and he warned, "Easy—it's hot."

"Why is it," she wondered aloud, savoring her sip like a pilgrim at the font, "—that the only things that sound appetizin' to me are the things I'm not supposed to be eatin'?"

"God's cruel joke," he suggested. She'd made him promise never to mention that she was thin, and needed to eat more; she got enough of that sauce from Acton and Reynolds, and it was more than a body could bear.

She took another sip, even though the first one had burnt her tongue. "What's afoot?"

"The Drake angle."

He needn't say more, and she nodded, suddenly somber. Williams had come to the same conclusion she had; if Maguire wanted to kill Drake, it was with good reason. She slowly shook her head. "I looked very carefully into the pawn broker's death, Thomas; it was the only Maguire story where Drake was a potential killer, and I couldn't find anythin' the least bit murky about it." It went without saying that their concerns would not be discussed with anyone else—Drake was a DCI, after all. Talk about bad public relations, that would be a topper.

Williams thought about it, absently fiddling with the sugar packets. "Could it be another case?"

With some regret, Doyle shook her head. "The others don't fit the profile, Thomas; Maguire's victims got off, thanks to the newspaper's manipulation of public sympathy. The only case that fits that m.o. is the pawn broker's death, and the video shows that the man went after Drake first—no doubt thinkin' he was the robber—and that Drake just defended himself."

With a glance at the door, Williams leaned forward. "You're forgetting that the profile has two parts; the person got off, but a more recent murder showed that he was guilty in the first place."

Actually, Doyle had been striving mightily to forget this unfortunate fact. In the other Maguire murders, the victims had all gone on to kill again, which showed—to Maguire's remorse, apparently—that the suspect had been guilty the first time around. Each had a second, more recent murder that had triggered Maguire's vigilantism.

She leaned in also, and lowered her voice, "Should we look into it, d'you think? We could start with this year's firearms report; that shouldn't be difficult to do." Any officer who fired a weapon was compelled to complete reams of paperwork, and the report was carefully reviewed by the Detective Chief Superintendent, who was the top law enforcement officer at the Met. However, DCIs like Acton and Drake were rarely in a firearms situation, because they were not usually in the trenches, so to speak. For that matter, even PCs were not likely to discharge a firearm; the use of weapons by police was carefully controlled.

Williams kept his neutral gaze on the table. "Perhaps you should speak to Acton about it."

Doyle immediately understood this to mean Williams didn't wish to speak to Acton himself, and that this particular request must be the reason for this off-premises meeting. It might have something to do with Acton's illegal guns-running—perhaps Williams thought that Drake was involved, somehow. Drake's victim was a pawn broker, after all, and pawn brokers were notorious for black market. Doyle appreciated the delicacy of Williams' position and the reason for his request; he would not want to ask Acton to look into deeds committed by Drake which Williams was well-aware Acton was committing himself on a regular basis. And as an added caution, Acton was Doyle's husband, so he had to be careful about what he said.

"All right," she agreed. "Do I mention your name?"

"Use your judgment."

She nodded, and they sat for a few quiet moments, thinking it over, as the rain pattered against the windows. Doyle had to admit she had a hard time imagining Drake taking the trouble of murdering anyone; he was a political creature, self-absorbed and careful not to exert himself overmuch. It didn't make a lot of sense to her.

Williams interrupted her musings. "There's another favor I'd like to ask."

"Ask away," she said readily, hoping it was something easier than the last favor.

"Morgan Percy has asked to meet with me away from chambers, and off the record; she says she may have information about a case, but is not sure how to go about it."

Doyle was suddenly on high alert. Williams was asking because their training told them it was best to have a third party present at any off-the-record meeting with criminal defense personnel, in the event the officer was being set up for a charge of impropriety. On the other hand, Doyle knew there was something smoky about Percy's place of employment. Percy was a junior barrister at one of the prestigious Inns of Court, and Doyle and Williams had visited the place a few months ago, trying to track down the vigilante killer. At the time, Doyle had the feeling that the chambers was awash in secrets, a feeling strengthened by the discovery that Percy's senior barrister, Mr. Moran, was staggering drunk by mid-morning.

"Of course I'll come along with you, although Percy'll be thinkin' me a dog-in-the-manger." It had been evident that Percy found DI Williams very attractive, and small blame to her; Williams was a fine specimen.

If she'd hoped to provoke a response from him, she was to be disappointed. "Thanks; when are you available?"

"My calendar is clear," Doyle replied in a regretful tone. "I have officially solved myself out of my last assignment." Now that the Maguire case had concluded, she'd have to find another task—and that was not as easy as it sounded. Her hyper-protective, certifiable husband did not want her working out in the field where she might be exposed to danger, especially now that there was a bun in the oven. She had little choice; her hyper-protective, certifiable husband also controlled her case load. Checkmate.

"Thanks Kath; can we go tomorrow morning? Munoz and I are doing interviews on the Wexton Prison case this afternoon."

"Right then," she agreed, privately hoping she wouldn't be sick. Mornings were the worst—next to evenings and afternoons.

# 3

Later that day, Doyle stood beside Acton and the coroner, as they somberly contemplated the dead SOCO photographer, lying in her bleak stainless steel drawer in the morgue. Law enforcement necessarily involved personal risk; still, it was never easy to lose one of their own, and one would think a scene of crime officer—and a photographer, to boot—would not be in any particular danger. Upon hearing the news, Doyle had sacrificed her lunch hour to visit the decedent—not much of a sacrifice, really, since she'd no appetite to speak of in the first place. And despite the fact he was hip deep in high-profile cases, Acton had offered to accompany her, and so here they were, taking a long, dispassionate look at the remains of the blonde woman in her thirties, who'd evidently met a bad end. The lividity marks showed she'd died prone on her back, and the bruise patterns indicated one or more blows to the forehead. After a small silence, Doyle asked Acton, "Do we have a preliminary?"

"Found dead in her flat; reported by a neighbor who noticed the smell. Possible domestic violence; the neighbor remembers hearing an altercation with a man."

Dr. Hsu indicated with a finger, "Cause of death was blunt force trauma; fractures to the frontal bone, and supraorbital process."

Acton nodded. "She faced her killer, then. Defensive wounds?" If there had been a face-to-face battle, the chances were good that the woman would have helpful DNA on her hands or arms.

"None apparent," was the coroner's regretful answer. "And although we took swabs from under her nails, preliminaries indicate that she was wearing latex gloves, even though there were none at the scene. Some spot bruising on her forearms—nothing of significance."

"Perhaps because she warded off the blows?" Doyle demonstrated by raising her arms and crossing them. "Otherwise, she just let someone come up and conk her in the face, which seems unlikely."

"Only spot bruising on her arms," Acton reminded her. "Therefore, not from blows."

Doyle frowned as she considered this paradox—paradox being a vocabulary word—but Acton was apparently following his own train of thought.

"Was she reclining when struck?"

"Upright," the coroner replied. "Then fell back."

"Sexual activity?"

"Nothing evident."

"Was she bound?"

"No—no bruising at the wrists."

"Tox?"

"Prelim screen shows no drugs or alcohol."

Acton was silent for a moment, and Doyle took the opportunity to ask, "Who's been assigned to the case? And have we any likely suspects?"

Acton replied, "DI Chiu is the crime scene manager. No obvious suspects; no indication there was a steady boyfriend."

Doyle made a wry mouth. "Not a surprise, my friend. She carried a crackin' torch for you, you know."

He did not disclaim, but remained thoughtful. "That doesn't mean she didn't have a boyfriend—or someone."

But Doyle shook her head doubtfully. "With her, I'm not so sure; she was the reclusive type—I imagine she rarely went anywhere. She probably did those role-playin' video games, and kept a cat."

Dr. Hsu lifted the corpse's hand. "The cat had started in on her fingers." It was an unfortunate truism that when cats were hungry, they were not sentimental creatures.

"No sign that the motive was robbery," Acton noted. "But it may be helpful to delve into that aspect, and take another careful look 'round."

Doyle wasn't sure she followed him. "And why is that?"

He crossed his arms, his hooded gaze on the woman's remains. "She was struck facing her attacker, yet there are no signs that she attempted to ward off the blow. What does that tell you?"

The penny dropped, and Doyle looked up at him. "She couldn't see him."

He nodded. "So it was either dark, or she was blindfolded. But she was upright, not bound, and we've ruled out sex play, so it must have been dark. He may have been lying in wait."

Doyle knit her brow, considering this. "But there were reports of a verbal altercation."

"Indeed."

"Then—then I suppose we're speakin' of two different people?"

"Perhaps," said Acton, who was not a leaper-to-conclusions.

At Acton's signal, the coroner moved in to zip the bag and re-shelve the corpse, and Doyle took the opportunity to observe in a low voice, "I don't know, Michael; it doesn't seem in keepin'—that she had a fight with someone outside her flat, and then got coshed by some-one else, waitin' inside. Some people—" she tried to put her instinct into words. "Some people are lookin' to get themselves murdered, and some people are not. She's one of the nots."

"Yet here she is," he gently pointed out.

Stubbornly, she persisted. "I'm only spoutin' your theory, my friend; if the facts don't fit the usual motivations, then attention should be paid. The SOCO people are inclined to blather in their cups—perhaps she said the wrong thing to the wrong person, and this was a containment murder; a murder to contain any further spilling-of-the-beans. It may be useful to take a peek at her recent caseload."

Acton made no immediate response, and she eyed him, aware that the dead woman was willing to work off the grid for Acton, so to speak, and on at least one occasion had manipulated evidence for him. Hopefully, I am not yet again investigating a murder that my own husband committed, she thought crossly, and briefly toyed with the idea of asking him outright. Instead, she asked, "Was she doing anythin' for you on the side, Michael?"

He was amused, and glanced at her. "Is that a euphemism?"

"No, it is not." She was not in a joking mood, a rarity for her.

"No, on both counts." He paused. "I discouraged any attempts to communicate outside of work, and she was someone who didn't want to be rebuked."

No, thought Doyle; she was the type who was content to entertain fantasies, rather than act on them. "Can you put me on the case? I always felt a bit sorry for her, and now I'm sorrier still."

He met her eye, and Doyle knew exactly what he was thinking. "I'll be safe as houses, Michael—and I'm dyin' for a new assignment. I'll just go ask a few questions, have a look round her flat, and see what there is to see." Inspired, she added, "I need somethin' to take my mind off the mornin' sickness; I'll feel better if I'm doin' good works."

"Right, then. But no heroics."

"Not to worry; I am in no shape, my friend."

Acton had to leave after taking a call on some urgent matter, so Doyle rang up DI Chiu with an eye to going out immediately to interview the neighbors—it was important to move quickly, before any leads went cold.

But when she picked up, Chiu was not necessarily pleased to hear that Doyle was to join her team. "The PCs have already done a preliminary, DS Doyle."

"I know, ma'am, but I knew the victim, and I'd like to lend a hand." Doyle then played her trump. "DCI Acton is the SIO, and he's given the go-ahead."

There was a slight pause. "I will meet you there, then."

Doyle copied the address, and then immediately called Williams as she made her way up the stairs from the morgue. "Hey."

"Can't talk long; I'm heading into the interview room."

"I'll make it quick; tell me about DI Chiu."

"Smart. Doesn't suffer fools."

Oh-oh, thought Doyle. "Well, aside from that, why wouldn't she like me?"

"Not a clue, Kath; maybe she's territorial, and doesn't like the Acton connection."

"There's not the smallest chance I'd be promoted over her, for heaven's sake."

"I've got to go—I'll ring you later."

"It's not important, Thomas, I'll see you tomorrow." Thoughtfully, Doyle rang off and headed outside, hoping the victim's flat had been aired out—the scent of decomposition always set her off, nowadays, and she didn't want to give her husband any excuse to take her off her only remaining case.

# 4

D S Syed, the Evidence Officer, was conferring with DI Chiu when Doyle arrived at the SOCO's flat, and so Doyle pulled out her occurrence book and began making notes, whilst they finished up their conversation. The flat was in a respectable building in a quiet area of the city, but the interior was what Doyle had anticipated—cluttered and disorganized; the furniture rather shabby, and the kitchen sink filled with unwashed dishes. As always, Doyle felt a pang of sympathy for the murder victim, who had to suffer not only the indignity of being murdered, but the indignity of having strangers comb through the leftovers of one's life.

The EO was saying to Chiu, "Nothing that stands out on personal electronics; no dating sites or unusual emails. We're looking through her mobile records. Not a lot of calls, though, so it shouldn't take long."

Thinking of Acton's theory, Doyle ventured, "Has burglary been ruled out?"

Syed shook his head. "Burglary seems unlikely; there's no sign of forced entry, and the victim's wallet was laying on the sofa."

Chiu took the opportunity to point out in a neutral tone, "You may wish to familiarize yourself with the preliminary report, DS Doyle."

Feeling herself blush, Doyle explained, "It's only that DCI Acton wondered if she was struck in the dark, ma'am, and didn't see it comin'. She was smacked right in the face, but there were no defensive wounds, as though he caught her completely by surprise."

Chiu considered this theory for a moment, her level gaze surveying the flat, and to her credit, she appeared willing to reassess. "The victim was killed in the spare bedroom—perhaps she heard something, surprised an intruder, he struck her down, and then fled in a panic without stealing anything. It's possible."

But the EO was forced to poke a major hole in the working theory. "Remember that he took the victim's latex gloves with him, on his way out. Doesn't sound very panicked."

Doyle knit her brow at this strange little wrinkle. "So it's true—she was wearin' latex gloves?"

Syed nodded. "Trace found the powder residue that would be inside the gloves—but nothing else on her hands or under her nails; she was completely clean. Since there were no discarded gloves in the flat, we can presume the gloves were removed post-mortem, and taken away."

Without a blink, Chiu accepted this rather bizarre fact, and adjusted her theory. "Perhaps she was cleaning when she heard him. Her attacker took the gloves because he was worried that his DNA was on them."

Doyle reminded her, "There were no signs of a defensive struggle, ma'am." With a nod, she indicated the messy kitchen. "And it doesn't much look like she was doin' the dishes; or cleanin'."

It seemed clear that Chiu had re-assessed Doyle's potential contribution to the case, and was now listening to her suggestions with bit more attention. "Yes—that's true. She must have been wearing gloves for some other reason, then heard the intruder knocking around in the spare room, and gone in to investigate."

With obvious regret, the EO poked yet another hole in yet another theory. "Then why wouldn't she have turned on the lights?"

They thought about this puzzle for a moment, and Doyle was forced to concede, "One of these assumptions must be wrong, then. Perhaps we should be lookin' at it from the other end—circumstantial evidence, instead of forensics. Were all personal papers gathered up?" Doyle was half-dreading that the woman kept an Acton scrapbook; no question she was one of his biggest fans.

Instead, the EO offered up a small smile. "She had your newspaper clipping on her fridge, Officer Doyle."

No need to ask which one; a few months ago, Doyle had jumped off Greyfriars Bridge into the Thames to save Munoz, her colleague. To her extreme embarrassment, she was now something of a local hero, and recognized by well-wishers nearly everywhere she went. Ironically, the glowing newspaper article posted on the SOCO's fridge had been written by Kevin Maguire, the vigilante killer who'd just died in custody.

"Not a lot of circumstantial evidence so far," Chiu continued. "No current or ex-boyfriends, and she hadn't a lot of money. Has trace come up with anything unusual?"

The EO shook his head. "It's a tough one for trace; cat hairs and other miscellaneous fibers on everything—it would be a long slog to try to isolate anything of interest, and we wouldn't know where to start. It's a shame she was killed with blunt force to the frontal lobe; not much blood spatter."

The two other detectives nodded at this seemingly callous remark; if a victim bled, it enhanced the chances that they could pick up footprints, or blood transfer fingerprints left behind. Messy murder scenes usually made their work miles easier.

Carefully, Doyle stepped over to look through the door into the spare bedroom, where the body was found, but the room was semi-empty, and held no spare bed. Instead, in one corner was a tall, carpeted cat's tower. "That's a bit odd, don't you think, ma'am? The rest of the place is so cluttered—you'd think the spare room would be packed to the gills."

"Perhaps the cat wouldn't have it," joked the EO.

Doyle smiled. "There's your suspect, then; the cat. Has he fled the scene?"

"The Animal Care Centre took him to the Metro shelter," said Chiu, who was not the joking-about type. "The SOCO's next of kin is her father, who lives in Liverpool. He's been notified, and will come to identify her this afternoon. I'll speak with him, to see if he can shed any light." She shut down her tablet, and nodded to Doyle. "Let's see if any neighbors are home; someone may have remembered something new, since the time the PCs took their original statements."

Looking self-conscious, the EO ventured, "Before you leave, do you think I could have a snap, Officer Doyle?"

Well-used to it, Doyle dutifully smiled while the man stood beside her, and held up his mobile to take a photograph. "My daughter will be thrilled—she wants to be a police officer, when she grows up."

"Well then; that is excellent." Doyle wondered whether the unborn Mary would also aspire to such a career—although it seemed unlikely that the Honorable Mary Sinclair, daughter of the fourteenth Lord Acton, would be grubbing around, knee-deep in decaying bodies. Reminded, she frowned, slightly. "That's odd; I don't smell decomp in here."

Syed affirmed, "No—the heat was off, and it was cold, so not a lot of decomposition. And she was only here for about twenty hours, after time of death."

"But—but didn't the neighbor report the smell of decomp?"

Doyle caught a flash of grudging approval from Chiu, who opened her tablet to re-check her notes. "Yes—the widow next door complained of the smell; a Mrs. Addersley. Let's go see if she's home."

In response to their knock, a well-dressed, middle-aged woman promptly answered the door, and addressed them in a brisk tone. "You are here about the murder, I suppose."

That's odd, thought Doyle in surprise; and on two different counts. A bit bemused, she followed Chiu into the woman's flat, and took a proffered seat on the sofa, her scalp prickling as it did when her intuitive abilities were alerting her to be wary.

The witness didn't appear threatening, though, as she crossed her hands on her lap, and looked to Chiu with serene coldness, ignoring Doyle as though she weren't there. Fortyish, thought Doyle, and very well turned-out. She looked like she took good care of her skin, and didn't go out in the sun, much.

"I understand you contacted the police about your neighbor," Chiu began.

Addersley nodded. "Yes; I noticed she didn't leave for work that morning—I always hear the door shut. So I wondered if she was ill, but she didn't answer the door when I knocked. When she didn't go to work the next day, I was worried enough to call—she never missed work."

Mother a' mercy, thought Doyle as she sat in stupefied astonishment next to Chiu; not a blessed thing the witness had said was true.

Chiu checked her notes, and continued, "I understand you heard an altercation earlier this week. Can you tell us about it?"

Her hands still crossed, the witness answered without hesitation. "Yes; she had a fight with a man a few nights ago—before she was killed. It must have been that man she was dating; he was a rough sort. I heard him threaten her. He was angry that she didn't want to see him again, and that she wouldn't let him in." She paused. "I was going to call the police, but it didn't sound violent, and I didn't want to embarrass her. Now, of course, I wish I had."

"Description?" asked Chiu, her fingers poised. Doyle said nothing, because there had been no such person.

"A dark-haired man; mid-height." The witness made a vague, apologetic gesture with her graceful hands. "I wish I knew more, but I only got a glimpse."

"How long were they dating?"

The woman considered. "A few weeks? I'm afraid I cannot be certain, I didn't want to pry."

Doyle spoke up. "How long have you lived here, Mrs. Addersley?"

For the first time, the woman's gaze rested on Doyle. "Three years, Officer Doyle."

Doyle was surprised into silence; the woman knew her name—even though they'd not been introduced—and aside from that, she didn't like her very much. Of course, Doyle was recognizable from the bridge-jumping incident—and some people were prejudiced against the Irish—but it seemed more personal than that. Not to mention that the witness continued to lie like the second death.

Doyle could sense that Chiu was impatient with her for interrupting the pertinent line of questioning, and the DI went back to pick up the thread. "During the argument, did you hear her say the man's name? Or did you notice a car, perhaps?"

"I'm afraid not. If only I'd known—"

Chiu was quick to provide comfort. "You mustn't feel badly, Mrs. Addersley; hindsight is always perfect, after all. How well did you know the victim—can you give us any insight into her habits?"

"Just to say hello in the hall; she kept to herself, mostly."

Chiu paused to make a note whilst Doyle sat and stewed, wondering if she should make an attempt to trip up the witness in front of Chiu, or whether she should just button her lip for the present, and then lay the whole before Acton. I'll speak with Acton—and as soon as I can, she decided. This type of dilemma cropped up from time to time; she couldn't disclose why she was aware that lies were being told, but the situation required immediate action.

After the witness confessed that she could recall no further details, Chiu stood and handed over her card. "Thank you, Mrs. Addersley; please don't hesitate to call if you can think of anything else."

"I will. It is a very tragic situation." Whilst telling this particular untruth, the woman's gaze rested for the barest moment on Doyle, who again caught a well-concealed flash of—of what? Anger? Bitterness? Perhaps the woman's deceased husband had been killed by an Irishman, or something; no mistaking that she was like a shard of frozen ice, under that well-groomed exterior.

Doyle followed Chiu down the hallway, furiously trying to understand why this particular witness had decided that the best course of action was to lie to the police, with the obvious answer being that she was complicit in the crime—after all, the woman had been striving mightily to cast blame elsewhere. It seemed a bit unlikely, though; the widow seemed too refined to be lurking about in the dark, waiting to cosh her neighbor—although any first-year detective could tell you that disputes between neighbors oftentimes erupted into murder.

Her thoughts were interrupted by an elderly man, shuffling toward them from the other direction, as they approached the lift. He carried a satchel over his shoulder, as though he were headed to the grocers, and nodded to them, speaking a little loudly in the manner of someone hard of hearing. "Good thing they got the smell off the carpet, what?"

"What sort of smell?" This seemed of interest, as Doyle was reminded that while there'd not been any decomp to speak of, Mrs. Addersley had reported an unusual smell.

"Eh?" said the gentleman.

"What sort of smell?" Doyle asked again, a bit louder.

"That cleaning smell." The man made a face, which served to emphasize his deep wrinkles. "Can't mistake it."

Doyle and Chiu regarded him for a moment, and Doyle knew they were both trying to decide if he was worth the trouble of questioning—the elderly tended not to be good witnesses. Chiu apparently decided to follow up, and raised her voice. "Can you describe the smell, sir?"

Shaggy white brows were raised while this question was considered, and the man waved a bony, age-spotted hand in a vague gesture. "Oh, you know—chemicals."

"Bleach?" Doyle prompted, when nothing further seemed to be forthcoming. Perhaps the killer had thought of using bleach to clean up the site—although there'd been no smell of it in the flat.

"No, no—not bleach; the other one, the one that smells sweet. My late wife used it to polish the furniture." He sighed, his thin chest rising and falling. "Can't mistake it—it brings back memories."

A widower, thought Doyle with sympathy—and lonely, poor man. She'd gained the impression that he had no particular errand to run, but instead sought an excuse to come out to speak with them.

"Someone spilled chemicals, here in the hallway?" asked Chiu, her gaze surveying the carpeting.

The man indicated with a crooked finger. "There. Down by the rubbish chute."

Chiu checked her notes. "You are Mr. Huse? Do you mind if we ask some questions?"

But in the manner of the elderly, Mr. Huse wanted to ask his own questions. "Do they know who killed her, yet? Hard to believe such a thing could happen here—what's the world coming to?"

But Chiu was not one to wax philosophical. "I am afraid I'm not at liberty to discuss a pending investigation, sir. Have you thought of anything that might be of interest, since your interview?"

The man shifted his feet. "I know she had a cat. A great, grey cat."

Ah, thought Doyle.

"Yes, she had a cat," Chiu affirmed with just a hint of impatience. "Did you ever run into her boyfriend, coming in or out?"

But the witness was not going to be led, and continued in his over-loud voice, "Do you know what happened to the cat? Sometimes she'd have me come in and feed it, if she was going to be late. I have a spare key."

Although it was hard to imagine Mr. Huse hefting a blunt instrument, there was no shirking this very interesting fact, and Chiu's voice suddenly became even more businesslike, if it was possible. "I understand you were out of town the night of the murder, Mr. Huse. Is there anyone who could verify this?"

He nodded readily. "Oh, yes. Visiting my sister."

Doyle asked, "Did you leave the key with anyone else, whilst you were away?"

Impatient, the man glanced toward the cordoned-off door at the end of the hall. "Don't be daft; of course not. The cat's not dead too, is he?"

Doyle decided to cut to the nub of this little encounter. "Would it be possible for you to take the cat in, Mr. Huse? He has no home, and I'm thinkin' it would be a great kindness."

The man took an embarrassed glance down the hall toward his own flat, his cheeks a bit pink. "Never had a cat—but he was a nice animal. I suppose I could, if no one else will."

"Well, it's a kind man, you are. Should I retrieve him from the shelter, and bring him back, then?"

The man nodded briefly, his spare frame emanating carefully suppressed pleasure. "Can you bring him tomorrow? Give me a day to buy the necessary."

Chiu was barely suppressing her irritation at this deviation from the task at hand. "Mr. Huse; did you ever see any men, coming in or out of the decedent's flat?"

"Oh, no," he said bluntly, with a definitive shake of his head. "She liked the film stars; would never make a push at a real man."

Much struck by this, Doyle could only agree; the SOCO photographer was the type to fantasize, rather than focus on an eligible man—her crush on Acton only served as an example. After confirming Huse's phone number against the preliminary report, Doyle congratulated herself on having a ready excuse to come back tomorrow without Chiu. Something was very smoky here, starting with the serial liar living next door to the kill site.

# 5

Once out on the pavement, Chiu paused for a moment. "You believed Mr. Huse about the boyfriend, rather than Mrs. Addersley. Why was this?"

As this question was one that should not be answered honestly, Doyle hedged. "I don't know, ma'am—it seemed strange that Mrs. Addersley opened the door to us without first checkin' who it was, considerin' there's an unsolved murder, right next door."

But Chiu did not deem this significant. "She probably heard us knocking about, and had an ear to the door."

Doyle persisted, "And the preliminary report said she was elderly."

"Did it? She may have refused to state her age. And if it was a young PC, he probably thought anyone over thirty was elderly."

"I suppose." Doyle gave it up, and instead offered, "I knew the SOCO—not well, but well enough—and I think Mr. Huse had the right of it. I doubt very much she had a boyfriend, and Mr. Huse is just the type who'd be keepin' a close eye on the comin's and goin's." Much struck, she added, "And if there was a boyfriend, wouldn't he have been the one asked to care for the cat?"

Chiu conceded this point with a slight nod. "True. What of the argument in the hallway, then? Who was that?"

Doyle frowned, thinking about it. "It was someone she didn't want to allow into her flat; otherwise she'd have moved the brangle inside, so as to keep it quiet. It may have been someone she feared, and since she wound up dead, it may well have been the killer."

Chiu thought this over. "Mrs. Addersley seemed credible, but go ahead and run a background on her to see what comes up—and may as well add everyone else in the building, since we haven't a lead. And please check for CCTV at the street level—men coming in who weren't tenants."

"Yes ma'am; that seems a good place to start." Doyle wanted to sound willing, since thus far she'd been a bit contrary, and she truly didn't want to be thrown off this case; not until she'd had a chance to come back, and nose around.

Apparently, Chiu was also worried that she was being too hard on her junior colleague, especially considering her junior colleague had some illustrious connections. Therefore, in a semi-friendly fashion, she offered, "Can I give you a lift back to the Met?"

"Yes, if you wouldn't mind; I should meet up with DCI Acton." Doyle was in a fever to fill him in on the strange matter of the lying next door neighbor.

But as they opened the doors to the unmarked, Chiu gave her a glance. "Isn't he at Wexton?"

At Doyle's blank look, Chiu explained, "You haven't heard? There was a murder in the holding area at Wexton Prison."

Doyle paused in surprise. "No ma'am; I hadn't heard." The prison was a medium security facility not far from London, and there had long been rumors of corruption in connection with it. Thus far, however, there'd been a code of silence amongst the prison personnel, and little progress had been made. Acton was patient, though; in this type of situation, all it took was for one nervous Nelly to start talking in exchange for leniency, and the other suspects would immediately fall in line, so as not to be the last one left, with nothing to offer the police. A murder in prison was, unfortunately, not a rarity, but since Acton had jumped on this one, he must believe that it was connected to his corruption case. It also meant he'd have no time to listen to her paltry concerns about a lying witness; best put it aside for the moment, and offer to help him. As Chiu drove out into traffic, Doyle texted, "Need me?"

Within seconds, Acton rang her up. "I'll have a suspect in Detention in twenty minutes, and I'd like to go after him as soon as possible. Can you observe from the gallery?"

This meant that Acton needed a truth-detector, and Doyle replied, "Let me check with DI Chiu." She turned to Chiu, who gave her a look that indicated she was well-aware her permission was superfluous. "Right; I'll be there."

"Is DI Chiu available? She may be of use."

Doyle covered the mobile, and asked, "Can you come in to help DCI Acton with an interrogation?"

"Of course."

Doyle informed Acton they were on their way, and then rang off. Doyle knew Chiu was not happy about being called in to help Acton, although you wouldn't know it from her demeanor. After a small silence, the woman remarked, "The suspect must be Chinese."

Here was a flippin' minefield, and Doyle wasn't certain what was best to say. "Oh—d'you think so?"

But her superior officer had already thought the better of her remark, and glanced over at Doyle. "It's a good tactic, if that is the case. DCI Acton knows what he's doing."

"No argument here, ma'am." Prickly, she is, thought Doyle; and wary about having the DCI's annoying wife on the case, but aware that the aforesaid annoying wife had a record of solving a thorny case or two.

"Do you think Mr. Huse is harmless? He did have a key."

"I do, ma'am," said Doyle absently, gazing out the window because they'd turned into the utility parking garage, and the smell of gas fumes always made her feel nauseous. "I think the SOCO enlisted his help with her cat, because she knew that he was lonely."

"Are you really going to bring him the cat?" Chiu glanced at her with a hint of incredulity.

"I am," said Doyle. "It's important." She paused, her scalp prickling as it did when her intuition was making a leap. Surprised, she tried to catch at the elusive feeling—why would it be important that the cat be given to the neighbor?

Chiu interrupted her thoughts. "Definitely important for the cat; they don't last long at the Metro shelter." Rather abruptly, she then asked, "Have you worked on the Wexton Prison corruption case?"

Thankfully, they'd parked the car, and immediately Doyle got out and stood up, breathing in the musty concrete smell and rummaging in her rucksack for a lemon drop, which sometimes seemed to help. "No, I haven't, ma'am; DI Williams has been doin' the legwork, with an assist from DS Munoz."

Chiu opened the car door, and took a quick look in the rear view mirror, to smooth her hair back. "I wish I had some background on the case, but I suppose DCI Acton will fill me in."

Why, I believe she's a bit nervous, thought Doyle; I always forget that everyone is terrified of Acton, except me. Again, her scalp prickled, but this thought didn't seem very significant; small wonder everyone was terrified of Acton, they called him "Holmes" behind his back, and he was not one to fraternize with the foot soldiers.

As she accompanied Chiu over to the lift, Doyle strove to remember what her better half had said about the Wexton Prison investigation—unfortunately, she tended to not pay close attention, when she didn't think it was important. Or when she wasn't feeling well, which was nearly all the time, nowadays. "It's a bribery-corruption case; they're keepin' it fairly quiet, because Acton thinks at least one judge is involved." This, of course, was a matter for no little concern; the public needed to have the general conviction that the justice system was indeed just. A corruption scandal such as this one would undermine everyone's faith in law enforcement, and a cynical public could react by second-guessing every action taken by the Crown's prosecutors for years to come. "And I think they're havin' trouble finding a suspect who's willin' to grass, so we must be dealin' with some ugly customers."

"Does he have a working theory?"

"I'm not sure. I imagine it's your usual rig, though; money is bein' channeled to certain persons in exchange for lenient sentences, or outright acquittals." Doyle knit her brow, trying to remember what Acton had intimated. "It's a tough case to crack, because the reason that a criminal is given a soft sentence—or gets off on an acquittal—is not usually a matter of record. You have to try to weed out those cases where the prosecution genuinely overestimated the strength of its evidence, or where a key witness genuinely changed his story, and instead try to find cases where an acquittal or light sentence seemed to come from out of the clear blue."

DI Chiu stepped into the garage lift and pressed the button. "I have every confidence that DCI Acton will sort it out."

Doyle stood beside her in silence, surprised to discover that this testament of faith was not exactly true.

# 6

"RU here?"

Doyle had settled into the gallery next to the interrogation room, watching Acton and Chiu through the one-way mirror and wishing she felt better—once something triggered the nausea, it was tough to shake it, and sooner or later she'd be retching miserably in a corner somewhere. Meanwhile, Acton had paused to text her, in between having a low-voiced conversation with the suspect's solicitor.

"Yes, sir," she texted back.

"Did U eat?"

Knocker, she thought. "Yes. Pay attention."

He looked up again, and listened to whatever it was the solicitor was telling him. Interesting, she thought; the solicitor seemed nervous to her—usually defense solicitors were hard to shake, as false bravado was their stock-in-trade.

Her thoughts were interrupted by the entrance into the gallery of Detective Sergeant Isabel Munoz, who immediately affected outrage. "What are *you* doing here? This is my case."

Doyle wasn't having it, being as she didn't feel well enough to humor stupid Munoz. "No, this is Williams's case, and I'll listen to the interrogation if I feel like it."

But a new hazard had appeared on the horizon, as Munoz paused to frown incredulously at the tableau beyond the glass. "Why is *Chiu* in on the interrogation?"

"Because she's Chinese, apparently."

Munoz sank down, emanating rage and chagrin. "That is *so* unfair. She's on probation."

Doyle raised her brows. "Is she?"

"Well; that's the rumor, anyway—dereliction of duty. Don't say I said."

Seizing on the chance to feel superior, Doyle remonstrated, "The reason you are not in on the interrogation, Munoz, is because you blurt out things like *that*."

The other girl tossed her hair over her shoulders, unrepentant. "You should know all the rumors; you're married to Acton."

"He never speaks of such things, and I've told you a *million* times, Izzy."

"Speaks of what things?" DI Williams approached to pull up a chair on the tier behind them.

"Nothing," said both girls immediately.

To change the subject, Doyle asked, "Who was killed at Wexton Prison today, d'you know?"

Williams leaned in so his head was between them, as they watched the figures in the interrogation room. "A new prisoner was being processed, and there are reports that he was demanding to speak to the women's matron. Next thing we know, he's dead on the floor of the holding cell—took a shiv in the back."

This was not exactly shocking; they'd heard many a tale about the arsenal of weapons that could be unearthed in any garden-variety Class B prison. Munoz tilted her head toward the table in the interrogation room, beyond the glass. "So who's the suspect, then? Another prisoner?"

"No—that's the twist. Supposedly, no one was in the holding cell with the victim, no one claims to have heard or seen anything, and the CCTV was not functioning. But an alert prison officer noticed inert drops of blood on another guard's trouser cuff, and placed him under arrest. The trousers are being tested for a match to the victim's blood; and the guard immediately lawyered up. He's the one being interrogated."

"Acton must think it's a containment murder, then," Munoz decided. "The prisoner who was killed was about to reveal something about the corruption scandal, and had to be silenced by someone on the inside."

"That seems to be the theory," Williams agreed.

Doyle made a face. "Faith, it doesn't look good—yet another death in custody."

Williams shrugged. "This one's not on the Yard's watch, at least. And it may be the break we needed on this case; this seems a little too panicky, and Acton wants to see if he can shake the suspect by moving on it quickly."

"What was the victim going to prison for?" asked Munoz, which seemed a very good question, and Doyle was annoyed she hadn't asked this herself.

"White-collar embezzlement. Three year sentence."

"And why would a male detainee want to be seein' a prison matron?" added Doyle. "That seems odd." Wexton Prison had separate facilities for female inmates, but the men greatly outnumbered the women.

"We're bringing in the matron, to find out if she can shed some light. There's no obvious connection; she's not a relative, or a known acquaintance."

"Can I be in on *that* interrogation, or is she Chinese, too?" Munoz was sulking to beat the band, although to give the devil her due, she always managed to look sultry whilst sulking.

But Williams was immune to sulking, as Doyle knew from past experience. "Give it up, Munoz; have you noticed that it's my case, and even I'm not in on this interrogation? Besides, you do better with men; women are intimidated by you."

Slightly mollified, Munoz leaned back into her chair, which had the added benefit of brushing her arm against Williams' leg. "A prison matron? Unlikely she's the type to be intimidated by anything."

"Whist, here comes the suspect," Doyle warned. She needed to concentrate, and oftentimes it was difficult from this distance; she wanted no distractions.

The suspect was escorted into the interrogation room, wearing the standard-issue prisoner's jump suit, since his uniform had been confiscated. He did appear to be of Chinese ancestry; a stocky, mid-sized man whose stoic appearance concealed what Doyle knew was his abject misery. Acton introduced himself and Chiu, and then began his interrogation.

"Officer Zao, how long have you been a British citizen?"

The suspect raised his eyes briefly from the table; a bit startled. Oftentimes an interrogation would commence with a diversion—not what the suspect was expecting, so as to shake him up a bit. Doyle had to admit she wasn't expecting this particular question, either.

After glancing for a moment at his solicitor, the man reluctantly answered, "Three years."

Surprised, Doyle leaned forward so as to focus. It was not true, which seemed a foolish move on the suspect's part; such a thing was easily verifiable.

Acton, however, made no attempt to pursue this topic, and instead asked, "You have a sister who is living in Epping, I understand." For the briefest moment, he glanced at Chiu, giving the impression that she'd verified this fact.

Doyle knew the suspect was startled, even though his expression did not change, and the man's gaze rested on Chiu for the first time. For her part, the DI did not betray by the flicker of an eyelash that she had no idea what Acton was talking about.

"And how is this relevant?" Doyle could sense that the solicitor was very uneasy, although his manner was slightly bored.

But Acton was on to the next topic. "A death in custody is a matter of grave concern. Are you aware of any other deaths at Wexton Prison, Officer Zao?"

The solicitor made an incredulous sound of impatience. "*How* is this relevant?"

Acton answered without taking his gaze from the suspect's. "I am looking for a pattern."

"Answer," advised the solicitor, with a careless shrug meant to indicate that they were on a wild goose chase.

But Doyle was aware that the solicitor was shaken, and listening very carefully to his client's answers. Acton knows something, she thought; and the solicitor is very much afraid about whatever it is.

The prisoner replied with palpable reluctance. "There was a death—on the women's side, last year." He paused, his gaze fixed on the table. "A prisoner fight; but I had nothing to do with it." This was not true.

Acton added, almost matter-of-factly, "And Solonik. Solonik was killed, also."

Doyle blinked, as this seemed off-topic. Solonik had been a Russian crime syndicate kingpin, dabbling in blackmail and weapons smuggling. The man had crossed swords with Acton—never a good idea—and had wound up in prison, sentenced for a murder he didn't actually commit. Unfortunately, this gave the aforesaid Solonik plenty of time to plot his revenge, and he'd been masterminding a plan to ruin Acton by trying to blackmail the fair Doyle. Just when she feared she'd have to confess what had been going on to Acton, the mighty Solonik had been killed in prison, and all vengeance plots had died along with him. It was amazing, sometimes, how things just worked out for the best.

At the mention of Solonik's name, Doyle could sense Zao's flare of strong emotion, quickly suppressed. "Yes—I'd forgotten; I was off that week." This was true.

"I suppose no one was surprised that Solonik met a bad end."

"Don't answer," advised the solicitor with an impatient gesture. "Someday we'll get to the point."

Acton leaned forward in his chair, as though conceding that he needed to focus, which was laughable, as Acton was always focused like a laser beam. Spreading them out on the table, he displayed several photos of the decedent, lying in a pool of blood on the concrete holding cell floor. "Were you involved in processing this prisoner?"

"No, I wasn't, sir."

Doyle blinked. He's respectful, all of a sudden, she thought with surprise. That's interesting.

"Do you know why he was asking to speak to the matron from the women's prison?"

"No, sir." Doyle frowned slightly; this was not exactly true, and it was not exactly false.

"Were you in the cell when he died?"

"No, sir; I came on the scene afterward. I checked for a pulse, and called for the medics."

This was not true, and seemed to be an attempt to explain the blood on his trouser cuff. It wouldn't be helpful, though; Williams had said that the blood on the trousers consisted of inert, round drops, which meant they fell from almost directly overhead—the victim was standing whilst bleeding. On the other hand, if Zao had knifed him himself, there would have been more than a little blood on his clothing—stab wounds were very messy affairs.

"Do you know why the CCTV in the holding cell area was not functioning?"

"No, sir—I don't."

Not true. More or less a serial liar, was our Mr. Zao, and Doyle was getting more than her share this fine day. Except for the whole Chinese thing, he could be related to Mrs. Addersley, with her fake story about how-the-nonexistent-boyfriend-done-it.

With a show of impatience, the solicitor spread his hands. "So; why exactly are we here? My client has an exemplary record—"

"Your client has been cautioned, twice."

"Minor rule infractions." Assuming a confident manner that masked his uneasiness, the solicitor snapped his file shut, and rose to leave. "You've got nothing, and there's no point in even putting a hold on him. I think the CID owes Officer Zao an apology."

But the prisoner had not stood. "I'd like to enter a plea," he said to Acton. "sir."

# 7

The gallery sat for a moment in stunned silence. "Does any-body know what just happened, here?" asked Munoz.

With a sound of satisfaction, Williams swiftly rose from his chair. "Cheers—I've got to go make a call." As he left, he reminded Doyle over his shoulder, "I'll text you about our interview tomorrow."

"What interview?" asked Munoz, immediately suspicious.

"He's got a witness who wants to talk off-campus." Best not men-tion to Munoz that the witness was an attractive young woman, and interested in the worthy DI Williams.

"On the Wexton Prison case?"

Munoz was being territorial again, and so Doyle soothed her as best she could. "He doesn't really know, Munoz; he wants me along because he doesn't want to be set up."

"He never asks *me* to be a third."

"That's because if you came along, he'd be needin' a fourth, to keep you at arm's length."

Hotly, the other girl retorted, "Come off it, Doyle; I know how to be professional—he *never* even gives me a chance." With an annoyed gesture, she gathered up her rucksack. "Fine. I'll go see if any help is needed with Zao."

This was a thinly-veiled attempt to slice a share of the glory, and Doyle was annoyed in turn, since Acton had kept her well-away from this whole prison case, and now it had taken a very interesting turn. "I don't know what you think you can do to help; they'll be keepin' him under lock and key til he's sung his song."

"Chiu is *not* taking over my case."

"We're all on the same side, Munoz." Doyle paused to text Acton on his private line, "Beware the solicitor." The man was a dirty dish, if ever there was one, and a liar in his own right—although there was not a lot Acton could do to try to come between a solicitor and his client.

Acton's text came back immediately. "Matron?"

Frowning, Doyle paused to remember the question and response from the interrogation, and then texted, "Zao knows something, but not everything."

"Zao citizenship?"

Trying to keep up, Doyle texted back, "N/T," not true.

"What's Acton saying?" On her way out the door, Munoz had paused to watch Doyle.

Doyle looked up. "He's sayin' he thinks Chiu's a genius, and she should be assigned to all his cases."

"Not *funny*, Doyle."

As the other girl shut the door with a semi-slam, Doyle turned back to her mobile and made one more attempt to get in on the action. "Need me to listen in?"

Instead, her mobile pinged with the instruction: "Home, please. Eat and rest."

Doyle took a reluctant breath, and reminded herself that she shouldn't worry her husband, he had enough going on—although it was hard to be a witness to this case-breaker, or whatever it was that had happened, here—and not want to be in the thick of it. "Right. See u there."

She sat in the dim room, and stared at the mobile screen for a moment, brushing her thumb over it absently. She could always do research from home, in a restful sort of way. Research was tedious and mind-numbing, but at least it was useful, and would cause no undue anxiety to her better half. She could put a report together about the SOCO's murder—since Chiu was apparently too busy being Chinese to do it herself—and she could also go over the search criteria she'd established to try to figure out which of the Crown Court judges might be involved in the Wexton Prison corruption case. Perhaps something would leap out at her; sometimes it did. With another sigh, she rang up the driving service, and asked that they come to fetch her home.

She arrived at the flat to find Reynolds cooking up some concoction on the stove. "What are you brewin', my friend? Not more poison, I hope?" The domestic whom Reynolds had replaced had tried to poison the fair Doyle.

"Certainly not, madam," said Reynolds severely. The servant did not always appreciate Doyle's sense of humor. "I am making a beef broth to soak the toast in; we think it may serve."

Doyle was not so certain, if it tasted anything like it smelt. "I did have a banana at lunch." This was technically true; she wouldn't mention it didn't stay down—she positively *longed* for Williams and his contraband, but he was off working on this very interesting case whilst she was fighting nausea at home. "I don't want to hurt your feelin's, Reynolds, but the smell alone is makin' me sick."

He immediately disposed of the broth, and insisted she lie down on the sofa. "Iced ginger tea," she suggested, just so he wouldn't hover over her. "And I'll be needin' my laptop, if you don't mind—I'm to make myself useful."

Doyle spent the next hour propped up on the sofa, typing up the report for the SOCO's murder, and reviewing the original interviews done by the PCs. She didn't want the woman's murder to be lost in the shuffle, now that things were finally moving on the more important Wexton Prison case, and besides, she has nothing else to work on, at the moment. Looking over the notes for Mrs. Addersley's original interview, she saw what she'd remembered—the woman was described as "elderly." The notes said that she'd been worried about the decedent, although it was not made clear why she was worried.

The report also said that the neighbor had noticed an odd smell. Further questioning had revealed that there'd been an argument in the hallway with an older man, three days earlier.

Doyle paused, frowning. Unlikely Addersley would have referred to the unknown man as "older" if it were a known boyfriend, even if the boyfriend were indeed older—it sounded more as though she was describing a stranger. And besides, Doyle had the distinct impression that the witness was telling lie after lie—although sometimes Doyle got her wires crossed. But what was the point of lying? Doyle had discovered—being how she was—that there was the occasional person who lied for sport, about anything and everything. She didn't know the psychology, but imagined it was some sort of personality disorder that made the person feel superior. It seemed odd, though, to want to lie to the police about your neighbor's murder.

Mr. Huse knew about the smell, also, although it didn't sound like it was decomp—he'd described the smell as sweet. So what was the smell? And who was the arguer-in-the-hallway?

She called out, "Reynolds, how old would a woman have to be for you to be describin' her as 'elderly'?"

The servant paused in his dinner preparations to consider this inquiry. "I would try to avoid such an adjective at all costs, madam."

Of course he would, the knocker. Possessing her soul in patience, Doyle persisted, "Pretend the police were askin', and you had to come up with a cut-off, so to speak."

"Eighty," he decided.

Doyle nodded absently. "That's what I think, too. Now, how old would a man be for a woman to describe him as 'older' with respect to a thirty-five year old woman?"

Reynolds sounded disapproving. "Is this one of those magazine quizzes, madam?"

"No, this is police work, Reynolds; I wouldn't be botherin' you, else."

He considered this. "Fifty?"

"Somethin's not right, here." She frowned into the laptop screen. "The witness completely changed her story from two days ago."

Oven mitts on, Reynolds carefully transferred the baking dish into the oven. "Perhaps someone got to her, madam."

But Doyle couldn't see it. "This witness seemed very self-assured, and not the gettin'-to type. She certainly didn't like me, much." Thoughtfully, she closed her laptop, and decided she'd go over tomorrow to deliver the cat, and see what transpired; perhaps the woman would tell yet a third version of her story, and then Doyle would know that she was just a lying liar who lied. Reminded, she rang up the Metro animal shelter, and spoke to a volunteer about the cat, explaining she'd deliver it to a new home tomorrow, and to please not give it the gas in the meantime. The volunteer was one of those people who gushed about Doyle's kindness and general merit, and so she hadn't the heart to tell her the cat was merely a ploy to nose around a crime scene.

"You will be bringing a cat home, madam?" Reynolds' voice was carefully neutral when she rang off.

"No—I'm deliverin' it to a man I met at the crime scene."

There was a pause. "You will mention this to Lord Acton?"

Surprised, she lifted her head to consider him. "Unsnabble, Reynolds. What's up?"

The manservant carefully folded the dish cloth. "I believe women in your condition are not supposed to handle cats."

She stared at him. "Truly?"

"Ask Lord Acton," said Reynolds. "But I believe that is the case."

"Well, I need to deliver this cat," she said aloud, and then wondered again why this was so. "I would put him in one of those carry-cases, anyway—I'm not going to wrestle a cat onto the tube; mayhem would be the certain result."

Reynolds eyed her doubtfully. "How large is the animal, madam?"

"I've no idea," Doyle replied absently. "Apparently, he sheds a lot."

"I shall accompany you, then."

Hiding a smile at the stoicism behind this pronouncement, she replied, "That's a kind offer, Reynolds, but no one is goin' to tell me anythin' of interest if my butler is standin' there with me."

Understandably, Reynolds was confused. "You are engaging this cat in your detective work, madam?"

"Aye, that." She nodded with certainty. "That cat knows a thing or two, he does."

# 8

"Couldn't stand the broth," Doyle confessed, when Acton came through the door. "Not Reynolds' fault."

"That is a shame; you need more protein." He bent to kiss her.

"I'll work on it," she promised. "I'll try chicken soup, later." He was dubious, but said nothing—the last attempt at chicken soup had not gone well at all.

After hanging up Acton's coat, Reynolds retreated to the kitchen to assemble dinner, while Acton walked over to stand before the windows, deep in thought. Interesting, Doyle thought as she watched him; he doesn't want to talk about this Wexton Prison case—or at least not with me. And he looks weary, poor man. She decided that, as his helpmeet, she should make an attempt to take his mind off his troubles. "Can you come into the bedroom, for a mo? I want to show you somethin'."

Acton cast a meaningful glance in Reynolds' direction, and she made a face to let him know that it wasn't *that*—and now she'd better make good on that later, after getting his hopes up. Instead, she led him to the bed, and instructed that he should lie down next to her, so that they were both on their stomachs, face-to-face. Taking his hand, she slid it beneath her abdomen. "Tell me if you can feel this." She positioned her own hand next to his and waited.

"There," she said. "Did you feel that?"

"No."

She readjusted his hand. "It's not obvious," she cautioned. "Stay very still."

They waited, and suddenly he smiled. "Yes," he said.

"Can you feel it?"

"Yes," he said again. "Mary."

"Mary," she agreed, and found that her eyes had filled with tears. He pulled her to him, and they lay cradled together, even though they still had their shoes on. Worth every nauseous moment, she thought; thank You, thank You, thank You.

She wasn't aware she'd dozed off, until she leapt up with a gasp, standing beside the bed, and gazing with wide eyes at the far wall. Acton scrambled up with her, and pulled her to him. "It's all right, Kathleen; you were dreaming, again."

Reynolds appeared in the entryway, alarmed, and Doyle stared at him, her heart beating in her ears, as the vision of the barricaded door faded from her mind.

Acton held her close. "Who is it? Did you see, this time?"

Shaking her head, she closed her eyes, and felt like an idiot. "He's on the other side of the door, so I never see him—but I think it's someone we know." She waited, willing herself to have one of her leaps of recognition, but it didn't come, and so she made a sound of extreme frustration. "I'm flummoxed—can't come up with a scrap."

"Does he have a weapon?"

"Yes," she answered immediately. "He does."

Reynolds regarded her consideringly. "I will check the alarm system," he decided, and went off.

Acton stroked Doyle's hair. "Anything else?"

She teetered on the edge of confessing that it may be Williams who was barricading the door, but then he'd know that she'd left out that little detail before, and he might think she was trying to hide something, which, in fact, she was. Acton knew about Williams' feelings for her, and did not appear to be overly concerned, but you never knew, with him; she didn't want him to snap, one day, and strangle poor Williams. And this was exactly why the nuns taught you that honesty was the best policy. "It just seems to be more and more—" she tried to think of the right word.

"Exigent?"

With a sigh, she looked up at him. "I haven't a *clue* what that means, Michael."

"More and more alarming."

Thinking about it, she slowly shook her head. "I don't know about that; I'm not afraid when I'm in the dream—not truly. I just wish I weren't so dense. I need a translator, or somethin'."

Resting his chin on the top of her head, he ran his warm hands up and down her back. "You must try to remain calm, Kathleen; else you'll alarm Mary."

"I'm that sorry. It's a crackin' annoyance, mainly."

He squeezed his arms around her, briefly. "Shall we have some dinner, and try to sort it out?"

"Could I have some coffee, d'you suppose?" She tried to sound semi-pathetic.

He turned, and tucked her under his arm. "You may have anything you like."

They adjourned to the kitchen table, where Doyle sipped a blessedly strong cup of coffee, and Reynolds served Acton his dinner. The servant had been thoughtfully quiet, but now offered, "Do you think it was Detective Samuels, madam?" Samuels was a fellow DC who had threatened Doyle, and then had ended up dead on the street from some sort of seizure.

"No," she said with certainty. "Not Samuels."

She could feel Acton slant a glance at Reynolds, and no more questions were asked, which was just fine with her, as she'd decided to take the bull by the horns, and quiz Acton about his Wexton Prison case. "What exactly happened durin' Zao's interrogation today, Michael? It made no sense a'tall, from where I was sittin'."

Acton marshaled his thoughts for a moment. "The suspect was under enormous pressure not to talk, and so I attempted to relieve that pressure."

Doyle eyed him over the brim of her cup. "You shook him up a bit, with your talk of Solonik's bein' killed in prison." Once again, she thanked God fasting for whoever instigated the prison fight—not that she would ever wish death on anyone, she offered up hastily—but Solonik's demise was a very convenient turn of events. In truth, his death was so convenient that Doyle had been worried that Acton murdered Solonik himself, but he'd assured her that he hadn't, and he'd been speaking the truth.

"Yes; I suppose that is true."

There was a small silence, and—as her better half was not being forthcoming—she prompted, "And there was somethin' about his sister, which seemed to surprise him."

Acton offered her a forkful of his pasta, and with a show of cooperation, she accepted it, even though it tasted like sawdust. He took a bite himself, and then disclosed, "Zao was cooperating in the corruption scheme—and in the murder—because his younger sister was being threatened."

She stared at him. "Oh—oh that is *despicable,* Michael."

"Yes," he agreed briefly, and went back to address his dinner.

Honestly; it was like being married to the sphinx. "So—you were lettin' him know that his sister would be protected? Is that why Williams leapt up to leave? And what was Chiu's part, in this little holy show?"

He considered for a moment, winding his pasta against a spoon. "Many Chinese operate on a caste system; she has a royal attribute, and therefore her presence was helpful, so as to apply additional pressure."

But this seemed a bridge too far for Doyle, who stared at him in frank disbelief. "You're not tryin' to tell me that Chiu is *royalty?*"

"No; but she is of a particular caste. Many Chinese work within their own concepts of justice, and the English common law has little effect, one way or the other."

This was so interesting that she absently ate another bite, when he offered it. "So will Zao feel confident enough to grass on the others, d'you think? I hope he fingers the judges involved—I'm not havin' much luck with my research."

Acton shrugged slightly. "Zao would not be someone who knows much; he's a foot soldier, but oftentimes the foot soldiers will eavesdrop, so as to hedge their bets. We shall see."

Doyle lowered her voice. "Do you think he would truly give testimony against the others? Won't he be worried that he'll wind up a dead man?"

"I think it more likely his solicitor will wind up a dead man."

Astonished, Doyle stared at Acton as he offered another bite, and it belatedly occurred to her that he was giving her bits of information only when she ate—like she was that dog in that famous experiment, whatever its name was. Nevertheless, she resolutely chewed and swallowed. "And why is that?"

"I rather think the solicitor is a marked man," was the only reply she received, and then he changed the subject. "I believe you were thinking that Judge Colcombe may have been one of the judges involved—no luck tying him to anything?"

"Well, his name comes up more often than most, but that wouldn't be much help, would it?" Colcombe did seem to have more than his fair share of unexpected acquittals, but he'd died several years ago—a heart condition, no doubt aggravated by the fact that he was being discreetly investigated by Judicial Standards. "And truly, it's hard to find a pattern that you could shake a stick at, Michael. The judges who handle the more serious crimes seem to have the most surprise acquittals, but that would make sense—there are better quality barristers handlin' the defense."

Acton nodded, and then offered thoughtfully, "Narrow the search to female suspects, please, and let's see what develops." He offered another forkful.

"Women? All right." Dutifully, she ate the pasta, and wondered where this thought had come from, and also wondered how she was going to perform this particular task; trials were not divided up by gender—the same judges would handle female and male suspects without any distinction, although the overwhelming majority of felons were male. She then added, "This recent victim at Wexton Prison was there for white-collar embezzlement; should I run a search on that, too?"

"No," he said. "I've already done so."

This was of interest, and so she prompted, "Anythin'?"

He met her gaze, and hesitated. Saints, she thought in surprise; he doesn't know what to tell me, because he's worried I'll catch him in a lie.

"Yes, there is something there. But I'd rather not say, and it is important that there be no traceable record of anyone looking into these particular commonalities. I'll have your promise that you will not pursue it."

She nodded, matching his serious mood. It seemed evident that he was on to something, but didn't want to give the villains any clues that they'd been twigged, whilst a trap was being set up. "All right, then." She then added diffidently, "D'you suppose I could help with some of the field work, then? Perhaps I could run a false flag operation." A false flag operation was an investigation that was a pretense, so as to make the suspect think they were unaware of his misdeeds, while actually, they were closing in on him. "I could interview personnel, and ask misdirection questions."

But he shook his head. "No. I cannot like your dreams."

She was surprised; he was not one to be fanciful. She noticed that Reynolds, coming in to clear the plates, slanted her his own glance. So—she'd spooked them, what with her wild talk of armed danger. It's exactly what I deserve for gabbling off every stray thought that crosses my mind, she thought a bit glumly; let this be a lesson.

# 9

Despite the important developments on the Wexton Prison case, the next morning Acton waited for Doyle, so that he could drive her in to work. Doyle was almost sorry for it, because she knew what was coming. The pasta hadn't stayed down last night, and despite her overtures in bed, Acton had been firmly committed to ceding his position to the heating pad—a true measure of his concern.

As he maneuvered them through the morning traffic, he said quietly, "I'd like to take you in to see Dr. Easton this afternoon, if you are available."

"Of course I'm available," she answered crossly, then closed her lips on any further complaints she'd been about to make about being taken out of the field.

He reached over to clasp her hand. "Perhaps it will be the last time." Dr. Easton had decided Doyle should be administered intravenous glucose with vitamins whenever she was unable to keep any food down for more than two days. She had endured the procedure twice already, and profoundly hated it—she had a dread of medical procedures in general, and needles in particular. Best not to think about how she was going to handle childbirth, which she was well-aware would involve both.

Miserable, she gazed out the window at the passing scenery, sick to death of feeling wretched, and sick to death of fretting Acton, who had better things to do than play nursemaid to the likes of her. To her horror, she started to cry; holding her hand over her eyes in shame, and trying without much success to stifle her sobs.

With one hand rubbing her back, Acton negotiated his way to the side of the road, and then gathered her into his arms, making soothing sounds that were very unlike her buttoned-up husband.

Mortified that she was behaving so badly, she wiped her cheeks with the palm of her hand, and tried to muster up a smile. "I am *wretchedly* sorry, Michael; of course I will go. I'm just feelin' a bit blue."

"No; you needn't go today."

She hovered between accepting this reprieve, and being a grown-up, and it was a near-run thing. "Fine; I'll just go without you, then."

"We'll wait another day or two, and see."

This seemed an acceptable compromise, and she nodded into his shoulder, adding unnecessarily, "I hate the doctor's."

"I know, but we should take advantage of the technology that is available; it is there to help."

This was undeniably true, and she was ashamed again, as he re-started the car, and pulled out into traffic. The obstetrician had also recommended an ultrasound, to check the baby's development. No needles, Acton had pointed out, and they would be able to see the baby; make out arms and legs. Doyle was thinking it over.

"Are you well enough to go into work? I can take you back home."

"I am fine, Michael. And I have to be a third on an interview with Williams, anyway." She omitted any mention of the cat delivery, being as how she was worried he'd forbid her, and it was important, for reasons unknown, that she deliver the stupid cat to Mr. Huse.

Reminded, she told him, "Chiu and I interviewed the SOCO's next-door neighbor yesterday—the reportin' witness—and she was lyin' like the serpent in the garden. I meant to tell you, and then I forgot, in all the Wexton Prison excitement."

Acton found this of interest, and tilted his head as he turned the car into the parking garage. "Is the neighbor a potential suspect?"

"No—or at least, there's not a whiff of motive. Very unlikely she was lyin' in wait to cosh the SOCO in the dark."

"Then why lie to the police? Did she have a key to the flat?"

Doyle blew out a breath. "Oh. We didn't ask, I'm afraid. Although another neighbor—a nice little old man—said he had a key so as to take care of the cat, but he didn't seem a likely cosher, either."

Acton considered this as he parked the car. "What did the first neighbor lie about?"

Shaking her head in bewilderment, Doyle held up her palms. "Everythin'. She said the SOCO had a boyfriend, described him, and said they'd argued in the hallway—castin' blame, she was. None of it was true, but there was nothin' I could say at the time, so I thought I'd tell you."

Thoughtfully, he rested his gaze on the concrete wall that faced them. "Anything in the background check?"

"Nothin'—she's as clean as the robes of the just. There's a discrepancy in the original report about how old she is, though."

He glanced at her. "Could she be an inveterate liar?"

Doyle wasn't certain what "inveterate" meant, but took his meaning. "I wondered about that, but she didn't seem the type." She paused, because there was something else she wanted to tell him about the neighbor, but she couldn't remember what it was.

Acton reached behind the seat to lift his valise, apparently having come to a decision. "Since she was trying to cast blame, she may have been covering for someone else. Let's find an excuse to interview her again—perhaps you can gather together some suspect photos to show her. I should be free for a time tomorrow afternoon, and I will accompany you."

While this was welcome news—and greatly appreciated, since the SOCO's case was far down in the pecking order—it was also news that caused a small qualm in Doyle's breast. "That would be excellent, Michael, but could you please not mention it to Chiu? I don't want to miff her—she already thinks me an idiot."

Acton paused with his hand on the door, his level gaze on hers, and Doyle immediately regretted her error—her wretched, *wretched* tongue. "I shouldn't have said, Michael. *Please* don't take it out on her; you make her nervous enough already."

But Acton was not one to allow such heresy to go unpunished. "You are a good detective, Kathleen; if she is prejudiced against you, I should appoint a different CSM."

"No, you shouldn't," she retorted in exasperation. "For heaven's sake, Michael; I don't want to be always watchin' what I say around you."

There was a small pause. "Fair enough."

"Sometimes, I just have to blow off a little steam," she explained.

Smiling, he opened the car door. "Is that so? You astonish me."

"Knocker." Grabbing his arm, she pulled him over to kiss him, one last time.

Doyle settled in to her desk with her mood much improved—not only had she avoided going to the doctor's, she'd enlisted Acton's help in the SOCO case. Oftentimes when the renowned chief inspector showed up, those witnesses who weren't cooperating became a bit less defiant, and a bit more worried about winding up in the nick. Of course, Doyle herself was now rather renowned, although Mrs. Addersley certainly wasn't impressed—that's it, she thought suddenly, sitting upright. That's what I forgot to tell Acton—the witness didn't like me much, and by not much, I mean not at all.

Since there was no apparent reason for this prejudice—it was not as though the witness hailed from Ulster, or something—Doyle pulled up the SOCO's file for a look-see.

She was interrupted in this endeavor by Munoz, who leaned into the cubicle's entrance. "When were you going to mention that you're pregnant?"

Unaccountably pleased, Doyle couldn't contain her smile. "Can you tell, then?"

"The coffee is a dead giveaway."

The smile faded. "Saints and holy angels, I miss coffee."

Munoz took a lingering sip from her own cup. "Are you going to quit?"

"No, I am not going to quit." Doyle tried not to bristle, and conceded, "I may have to cut back on hours."

"Don't let them try to put you in PR," warned Munoz.

This was actually a fair point; Munoz had signed on to the Met's public relations team, and the last thing either of them wanted was to be paired up like a raree show, and have to recite the bridge-jumping incident on a weekly basis.

Reminded, Munoz continued, "Guess who was at the community outreach last night? Remember the witness who came in on the turf war cases—Gerry Lestrade? The one with the nice watch?"

Doyle was instantly on high alert. Gerry Lestrade was actually Philippe Savoie's brother, and Philippe Savoie was a French criminal-kingpin type who'd given Doyle some aid when the evil Solonik was trying to do his worst. Before Doyle knew of the family connection between Lestrade and Savoie, she and Munoz had interviewed Lestrade, when the man was nosing around the Met, trying to figure out why the turf wars were depleting the ranks of London's underworld. To Munoz, however, he was just another witness.

Doyle pretended a mild interest. "Was he indeed? Did he remember you?"

Munoz drew down her mouth in amused irritation. "He was cheeky—he kept asking me questions about the bridge-jumping incident, because he knew I didn't want to answer them."

"Brave man. Did you rear up and smite him?"

"I didn't give him the satisfaction. He was there with another man, and they seemed pretty thick with the minister's secretary. It was a little strange; he didn't seem the well-connected type, back when we interviewed him."

This was an alarming little piece of information; the companion might be Savoie himself, and it did not bode well that blacklegs like the Savoie brothers were hanging about with a government official. Doyle swallowed and asked in a faint voice, "Oh? Which minister's secretary is that?"

"The Home Office's Minister for Immigration, of course—it was a community outreach, stupid." Munoz tossed her hair over her shoulder in a self-important gesture. "They want to reassure the immigrant communities that the new minister will do a better job than the old one did of protecting them from protection rackets, and such. I think the man that was with them was from the Cabinet Office."

The outreach to the immigrant community was much needed, as the former minister for immigration had been caught up in some sort of scandal, and then had promptly killed himself before the particulars could be sorted out. Still and all, it didn't bode well if the likes of Gerry Lestrade was hanging around with someone from the Cabinet Office. "Why do you suppose Lestrade was there?"

Munoz shrugged. "I don't know, but he's involved, somehow."

I have to tell Acton, Doyle thought in acute dismay. If Savoie and his brother were currying favor with the new minister's people, it was for no good reason. It would be a delicate matter, as Acton was unaware she'd shared a brief but intense adventure with the notorious Philippe Savoie. Nothin' for it, though; this little development was not something that could be ignored.

Her mobile pinged, and she saw that it was Williams. "20 min?"

She texted "OK," as Munoz looked on with interest. "Any news about the prison matron?"

Doyle looked up. "No—did they bring her into interrogation?" Acton hadn't mentioned it this morning.

"They can't find her, last I heard."

Doyle met Munoz's sober gaze as both girls contemplated this unwelcome news. "Faith, Munoz; I hope she's not another containment murder."

Munoz shrugged, as she turned to leave. "On the other hand, she may have gone to ground, so as to avoid that fate. I'm to visit a few of her neighbors this morning, and try to track her down before the bad guys do."

"Good luck."

Munoz made a negligent gesture with her coffee cup in the general direction of Doyle's abdomen. "Good luck to you, too."

Doyle's mobile rang, and she saw it was Chiu. Thinking to sound up-to-speed, she answered, "Hallo, ma'am; have they managed to run down the missin' matron yet?"

"No, but I wanted to ask if you would interview the SOCO's father; he'll be at her flat this afternoon, packing up, and I know you were going to deliver the cat. I am going to be needed on the Wexton Prison case again."

"Oh—oh, of course, ma'am." Doyle wondered if the DI's reassignment had anything to do with her own thoughtless comment to Acton about working with Chiu, but decided that it didn't matter; the dead SOCO's case deserved equal attention, and maybe Chiu would get a chance to get out of the doghouse, if she did a good job working with Acton.

Chiu continued, "I met the father at the morgue this morning for the ID. It turns out he was the one who was arguing in the hallway with her—so that lead from the neighbor sounds like a dead end. He has an alibi for time of death, but I thought you could follow up with him; I told him you'd be by."

Doyle took down the father's mobile number, and rang off thoughtfully. One would think that an argument with one's father would not sound at all like an argument with one's boyfriend, and so here was another discrepancy to be laid at Mrs. Addersley's deceitful door. She was tempted to try to speak to the woman again when she went over there today, but best wait for Acton, who wanted to use photos as a pretext, so the witness wouldn't know they were suspicious. And besides, Doyle wanted Acton to judge the witness for himself; he was very long-headed, was Acton.

With a sigh, she gathered up her rucksack. Since Munoz knew that she was pregnant, it was only a matter of days before the entire organization was made aware; therefore she'd best tell her supervisor without delay.

# 10

Inspector Habib was entering data on his laptop, and looked up when Doyle appeared at his workstation. "DS Doyle; my congratulations on the Maguire catch."

As the suspect had died in custody, Doyle wasn't certain that congratulations were in order, but accepted the accolade anyway, being as she'd caught him in a good mood. "It was an interestin' case, sir."

"And DCI Drake must be very grateful to you."

"Yes—why yes, of course." Doyle was suddenly struck by the fact that she hadn't heard a word from the aforesaid DCI, despite the fact that she'd undoubtedly saved his life. Without her legwork, he'd have gone to meet Maguire all unknowing that he was going to his doom, and she drew the immediate conclusion that Drake was avoiding her because he feared that she knew the reason he had been targeted. Her scalp began to prickle, as it did when her intuition was making a leap—she should keep digging at this; it was important, for some reason.

Habib had asked a question, but she wasn't paying attention, and so she tried to retrench. "What was that, sir?"

"Your caseload? I understand that you are giving support on the Wexton Prison case."

On the contrary, it seemed that Acton wanted to keep her well-away from the Wexton Prison case, but she did not disclaim. "And

I'm on the SOCO's case, also, sir. DI Chiu was pulled into the Wexton Prison case, and so I'm doin' some legwork, there."

The Pakistani man raised his brows. "DI Chiu is now assigned to the Wexton Prison case?"

Doyle could sense a flare of chagrin from her supervisor, and so assured him, "The suspect was Chinese, and it was thought she might be helpful, in that regard."

DI Habib, who knew his tribes, nodded in resigned understanding. "Ah—yes, I see."

Doyle mentally girded her loins. "I wanted you to be aware, sir, that I am goin' to be havin' a baby."

His reaction to this rather bald revelation surprised her; he positively beamed, as he leapt to his feet. "That is indeed wonderful news, DS Doyle. My congratulations to you and to the chief inspector." She had the impression he almost unbent enough to embrace her, but refrained at the last minute. "You are feeling well, I hope?"

"As well as can be expected," she hedged.

Still smiling, he nodded in his quick, bird-like manner. "You must not hesitate to let me know if you need to rest. Your health must be a priority."

"I will, sir."

Having managed to weasel out of any tedious assignments, Doyle took her leave, and made her way down to meet Williams at the utility garage. Interesting, she thought; Habib was sincerely delighted—she believed he longed to be a father, himself. The man was for all intents married to his job, and if he had a social life, no one knew of it. He had an enormous crush on Munoz, but that didn't really count, as everyone else did, too. I hope he gets his wish, she thought charitably; I imagine he would be a good father. She thought about Acton, who also seemed delighted in his own way—faith, he'd pulled out the pregnancy treatise yet again last night, and pored over it like a hermit with the holy writ.

Before she'd had the miscarriage—when she was pregnant the first time around—she'd been a bit apprehensive about his reaction,

Acton's being how he was. Apparently, though, her husband did not view the baby as a rival for her affections, and it was not going to be a problem. It was interesting how fatherhood could transform men— why, even Solonik, who'd been a cold-blooded killer, had a weak spot for his son. Acton had taken ruthless advantage of it of course; in his own way, he was as cold-blooded as Solonik. Doyle decided she didn't want to pursue this line of thought, and therefore was relieved when she spotted Williams, waiting for her near the lifts, with an extra cup of coffee in his hand.

Doyle hesitated, remembering she'd had coffee last night, but decided—as her mother would say—that she may as well be hung for a sheep as a lamb, and gratefully took it, as they stepped into the lift. "Do we have a protocol?"

"Not as yet; I honestly have no idea what this is about. Percy wanted to meet off- premises, though, so it must be a delicate situation." He checked his mobile for the time. "She has a court appearance, and then she'll be waiting at a pastry shop near the Old Bailey."

As they walked over to the vehicle, Doyle teased, "I'm to stick to you like a burr, and slap her hand away, if she tries anythin'."

He smiled his rare, lopsided smile as he opened the car door. "I would appreciate it."

A few months ago, they'd met the junior barrister at the Inns of Court, when they were investigating the Maguire murders. Percy was attractive and competent, and had traded a few jibes with Williams in the time-honored manner of defense personnel when dealing with prosecution personnel. At the time, Doyle had gained the impression she was mightily attracted to her counterpart, and the girl was probably hoping Williams would take this opportunity to further their acquaintanceship. DI Williams, however, was well-experienced in thwarting the best-laid plans of many a maiden. Personally, Doyle thought Percy might be a good match for him, but as she'd not been consulted, she kept this opinion to herself.

As he drove, Williams observed, "You're beginning to look a little different."

"Thicker, you mean, but are too nice to say."

He gave her an assessing glance. "Not very noticeable, as yet."

She smiled as she sipped her coffee. "I told Habib today. He could have done the deed himself, he was that happy."

"Now, there's an image that would have been better left unspoken."

She chuckled, and looked at the window for a moment, so as to control her queasiness. "I haven't had a chance to discuss the Drake angle with Acton, but it does seem a little strange that Drake never contacted me, after Maguire was taken down. It's almost as though he's worried that I know the reason Maguire wanted to do him in."

Her companion chose his words carefully. "I was wondering—I was wondering if perhaps there was a Drake connection to the Wexton Prison case, and that's what Maguire knew."

Doyle glanced at him in complete surprise, forgetting for the moment that she was queasy. "Truly? D'you think Drake was involved in the corruption scheme? How would that work—he's prosecution, not defense."

"I was thinking more about the sex trafficking angle."

Once again, she stared at him in astonishment. "*Is* there a sex traffickin' angle?"

"Acton hasn't said?"

She lowered her cup to her lap. "Thomas, I am too dense to understand this; please speak plainly."

But Williams was regretting the disclosure, and said only, "I shouldn't have mentioned it, Kath. Promise you'll say nothing; it's being kept very quiet."

Frowning, she considered what he'd said for a moment. "I thought the Wexton Prison case had somethin' to do with embezzlement. Acton was nervous about me doin' an embezzlement search, and leavin' a trail so as to alert the villains that we were on to them."

He glanced over at her in alarm. "Listen to him, Kath; remember these are the people that threaten female relatives."

"Oh—oh, that's right; small wonder Acton wants me well-away from it. But what does embezzlement have to do with sex traffickin'?"

"Don't ask."

Annoyed, she crossed her arms. "Honestly; everyone thinks I'm a baby."

"In some ways, you *are* a baby," was the unapologetic reply.

Doyle turned her head to gaze out the window at the passing scenery, but decided she couldn't sulk just yet, as she still needed some questions answered. "Does the sex traffickin' ring involve immigrant women?" She was thinking about Lestrade, hanging about with the new minister's people, at the community outreach.

He glanced over at her, wary. "Why? What have you heard?"

But she was annoyed with him, and shrugged a shoulder. "Only that I've somethin' to tell Acton—but don't worry; I'll not implicate you and your *precious* secrets."

"Kath—"

She retorted hotly, "I can be discreet, y'know; I'm not a constant gabbler, despite all indications."

"It's not my place," he said firmly. "Please don't put me in the middle, again."

She was instantly remorseful, and subsided. Whilst Williams was loyal to Acton, he'd helped her out with the Savoie problem without telling her husband, and she could appreciate that he wanted to avoid a similar situation at all costs. Best not mention to Williams that Savoie may be involved in the current sticky situation; mental note. "Sorry," she apologized. "It's out of sorts, I am."

"My fault." He placed a hand over hers for a moment. "I shouldn't have said anything to begin with."

Into the ensuing silence, she suddenly remarked, "He's worried about this case, you know—the Wexton Prison one."

But Williams was not going to allow any more insights, and instead observed, "At least we've had a breakthrough with Zao; with any luck it will start to unravel, now."

They parked at their destination, and ventured into the small pastry shop, unpopulated at this time of day, which was undoubtedly why it was chosen for the rendezvous point. A glass case displayed a wide variety of bakery items along one side of the interior, and several small tables lined the opposite wall. Percy was already seated at one of these near the back, and stood to greet them. On shaking Percy's hand, Doyle caught a small flare of chagrin, but the girl gave no outward sign of her disappointment that Williams was accompanied by a gooseberry.

They settled in across from the junior barrister, and she began without preamble. "Thank you for coming; I felt I needed to come forward, but it is a sensitive subject, and I wasn't certain how to go about it."

"What's happened?" asked Williams.

"The barrister I worked for—Mr. Moran—passed away recently." She paused. "He'd not been in good health for some time."

Doyle remembered meeting him; Moran was a well-respected criminal defense barrister with a thriving practice, yet he'd been swilking drunk at ten in the morning. Not a surprise that his health had not been good.

In his best detective manner, Williams asked, "Was there anything unusual about his death?"

"No," the other said. "I am concerned about something he made reference to—oh, weeks ago."

Doyle's ears pricked up. When Percy said there was nothing unusual about Moran's death, she was not telling the truth.

Percy continued, "Mr. Moran had just won a difficult case—was awarded an acquittal, where it looked unlikely. He was trying fewer and fewer cases, and so it was quite an occasion. We all went over to the pub to celebrate, and Mr. Moran had a few drinks." She paused and glanced up at Williams. "He turned rather melancholy, and said something about Whitteside treating him like a supplicant, and not being a gentleman about it, like Colcombe was."

Williams and Doyle digested this disclosure in silence for a moment. Colcombe was the judge, now dead, who'd had the most suspicious record of surprise acquittals and soft sentences. Whitteside, on the other hand, was a brand new judge, recently assigned to the prestigious Crown Court, and handling major crimes.

Williams asked, "And what did you believe he meant when he said this?"

"I think," she said slowly, "that he was referring to the taking of bribes."

Mother a' mercy, thought Doyle in astonishment; while Acton is beating the bushes, I fall into a case-breaker whilst minding Williams' virtue.

# 11

"Is it possible," asked Williams in a level voice, "that you misunderstood? That he meant Judge Whitteside wasn't as respectful toward him as Judge Colcombe?"

"No," Percy replied in a quiet voice. "It wasn't that type of remark." She paused. "I don't think he would have said it, except that he was in his cups."

"And the sensitive part," inserted Doyle at this point, "is that he implicated himself."

Percy dropped her gaze to the table. "Yes."

The last time she and Percy had met, Doyle had been impressed by the girl's loyalty in what seemed to be a largely disloyal world. She understood the current dilemma; Percy hated to besmirch her former mentor's reputation, but could not stand by, if she thought she had information that might be important. It was a difficult situation for anyone who wanted to protect the persons involved, but who also wanted to protect the justice system.

"Who was the defendant in Moran's surprise acquittal—the one you were celebratin'?" Doyle asked. "Was it a woman?"

Both Williams and Percy looked at her in surprise. "It's a theory," she offered a bit lamely, hoping that neither would ask exactly what Acton's theory was, since she didn't know it, herself. Maybe it was true that she was a gabbler, after all.

"Yes, it was a woman." Percy paused, and glanced at Williams. "I suppose you will want to know the details."

The girl's unhappiness was apparent, and Williams leaned forward, sympathetic. "I don't know how we can proceed without implicating Moran. I'm sorry; if there's any way to contain the damage, I'll do my best."

The other girl nodded, and Williams continued, "Can you think of another source of information in your chambers—perhaps closed files involving Judge Colcombe? Or other people on staff who might have known about this, or participated?" Williams was following the book, trying to find a trail of hard evidence that would support the dead man's remark, as the remark alone was probably not enough.

"No." Percy shook her head.

Again with the lying, thought Doyle in surprise. Merciful mother, what am I to do? Testing it out, she asked, "Do you know of any court personnel who may have been involved?"

"No. I am only allowed to sit second chair on occasion—usually summary offenses—and so I'm not very familiar with court personnel."

"Have you heard any rumors?" Williams persisted. "If we can track down other concrete leads, it would help us take the onus off Moran."

Good one, thought Doyle; appeal to the girl's loyalty.

"It wouldn't feel right to say," she replied steadily. "I'd rather deal in evidence, not in rumors."

"On the other hand, a lot of what we do is based on guesswork," Williams countered. "Were there any other unexpected acquittals in your chambers? Within—let's say—the last five years?"

The girl thought about it for a moment, and then seemed to come to a decision. "Let me double-check. I'll make a list, but I don't want to send anything electronically."

"Understood," Williams agreed. "Let me know when you have it ready, and I'll meet up with you."

Ah, thought Doyle; Williams is a wily one—he's playing the let's-meet-without-the-Irish-baggage card.

Now that she'd decided to help the enemy, Percy ventured a small smile. "I'll try to get it to you tomorrow."

As a course of action had been decided upon, they all rose. "We are grateful that you came forward." Williams said, offering her his hand. "I know it was difficult."

"It was," Percy agreed. "But I'm glad I did; it was bothering me, and I didn't like having a guilty conscience." She checked the time, and her eyes could not help straying to him. "Time for lunch. Would you care to join me? There's a little café a block away—it never takes long."

But Williams was not going to bestow his presence until he got his list, and so shook his head with regret. "I'm afraid I'm due at an interview."

Percy courteously included Doyle, who decided it would behoove her to spend some more time with the fair Ms. Percy of the contradictions. "I'll go with you."

She could feel Williams' surprise as they walked toward the door, and he asked, "Do you have any money?" Doyle was notorious for continually being short of cash.

"I do," she replied, and hoped it was true. "See you later, sir." After giving her a look, Williams took his leave.

"Let me make a quick call to the Met, to let them know that I'm takin' a lunch," Doyle told Percy. "It will just take a second." She walked a few steps away, and called Williams.

"Yeeees?" He was annoyed with her.

"Thomas, it is important you don't speak to anyone else about this before we've had a chance to confer."

"Oh? What's up?"

"Can't talk now, but its *inperative.*"

"Imperative, Kath. Right then; call me when you're done, I'll see where I am."

Doyle rang off, and walked back to Percy. "Ready to go," she said brightly.

They walked to the café, and on the way Doyle asked the other girl general questions about her work. She could feel Percy's wariness relax, and by the time they were seated, the two were conversing in a friendly fashion.

Doyle looked over the menu and tried mightily to find something that sounded remotely appetizing. Percy ordered a watercress salad, and Doyle ordered plain toast, dry. In a sympathetic manner, Percy leaned forward. "If you are short on money, I'll be happy to lend you some."

Doyle smiled her appreciation. "Not the problem, I'm afraid. I'm pregnant, and I've been sick as a cat; I'll stick to toast so as not to disgrace myself—here's hopin'."

"Oh—oh, congratulations."

Doyle valiantly sipped some lemon water, and felt Percy's silent perusal for a few moments. The other girl then asked, "Where are you from?"

"From Dublin, I am." Can't hide this accent under a bushel.

"How did you two meet?"

"We met at work," Doyle replied briefly, and lifted her glass to drink again. She avoided all questions that probed into her courtship with Acton, being as how there really wasn't one, to speak of.

"Will you marry, do you think?"

Doyle's gaze snapped to Percy's in surprise, and she set down the glass. "We *are* married."

"Oh." The other girl was surprised in turn. "Sorry—he doesn't wear a ring."

The light dawned, and Doyle explained, "I'm married to DCI Acton."

Percy was clearly astonished. "You are married to Chief Inspector *Acton?*"

"The eighth wonder of the world," Doyle agreed. Serves you right, you vain knocker; thinking you're world-famous, or something.

"I—I beg your pardon," Percy stammered. "I assumed. . ." She decided she didn't want to finish the sentence. Fortunately, the waiter came with their lunch, and the subject was dropped.

Doyle regarded the toast, tastefully arranged on her plate, and steeled herself, bringing to mind Dr. Easton, and his evil needle. Percy reached into her tote bag, and pulled out a small jar, which she opened, and placed on the table. An intriguing aroma wafted over. "What's that?" asked Doyle. "Sauce?"

"It's my guilty secret," Percy replied with a smile. "It's peanut butter."

"Peanut butter? It doesn't much look like butter."

"It's *huge* in the states, which is where I discovered it. Its mashed peanuts, with sugar and salt. I'm addicted now; I spread it on bread." She demonstrated. "Would you like a taste?"

"Yes," said Doyle.

# 12

Doyle waited on a bench inside the café's waiting area, watching out the window for Williams. She'd already called Reynolds, and informed him of the latest miraculous development. "It's called 'peanut butter.' The jar has a red lid. Buy lots."

"Certainly, madam," Reynolds had said. "Anything else?"

"I think you can spread it on many different things," offered Doyle. "Use your judgment."

"Perhaps we will start with melba toast," he'd suggested, as though it were a rare delicacy.

"Can't wait," she'd replied, and had rung off.

She texted Acton, who was in the midst of Wexton Prison-related meetings with the DCS and the Prison Board. "Have a million things to tell u."

The response came almost immediately. "I can spare 10 min."

Not unexpected that he was busy, poor man. She thought about it for a moment, then texted, "No worries—can wait."

Sheathing her mobile, she settled in to watch the traffic go by. After Percy left to go back to work, Doyle called Williams, and asked if he could pick her up, and drive her to the Metro animal shelter, since she needed to speak with him. Best not mention to Williams that Percy thought they were a couple—she didn't like to think they gave off that impression. After Percy had watched Doyle devour her peanut butter, the other girl felt emboldened enough to ask causally about Williams.

"He's a good friend," Doyle had explained, licking her fingers. "I'd rather not be talkin' about him in his absence." Percy had taken the rebuff in good part, but her mood had improved considerably after Doyle's revelation. She'll make a run at him—she's smitten, thought Doyle, and he's half-way there, himself. Unfortunately, it was now time for the fair Doyle to throw some cold water on this promising romance.

Seeing the unmarked coming down the road, she went to stand at the curb, so he wouldn't have to pull over. Williams leaned over to open the door for her, and she slid in. "I didn't talk about you," she said immediately.

"I appreciate that," he replied a bit grimly. "What was this about?"

"Don't be angry, Thomas. I needed to sound her out about somethin'."

"All right, let's hear it."

She considered. "Perhaps you shouldn't be drivin'."

She saw him press his lips together. "Is this going to be worse than Savoie?" Williams had been nearly apoplectic, when he'd discovered that Doyle was hip-deep in clandestine dealings with the notorious Frenchman.

"I don't think so," she said cautiously.

"Then do your worst, I won't crash the car."

"Percy's not telling us everythin' she knows about the Wexton Prison case, and I think she knows quite a bit."

He glanced over at her in surprise. "Oh?"

"Yes. I'm that sorry; she seems very nice." She glanced sidelong at him, but he did not respond, as he was thinking over what she'd said. Here we go, she thought; nothin' for it.

"How do you know this?"

Doyle swallowed. "Well, when she said that there was nothin' unusual about Moran's death—that it was not unexpected—she was lyin'. And since he was startin' to blather in his cups about the bribery scandal, I wouldn't be surprised if Moran's death was yet another containment murder. And she lied about several other things also, like when she said there were no files in their chambers that would contain relevant information, and when she said she didn't know of any court personnel who'd know about the scandal."

His brow furrowed, Williams glanced over at her. "How do you know she was lying?"

"I can tell. I have a knack, or somethin'."

There was an incredulous pause. "You *know* when someone is lying?"

"Yes; well—most times."

He turned to look at her for a long moment.

"Watch the road, Thomas."

"Does Acton know this?"

"Yes, of course," she replied, nettled. "And you must'nt mention it to anyone—not even Acton, because he doesn't want anyone else to know."

There was a pause. "I don't believe you."

Her eyes slid over to him. "Yes, you do."

He was silent for a moment. "I have an extra vertebra in my back. I've never had my wisdom teeth pulled."

"Thomas," she protested, thoroughly annoyed. "It's *not* a parlor trick." After a small pause, she added, "And the vertebra thing is true, but the wisdom teeth is not."

"Holy *Christ*."

"You mustn't blaspheme, Thomas." He'd picked up this bad habit from Acton, unfortunately. "So if we can get back to the subject at hand, we have a problem."

Williams was still struggling to maintain his composure, but after a moment he asked, "Was Percy lying about Whitteside?"

"No. Moran did indeed make the comment. And there was somethin' else—" she frowned, trying to remember. "When Percy said it was difficult to come forward, that was not true, either."

Surprised, he raised his brows. "So the whole thing's a set-up, then? Are we being manipulated?"

"I don't know. I wish I did. I tried to get her to talk about it at lunch, but she was close as an oyster."

"I think," he said slowly, "that we tell Acton." He paused. "But I suppose it has to be you that tells him."

She glanced at him, and said gently, "I wanted to let you know; she may be in the thick of it."

"You did right."

He drove, and seemed disinclined to speak any more on the subject. She ventured, "It may not be as bad as it looks."

"I would appreciate it if you allow me to handle my own affairs, Kath."

Thus rebuked, she subsided into silence, and after a moment he reached to squeeze her arm. "My turn to be sorry. Mainly, I'm annoyed because you're not jealous in the least."

"Nor should I be," she retorted. "And you promised you were not goin' to do this to me."

He ran a hand through his hair, and made as if to respond, but said nothing, and they fell into an uncomfortable silence. As Doyle was not one for uncomfortable silences, she said rather defensively, "I only want you to be happy."

"Allow me to decide things for myself, please."

Biting back a retort, she decided she'd best hold her tongue for a change, lest the emotions that were now thick in the car get out of hand. She'd forgotten that she should tread carefully around Williams, which was annoying in its own way, because she was not very good at watching what she said.

His mobile pinged, and he answered. "Williams." He listened, then said, "Yes, sir; I'm dropping off DS Doyle, then I'll be over straightaway." He listened, then handed the mobile over. "He'd like to speak to you."

"Ho," she said into the mobile. "Are you knockin' any heads together?"

"Matters are progressing, I think. How are you feeling?"

"I am well. I am startin' to think you like Chiu more than you like me, though."

"I'd be no better off. She likes Chinese food, too."

She smiled. "Good one."

"Are you heading back to the Met, or going home?"

"Do you need me?" She carefully sidestepped any cat-delivery explanations.

"I'd like to have you listen in to Zao's solicitor, but I'm not sure how I can arrange for it. Let me think about it."

"The one who is doomed?" she teased.

"That's the one," he replied matter-of-factly. "Please give me Williams again."

Williams pulled in to park in front of the Metro animal shelter, and after he'd hung up with Acton, he contemplated his hands on the steering wheel for a long moment. "I should go; are we all right?"

"We are, and we always will be," she assured him as she got out of the car. "I'm that sorry I'm such a crackin' knocker."

He leaned out the window. "No more than I am. You'll tell Acton?"

"As soon as I run my cat-errand. Thanks for the lift." She straightened up, and then paused in astonishment, as the woman coming out of the building was Cassie Masterson.

Masterson saw her at the same time, and there was an excruciatingly awkward moment; the other woman was a disgraced newspaper reporter who had been about to write an exposé about Acton, but Acton had turned the tables by pretending to pursue her. He'd manipulated her into stalling the story long enough to exact a thorough revenge, and now she'd lost all credibility, and was out of a job. As part of this scheme, Doyle had been forced to stand by while Acton pretended a romantic interest in the woman; it was a thoroughly forgettable experience.

Masterson's gaze rested on Williams, and she smiled ironically. "I shouldn't be surprised, I suppose, to discover that you two are in cahoots."

Williams, ever the gentleman, said politely, "I hope you've found another position, Cassie."

"Still searching," she replied. "But I will definitely be more careful; lesson learned." She glanced over at Doyle again, her expression mocking. "No hard feelings, I hope?"

"You were a fool, pursuin' another woman's husband," Doyle retorted, trying to keep her temper in check. "Drinkin' from another's cistern."

"As I said, lesson learned," Masterson replied with a graceful shrug.

As the other woman turned to walk away, Williams grasped Doyle's arm from the car window and murmured, "Count to ten."

But Doyle continued incensed, as Masterson's figure disappeared into the crowd. "How can she be so casual? She tried to ruin our lives."

"You won; she lost. She acknowledges it; everyone moves on."

"She actually thought Acton would divorce *me* and marry *her*." Doyle could not let it go.

"It only shows how delusional she was; Acton will never marry anyone but you—that much is obvious."

"*Stupid* brasser," pronounced Doyle with satisfaction.

"Lesson learned," he replied mildly, and started the car.

# 13

Doyle set the cat carrier down in the hallway, overheated and thoroughly frustrated, and knocked on Mr. Huse's door. She'd phoned the man repeatedly to let him know she was on the way, but had gotten voice mail every time, and she wondered if perhaps he couldn't hear the phone; he did seem hard of hearing.

The cat hadn't taken kindly to being lugged around in the carrier, and had yowled in protest on the tube, which thankfully hadn't been very crowded. Still and all, a very forgettable experience, and Doyle was half-inclined to push the beast down the rubbish chute, and call it a day.

"Mr. Huse," she said loudly, knocking again. "It's Officer Doyle."

The door didn't open; instead, the SOCO's door at the end of the hall opened, and a heavy-set, older man stood framed within it. "So it's you, is it?"

Doyle willingly abandoned the stupid cat to approach the man she presumed was the SOCO's father. "My sincere condolences for your loss, sir."

"Off-i-cer Doyle." The man eyed her sourly. "She thought you were really something—a girl hero."

As this was said in a mocking tone, Doyle was a bit taken aback. "We were friends," she offered, and hoped it wasn't a sin to fib about the dead.

The man shrugged, and retreated back into his daughter's flat. "Not a lot here; all the equipment is gone."

A cold one, Doyle concluded; selfish and mean. Probably not a killer, though; Chiu said he had an alibi, and in truth, he was the sort who wouldn't bestir himself enough to murder his poor daughter. Changing her manner from sympathetic to brisk, Doyle said, "I understood you had a fallin' out with your daughter last week. The neighbor said you had an argument in the hallway."

"I already told the China lady," he protested with the wave of a ham-sized hand. "It weren't a big deal; she wouldn't let me in—didn't want me to see what she was working on." He shook his grizzled head. "Daft, she was. I told her to stop all her nonsense, and get back to Liverpool; her sister needed help with her kids."

Although Doyle was inclined to hotly defend the decedent to her uncaring parent—faith, it was turning out to be a very contentious day—her scalp started prickling, so instead, she tempered her reaction, and asked, "What was it that your daughter was workin' on, sir?" There'd been nothing in the flat that seemed related to a project, work-connected or otherwise.

The man shook his head and shrugged. "Ha; *I* don't know what it was, she wouldn't let me see—didn't you hear me? She was going to be a hero, though, just like you. Some hero." He made a gesture that indicated the empty flat. "Look where it got her."

This is important, Doyle thought in surprise, her instinct prodding her; I wonder why? "You've no idea what she was talkin' about? It may be a clue, to help solve her murder."

The man raised both hands in disgust. "She always had big dreams that went nowhere. This time she thought she'd break a massive story, and her snap would be in all the papers with that famous detective—that Lord what's-his-name."

Doyle stared at him. If I were Williams, she thought, I'd say "Holy Christ."

"So what's with the cat—is it a police cat?" The man peered around her at the pet carrier in the hallway, clearly tired of discussing the dead daughter, who hadn't left much of value in her flat.

As the cat yowled in frustrated outrage, Doyle tried to pull her scattered wits together. "Oh—it was your daughter's cat. Her neighbor, Mr. Huse, is going to take him in."

But her companion only seemed to find this amusing. "Ha; no he's not. He's dead, too."

"Dead?" Doyle stared at him incredulously. "Are you sure?"

"The building manager told me when I came to get the key; said he couldn't believe it—two people dead on the same floor in the same week."

"A moment, please." Her mouth dry, Doyle stepped aside, and pulled her mobile to call Chiu, only to be sent to voice mail. After hesitating for a moment, she rang up Acton on their private line, and he, bless him, answered immediately. "Kathleen."

She could hear voices in the background, and said quickly. "I'm sorry to be botherin' you, but I'm at the SOCO's flat and somethin's come up; a witness is now dead—not the one who was lyin', the other one—and I think there's somethin' here." As the SOCO's father was within earshot, she added with meaning, "It's one of those things. I'd like to re-seal the flat, and bring in the SOCOs again, for another look round."

"Can't you speak over the phone?" He must have sensed there was someone listening.

"I don't know what I've got, yet," she admitted. "But I wouldn't be surprised if it's connected to somethin' big, and that we're lookin' at a couple of containment murders."

"Right; can you wait? I should be free in an hour or two."

"I'm that sorry to pull you away, Michael, but I think it's important."

"Don't worry; I'll see you soon."

After she rang off, Doyle pulled her occurrence book out of her rucksack, and began scribbling notes, trying to remember the bits and pieces of information that she hadn't thought were very important, up to now.

Watching her with open annoyance, the SOCO's father protested, "Here now; you're not going to shut the place down again?"

Thoroughly irritated, Doyle decided that a small abuse of power would not be out of line. "Yes. And in the meantime, you are goin' to sit at the table and write out a statement of everythin' your daughter said to you over the past two months, together with the dates and times."

The man blustered in disdain, "How am I supposed to remember all that?"

"Because otherwise you are goin' to the nick for obstruction of justice, that's how."

As was the case with all bullies, he buckled under pressure, and retreated with a show of reluctance. "All right; all right; I think there's a pad here, somewhere."

Alert, Doyle asked, "Is there? Don't use it; I'll want to test it for impressions." Oftentimes the writings from a torn-off page could be discerned on the blank page beneath. "Don't touch anythin', and call the manager to come up here."

While she waited, Doyle rang up Syed, the evidence officer on the case, to explain that she wanted to re-open the forensics investigation at the SOCO's flat. Fortunately, he was willing to indulge her, even though she could hear in his voice that he wasn't certain there was much call for it. She explained, "I think there is somethin' here that's bein' covered up—somethin' that was removed from her flat. D'you know who she was friendly with, within the unit? I'm hearin' that she had a project she was workin' on—somethin' mysterious, that she thought was very important. D'you know anythin' about it?"

He thought about it for a moment. "Occasionally, she'd go out for drinks with everyone, but I don't remember her saying anything unusual." He hesitated, embarrassed. "She rather admired your husband."

Doyle said fairly, "Can't be blamin' her; I rather admire him, myself."

"Yes; well, she was a bit—immature, I suppose, despite the type of work we do."

"Can you ask around for me? Find out if she had any secrets, or dropped any hints? I think it's important."

"Will do."

After she rang off, Doyle turned to ask the dead girl's father, "Are there any other relatives your daughter may have spoken to about this—about her secret project? Or can you name any of her close friends?"

But he continued uncooperative, and shrugged without even looking up from his task. "No. Her mum's dead, and she kept to herself, as far as I know."

Like me, thought Doyle—except in my case a certain chief inspector swooped in to save me from myself; it's a shame no one did the same for her. "Keep writing," she directed. "Lord what's-his-name is comin', and he'll be wantin' to ask you a few questions."

# 14

T wo hours later, Doyle was in the SOCO's spare room, trying to make her case to Chiu and Syed while Acton listened
without comment. It was not necessarily going well, but as
she was the bridge-jumper, and married to a peer of the realm who
appeared to find her credible, they were careful not to express open
doubt. The cat carrier was now situated on the kitchen counter, with
its occupant still yowling in protest at his involuntary confinement.

Doyle explained rather lamely, "The victim's father said she
wouldn't let him go inside—said she was workin' on a project that she
didn't want anyone to see. They were arguin' in the hallway about it."

"It weren't a big deal," the man called out defensively, from his
position at the kitchen table. "A little brangle—not *that* loud."

"That's enough from you," said Acton in a tone that brooked no
argument, and Doyle noted that both the man and the cat went silent.

The building's manager offered, "The argument was loud enough
that Mrs. Addersley heard it—she rang me up." The manager was a
rather vacuous young man who was related to the building's own-
er, and Doyle surmised that he was probably a shirt-tail relative who
needed a little help in keeping body and soul together. He was not
very bright, but appeared very interested in the dramatic events unfolding in the formerly quiet residential building, his mouth slightly

agape, as he watched from his post at the door. "Do you mind if I feed the cat?"

"Please do so," said Acton, and the young man rummaged in a cupboard until he found a tin of cat food.

Trying to keep her report going, despite these various interruptions, Doyle persisted, "Yesterday, Mr. Huse was speakin' loudly in the hallway because he was hard of hearin'. He told me that he'd been given a key to take care of the cat—meanin' he announced to anyone listenin' that he'd been into the victim's flat, and knew what was inside." She made a gesture that encompassed their surroundings. "And the spare room looks to me like it shouldn't be empty, as compared to the rest of the flat."

Arms crossed, Acton bowed his head. "So you believe the killer heard the SOCO's argument with her father, and as a result, killed her. The killer removed the incriminating evidence, then heard Huse speaking with you, and—realizing that he was a witness as to whatever was in the flat, murdered him in turn."

"I—I suppose so," Doyle faltered, realizing this did not sound very plausible. "Or the killer found out about the project some other way. But I can't think it's a coincidence that Mr. Huse is now dead."

"He was pretty old," the manager offered doubtfully.

"So it was the same killer for both, and your theory points to one of the neighbors?" Chiu's voice held a hint of skepticism. "It seems strange that the SOCO would be working up a case without reporting it to the Met—a case against a neighbor on her own floor."

"It does seem a bit strange," Doyle agreed, wishing she had better answers—truly, it didn't make a lot of sense. "Perhaps we should speak to Mrs. Addersley again." Doyle met Acton's eye to remind him that the woman had lied to the police.

"An unlikely suspect," Acton pointed out reasonably. "She is the one who alerted the manager about the argument, and then alerted the police about the possible murder."

"And she's pretty old, too," the manager chimed in, as he tentatively stroked the cat.

Both Chiu and Doyle turned to stare at him. "How old is she?" asked Chiu. "How old is Mrs. Addersley?"

The manager made a face indicating great thought, then guessed, "Seventy? Eighty?"

Doyle looked at Acton. "The woman we interviewed wasn't much over forty."

Acton straightened up. "Then I suggest we go speak with her."

"You can't speak to her," the manager advised. "She left me a note saying she'd gone to visit her son in the Cotswolds. Not sure when she'd be back." He paused, because the law enforcement personnel had all stopped to stare at him, yet again.

"Is that so?" asked Acton. "Do you have an address?"

Sorry to disappoint, the young man shook his head. "No, sir—no address."

"Do you have a photo of the woman?"

Again, he shook his head with regret. "No, sir—no photo."

"Well then; I imagine you have a key?"

"Can we do that?" the manager asked doubtfully. "Just go in?"

"Indeed we can," said Acton, and made a gesture indicating they were to go next door.

As he went through his keys, the young man explained apologetically, "It's only that Mrs. Addersley is the nervous type—she tends to complain. But if it's the police—"

Reminded, Doyle asked, "She also complained about the smell in the hallway—did you know about it?"

"Oh, sure." He knocked loudly on Mrs. Addersley's door. "It was nasty. Someone must have spilled, when they were using the rubbish chute—I had to have the carpet cleaned."

"What did it smell like?" Doyle persisted. "Bleach?"

"No—kind of like scented candles, or something." The man inserted his key to open the door.

Acton indicated that the manager was to stay back, and the others carefully stepped into the empty flat. It looked the same as it had when Doyle had been there last—very neat, with porcelain bric-a-brac on shelves and tabletops.

"No photos on display," observed Acton, who pulled a pair of gloves from Doyle's rucksack. "Let's look for some."

Doyle offered, "I think the smell in the hallway was connected to the murder, but I'm not sure how. The neighbors noticed it only after the estimated time of death." She paused, thinking about it. "I assumed it was bleach, to scrub the site, but Mr. Huse said no—he said it was sweet, and reminded him of his late wife. He said she used something similar to polish the furniture."

This remark had a profound effect on Acton, who stilled, and then slowly straightened up. "A darkroom. It was benzene; the SOCO must have had a darkroom in the spare room."

"A darkroom?" exclaimed the EO, his brows raised in surprise. "No one has a darkroom for photography anymore, everything is digital."

"Not," said Acton slowly, "if you wanted to ensure that no one else would see what you were developing." In a brisk tone, he began giving orders. "I'll want this flat processed, and let's take a look at the late Mr. Huse—see if there's anything suspicious about his death. I'll want someone to contact the rubbish contractor, to see if we can trace the dump site; we'll want to see if any photographic prints were disposed of, or negatives of the prints." He paused, thinking. "Let's look through the victim's records and receipts, find out where she bought her photography equipment—she may have spoken of her project to fellow enthusiasts." He glanced at Chiu. "We've already looked through her media?"

"Yes, sir," said Chiu, typing quickly on her mobile.

"There was a pad of paper in the flat," Doyle offered. "There may be markin's on it."

"Bag it, please," said Acton. "We'll send out an All Ports Warning on the false Mrs. Addersley; if nothing else, we can bring her in, and hold her on obstruction of justice."

Chiu was typing furiously with her thumbs. "Description is fortyish, Caucasian, about one-thirty pounds, five foot four; dark hair, dark eyes. Well-groomed."

"She seemed very refined; she had beautifully manicured nails," Doyle offered. Doyle bit her own nails to the quick, and so she always noticed. "And lovely earrin's."

She caught a flare of impatience from Chiu. "Can you add anything to the physical description, DS Doyle?"

"Tell me about the earrings," said Acton.

Oh-oh, thought Doyle; I am slated to receive some lovely earrings from my over-fond spouse who is always looking for an excuse to give me something expensive. "They were that blue stone, that lapil—"

"Lapis?" asked Chiu impatiently.

"Why, that sounds like the lady from the council," ventured the manager. "I asked her about her earrings—thought my mum would like some."

Into the sudden silence, Acton tilted his head in invitation. "Tell us, if you would, about the lady from the council."

The young man shifted his feet, made uncomfortable by the attention. "She came by—oh, maybe a week ago. The council was looking for flats to place prison parolees. I told her we didn't have any vacancies—not that I'd put any parolees here, Mrs. Addersley would never let me hear the end of it."

"What did the woman look like?" Chiu asked him briskly. "Did she leave a card?"

But Doyle was distracted by the sudden flare of emotion she was picking up from her usually emotionless husband, who had pulled out his own mobile, and was scrolling with his thumb. He paused, and showed the other man a photo of a dark-haired woman. "Is this she?"

"Why—why yes," the man replied in surprise. "That's the lady from the council."

Silence reigned, and Doyle finally couldn't contain herself. "Who is it, then?"

"The missing prison matron," said Acton.

# 15

Acton was on the phone at the SOCO's flat, trying to track down the waste management supervisor who would know the dump site location for the rubbish from the building. Doyle listened from the kitchen table, and decided he was a very patient man; she'd be threatening arrest if she'd been shunted about as much as he had.

Syed and the SOCO team had been combing through Mrs. Addersley's flat next door, and Doyle was hoping they could head for home soon—she was that tired, what with splicing together two apparently unrelated murder cases—three, if you threw in poor Mr. Huse. A good day's work, if she did say so herself.

The SOCO's father had been released, and the place was now blessedly silent, because the manager had asked shyly if he could keep the cat. Doyle was more than happy to let him take the wretched creature, being as she'd didn't know if she had the wherewithal to take it back to an uncertain fate at the animal shelter. All in all, a very lucky animal.

So that she wouldn't forget, whilst she waited for Acton to finish up, she ran a background check on Morgan-Percy-of-the-untruths, and her deceased mentor, Mr. Moran. Percy had dabbled in activism at university—she was worried about animal testing, it seemed—but didn't have an arrest record. She'd done well at university, and volunteered with various organizations designed to provide legal representation to the poor. After graduation, she'd then been offered the prized position as a junior barrister in Moran's chambers. Doyle wondered if the girl was related to Moran in some way—she'd had a sense that there was something along those lines—but she found no indication. All in all, very routine.

Doyle then checked for articles about Moran's recent death. Again, nothing startling; he had a chronic heart condition—probably aggravated by alcohol abuse—and had died of a heart attack, although the particulars were not disclosed. Many in the legal community had attended his funeral; he was well-respected, and had been a fixture at the Crown Court for many years.

She stared at the screen, deep in thought, and then realized that the screen reflected Acton, standing behind her. She smiled at the reflection.

"I didn't want to interrupt," he said. "You've done exceptional work today."

"It's a case-breaker, I am." She turned to face him. "How goes the rubbish?"

"I don't have high hopes; I imagine any prints or negatives were carefully destroyed, and the darkroom equipment was then pitched down the chute. I'll have a team out to the refuse site at first light, to have a look."

"Don't send poor Williams, please; he's already havin' a bad week."

"Oh? How so?"

Belatedly, Doyle realized she may have to omit certain details from her recital. "He interviewed Morgan Percy this mornin'—she wanted to speak to him away from chambers. She thinks Moran and Colcombe may have been involved in the corruption scandal, and she added the new judge—Judge Whitteside—but she wasn't tellin' the truth on a couple of points, Michael." Doyle frowned, remembering. "She lied when she said that Moran's death was not suspicious or unusual. And also when she said there was no indication that others from the chambers were involved in the scandal."

This caught his interest, and he leaned against the table and crossed his arms. "So she was either involved herself—which seems unlikely, as she is a junior—or is covering for someone."

She sighed. "Yes, I suppose so."

He raised his brows, reading her tone. "You don't think so?"

"No—I imagine that's the case. It's just a shame; she seems a decent sort. She fancies Williams."

He considered this for a silent moment. "Is the attraction mutual?"

This was a surprise, that Acton could be sidetracked by Williams's love life, such as it was. Carefully, she offered, "He's not one to say, but I think there is somethin'—please don't mention it; I shouldn't be tellin' tales."

Absently, he gazed out the windows—it was starting to rain again, and because he did not immediately comment, she prompted, "Did you already know Moran's chambers were involved in the corruption scheme?"

He brought his attention back to her, and gave her one of his patented non-answers. "I'll look into it; say nothing, if you would."

"I would," she agreed. "I also ran the program you suggested, to compare unexpected acquittals by gender—no easy task, my friend, especially when the suspect's name is foreign, and I haven't a clue about the gender. It turns out that Colcombe had a much higher-than-average record of female acquittals."

Acton nodded as though he was expecting this. "Were the females usually foreigners?"

She gave him a look. "All right then; I'll run it." She had a sneaking suspicion that Acton was giving her busy-work, and so asked, "What is the workin' theory, if I may be askin'?"

He replied evenly, "I believe the prison corruption scandal is also a sex scandal."

She stared at him for a moment, remembering what Williams had implied. "The immigrant sex slavery ring? *That's* connected to this?"

"I would not be surprised."

"And who is it who's havin' sex?" Doyle was at sea.

"We shall see," was all he would say.

"I'm not goin' to keep breakin' all your cases for you if you keep me in the dark, Michael," she replied crossly. "Honestly."

In a conciliatory gesture, he placed a hand on her shoulder and gently squeezed. "I am sorry, Kathleen. I don't like this case, and I don't like your dreams."

But she reminded him, "The dreams aren't really nightmares, Michael—they're more puzzlin', than anythin'."

"They're a little ominous, you must admit."

Doyle found this unfair, but knew they'd be no budging Acton if he was worried about her safety, and so she tried a different tack. "Well—can you at least tell me how the prison matron is connected to this case? D'you think she coshed the SOCO, because she realized the SOCO was workin' on the secret photographs, whatever they were?"

"We can't yet be certain that the matron was the SOCO's killer."

Doyle eyed him, as this remark seemed to be a bit too cautious, even for Acton. "If she's killin' all the neighbors, and leadin' the police astray, it does seem likely, my friend."

"That is precisely the point; the matron has gone to bold lengths, and taken great pains to contain the fallout—to cover up the original reason for the murder. Yet, if she is indeed carrying out these containment murders, why did she miss the main chance?"

Doyle knit her brow, not quite following, and he patiently explained, "The darkroom threatened exposure of the incriminating prints, so it disappeared without a trace. The real Mrs. Addersley, who was worried for some undisclosed reason, also disappeared without a trace. Mr. Huse knew of the darkroom, and so he was also killed—although his death would have been overlooked, but for you."

"And the cat," she added fairly.

"And the cat." He met her eyes. "So there was a very thorough cover-up to avoid any trace of the SOCO's secret project, except for one thing."

The light dawned, and Doyle saw what he meant. "The SOCO's body was left in her flat, plain as day." She frowned. "So someone else killed the SOCO, and the matron came in to scrub the scene?"

"Perhaps. Or another possible explanation is that the body was deliberately left to send a message—as a warning to another player."

She thought about this for a minute. "The SOCO's body was left to make sure that the others who are bein' coerced by these villains don't get any heroic ideas—is that what you mean?"

"Yes—something like that. In any event, little more can be accomplished tonight, so let's head home, and find you something for dinner."

"I've already arranged for my dinner," she said airily, shutting down her laptop. "Look to yourself."

She wouldn't answer any further questions, but immediately upon arrival at their flat, addressed Reynolds with a great deal of eagerness. "Did you get it?"

The manservant bowed slightly. "Yes, madam. Would you care to partake?"

"Please."

With a flourish, Reynolds produced a small plate of toast triangles, artfully arranged and topped with peanut butter.

"Good God," said Acton. "What is that?"

"I have found somethin' I can eat," Doyle told him proudly. "It's peanut butter." After giving him an abbreviated version of her experience at lunch, she concluded, "It's the strangest thing; I could eat the whole jar with a spoon." She promptly bit into a slice to demonstrate, and then offered it up to him. "Will you be wantin' a taste?"

He leaned over to kiss her. "That's close enough."

"Milk," she decided, licking her fingers. "I'd like some milk."

They had their dinner, and after Reynolds had cleaned up and gone home, Doyle sat on the sofa gazing at the fire, while Acton worked at his desk. She felt much better—amazing, the difference a bit of food could make. When Reynolds had presented Acton with his lamb chops, however, she'd left the table—apparently she'd no appetite for anything other than peanut butter. And Williams's coffee, of course; between the two, hopefully it was life-sustaining. I've turned a corner, she thought; everything's going to be miles easier from here on out. Now I have only to soothe Acton, who is all worked up about this case, for reasons that he is unwilling to disclose. And he's worked up about my dreams, too. She glanced over to where he sat, reviewing some documents that he'd pulled out of a manila envelope, and decided that it wouldn't hurt to get him worked up about something else, for a change.

As she was well-versed in the working-up of her husband, she stood, stretched, and then walked over to stand behind him, running her hands down his chest. He immediately logged off—always one to take a hint, was Acton. Rising, he took her in his arms as she began unbuttoning his shirt and placing the occasional kiss on the skin thus exposed. "I've my appetite back, I think; let me check."

"If you're too tired, Kathleen, you needn't humor me."

She gave him points for sounding sincere, even though he was pulling off her shirt with no further ado. "I'll humor you one, I will."

"If you wouldn't mind."

She laughed, and he swung her up to carry her to the bedroom—she was almost surprised to discover that she was eager for sex; it had been awhile since she'd felt like her old self, and it was past time to make it up to her better half.

A very satisfying space of time later, she lay on her side, with her back cradled against his chest and the covers in disarray on the floor. "How long has it been since you've had a drink?"

"A while," he replied in a neutral tone, stroking her arms.

"Good father." She could feel him smile, and added, "You may be needin' one; I ran into Cassie Masterson today."

He stopped his movements. "Oh? Was it contrived?"

"No, I don't think so. I was walkin' into the animal shelter with Williams, and she was walkin' out; she was genuinely surprised to see me."

"And?"

"She said somethin' about how I'd won, and she'd lost, and hoped there were no hard feelin's. So I wished her well."

He chuckled, deep in his chest, and she admitted, "Williams had to hold me back."

"You could take her."

"Considerin' you almost did, Michael."

"Unfair," he said mildly.

Turning over to face him, she ran her thumb across his chin, and he bent his head to kiss it. "You know, Michael, for an unemployed journalist, she was wearin' a very expensive suit of clothes—looked very smart."

"Solonik's money, no doubt. He was paying her a fortune to do the exposé about me."

She thought about this, fingering his ear so that he flinched away, because it tickled. "Do you think they were married, Masterson and Solonik?"

He was surprised by the question. "No, Solonik never married." He seemed certain, and he probably would be, having done a thorough search for potential blackmail material.

"It's just that I'm rememberin' our lovely visit to Trestles, and how Masterson was lyin' when she said she'd never married."

"I have married." Acton leaned in to place his mouth against her throat.

"I see where this is goin'," she sighed, and settled in.

# 16

That night, Doyle had the dream. Again, the man was fortifying the door against the danger, whilst she observed from a small distance. "Thomas?" she asked tentatively, but the man did not respond.

"*Cherchez la femme.*"

With a start, she looked beside her, and saw Maguire, the newspaper reporter—only as he had been when she first met him; healthy and overweight and rumpled. Smiling, she greeted him. "I'm that glad to see you; fill me in on all this, my friend."

But he only shrugged in his cynical manner, and jerked his head toward the man at the door. "You'd better help him. It's another containment murder."

Puzzled, Doyle looked toward the young man. "Oh? I don't understand—what am I supposed to do?"

She woke with a gasp, and sat up, gazing into the darkness. Acton rolled over and turned on the light, then propped himself up on an elbow to scrutinize her carefully. "Tell me."

She closed her eyes, and tried to describe what had happened, but didn't mention that she wondered if the man might be Williams. That part, she decided hastily, didn't seem important, and he hadn't responded to Williams' name, after all.

He listened without comment, and so she asked, "What does that mean, Michael—*cherchez la femme?*"

"Roughly, it means 'Look to the woman.'"

She knit her brow. "Is the danger female, then? Perhaps the prison matron?"

Acton tilted his head, unable to commit to this theory. "Maguire was referring to you, when he said it."

"Oh." Doyle had forgotten. "Am *I* the danger, then?"

"Do you think—" he paused for a moment, as though reluctant to say, but then continued, "Do you think the man in danger is Howard?"

This was not a bad guess; Doyle wasn't certain who Howard was, when he'd come to visit them at Trestles a few months ago, she'd only known that he was some important Home Office official, and that Acton was investigating him for a sensitive political case. Howard was about to be quietly arrested, when Doyle had warned Acton that her instinct told her Howard was good and true, and that the evildoers were framing him up, so as to stop his investigation. She didn't know what had happened since—Acton hadn't mentioned him again until now—but it made sense that perhaps Howard was the target of a containment murder.

"Not Howard," she told him with regret. "I wish it were; then all would be clear."

He lay back down, and pulled her against him, reaching over to turn off the light. "Keep me posted, will you?"

The next day at work, Doyle rang up Williams, resolute, but feeling a bit foolish.

He answered, but it sounded like he was walking. "Hey."

"Hey yourself."

"Am I to discourage the contraband?"

"No—but on pain of death, Thomas, no more than a small cup, every two days. This poor child will be born with the willies, else."

"Understood; when and where?"

"I'm really callin' about somethin' else." There was a pause, whilst she tried to decide how to raise the subject without sounding like a madwoman.

He prompted her, "And that would be?"

"How is your health?"

He was surprised by the question, as well he should be. He was diabetic, and didn't like to talk about it.

"My health is good. How is your health?"

"Don't change the subject, Thomas. I am—I am checkin' to make sure you're not bein' careless."

"What is this about, Kath?" He was a remarkably patient man, truly.

She chose her words slowly. "Do you need help in any way? From me, I mean?" She paused, but there was nothin' for it. "D'you think anyone would be wantin' to murder you?"

She could hear echoing voices in the background; it sounded like he was in a hallway. "Have you taken up drinking, Kath? Because gestation is really not a good time."

"I don't drink," she reminded him crossly. "And I'm tryin' to offer my help, here."

"I appreciate that." She could tell he was trying not to laugh. "Is there something I should know? Are you in trouble again?"

Stung, she replied hotly, "You make it sound like I'm always in trouble, Thomas. I'm not so very helpless, you know."

"I have to go; text me when you decide what we are talking about."

She rang off, thinking that didn't go very well at all. She was reluctant to tell him about the dream, being as she'd already shaken him up once this week, and she truly wasn't certain that the dream was about him, in the first place.

Habib presented himself at the entry to her cubicle, holding a message receipt. "DS Doyle; I had a call from a potential witness, asking for you. Since you were speaking on the telephone, I took down his information."

"Thank you, sir," said Doyle, hoping he wasn't listening to her conversation with Williams. No privacy at all, in the land of the cubicles. The name on the message was unfamiliar, and so she asked, "Any clue about what he wanted, sir?"

"He wished to speak directly to you, and was reluctant to say anything further." Habib attempted a joking manner. "It is indeed fortunate that DS Munoz is not here, or she would pre-empt you." This in reference to the anonymous witness, who'd prompted the bridge-jumping incident.

She's a poacher, that one," Doyle agreed, and then to avoid any further discussion of stupid Munoz, began ringing up the witness—Dr. Jeremy Harding, the message said. A receptionist answered the phone, and Doyle explained she was returning a call, and wasn't certain why the doctor had contacted her. She didn't like to state she was with the police, in case it was something the witness wanted kept quiet.

After a moment, the doctor himself came on the line. "Ms. Doyle, thank you for returning my call. I must give you some information, and I would like to speak with you privately at your earliest convenience."

Doyle poised her pencil. "May I ask what this is regardin'?"

"I'm afraid I cannot say over the phone."

This seemed a bit unlikely, unless he was afraid of being overheard. "Would you like to come by headquarters, and make a statement?"

"No—I'm afraid not. I must stress it is a private matter."

Doyle's antennae quivered; something was not right, and she was not about to go meet a witness willy-nilly—she'd learned a hard lesson at Greyfriars Bridge. After agreeing to come to Harding's offices that afternoon, she rang off, and immediately texted Williams. "Ring me." She would take no chances.

Munoz came by, and paused to cross her arms on the top of Doyle's cubicle wall. She was in an uncharacteristically benign mood, and full of news. "Remember that witness, Gerry Lestrade? The one that was baiting me at the community outreach?"

No, thought Doyle, reading her aright. No, no, no, *no.*

"I'm going out for coffee with him."

Thoroughly dismayed, Doyle swallowed, and knit her brow. "D'you *truly* think that's wise, Munoz? He was a bit sketchy, as I recall."

But the beauty only examined her nails, unperturbed. "Not if he's hanging about with a minister's secretary, he isn't. I thought I'd give him a chance—he keeps turning up."

Holy Mother of God, thought Doyle in abject horror; it wants only this. "Let's go out to lunch, Munoz; we haven't had a chance to stop traffic in a while."

"You can't eat anything," Munoz accused.

"Not true: I can eat; and—and I think Williams wants to come."

Munoz gave her a skeptical look. "Williams wants to meet us for lunch?"

If he doesn't kill me first, thought Doyle. "Yes, indeed he does." She decided Williams would appreciate safety in numbers, and added, "And I'll see if the transfer from MI-5 wants to come; he seems nice enough." After DC Samuels had met his untimely end, their numbers were depleted, and so the unit had taken a temporary transfer from counter-terrorism.

"Don't make it sound like I asked for him," said Munoz, who encouraged only those victims she'd carefully vetted herself. She flipped her hair back and wandered off, saying over her shoulder, "Text me when you're ready."

Doyle then called the transfer, Officer Gabriel, and invited him to join them at the pub, which was a short walk from the building. He seemed pleased to be included; hopefully he could help distract Munoz from her chosen course.

As soon as she rang off, Williams called her. "I'm free; are we going to have another obscure conversation?"

"No," she replied crossly. "You are not appreciative enough. Instead I was wonderin' if you could accompany me to a witness interview." Doyle explained the call from Dr. Harding. "I don't like it; I've had my fill of mysterious witnesses."

"Do you think it's about the Wexton Prison case?"

"Maybe. I'm just a bit uneasy; he doesn't want to tell me anythin' over the phone. He says it won't take long." She then added in an over-casual manner, "Oh, and we're havin' lunch with Munoz, at the pub."

There was an ominous silence.

"I need to distract her, Thomas. She's interested in someone *completely* unsuitable."

But he wasn't buying it. "Not Munoz; she's not going to waste her time on someone completely unsuitable."

"*Please*, Thomas; I promise I'll slap her hand away, too."

"All right, but you'll be busy."

She had to smile. "Truly? I'm a bit shocked, Thomas. Irresistible, is what you are; perhaps you shouldn't work out so much."

"Sit between us," he instructed, and rang off.

# 17

Doyle and Munoz went by Officer Gabriel's desk to pick him up on the way to lunch. He was of mixed race; his mother was Persian, and his father English, and the result was rather attractive, with pale skin but dark, heavy eyebrows and dark eyes. He seemed very affable, and shook Munoz's hand without any outward indication that he'd instantly become her slave, which was actually a bit disappointing, for a change.

"I'm very pleased to meet you both; your fame precedes you."

"Never speak of it again," Munoz directed in a curt tone.

"Right, then," he said easily. "A sore subject."

"Not that DS Munoz is being unfriendly," Doyle hurriedly assured him, as the other girl headed down the hallway. "She's just being modest."

"Good *God*," threw Munoz over her shoulder.

"She's truly *very* nice," whispered Doyle in an aside. "Pay no attention."

As they made their way out of the building, Munoz gave Doyle a sidelong glance. "I hope you don't mind; Lizzie from the lab will be joining us."

On the other hand, perhaps there was no point in even pretending that Munoz was nice. She'd hinted in the past that Acton was on intimate terms with Lizzie, and no doubt had invited the other girl so as to stir up trouble. "That's just grand," said Doyle with a bright smile for Gabriel's benefit. "The more, the merrier."

To her immense surprise, however, she discovered that Lizzie from the lab was the woman who had acted the role of her maidservant, when Doyle had visited Trestles on that never-to-be-forgotten occasion.

"Lizzie Mathis," the young woman said, taking Doyle's hand without a hint of recognition.

"I am that pleased to meet you," said Doyle in return, vowing to blister Acton at her earliest opportunity. Mathis was intelligent and reserved, and just the type of person her husband would enlist to assist him in his shadowy doings, but nonetheless it was a crackin' annoyance that Doyle hadn't been informed of the woman's dual role.

"How do you like forensics?" asked Gabriel with a show of interest. "I was tempted to go that route, myself."

"It is a very fluid field, right now," the girl replied. "There are amazing advances on the horizon; ID by antibodies, or retinal scan, for example."

"Munoz is very interested in forensics, also," Doyle informed Gabriel, who was unaccountably talking to the boring Mathis. "Aren't you, Munoz?"

But Munoz had been checking her mobile for messages, and was not paying attention. "New homicide," she announced. "Victim is a nun. Who would kill a nun?"

"A religious kook?" suggested Gabriel. "A religious kook with a grudge?"

"She wasn't wearing a habit at the time, though." Munoz frowned as she thumbed through the preliminary report.

Doyle asked, "Was she in the wrong place at the wrong time?" This was an unfortunate but all-too-often occurrence; tourists or other naïve souls would wander into dangerous territory, all unknowing.

"I don't know—if it's in Drake's jurisdiction, maybe I can get assigned."

"Have you worked with DCI Drake?" asked Gabriel. "I'm supposed to help out with his major crimes case load."

"Yes, I've worked with him," Munoz replied in a diplomatic tone. "Just be sure you make him look good."

While the others all smiled, Doyle was reminded that Drake still had a cloud hanging over him, so to speak, and that she should have asked Maguire about it in her dream, while she'd had the chance. The problem was, she never felt as though she was a participant in the dreams—not really. It was more as though she was merely an observer—as though she was watching something unfold that didn't concern her.

Her thoughts were interrupted by their arrival at the pub. The crowd was thin—as the weather was cold—and so they easily secured a large corner table. Doyle saved a seat for Williams, who arrived just as the bangers and mash were being served. With a deliberate motion, Doyle began applying peanut butter to toast, and tried to avoid inhaling the scent of the bangers, which were stomach-turning greasy.

"Do you miss counter-terrorism?" asked Munoz of Gabriel.

He thought about it as he rested a fork. "It's interesting, but it's nerve-wracking too. I'm enjoying the change of pace over here, I must say."

"Do you need to know languages?" asked Doyle, who didn't, and wished she did. English was tough enough.

"I know Farsi, and Arabic," he admitted. "It's helpful, and no doubt one of the main reasons I was recruited."

"Munoz knows Spanish," Doyle offered, trying to boost her stock.

But the beauty's thoughts were clearly elsewhere. "Do you know any French?" she asked with a hint of wistfulness. "I wish I knew some French."

"Some, but I'm not proficient." Gabriel turned to Doyle, who was eyeing Munoz with deep dismay. "Do you speak any Gaelic?"

Doyle nodded. "I was taught at school. I'm rusty, though; it isn't spoken as much in Dublin—mainly in the far west, instead."

"It's useful in counter-terrorism; often the communication is in Gaelic, and it's tough to find a translator who's willing to grass."

Doyle tried not to look conscious on behalf of her countrymen, and Mathis, who'd been quiet up to this point, said to Gabriel, "You may not be aware that DS Doyle is married to DCI Acton."

Gabriel grimaced good-naturedly. "Put a foot in it there; no offense meant. I serve as a translator, myself."

"Sometimes Acton needs one, with me," Doyle replied easily, and everyone laughed.

Munoz decided it was time to change the subject to one that featured herself. "I've been assigned to a task force that's supposed to pull together a report and recommendation on how to avoid deaths in custody."

"There's nothing worse than a task force," observed Williams with sympathy. "It's usually nothing but a time-suck, and no one really wants to hear the truth, anyway. Who's the lead?"

"I don't even know yet. The brass are rushing it together to stem the bad press. They want to show that every effort is being made."

"Best investigate Williams, then," Doyle pointed out, teasing. "It's a hazard, he is."

"I've only lost the one," Williams defended himself. "Surely that's not so bad."

"Someone died in custody? What happened?" asked Gabriel.

"A suspect died in the back seat of the unmarked, as I was taking him in for booking. CPR in the back seat; I don't recommend the experience."

"Did they find any trace poison on his hands?" asked Doyle.

Williams glanced at Mathis for confirmation. "Not that I am aware."

Doyle knit her brow. "Oh. I was thinkin' that maybe he did himself in."

Mathis offered, "I believe the suspect died of a heart attack, brought on by stress and complications from cancer."

Interestingly enough, this was not true. In a casual manner, Doyle continued, "Did they autopsy, then?"

Mathis shook her head. "The family requested immediate cremation, and considering his general health, an autopsy wouldn't have been worth the expense."

Doyle knew this was not true even without her perceptive ability; Maguire had no family in the picture. I wonder, she thought, what this is all about. She recalled Williams' hesitant questions about whether Acton would cover up evidence to protect Drake, and decided she'd best find out what her husband was up to—hard to imagine he'd protect Drake, if Drake was a murderer, but on the other hand, it couldn't be a coincidence that Drake was avoiding her, and Acton's henchwoman was sitting here, lying about Maguire's cause of death.

Munoz asked Gabriel, "What type of cases has Drake put you on, so far? Any homicides?" Munoz was always laboring under the conviction that everyone handled homicides except her.

"Yes indeed, although it's a grisly subject for the lunch table."

"Do your worst; we can handle it." Munoz teased him with her slow smile, but Doyle could tell her heart wasn't in it; she was too busy thinking about her upcoming date with Doyle's worst nightmare.

"A woman in King's Cross was murdered for her fetus."

"Oh," said Munoz, who despite her brave talk, was a bit shocked. "Did the baby live?"

"We don't know," Gabriel admitted. "We haven't identified the suspect, nor found the baby."

"First nuns, and now pregnant mothers," Munoz observed. "What's *with* everyone?"

Doyle kept her gaze on the table, and fought nausea. Don't think about the stolen fetus, she thought, and then naturally could not stop thinking about it. She rose. "I'll be right back," she said easily, and made her way to the loo, where she was promptly as sick as a cat.

She was standing before the mirror, patting a wet paper towel on her face and neck, when Munoz entered, looking self-conscious. "Williams said I should check on you. Are you all right?"

"Mornin' sickness," Doyle replied with a smile. "Sometimes it hits when you least expect it."

"What should I do? Do you want to lie down?" Munoz was clearly unused to her role as handmaiden.

"I'll be all right now; it passes very quickly," Doyle lied. Best not educate Munoz too thoroughly on the perils of pregnancy.

"You're pale," said Munoz critically. "Here, use my lipstick."

Doyle was touched, and dutifully dabbed on just a bit of color. "Better," said Munoz. "You're normally so pale, anyway, that it's not very noticeable."

"You're a rare treat, Munoz," said Doyle. "I don't tell you near enough."

"Just doing what I can," the other girl replied modestly.

They returned to the table, where Gabriel immediately apologized. "If I'd known you were expecting, believe me, I wouldn't have said anything."

"Oh, no," Doyle assured him. "It's the smell of the bangers; I've been fightin' it since I walked through the door."

"When are you due?" asked Mathis.

"Summer," said Doyle. "I'm waitin' for the day when I'm not sufferin' from the mornin' sickness."

"Will the baby have a title?" Munoz asked the question with just a tinge of bitterness— she was never going to get over letting Acton slip through her fingers.

"I think it's an 'Honorable,'" Doyle replied vaguely. Acton had explained it once, but as she hadn't been paying attention, she wasn't certain.

"You don't know whether boy or girl?" asked Mathis.

"No." Doyle didn't want to start discussing ultrasounds, and instead said, "Time will tell."

Munoz sank back against the seat. "Hard to imagine Holmes with a baby." "Holmes" was Acton's nickname, although no one would dare say it to his face.

"Well, you learn quickly," offered Gabriel with a smile. "I have a baby sister, myself. She was something of a surprise, but we all pitched in to help."

"How lovely," Doyle enthused in Munoz's direction. "A devoted family man."

But Munoz hadn't heard, because she was checking her messages, yet again.

# 18

"What d'you think of Mathis?" Doyle asked Williams, as he drove her to the Dr. Harding interview. Mainly, she wanted to see if Williams was aware of the woman's role as a fellow doer-of-shadowy-deeds.

Williams, true to form, was reluctant to engage in gossip. "Nice enough. A little dry."

Doyle teased, "Was she tryin' to play footsie with you?"

He smiled at the idea. "No."

"Well, then; not so irresistible."

"I already knew I wasn't irresistible." He gave her a look.

"Touché," she replied, proud that she'd used the word correctly, and equally proud that Williams could joke about the subject, after their strained conversation of the day before. She was quiet for a moment, and then asked in a diffident tone, "D'you suppose Mathis would falsify evidence?"

Williams was taken off-guard, and said carefully, "What makes you ask such a thing?"

"Nothing—just a thought." Williams had given her an equivocal reply, so she already had her answer. Honestly; half of her job was figuring out what her renegade husband was up to, which brought her to the next subject. "Acton said somethin' about the Wexton

Prison case bein' connected to the immigrant sex slavery case, so you needn't be worried about sayin' somethin' you oughtn't, anymore."

"I'm sorry, Kath, but it's all being kept very quiet."

"Meaning they're hopin' to snag a few big fish, before it's over." This was guesswork on her part, but it didn't take a genius to put two and two together; she hadn't heard a whisper about this, and Acton was on pins and needles, although he was trying to hide it from her. "Who is havin' sex with who?"

"Whom, Kath."

"Fine, then; who is havin' sex with whom?" Faith, what a bunch of sticklers these stupid English-speakers were.

"I think that is unclear. Or at least, I haven't been informed."

This was true. Nevertheless, the scheme was beginning to take shape in her mind, and she began to voice a working theory aloud, just to see how it sounded. "Zao had to cooperate because they'd threatened his sister—presumably with bein' forced into the sex ring. He also lied about bein' a citizen at his interview—he's not really a citizen. I imagine that's the reason this ring is so hard to crack; they draw immigrants in, with promises of a job in government, and phony citizenship papers, then force them to cooperate in—in whatever the corruption ring has as its aim—by threatenin' to report them to immigration. Or—if they need to pull out the big guns—threatenin' to force their wives, daughters or sisters into the sex ring. It's all done by blackmail—faith, a crackin' nasty brand of blackmail."

Warming to this theme, she straightened up in her seat. "That's why Acton wanted to know about female acquittals; they probably bring the women in on a phony arrest to force the men-folk to do what they're told. And it's done right in front of our faces, through government channels, so that everyone else who's involved can see they mean business, and no one dares to grass on them."

"That sounds about right," Williams agreed. "We're dealing with some very ruthless people."

"Who?" she asked, frowning. "And what is the object? It seems a lot of trouble to take, just to run a prostitution ring."

"Money," said Williams. "Money is always at the root of these rigs—and the complicit judges are being cut in, to get their share."

But Doyle shook her head slightly. "I think it's about somethin' more important than money, Thomas. And I think Acton knows what it is." Doyle's scalp prickled, and she remembered Howard, the Home Office official, and the knight who'd visited her dreams at Trestles. "It has to do with the good of the country."

"The good of the country?" He glanced over at her. "What do you mean?"

"Nothin'," she said absently, but knew that it wasn't nothing; knew that it was all connected, somehow—small wonder that Acton was stewing like a barleycorn. "What's happening with Zao, the prison guard?"

As he slowed to turn onto Harley Street, Williams replied, "There's a rumor going around that he's ready to name names—so they're taking their time to hammer out the plea negotiation."

She slanted him a glance, because there was something in his tone that made her antennae quiver. "Best hurry along, then; our friend Zao has got a target on his back."

"I'm sure everyone is aware, and he's being carefully guarded. And at least the sister is now safe."

"Good one, Thomas," she said, smiling at him.

"Sometimes, the good guys win one."

The witness's address proved to be an upscale medical offices building, and Doyle read the brass plaque that identified Dr. Harding as a psychiatrist. After entering the tasteful and muted reception area, Doyle spoke to the very refined receptionist, who in turn informed the doctor of their arrival.

When the doctor entered, he looked a bit taken aback, when they introduced themselves. He was a slim, short man, who sported spectacles and a trimmed beard, in the best tradition. "I'm sorry, officer," he said to Williams. "I should have made it clearer; this is not a police matter, it is a personal matter, and I'm afraid I can speak only to Ms. Doyle."

This was unexpected, particularly because the doctor was lying when he said it was a personal matter, and Doyle's scalp was prickling to beat the band. She turned to Williams. "Oh—right, then; would you mind waitin' for me, Officer Savoie?"

"Right," he replied, meeting her eyes. She knew he would text her in a few minutes, as she'd asked him to do when she'd met with Savoie. As was the case then, if she didn't answer, he'd come in to rescue her.

Doyle followed the doctor into his office, her footsteps sounding over-loud in the quiet room, and he indicated a chair across from his desk. I wonder what this is about, she thought. Her instinct was banging about, warning her to be wary, and her instinct was rarely wrong.

He began without preamble, "Your husband was my patient for several months, earlier this year."

Doyle stared at him in surprise. When she'd been pregnant the first time, Acton decided he should seek treatment for his obsessive condition—which was a measure of his devotion to her, because Acton was a very private person, and with good reason. Although she was not aware of the particulars, the therapy had not gone well; Acton's drinking had worsened, and finally he'd stopped going altogether.

"I see," she said to the doctor, although she didn't see at all. Her mobile vibrated, and she quickly texted "OK" to Williams in reply.

"I am required by law to inform you that—based on a reasonable medical probability—I believe you stand in danger from my former patient."

Doyle blinked, and then gazed at him blankly. "What?"

With careful fingers, the doctor adjusted the bracket clock on his desk. "Normally, treatment is strictly a private matter between myself and the patient. However, if I believe there is a danger to a specific person, I am obligated by law to inform that person of the potential danger."

She continued to stare at him. "You're sayin' you believe Acton may do me harm."

"Yes." He nodded slowly, for emphasis. "I'm sorry to have to tell you, but it is imperative that you be informed. You are in grave danger."

They regarded each other; Doyle thinking furiously. "I see," she said again. "And why did you wait so long to be tellin' me this?"

The man clasped his hands on the desk, and bowed his head. "It has come to my attention that you are pregnant. I believe the pregnancy could trigger a violent reaction."

But rather than betray any alarm, Doyle asked, "Who else knows of this?"

He adjusted his glasses, puzzled. "I'm—I'm not certain what you mean, Ms. Doyle."

"Are you required to inform the police, or anyone else of this—this concern of yours?"

This was apparently not the reaction he expected, and he frowned, and cleared his throat. "Well—I am obligated by law to make a record, to show that I made this disclosure to you today, but there is no requirement that I inform law enforcement. That is strictly for you to decide."

Nothin' for it, thought Doyle; another *flippin'* crisis, and no rest for the weary. "Is this conversation bein' monitored, or recorded?"

He stared at her for a moment. "No—no; of course not. I'm not sure you understand what I am telling you—"

"Doctor," she interrupted, "I am a fair-minded person, and so I will give you one chance to tell me who put you up to this."

He placed his palms against the surface of the desk, and Doyle knew he was trying to suppress his alarm. "I assure you, Ms. Doyle, it is a valid concern, and the law must be obeyed." For the first time, his self-possessed manner faltered a bit—not that Doyle needed to confirm what she already knew.

"You should be heartily ashamed of yourself, then, and let this be a lesson to you." Bending down, she pulled her gun from her ankle holster, and then stood to aim it at him. The doctor gaped at her.

"Keep your hands where I can see them, and stand up slowly."

"What—what are you doing?" he stammered.

"I'm turnin' the tables. You've assaulted me." She pulled her ponytail band so that her hair came loose, then pinched the side of her neck.

He stared, blustering and incredulous. "Young woman; it is your word against mine, and I assure you, no one will believe you."

"You forget that I'm the famous bridge-jumper; there's not a soul in London who won't believe me, when you are in the dock for attempted rape."

He blanched, as she bit her lower lip until she tasted blood. Her mobile vibrated, and she carefully raised it up to her line of sight, next to the gun, and texted: "tcall." T Call was police shorthand, indicating that an immediate response was required. Within seconds, the office door burst open, and Williams came through, a gun held before him at arm's length, aimed at the doctor's forehead. "Police," he announced unnecessarily; "Don't move." There was a small, horrified shriek from the receptionist in the outer room.

"Shut the door," Doyle directed, and Williams kicked it closed.

She then asked Williams, "Is there a longer sentence for assaultin' a police officer, or for attempted rape?"

"Assault," said Williams grimly, and with a click, he pulled the loading mechanism back on his pistol.

"Oh my God," the doctor gasped, "Wait, she's lying—"

"I think," said Doyle thoughtfully, "that he is resistin' arrest."

Williams obligingly holstered his gun, stepped to the doctor and—grasping his shirtfront—knocked him out with one blow. The man fell into a heap on the plush rug, and Williams stood over him, looking as though he hoped that a second dose would be needed.

Doyle was already calling Acton on his private line.

"Kathleen."

"Michael, it's a long story, but your psychiatrist was tryin' to frame you for somethin'. I've said he assaulted me—even though he didn't—and Williams has knocked him out." She paused. "We'll need the protocol."

Acton didn't miss a beat. "Cuff him, and bring him in, please; read him the caution and follow procedure, but don't call this in. I'll meet you in the utility garage. "

"Right." She rang off. "We're to cuff him and bring him in. Acton'll meet us in the garage."

Williams pulled a pair of flex cuffs from his belt loop, and bent to secure the suspect, as Doyle returned her weapon to her ankle holster. No point in attempting an explanation for her illegal weapon; it was a stand-off, as Williams had one, too.

Pulling the cuffs tight, he glanced over at her. "Exactly what happened here?"

She hesitated. "I'm not sure I can say, Thomas. It's that divided loyalties thing again."

"Understood." He straightened up. "Your lip is bleeding."

She dabbed at it with her wrist. "Self-inflicted; I had to make it look like an attack."

The doctor began to moan and recover consciousness, and Williams hauled him roughly to his feet. The dazed man was then paraded past the horrified receptionist and the next patient in the waiting room. "He won't be back today," Doyle announced unnecessarily. "He'll be all tied up."

# 19

cton was waiting in the parking garage, and approached the unmarked as they pulled in. There were security cameras in the garage, but no sound recording, and so he took Doyle by the elbow, and turned so they weren't facing the camera. "Let's have a report."

In a quick, whispering monotone she related, "He was giving me some warnin' under the law that you were a danger to me. He was lyin'; it was a set-up. I pretended he'd assaulted me, to gain some leverage."

"Did he do that to your lip?"

The question was asked in a conversational tone, but Doyle had much experience with her husband's conversational tone, and so was quick to respond. "No; strictly self-inflicted."

He gave her a quick, assessing glance, and directed, "Go to my office, please, and stay there until I come for you. I may send ERU to take some photos of you."

Doyle admitted, "I'd rather not bear false witness, Michael."

"It won't come to that." He then turned, and said to Williams and the doctor, "Come along, now."

"I insist on speaking to a solicitor, sir." Despite his brave words, Harding was a bit white around the mouth.

"We shall see," said Acton in a mild tone, and gestured for Williams to follow him.

Following instructions, Doyle went upstairs to Acton's office, trying to keep calm and trust her husband, even though this latest turn of events was nothing short of alarming. She knew that her first instinct was the correct one—someone had put the psychiatrist up to it, as he hadn't believed what he was saying. It was all rather ironic, actually; someone was trying to make it appear as though Acton was a dangerous character when in fact, Acton *was* a dangerous character—something the instigator of this little plot would no doubt soon find out.

When Doyle arrived at his office, Acton's assistant was waiting for her, discreetly hiding her avid curiosity. After explaining that someone from forensics would be along shortly, the girl quietly shut the office door behind Doyle with a last, sidelong glance. She's probably hoping my bleeding lip was the result of Acton giving me the back of his hand, Doyle thought; Acton's assistant was yet another workplace hazard.

To pass the time, she wandered over to her husband's desk, and noted with a smile that he had a new photograph of her. She was in three-quarter profile, her hair in a braid and blowing a bit, her cheeks flushed—the flag of Ireland, her mother used to say. Trestles? It looked like it was taken the morning Acton had given her a riding lesson at his estate. She picked up the photo, and fingered it fondly. The knocker was always taking snaps of her with his mobile; once it had nearly gotten her killed.

There was a tap at the door, and Doyle cautiously approached and asked who it was.

"Mathis, ma'am," the answer came. "I'm here to collect evidence."

Just crackin' grand, thought Doyle, and opened the door.

Mathis stepped inside, scrutinizing Doyle's swollen lip. "Ouch."

"Yes," agreed Doyle. "Ouch. I was that surprised to see you here, Mathis."

"I'm called into Trestles to help out on occasion," the girl answered evenly, and Doyle surmised this meant she acted as Acton's eyes and ears, when he wanted to keep tabs on his scheming mother and heir; Acton's assorted relatives were yet another cause for alarm in what seemed like an unending list.

Although Mathis carried an evidence kit and envelope, she made no attempt to recover evidence—which was a relief to Doyle, as there was none to collect. Instead, the two girls sat across from each other, saying nothing. I feel like Alice, after she'd gone through the looking-glass, thought Doyle. "Do you need me to make a statement, or anythin'?"

Mathis smiled in a reassuring manner. "No—not unless we hear word."

Annoyed that the other girl knew more about her husband's plan than she did, Doyle bit back a retort, and instead idly checked the messages on her mobile. She then decided she was being childish, and so put the mobile away, and set about trying to draw Mathis out in conversation. It was heavy going, as the girl didn't particularly like Doyle, and it was clear she would have been quite content to sit in silence. During the course of the labored conversation, Doyle noted that Williams' name came up more than once. Ah, thought Doyle; perhaps he is irresistible, after all.

They could finally hear Acton's voice outside, speaking with his assistant, and then he came through the door, his gaze on Doyle. "Are you all right?"

"Right as rain," she replied cheerfully, although it hurt her lip to smile.

"Thank you," he said to Mathis. "We won't require a report."

"Yes, sir." The girl rose, and left with no further ado.

"I would have liked a little warnin'," said Doyle with a significant look at the door, as soon as it clicked shut. "It gave me quite a turn when she popped up, like a jack-o'-the-clock."

He took her hands in his, and bent his head. "I asked her to keep an eye on you, and I knew you'd not appreciate it."

This was not surprising; Mathis had been given the same task at Trestles. "You should have told me," she insisted. "Otherwise—" she tried to explain why she was so annoyed. "Otherwise it makes me think you trust her more than you trust me—that she's on the inside, and I'm on the outside."

He met her gaze, startled. "Is she disrespectful to you?"

Doyle sighed, and reluctantly clambered off her high horse. "No—no, of course not. I don't like to be taken unawares, is all."

Gently, he pulled her into his arms, and rested his chin on her head. "Can you humor me in this?"

Of course she could; one of the hallmarks of this tangle of related cases was the threatening of female relatives. If Acton was in the process of exposing the plot, it was entirely possible the villains would go after the fair Doyle, so as to keep him in line. "Resting her cheek against his lapel, she assured him, "I'll take no chances, Michael. I'm bein' very careful—you should have seen how fast I was wavin' my fine weapon at the wicked doctor."

"That was quick thinking."

She smiled in relief—sometimes he was unhappy with her for behaving recklessly, without consulting him first. "There was nothin' for it; I thought drastic measures were needed, with no time lost." She leaned back to look up at him. "What did he say?"

"He is terrified he'll lose his license and his wife; it didn't take much persuasion to have him tell his tale."

"And what's the tale, then?"

"He says he was offered money to give you the statutory warning; he claims he was informed there was a valid concern."

Doyle made a derisive sound. "No, he knew better." She fingered his lapel. "Can you use him as the bait, in a trap and seizure?"

"It does not appear so; Harding was to have no further contact." He paused. "Did you mention to anyone that I'd sought therapy?"

"Of *course* not, Michael." Someone obviously knew, though, and was using it against him. Of course, Acton was a recognizable figure in London, and anyone may have seen him going in and out—the shrieking receptionist, for example, may have been unable to resist mentioning it to her mates. But the whole thing made little sense, when you thought about it. "What was the point of this little morality play? Were they tryin' to smear you? Or did they think I'd believe such a warnin', and flee from you in horror?"

But he was thinking along other lines, and said slowly, "I am wondering if you should start wearing a vest."

She blinked. A Kevlar vest was bulletproof; the latest models were lighter and easier to wear, but she was a small person, and it wouldn't be comfortable. On the other hand, if it meant her husband would be less inclined to appoint annoying babysitters to watch over her, she'd do it gladly, and never count the cost.

"Just as a precaution."

She eyed him, but as he offered nothing further, she asked the obvious. "So—d'you think this ploy was aimed at me? That I'm the one who's in some sort of danger?"

He leaned back to meet her eyes, intent. "Do you?"

This, of course, was the more pertinent question, and so she dutifully plumbed the depths of her feelings on the subject. "I don't think so—I didn't get that feelin', at the time. But I never get any warnin's anyway; I didn't get a warnin' with Owens, or Caroline—or Greyfriars Bridge." Which certainly seemed unfair, when you thought about it. She caught a wave of deep unhappiness from her husband, and mentally chided herself for bringing up all the assorted and sundry attempts on her life; he was a pig's whisper away from locking her up in a tower, and she shouldn't be reminding him that she was a bundle of bad luck.

He pointed out, "You are getting warnings now, though."

She knit her brow. "The dreams? I suppose, but mainly I feel like I'm as thick as a plank, and not understandin' whatever it is I'm supposed to be understandin'." She paused. "But I do know something; remember my dream at Trestles, when I said there was a woman who is not English, but everyone thinks she is?"

"I do."

"I think she's the *cherchez la femme* in all of this."

He ducked his chin and ran his hands along her arms. "We've run a thorough background check on the prison matron, and by all appearances she is English."

Doyle considered this. "Well, I'm not sure if that's who was meant, but she seems a likely candidate, what with her scrubbin' of crime scenes, and then goin' to ground. Munoz was in the field, checkin' in with the matron's neighbors, so she may have somethin' to report." The mention of Munoz brought to mind yet another crisis, and Doyle closed her eyes and rested her forehead against his shirtfront. "I have to tell you somethin' that you'll not be thankin' me for."

"Kathleen," he gently chided. "You should never be afraid to tell me anything, remember?"

A bit late for that, she thought, and soldiered on. "Remember that night when Samuels died, and the—the passer-by was there, the one who wanted to take my snap?"

"The one you said was affiliated with Philippe Savoie?"

She smiled into his chest. Trust Acton to make this easy for her; he'd never asked how she knew such a thing, and he didn't ask now. "Yes; the very same. It seems—" she took a breath. "His name is Gerry Lestrade, and it seems he's makin' a run at Munoz. I'm un-easy, because he's in thick with a minister's secretary from the Home Office."

If he was surprised by this revelation, he hid it well. "I will look into it. Please don't worry."

Immeasurably relieved to have gotten over that rough ground so lightly, she quickly changed the subject. "Are we goin' home, or do you have work to do?"

She could feel him turn his wrist to look at his watch. "I should stay to make some calls; I'm behind schedule, thanks to the good doctor."

"This only supports my theory, Michael, that doctors are a waste of time."

"You have an appointment in two days; have you been eating?"

She could have bitten her tongue for bringing up the subject— she was indeed as thick as a plank. Equivocating, she replied, "I had some peanut butter on toast, at lunch."

"You were sick at lunch."

After a silent moment, she stepped out of his embrace, and met his gaze with a chilly one of her own. "And how would you be knowin' that, if I may be askin'?"

She could see him pause, realizing she was annoyed. "Mathis," he confessed.

Doyle had already known it was Mathis; Williams would never grass on her, and the others had no contact with Acton. She tried to control her temper, but was only moderately successful. "I *don't* appreciate bein' spied on."

"My fault," he said immediately. "I should not have asked her."

With dawning anger, Doyle remembered the seemingly artless questions about Williams. "And my relationship with Williams is *none* of her business."

"Forgive me, Kathleen; I will speak with her."

But Doyle knew this would only make things worse. "No—she'd only think I'm a baby, and she'd be right. Instead I'll have your promise that you will *not* discuss me with her from here on out."

"You have it." His mobile pinged, and despite the fact they were in the midst of a rare argument, immediately, he drew it to answer. "Acton."

Oh-oh, she thought in dawning realization; he was stalling here with me, waiting for this call. Now what?

"Right; I'll be straight down." He rang off, and announced, "Zao has killed his solicitor."

Doyle stared in astonishment, as she watched him walk over to hoist his field kit. "Zao? I thought Zao was in custody."

"He is. The death occurred in Detention."

"Mother a' *mercy*," she breathed. "Another death in custody. What's my assignment?"

"You're to go home, I'm afraid."

"Oh, Michael—"

"I'm afraid that's an order, Kathleen." To take the sting out, he kissed her forehead before heading for the door. "I'll ask my assistant to call the driving service."

# 20

O n the ride home, Doyle was harboring some very disquieting
thoughts. Acton had predicted from the get-go that the solicitor was going to get himself killed. Acton had also given
Zao some sort of veiled assurance in his interview, an assurance that
made the suspect buck his solicitor's advice, and enter a guilty plea.
Then there was the strange delay in announcing the plea, whilst rumors swirled that Zao was about to name names—it was almost as
though they were encouraging an assassination attempt on Zao. But
instead of Zao's getting himself killed, he'd killed his nasty solicitor, and probably with immense satisfaction, if he'd been under the
thumb of these hateful people.

She closed her eyes, briefly, and conceded that it had Acton's fingerprints all over it. Acton was a master at turning the tables, and
now the vile threateners—who were openly abusing the system, so as
to keep everyone in line—had a fine taste of their own medicine. A
victim of the scheme had been allowed to take his revenge, a revenge
that was in full view of everyone who watched, so that a message was
sent to the villains and to the victims alike. Small wonder that Acton
had predicted with such confidence that the solicitor would be killed;
he'd been arranging for it himself.

Which brought up another disquieting thought; out of the clear
blue, Acton had mentioned Solonik's death during Zao's interview,

but it hadn't been out of the blue, not really—Acton never said anything out of the blue. Apparently Solonik's death could be laid at Acton's door, and everyone in London's underworld knew this. Acton had been reassuring Zao that he'd take care of him.

Michael, Michael, she thought; what am I going to do with you? Just when I think we're getting over all the commandments-breaking, you go out and break a few more.

As the town car pulled into the security garage, she decided that there was nothin' for it; she'd have to try to reason with him. He loved her, and she should try to influence him as best she could, and even though it hadn't seemed to work out very well thus far, she should keep trying.

Upon her entry into the flat, Reynolds expressed his dismay at the sight of Doyle's swollen lip. "Acton finally got sick o' my sauce, and clipped me," she confessed.

The servant did not deem this comment worthy of a response. "Can you eat, madam?"

Privately, Doyle couldn't wait for the glorious day when no one cared anymore. "I'll wait a bit, if you don't mind."

"What would you like to serve for dinner tomorrow, madam?" asked Reynolds. Timothy and Nanda were coming over.

"I know what I'll be havin'," groused Doyle, who continued out-of-sorts.

"Lord Acton never seems to indicate a preference," the servant mused.

With a mighty effort, Doyle shook off her sulks, and suggested, "Cornish game hens? I know his mother served them, at Trestles."

Reynolds immediately plucked up. "Is that so? Can you remember how they were dressed, madam?"

Doyle stared at him for a moment. "Well, they had those funny little paper things on their legs."

Reynolds solemnly bowed his head, but Doyle knew he was wanting to laugh out loud, which made her annoyed all over again, since he was the one who'd asked the absurd question, not her.

Wishing she had something to do, she pulled her mobile, but there were no new messages. She was tempted to turn on the telly, but decided she didn't want to be treated to the sight of the press all agog, whilst they interviewed Acton about another shocking death in custody—may as well find out what was going on straight from the source. She texted him, "Call when u have a mo. Just curious."

With gratifying promptness, he rang her up within the minute, and she asked, "How goes it? Did Zao confess, or is there no need?"

"We're almost done, but there may not be much of a case, here."

Doyle quirked her mouth to express her private lack of surprise, but asked with all sincerity, "Oh? How is that?"

"The two were meeting in the briefing room, and it appears the solicitor smuggled in a tincture of hydrogen cyanide to put in Zao's coffee. Instead, the tincture wound up in the solicitor's coffee, so by all appearances, it may have been death by accidental switch."

"And the briefin' room is the one place where there's no CCTV."

"No," he agreed, with all appearance of regret. "There cannot be; we are not allowed to listen in on attorney-client conversations."

Doyle noted that her husband had couched his words so that she couldn't spot a lie, but decided there was little point in calling him out. "Will you be home soon?"

"Another hour, perhaps."

It was just as well, she thought as she rang off; she needed some time to decide how best to handle her wayward husband's latest excursion into vigilante justice. The problem was, she could reason with him until she was blue in the face, and it probably wouldn't make a dent. He was a force unto himself, was Acton, and when he thought his methods might upset her, he simply didn't let her know what was afoot.

In a pensive mood, she wandered into the kitchen to behold Reynolds, bent over the counter, and studying a list.

"Do you remember, madam, how many courses were served at Trestles?"

"Reynolds," she warned in an ominous tone. "If you serve me a fish, I swear on all the holy relics I will swing it by the tail, and knock you down."

"Just so," he said, and crossed an item off the list.

With a sigh, she reined in her temper, and offered, "I know it's the first dinner party you're to handle for us, but I *promise* you it needn't be fancy—and Acton would never notice, anyway."

The servant looked up. "I must disagree, madam. There is little that Lord Acton does not notice."

She met his gaze for a moment, unable to refute this irrefutable fact. "Well then; he'll be pleased, as long as I am pleased."

As this was another irrefutable fact, the servant conceded the point with a nod. "We'll have a cover of soup, then, and the hens. Very simple."

"Perhaps a fruit pie for dessert?" This actually sounded rather good to her.

Reynolds offered smoothly, "A fruit compote, instead. Or perhaps a *torte*."

"I don't know what that means, Reynolds, but I'm partial to fruit pies, nowadays—the ones they sell at the convenience store; I think the crust is made with lots of lard."

There was the tiniest pause, whilst the servant hid his abject horror. "Very good, madam."

"You'll see," she teased. "Next we'll be havin' black puddin', with a full measure o' pig's blood."

"I quite look forward to it." The servant spoke this untruth without turning a hair, and Doyle smiled to herself, as she poured out a glass of milk.

When Acton came home, she covertly assessed his mood, and decided that—although he emanated a sense of satisfaction—he was also a bit preoccupied. He was almost constantly on his mobile, even during dinner, and it didn't sound as though he was necessarily talking to CID personnel, because he did a great deal more listening than speaking.

After Reynolds left for home, Acton retreated to his desk, and Doyle stayed out of his way, lying on the sofa with her own laptop and pretending to work, even though she had precious little to do. Instead, she idly watched him, as he studied his computer screen with an unreadable expression. He had an amazing capacity to handle a complicated caseload and, as Reynolds had noted, no detail would go unnoticed. A genius, she thought with pride—despite the occasional and troubling shirking of the law. I, on the other hand, am no genius, but he loves me regardless, being as he is a bit nicked.

She was tired; she didn't have the stamina she used to, what with this whole being-in-the-family-way business. Drowsy, she turned her face into the sofa back, and thought she could feel Mary moving— now that she knew what it felt like. She'd let Acton feel again, when he was ready to take a break.

She didn't realize she'd fallen asleep, until she began having the dream again. "Tiresome, is what this is," she said in the dream. "It's always the same thing, and I'm not understandin' it."

"Keep trying," Maguire replied. "It's important."

She watched the man barricading the door. "Who's on the other side? It's not the matron; instead, it's someone we know."

But Maguire only pronounced, "Some are dead, and some are not."

Doyle looked at him in exasperation. "That's not breakin' news, my friend."

"Oh yes, it is."

"You're no help whatsoever, is what you are," she retorted crossly. "The wretched press has done me no favors."

"I made you the bridge-jumper." Maguire countered. "And then your husband did me a favor, in his inimitable way."

As Doyle felt it might be bad form to take a swing at a ghost, she decided to ignore him, and instead marshaled all of her energy to take a step toward the man at the door. Striving mightily to focus, she asked, "What is it—can you tell me? Who is on the other side?"

The man did not respond, but straightened up to turn and face her. *Holy Mother of God,* she thought in complete astonishment; you're not Williams at all.

She woke, and leapt to her feet with a gasp, focusing with some difficulty on the room and on Acton, who had also leapt up from his desk, to come to her.

"It's all right, Kathleen; it's all right."

"*Tá sé ina buachaill—*"

Taking her in his arms, he said in a calming tone, "English, Kathleen; I can't understand you."

With a monumental effort, she gathered her scattered wits, her chest heaving. "We won't be needin' an ultrasound, Michael; tis a boy— tis a boy, an' he's *paarfect.* He's paarfect, wi' chestnut hair, an' me mather's eyes." She bent her head, and began to weep into his chest. "He's—he's so *beautiful,* Michael. But he needs help."

"You will be wearing a vest, starting tomorrow," said Acton.

# 21

Doyle held a coffee cup between her hands, as she'd decided that the circumstances warranted a bit of well-brewed comfort. Acton was seated across from her, knee to knee, and between them, they were trying to make sense of her dream.

"Do you think it's significant that it's Maguire?" he asked.

She contemplated her cup. "Yes, I do. What does 'inimitable' mean?"

He paused, surprised by the non sequitur. "It means unique; in a class of its own."

When she made no response, he leaned in to look at her lowered face, and prompted, "Who said 'inimitable,' Kathleen?"

"Maguire." She drew a breath. "He seems to think you killed him, Michael."

Now it was Acton's turn to make no response, and so she filled in the silence. "But he said you did him a favor. He wanted to die, I think, and knew you'd do the deed." She paused. "He knew you better than most."

"Kathleen—"

She lifted her face to his. "Were you tryin' to cover for Drake? Did you know why Maguire wanted to murder him, then?"

She could see that he was trying to decide whether to be honest with her, and was relieved to see that apparently, honesty won. "I could guess."

She ventured, "It has to do with this corruption-and-sex-slavery case, doesn't it?"

"Yes. Although—" he paused for a moment. "Although I believe Drake may have been an unwitting participant."

There was a small silence, whilst she struggled yet again with keeping her composure in the face of her husband's proclivity to go about killing people. He rarely opened up to her on this subject; rarely spoke of his shadowy activities, and so she wanted to stay level and calm, so as to keep this fragile conversation going. "So it was suicide-by-cop; Maguire knew he'd wind up as yet another death in custody."

"A containment death," he corrected her. "Unfortunate, but necessary."

She met his eyes, thinking about this. "Which scandal had to be contained? Drake's? Or were you afraid Maguire would reveal too much about—about your methods?"

He shook his head. "No; after what happened to Masterson, Maguire changed his mind about going public with any exposé about me."

"And I think he rather admired you," she added slowly. It was not surprising, truly; when you thought about it, Maguire and Acton had a lot in common. "And he liked me, too—he still does." She glanced up at him, genuinely curious. "Why was Maguire so certain that you'd do him in, if he went after Drake?"

Acton bent his head, and fingered her hands for a moment. "What would be the result, if the particulars of this corruption case came to light?"

She retorted without hesitation, "A passel of blacklegs would be packed off to prison, and a good riddance."

He shook his head slightly. "I meant the larger picture—what would happen to the Crown Court?"

She hadn't thought about this, and ventured, "I suppose all the questionable acquittals and soft sentences would be set aside, and all the suspects would have to be re-tried. They'd have to sort out the genuine results from the invalid results."

"But at what cost?"

Honestly, thought Doyle; it's as though he's the teacher and I'm the not-very-bright student. She thought about it some more. "The public would be horrified; everyone would think the system is crooked. The immigrant community would be up in arms."

"And?"

"And I don't know, Michael. Tell me."

He lifted his head to meet her gaze. "Every criminal case prosecuted during the past five years—ten?—would be the subject of an inquiry put forward by the defense. Those who were convicted would claim it was because they refused to sleep with any official you care to name—and they would be all too pleased to name names."

"Saints and holy angels," she breathed. "I see."

"Best left alone," he concluded mildly, as though they were discussing the weather.

Doyle, however, could not like this summary decision. "But who are we to shield the system from the consequences, Michael? Perhaps it would be best to expose this vile plot to the light of day, come what may. "

"No," he said with certainty. "It wouldn't."

"I worry about you, Michael," she continued softly. "Maguire, Zao's solicitor—and Solonik, I imagine. You canno' go on like this."

He dropped his gaze to her hands again, and she could feel him withdraw into himself. "I'd rather not discuss it, I'm afraid."

She leaned in, and persisted in a gentle tone, "D'you notice that I always manage to find out about it, despite your best efforts? And at the same time, I'm the only one in the world who might convince you to think twice? I don't think that's a coincidence, Michael—we both know I'm not that smart."

He raised his gaze to hers, but made no response, and she couldn't tell what he was thinking. He hadn't withdrawn his hands, though, so she carefully concluded, "Just think on it, please; it seems to me that some of these messages—or whatever they are—are not necessarily meant for me." Truth to tell, this was not the first time she'd had this unsettling thought; that perhaps her husband hadn't fallen for her at first sight—that instead, he'd been steered to her so that he could, in turn, be steered. It was a bit disheartening, so she didn't like to think about it.

"I will consider what you've said, Kathleen." This was true, but didn't mean much, and his tone held an underlying finality that told her the subject was closed. She was ashamed of herself for being relieved; she may be the only person who could force him to stop, but it was not in her nature to make demands. Besides, the ghosts at Trestles seemed to approve of his methods—although they were a bloody-minded group, to begin with.

He continued, "Is there anything else that Maguire said—can you remember?"

She nodded. "He did say somethin'—although it doesn't seem very helpful. He said, 'Some are dead, and some are not.'"

This seemed to catch her husband's attention, and he frowned, thinking it over. "What could it mean, do you have any ideas?"

"No," she confessed. "I told him that it didn't make any sense, but he seemed to think that it did." She paused, and then tried to explain, "It's very hard to have a sensible conversation; it's as though words aren't the preferred method of communication—instead it's all sounds and impressions." She gritted her teeth, and fought off the panicked feeling that always reared up. She knew—in the way that she knew things—that she was never supposed to discuss with anyone what it felt like to be a human tuning fork.

Leaning back, Acton crossed his arms, and drew his brows together. "So perhaps someone we believe dead is not."

She looked up. "Is Solonik dead—are we certain?"

His eyes were steady upon hers. "Definitely. Why?"

She contemplated her cup again. "That's what leapt to mind, I suppose. You said he was an expert at diggin' up blackmail, and this whole scheme seems to be based on a ruthless brand of blackmail—oh," she exclaimed, startled. "That's it—I knew it was about somethin' more important than money, and that's what's more important than money—reputation. One's good name is more important than money, which is the whole point of paying blackmail."

Acton lifted his chin slightly to disagree. "I would think it is about power. If the victims are exposed, they will be forced to give up their positions of power."

But Doyle could not concur. "I don't know, Michael—I don't think Mr. Moran was drinkin' himself to death worryin' about power. Reputation still matters to some people." She gazed out the windows for a moment. "I need to find out what happened to Mr. Moran; I think it's important, for some reason. Remember, Morgan Percy was lyin' when she said his death wasn't unusual."

He nodded. "And we should consider the possibility that Maguire meant that someone is dead whom we believe alive."

"Like the real Mrs. Addersley? But we already know she's dead."

His gaze rested on her. "We are not yet certain Mrs. Addersley is dead."

"Oh, she's dead, poor thing," Doyle confirmed absently. "I also need to find out what the SOCO discovered; I think that's the key to this puzzle."

He leaned forward to take her hand in his. "You must promise to check with me, before you do any more fieldwork on this case."

She gave him a look. "Then give me another assignment, Michael."

He ducked his chin in concession. "Fair enough; I'll give you an assignment tomorrow, after I see where we are on these cases."

"And don't give me busy-work," she warned. "There's something here—it's just out of reach. The SOCO, and Moran—and the prison matron, who's not who everyone thinks she is."

"Think about it tomorrow, please; tonight let's get you into bed."

With a smile, she took the hand that held hers, and pressed it against her abdomen. "Not Mary after all, Michael. Are you disappointed?"

"I'll come around."

She moved his hand to the side, trying to remember where the movement was. "We'll need another name; can't be callin' the poor boyo 'Mary'."

"Edward," he said. "Edward John."

"Oh." There was a small pause, then she added diplomatically, "Do you like that name?"

"My grandfather."

"The one from the Battle of Britain?" Acton's grandfather—two Lord Actons ago—had been a self-taught mechanic, helping the Royal Air Force during World War II.

"Yes."

Doyle was conflicted; if anyone had ever told her she would have a son with such an English-sounding name, she would have laughed in their face. She ventured, "What was your father's name?"

"No." the syllable was abrupt and vehement.

All right then, she thought—don't talk about his mysterious father, who disappeared many years ago; mental note. "Was 'John' your grandfather's middle name?"

"No; I thought we would honor Father John."

She smiled with delight; Father John was Doyle's priest, and was giving Acton instruction in Roman Catholicism. "He'll be over the moon, Michael—what a lovely idea." She paused, and then said firmly, so as to get used to it, "Edward." Edward obligingly gave the tiniest twitch, and they looked up in surprise to smile at each other. "We are so clever," she pronounced.

# 22

Her rucksack on her shoulder, Munoz paused at Doyle's cubicle entryway. "So; Holmes finally hauled off and belted you?"

"No," said Doyle, who was running a set of unbelievably boring statistics. "Holmes is not a belter."

"So what happened?"

Doyle paused. "An accident. I'd rather not discuss it." Let Munoz draw whatever lurid conclusion she liked; she was being tiresome— gloating, and full of herself. Acton had not yet come through with the promised new assignment, and the only reason Munoz had stuck her head in was to impress the lowly Doyle with her own importance. As a counter-tactic, Doyle refused to ask where the other girl was headed, since it seemed clear she was on the way to some interesting crime scene. I am going to go mad, Doyle thought, if I'm to watch Munoz solve all the interesting cases, whilst I bide my time at a desk, wearing a flippin' vest and not even having a *flippin'* latte to drown my sorrows. That morning she'd asked Habib for a new assignment, but Habib had only looked self-conscious, and given her a quarterly statistics sheet to run. It was clear that Acton had issued an order or two on the sly, and that the fair Doyle was to be kept in check.

"What are you doing, that's making you so sour?"

Munoz had no real interest, but was trying to prod Doyle into returning the question. Pigs would fly. "I am runnin' a statistics sheet, to correlate burglary patterns with major highways. Its facinatin' work."

Munoz could contain herself no longer. "I'm on undercover detail—they recruited me."

Doyle made a face that communicated her extreme disapproval. "I suppose it's no surprise that Vice recruited you."

The other girl looked upon Doyle with a full measure of disdain. "Not Vice, idiot—as if I'd pass as a prostitute."

"You could be one of those high-class prostitutes," Doyle insisted, looking up from her keyboard. "You'd pass muster."

Munoz was distracted into considering this. "Maybe."

"There you go."

But Munoz would not be led away from boasting of her triumph, and lowered her voice. "I was recruited by the Anti-Corruption Command."

This revelation did not improve Doyle's mood, and so with a mulish mouth, she turned back to her tedious assignment. "Well, if they're expectin' the likes of you to exercise some discretion, there's the end of the kingdom. It was nice while it lasted."

"It's not a kingdom; technically. It's a constitutional monarchy."

Crossly, Doyle punched in another data point. "A lot of Irish people wouldn't agree."

"And not-so-coincidentally, there're a lot of Irish people on the Watch List."

Holding on to her temper with both hands, Doyle changed the subject. "So, what's your cover? If you're not a prostitute, then you must be posin' as a dustman's apprentice—they've few other options."

Munoz was stung into replying, "No; I'm supposed to be a confused foreigner, with poor language skills. I'll use you as an inspiration."

Doyle checked herself before firing off the next volley. If Munoz—a beautiful girl, to give the devil her due—was posing as a vulnerable foreigner, this implied that she was working on the corruption-case-that-was-also-a-sex-slavery case, and with a twinge of alarm, Doyle was reminded of the girl's budding romance with Gerry Lestrade; a suitor who—from all appearances—seemed to be a little too friendly with the questionable immigration authorities. As a result, Doyle came out of her sulks long enough to caution, "You mustn't mention this assignment to anyone on the outside, you know."

Munoz gave her a look that was equal parts scorn and condescension. "I'm not that stupid, Doyle."

Doyle hoped not, but she'd already warned Acton about Lestrade, and presumably he was keeping tabs on that little tangle patch. In an attempt to further her own covert operation, Doyle asked with false heartiness, "What did you think of Gabriel? I think he rather liked you."

"Nice enough," said Munoz, with no real interest.

"Nice-lookin'," prompted Doyle.

"He has a live-in girlfriend."

"Ah." So much for that counter-plan.

"What did you think of Lizzie Mathis?" asked Munoz in return, with what could only be described as a knowing smirk.

"Not a lot," said Doyle. "Especially if she and Acton are havin' a torrid affair."

Munoz was stung. "Don't be an idiot, Doyle—I was only teasing you. If Acton was going to have a torrid affair with anyone, it would be me."

"Goes without sayin'," Doyle conceded. "I was just teasin', too."

Mollified, Munoz checked her mobile with a self-important gesture. "I'll be off; I'll let you know as much as I'm allowed to say."

"I thank you," Doyle replied with heavy irony. "I'll be anxiously awaitin' your return."

With a final flip of her hair, Munoz raised a hand in farewell, and moved on. Doyle sat and stewed for a moment, then called Williams.

"Hey."

"I am literally *dyin'* to go out in the field somewhere. D'you need me to interview someone? Anyone? I can't be still sittin' here when Munoz comes back, Thomas—she's bein' sufferable. "

"I think you mean insufferable, and as a matter of fact, I know someone who wants to interview you."

This was unexpected, and Doyle straightened up in surprise. "You do? Who?"

"Gabriel's little sister is doing a report for school about careers. He asked me if I would ask you to speak with her."

"Truly? Why didn't Gabriel ask me himself?"

"Terrified of you."

Doyle laughed. "I'm terrifyin', it's true. Of course I will; do I have to talk about the bridge-jumpin'?"

"I think that's the major draw, yes."

"Right, then. I will try to sound brave and useful."

"Excellent; I'll tell him."

"Back to the original subject, Thomas."

"I do have two interviews lined up; I'm checking in with those detainees who were in the prison's holding area when the female inmate was killed last year. Supposedly it was a fight, but Acton believes that particular death in custody is worth a second look. You may come along, if you like."

"Oh, *bless* you, Thomas. I'm wastin' away here." Acton could have no objection, certainly; she'd be with Williams, and besides, these were peripheral interviews concerning a long-cold case—there'd be small chance of running into trouble.

"Then let's go. We'll pick up some contraband on the way."

"You are a *saint,* is what you are. Meet you in ten."

As they drove to the first address on the list, Williams briefed her on the particulars. "There were four suspects in the processing area on the evening of the murder. They were all released ahead of schedule, and I think that's one of the things that interests Acton."

Doyle had a good guess as to what else had interested Acton. "Was our missin' matron on duty that day?"

"She was."

Doyle tried to decide if she felt well enough to make notes whilst they drove, and opted on the side of caution. "So there are four potential witnesses. Any of them immigrants?"

"Two yes, and two no. I've already interviewed one of each, but the other two were a little harder to track down."

They approached the address for the first witness on the list, a housing project teeming with less-affluent members of society. Doyle had a bad experience in a housing project like this one once, and instinctively stayed close to Williams—not a good memory, it was.

They knocked on the door, and it opened to reveal a young woman, heavily pregnant although she surely wasn't much older than twenty. Mother a' mercy; that'll be me, thought Doyle, trying not to goggle at the hugely protruding belly. How does one manage to move about?

The girl invited them in, and asked with no real conviction if they'd care for tea. When they declined, she sank into the well-worn sofa, and gathered her wrap around her tattooed shoulders—it was a bit chilly in the flat, and she wasn't wearing much. She then waited with no real interest for the two detectives to explain the reason for their visit.

In response to Williams's questions about the prison altercation, the witness made vague gestures, and seemed to have trouble concentrating. She'd been sent to Wexton Prison for a one-year sentence arising from narcotics trafficking. She'd spent only two hours in holding, and then they'd commuted her sentence, and released her on her own recognizance. She was aware of a commotion of sorts, but was vague about the details. She had no particular recollection of the matron.

Drugs, thought Doyle sadly, who'd seen this story a hundred times; drugs and prostitution, and a baby being born into it. As she and Williams descended the stairway back to the street, she sighed. "It's so sad, Thomas—that her life has been mapped out already, and there's little to prevent the certain misery to come."

"She made her choices; now she must live with them."

Doyle took a last glance over her shoulder at the children who were playing on the dilapidated playground. "It's a hard one you are, DI Williams."

"It's not so hard to make the right choices."

Doyle thought of her own mother, abandoned and with a baby. "Sometimes it is." She could feel his gaze resting on her, and added, "And in any event, the poor baby has no choice—at least mine will have himself a fightin' chance."

"It's a boy?" He smiled at her.

"'Tis." She smiled back.

"The ultrasound wasn't so bad, then?"

She hesitated, and then admitted, "I didn't have one—I just know that it's a boy."

He shook his head, as they came to the car. "I'm with Gabriel—you terrify me."

The next address was a small, terraced house in Earl's Court, a middle class neighborhood. A girl of about ten informed them that the witness was visiting next door, and went to fetch her, whilst they waited on the stoop.

"Are you followin' up on Mr. Moran?" Doyle asked, striving for a neutral tone. Williams hadn't said whether he'd gone to meet the fair Miss Percy, and beguile her list of suspicious cases from her.

"Yes," he said briefly.

Awaiting further explanation, she eyed him, but he refused to meet her gaze, instead watching the girl return with the witness. "You don't want to tell me, or you can't?"

"A little of both."

She didn't press him; she'd warned him about Percy, and he was nobody's fool, was Thomas Williams.

The witness was a plump, older woman, who paused to catch her breath at the base of the steps as she assessed the police officers who stood before her. Overall, she looked to be a very unlikely candidate for prison, but on second thought, there was a defiant gleam in her eye that made Doyle reassess. She looked a bit headstrong; a ruckus-raiser, as Doyle's mother used to say.

Without preamble, the witness said to Doyle, "You don't look old enough to be a detective, sweetheart. How old are you?"

"Almost turned twenty-five," Doyle replied a bit defensively. She was often mistaken for younger, and it never ceased to rankle.

"You're a baby," the woman pronounced. "And you should work on that accent." She then turned to Williams. "And you have all the girls after you, my fine fellow; I'd be after you myself, if I were twenty years younger."

"May we come in?" Williams gave the woman a charming smile, but apparently she was not as smitten as she professed.

"Not so fast; I know my rights. What's this all about?"

"We are investigating a death in custody that occurred last year, and we understand you were in the holding area for a time with the decedent."

With suddenly narrowed eyes, the witness looked them over for a second. She knows something, Doyle thought with surprise. "Any money in this?" the woman asked abruptly.

"I'm afraid that is out of the question," Williams said firmly. In truth, sometimes they did pay witnesses, but Williams must have decided he didn't want to pursue that particular path with this particular person. "We can bring you in to headquarters for questioning, or we can take a statement right now."

Apparently, the witness admired a forceful man, and gave him a look that could only be described as coy. "All right, all right; come in—can't fault me for trying."

After they were invited to have a seat at the kitchen table, Doyle leaned to pull her occurrence book out of her rucksack, and then caught a flare of surprise from Williams, seated beside her. She straightened up to find his unreadable gaze upon her, although she could feel he was hiding his intense dismay. "What?" she asked under her breath.

"Nothing," he replied, and turned to address the witness. "Did you notice anything unusual, the evening that you were in holding?"

"The girl that got killed wanted to have sex with a dead judge," the woman disclosed with a gleeful air. "I'd say that's unusual."

# 23

Doyle and Williams sat for a moment in silence, digesting the comment. The witness observed their reaction, and settled back into her chair, clearly enjoying herself.

"Tell us what happened, please," said Williams. "Step by step."

He already knows something about this, thought Doyle—he's not that surprised.

"I was supposed to serve a year for domestic violence—knocked the bastard clean out with a fire jack. But then they decided I could do probation, instead, and now I'm living with my niece." She sounded cheerfully unrepentant.

"Saints and angels," Doyle exclaimed in wonderment. "How did you manage that; didn't he see what you were about, comin' at him with a fire jack?"

"He was drunk as a wheelbarrow," the woman explained. Then, with a female-to-female look at Doyle, she added, "He had it coming."

Although Doyle was winding up to ask about the particulars, Williams steered them back to the task at hand. "When did you first see the prisoner—the one who was later killed?"

Crossing her arms, the witness studied the ceiling. "When they first brought me in, the girl was wailing and making a fuss—she was a foreigner, and it was hard to understand her. She wanted to see her baby, and said she wanted to have sex with a judge—although I am cleaning up her language a bit, seeing as you're so young." This as an aside to Doyle.

"I appreciate it, I do," said Doyle, who'd heard language at the Dublin fish market that would shock even this woman.

"The guard told her to be quiet, and that her judge was dead, but that didn't seem to put a stop to it—she just kept caterwauling."

Williams offered, "The prison record shows there was an altercation between the dead girl and another prisoner, while they were in holding."

"No sir," the witness said with finality. "The hoity-toity matron came and took her away. It was done quiet-like, and I thought it would be best to say nothing, and mind my own business."

Doyle—who'd learned a lesson from the two Mrs. Addersleys—decided to pin down a description. "What did the 'hoity-toity' matron look like? And what made her hoity-toity?"

The witness pursed her lips. "Didn't seem like someone who worked for a living, if you know what I mean. Nice-looking lady. Dark hair, dark eyes. Fortyish. Seemed foreign to me."

This was of interest, and Doyle asked, "Can you say where you think she was from?"

The witness contemplated the table for a moment, and then shrugged. "I dunno; she just seemed foreign to me. Lots of foreigners in this neighborhood."

Williams asked, "Did you hear or see anything afterward?"

"No—then they decided that I could be released. But I wasn't too surprised when I read in the papers that the crying girl was dead." She nodded sagely. "It was all very smoky, if you ask me."

Williams leaned forward and said with all seriousness, "It is very important that you keep this story to yourself. Have you told anyone else?"

"No—I'm no fool. I wouldn't have told you, except that you sweet-talked it out of me." She winked at him.

"We'd like you to come into headquarters with us for a statement—," Doyle began, but Williams raised a cautioning hand.

"No—we'll write out one here, for your signature." He handed her his card. "Don't speak to anyone but me about this, please. If you are contacted by anyone, pretend you have no idea what they're talking about, and then call me immediately."

The woman indicated Doyle with a nod of her head. "What about Molly Malone, here?"

Williams smiled. "Don't even talk to Molly."

"Just you and me, then," the woman agreed with a gleam. "Don't worry; I'll be keeping my mouth shut."

"Good girl," he said approvingly, and she grinned at him, exposing a questionable set of teeth.

After the statement was written out, and the witness cautioned yet again, they walked out to get back into the unmarked. Doyle was quiet, turning over this latest revelation in her mind, and trying not to be alarmed that Williams didn't even want the witness to come into headquarters. Surely, the Met hadn't been compromised by this corruption ring? She was still deep in thought when she realized—after a few moments—that Williams had not started the car. She looked over to see that he was sitting in the driver's seat, regarding her very seriously.

"Why are you wearing a vest?"

She blushed to the roots of her hair, and couldn't decide what to say, so she stammered, "Just a precaution I'm takin', is all."

He held her eyes with his own. "Kath, we are not going anywhere until you tell me why you are wearing a vest."

She took refuge in being offended. "It's none of your business, Thomas."

"Tell me."

Short of leaping out of the vehicle and making a run for it, she didn't see any other option. "I've been havin' dreams that the baby is in danger—or somethin'. It's truly not very clear."

He frowned, thinking this over. "Danger from who?"

"Whom," she corrected. "And that's just it; I don't know—I haven't a clue."

After a few moments of silence, he concluded, "And Acton is worried enough to have you wear a vest."

"Yes," she admitted.

He was angry, was DI Williams. "You should have told me, Kath."

"Thomas," she said reasonably. "How could I? It sounds absolutely crazy."

"I would never have taken you with me today, had I known this."

Now it was Doyle's turn to be angry. "You sound like Acton—I'm not going to be locked away for fear I'll stub a toe; I'll go barkin' mad, Thomas."

"This is not about just you anymore—remember? And Acton has every reason to be worried, this is an ugly set of customers we're dealing with."

But Doyle did not want to hear it, and retorted, "I'm not so very helpless, Thomas Williams."

"You don't always *think*, Kath." He ran a distracted hand through his hair.

Mulishly, she looked out the window. "Thinkin' is overrated."

"You are not this *stupid*; Christ, what am I going to do with you?"

Incensed, she turned on him. "I'm *not* yours to do anythin' with—somethin' you keep forgettin'."

There was a sudden silence, whilst she felt the full force of his hurt feelings, and wanted to bite her stupid, red-headed tongue. Stricken, she faltered, "Mother a' mercy, Thomas, but I'm an archwife. You—you mean the *world* to me." She paused. "I beg your pardon fastin'."

He turned to start the car. "It's all right, Kath, you're right; it's really none of my business."

Hard on the realization that he was right to be angry at her, and that she was a knocker, and that she'd hurt his wretched feelings, she dissolved into tears.

Alarmed, he looked over at her, hunched and weeping into her hands. "Oh—oh hey, Kath; it's OK, it's nothing." He pulled the car over again, and turned to place an awkward hand on her shoulder. "I'm the one who's sorry; I shouldn't have been so hard on you."

But Doyle was drowning in tears and remorse, and wouldn't hear it. "I—I shouldn't have come—you're right. I saw Munoz goin' out in the field and I—I couldn't bear it."

"You are twice the detective she is."

This was not true, of course, but had the beneficial effect of putting a halt to the waterworks, as she hid a smile, and wiped her eyes on her sleeve. "I'm *wretchedly* sorry I snapped at you, Thomas. Of course my business is your business—" she paused delicately, "—well, most things, leastways." With a sudden burst of clarity she added, "I've always been—well, I've always been a solitary soul, I suppose. I don't know how to do this friendship business, and I shouldn't be so abrupt with you, and so defensive."

"I understand, Kath. It can't be easy for someone like you to have friends."

With another rush of guilt, she realized he'd never pursued the subject of her perceptive ability, even though he must have been dying to know more. She wiped her eyes again. "Whist, Thomas; everythin' is a million times better since I met you. I'm sorry I hurt your feelin's."

He bent his head, and contemplated the cracked leather seat. "You were right, though—I keep overstepping, when I promised you I wouldn't. I want you to be happy, and even if that happiness doesn't lie within my own power, it doesn't change the fact that I want you to be happy."

"Oh—oh, you are so *good*." She said it with all sincerity and wonder. "I wish I was."

Meeting her gaze with his own, he asked, "Are we all right?"

"Or course we are. After Acton and this baby, you are a very close third—there's hardly any daylight between you."

Smiling, he turned to start the car. "I can't ask for more than that."

# 24

D oyle's mobile pinged, and she saw that it was Acton, calling her on his private line. "Michael," she answered. "Are you tryin' to keep track of your wayward wife?"

"Not so wayward, as long as you are being careful. You're with Williams?"

"Yes, I begged him to take me with him, but I shouldn't have, and I'm sorry if I worried you. We do have a good report, though."

"Are you all right?"

Apparently she hadn't been successful at trying to erase the recent crying jag from her voice. "I am indeed. We have a witness who will testify that the matron led the dead girl away, like a lamb to the slaughter. And that she thought the matron was a foreigner."

"Well done. Did we get a statement?"

"We did. DI Williams here seemed to think we shouldn't bring her in."

"No. In fact, we may have to put her in protective custody."

"Like me," Doyle joked with a false sense of heartiness.

But Doyle's husband cut to the root of her unhappiness with no further ado. "I have an assignment for you—this afternoon, if at all possible. There's a witness I'd like to you speak to—to see what there is to see. "

"Won't be as good as this one," Doyle cautioned. "This one brained her husband with a fire jack."

"Did she? I'd prefer that you didn't take a page."

"I suppose that depends; who's my interview?"

"I'd like you to interview Moran's widow."

Doyle leapt upon this plum assignment with all the fervor it deserved. "Oh—that is an *excellent* idea, Michael."

"She may not want to say much, even if she knows something."

Doyle could only agree. "I suppose I can't just ask her outright if her esteemed late husband was runnin' a sex slavery ring."

"I'd like you to keep this just between us, for now; don't even mention it to Habib."

This was a twist, and Doyle ventured, "Are you worried Mrs. Moran'll end up as another containment murder?"

"There's that, certainly. But a disposable mobile phone number was lifted from the pad of paper at the SOCO's flat, and I've traced the purchase of the phone to Mrs. Moran."

"Mother a' mercy," Doyle breathed in surprise. "That's a wrinkle— it all keeps comin' back to the SOCO."

"Indeed."

"And her cat." For heaven's sake, thought Doyle in exasperation; why is it I can't stop thinking about the stupid cat? "All right then, Michael, I'll go speak to the grievin' widow, and see what I can find out."

There was a small pause. "I have a lunch meeting in an hour, but shall I come fetch you first? We can pick up a jar of peanut butter."

Ah-ha, she thought; *that's* what this call is all about. Aloud, she said, "No thank you, Michael—I owe Williams a lunch. He had to remind me that I'm too reckless, and I took umbage—"

"Umbrage," Williams corrected in the background.

"—umbrage, and now I'm repentin' like a prophet in ashes."

"All right," Acton replied in a mild tone. "Don't forget to check in with me."

"Will do. See you later."

She rang off, and as Williams drove, he hunched his shoulders in exasperation. "I wish you hadn't mentioned our little—our little misunderstanding, Kath."

But Doyle only smiled out the window. "I had to, Thomas; Acton already knows about it. Don't look, but he has a man shadowin' me. He's probably a white male in his early thirties—he's had the assignment before. He's supposed to be keepin' me safe, so he must have reported to Acton that you were scoldin', and I was cryin'."

Without moving his head, William's eyes slid to his rear view mirror. "Why doesn't Acton want you to know you've got a shadow?"

"Because I had just had a temper tantrum about bein' spied on, that's why."

Williams took a deep, unhappy breath. "I look like an idiot."

"No, I'm the one who looks like an idiot. Just don't wave your weapon at me, and all will be well." Assuming a casual air, she admired the view out the window. Poor Acton; he'd been informed about the contretemps in the car, but couldn't ask her outright what had happened. And it hadn't helped matters that she'd flown the coop to begin with, but he loved her too much to give her a well-deserved scold. Williams had no such qualms—which was a good thing, actually; sometimes she needed a good bear-garden jawing, just to keep her in line.

"What's for lunch?"

She looked over at him, amused. "You're holdin' me to it?"

"It's our cover, now. And anyway, I'm hungry. It's exhausting work, trying to manage headstrong elderly ladies."

"As opposed to headstrong younger ones." He smiled, and she took the opportunity to observe, "You know, Thomas, if all the detainees who witnessed this little incident were allowed to go home, instead of serve their sentences, it is starting to look like this corruption scandal involves some higher-ups, doesn't it?"

He said carefully, "I would not be surprised."

She didn't press it, but hoped Acton's plan—whatever it was—was a good one. She didn't like to think about what would happen if he tried to nick a higher-up, and fell short.

Williams decided on fish and chips, and so they stopped at an open-air stand near the embankment, as it wasn't too cold to eat outside, and it would make matters easier for her shadow. Once seated on a bench, Doyle methodically spread peanut butter on Melba toast, and averted her eyes from the sight of Williams enthusiastically eating fried cod from a greasy newspaper.

Between bites, Williams took a causal survey of their surroundings. "Have you twigged the shadow?"

"Please don't even try, Thomas.  It could all get very awkward."

They ate in silence for a few moments, then he ventured, "Can you tell me more about the dreams?"

Immediately, her instinct rose up, warning her not to speak of it, and so she said only, "It's hard to understand, but the general gist is that the baby's in danger."

He thought about this, as he applied another liberal dose of malt vinegar. "But not you? Just the baby?"

"Yes—just the baby." Now that she thought about it, it did seem a little strange, that in the dreams it seemed clear it was not her problem— but it was not as though you could separate one from the other.

Williams asked, "Who is Acton's heir, do you know? It must have been a shock, that Acton is suddenly starting a family. Who's being cut out?"

Although her companion was watching carefully for her reaction, this thought hadn't even occurred to her, which only served as another example of why DI Williams was storming up through the ranks. "Acton's heir is Sir Stephen, a cousin. As vile as the day is long."

He addressed his fried cod again. "That would be someone who has a grudge against the baby, but not against you."

"I suppose that's true." She decided not to mention to Williams that the danger was female—at least according to Maguire—and that the dowager Lady Acton hated Doyle with the heat of a million suns. I imagine Acton has already thought of this, she thought, and that's another reason he's fretting about it. No doubt the other Lady Acton has a shadow assigned to her, too.

Williams' mobile pinged, and after checking the ID, he spoke to Gabriel about arranging to meet his sister for her interview. He turned to Doyle. "Are you free after Marnie gets out of school today? Gabriel says they can meet you at the pub."

Doyle made a face.

"Oh, sorry." He spoke again to Gabriel. "Somewhere less nausea-inducing; how about the canteen at headquarters? Marnie can have a tour."

This agreed upon, he rang off, and Doyle complained, "Saints, Thomas; I thought I was done with tellin' the sorry tale of leapin' from the stupid bridge."

"Cheer up; you would be telling it every week at the community outreaches, if the DCS had his way. Although Munoz would probably kill him, if he tried to set up such a thing, so there's that."

"I understand that Munoz's been given an undercover assignment." Doyle eyed him, and waited to see whether he'd give her any particulars, but he was by-the-book, was DI Williams.

"Sorry, I can't discuss it. Shall we head back? Your shadow must be getting hungry."

"Poor thing. I hope he's gettin' time-and-a-half."

Williams returned the vinegar bottle to the stand as they prepared to leave. "If I'm asked about this, what do I say?"

"Tell the truth and shame the devil, Thomas, but I doubt you'll be asked. How did you know I was wearin' a vest, anyway? Were you lookin' at somethin' you oughtn't?"

He glinted a smile at her. "There *is* more to see, nowadays."

"That's enough of your sauce, DI Williams; don't give my shadow any grist for the mill. Now stay a good arm's length away, keep your hands in plain sight, and let's slowly get back into the car."

As they headed back to the Met, Doyle reluctantly decided that—with respect to Munoz and her new assignment—the fair Doyle would have to intervene; the fact that the girl was working undercover made Lestrade's interest all the more ominous. She paused for a moment, trying to remember if 'ominous' meant what she thought it did, and decided that it did.  It was past time she stopped being such a baby, and tried to be *good* for a change, like Williams was. Therefore, once back at her desk, she dug into the very back of her top drawer, where a plain card displayed an international telephone number, next to a hand sketch of a goat. After walking over to an empty cubicle, and taking a careful look over her shoulder, she rang up Philippe Savoie.

# 25

Savoie answered in his usual brusque manner. "Yes?"

"Hallo," Doyle ventured. "It's me."

"Ah." He was very much amused. "You have changed your mind, yes?"

Savoie had suggested they have an affair, because—for reasons that were unclear— he was very fond of the fair Doyle. "No," she said bluntly. "But I have to speak to you about somethin' important."

"What is it?" He continued amused, as though he were enjoying himself hugely, which was a bit strange, as he was not someone who was easily amused. Perhaps he was drunk.

"I can't say until we meet." Belatedly, it occurred to her that this may not be feasible. "Are you still in London?"

"Yes, but I am very, very busy."

She had the impression he was teasing her, but she was in no mood to be teased. "It's about your brother; the one who's here in London." A bit crossly, she emphasized, "It's important, Philippe— don't be jokin' around."

"*Bien sûr*; we will meet. Not now, though."

Listening to the amusement in his voice, her scalp prickled, and she was so astonished that she nearly dropped the phone. She knew—in the way that she knew things—that Savoie was with Acton. Acton's flippin' lunch meeting was with Philippe *flippin'* Savoie.

"Hello? You are there?"

With a monumental effort, she pulled herself together. "Yes—sorry. Are you available later today?" Tiresome, is what it was; the interviews were piling up, but she decided she could squeeze in an underworld kingpin, as long as it didn't take too long—Savoie was not one for long conversations, anyway. "The usual place and time?" In the past, they'd met at the bookstore, a few blocks away from headquarters.

"*Bien.*" He rang off.

Slowly, Doyle replaced the receiver on the phone set, trying to make sense of it. Acton was meeting with Savoie, and he didn't want her to know of it. Of course, Acton wouldn't know that she was acquainted with Savoie, but it did seem ominous—second use of the word in ten minutes; a shame that it was needed yet again.

Was Acton aligned with Savoie? From what she'd gleaned, Savoie was running a smuggling rig, using horse trailers that traveled between racecourses. Doyle was aware that her husband was also running illegal weapons, although she'd never discussed it with him. Were the two men involved in a common enterprise? One could only imagine the fallout, if it were discovered that the illustrious chief inspector was collaborating with the notorious Philippe Savoie—but *surely* Acton didn't trust the Frenchman. On the other hand, perhaps Savoie was involved in the Wexton Prison case, and Acton was setting him up for an arrest.

This thought gave her pause. Savoie was a rum character, but he'd saved her life, once, and they were friends, in a strange way. It's that "friends" thing again, she thought with dismay—life was so much easier when I had no friends. Coming to a decision, she rose to her feet; she would meet with Savoie, and hopefully she wouldn't muck up whatever plan Acton was hatching—she'd be very careful.

Doyle next wandered over to Munoz's cubicle. "Munoz," she said with an attempt at friendliness. "How goes the undercover business?"

The other girl didn't look up from her typing. "I shouldn't have said anything—I thought you'd already know, through Acton. Obviously, he's aware you're a weak link."

"I am *not* a weak link, it's only that Acton is very by-the-book on classified matters." Doyle paused for a moment, hoping she wouldn't be struck by lightning, as a result of such an out-and-out untruth.

"I can't talk about the case with you, so go away."

"No, it's not that," said Doyle, trying to keep a firm grip on her temper. "I'm needin' some advice, is all. What if your husband had been involved in an illegal sex ring? Would you talk about it, or would you pretend you didn't know?"

Munoz immediately stopped typing, and smoothed her hair back. "Hold that thought, while I go track down Acton."

"It's not Acton, with the sex ring," Doyle said crossly. "Try to stay on-topic."

"Oh? Well, that's a shame," the other girl said with feigned regret. "It's always the quiet ones who are amazing in bed."

"Whist, Munoz; may I remind you that we're speakin' of my husband, here?"

"I thought we weren't," said Munoz, startled. "Good God, is he *really* operating a sex ring?"

"No, he is definitely not. But I am interviewin' a widow, and I'm afraid she'll pretend she knows nothin' of her late husband's misdeeds, because it's too embarrassin' to admit she knew."

Leaning back into her chair, Munoz considered this. "I think you approach her as if you assume she didn't know. She'll have to pretend to be outraged, and want to help you in any way she can."

"I see," said Doyle thoughtfully. "Box her into the virtuous corner."

"A very dull place, but I think she'll have no choice."

As Munoz turned back to her keyboard, Doyle took the bull by the horns. "So—how is our Mr. Lestrade?"

Munoz gave her a wicked glance. "Amazing."

"Oh—oh, I see; matters have progressed so quickly?"

"So far, so good," the other girl replied in a neutral tone that—much to her distress—didn't fool Doyle for a second.

"Well, you've got to be a bit careful, Munoz; there's always a chance that he's tryin' to winkle out your secrets."

"I don't think so—he never discusses work." She paused. "He likes to watch me sketch."

Worse and worse, thought Doyle in horror; she's smitten; and I'm not seeing wretched Savoie a wretched moment too soon.

Habib appeared, willing to latch on to any excuse to speak to Munoz. "What is this? We speak of suspect sketches?"

"*Amazing* sketches," Munoz confirmed with a glance at Doyle.

"More like sketchy sketches," Doyle countered crossly.

"Who is the suspect?" asked Habib, who was clearly at sea.

Munoz retorted, "I'll tell you who's suspect; Chelsea's entire back line."

Doyle understood this to be a reference to football, which meant she'd have nothing to contribute. Thank all the available saints that Acton was not a football enthusiast—although if he were, she'd probably have to pretend an interest, to humor him. After all, he humored her all the time—when he wasn't secretly meeting with enemies of the state, that was.

"The Chelsea team will play Man U next week; perhaps I can acquire tickets."

Doyle nearly fell over in surprise; Habib appeared to be asking the fair Munoz out on a date, and rather than await the certain snub, Doyle was desperate enough to help him clutch at this straw. "That sounds grand, Munoz; you can see whose team is the better."

Surprisingly, Munoz did not carve out Habib's heart on the spot, but instead slid a malicious glance toward Doyle. "My sister can get tickets through the council; we can all go."

Doyle had to admire this deft handling of the tricky situation; it was never wise to scorn a superior officer—as well she knew, having decided that marrying one was easier.

Munoz then asked with a hint of steel, "You'll come too, won't you Doyle?"

But Doyle was not one to buckle under duress. "Not I; I'm to avoid crowds, in my condition." This was actually true, but for other reasons; it was always difficult for someone like her to be in amongst a group of people who were emanating a wide variety of strong emotions.

To avoid Munoz's angry glare, she hastily asked, "How can she get tickets—does your sister know someone on the council?" The council was the Health Professions Council, and—come to think of it— the council had figured prominently in Doyle's cases lately. There'd been a murdered pedophile amongst its members, and the missing prison matron was pretending she was affiliated with the council. And Moran—she drew her brows together—Moran had been on the council's board, according to his obituary.

Munoz informed her, "Elena is doing an internship there. She's working on immigration issues."

Doyle thought this over, her scalp prickling; Acton famously didn't believe in coincidences. "Has she noticed anythin'—I don't know— *odd* over there?"

Both Munoz and Habib looked at Doyle in surprise, and Munoz shrugged. "Nothing other than the usual problems in dealing with wealthy do-gooders. There are factions that butt heads, of course."

"Can your sister certainly obtain tickets?" Habib was impatient with this work-talk, and wanted to get back to the outing-with-Munoz-talk. "I will be pleased to purchase them, if necessary."

With a palpable lack of enthusiasm, Munoz replied, "No, Elena can get the tickets, and what's more, they'll be good seats—I'll put her on it."

"I'll be off," said Doyle, as she checked her mobile for the time. "Keep me posted about Chelsea's back line."

"DS Doyle, perhaps you are forgetting that there is a sensitivity training scheduled for lunch," Habib reminded her, gently remonstrating.

"Oh—oh, well I have one of those classes that teaches you about childbirth," Doyle improvised. "La-something." She paused, thinking about it. "Lamorse."

"Oh, then by all means," said Habib, beaming. "Best of luck."

As Munoz shot her a darkling look, Doyle made her escape.

# 26

Doyle wound her scarf around the collar of her coat as she walked through the lobby, thinking about the coming interview with Mrs. Moran. Ex-wives, along with ex-girlfriends, were a detective's best friends, but a widow—one would think—would be very defensive about her late husband's reputation. Perhaps a peek into their bank records wouldn't be out of line; she'd see if Acton had already done so.

The desk sergeant called out a greeting, and she smiled in response, as she came to the lobby doors; the man had been a big fan ever since the bridge-jumping incident, and she was reminded of the dead SOCO, who thought she was going to be a hero, like Doyle. She must have caught wind of the Wexton Prison corruption ring, somehow, and was working to expose it—hence she was killed, to put a stop to her investigation. And since the SOCO had written Mrs. Moran's mobile number on her note pad as one of her last earthly actions, it placed a different light on the forthcoming interview—the SOCO may have been trying to contact the widow to discover what she knew about her husband's activities, or the widow may even have been involved in the SOCO's murder; best to keep an open mind. Doyle wondered how she'd manage to raise the subject of the murdered SOCO in the context of the vigilante murders, but decided—as she always did—that things seemed to work best when she didn't have any particular plan. She was an intuitive creature, and plans—like thinking—were overrated.

She'd dutifully rung up the driving service, but upon emerging onto the front pavement, she was treated to the welcome sight of Acton in the Range Rover, waiting for her at the curb.

Smiling with delight, she slid into the car, and wondered what had prompted this unlooked-for visitation. "What a nice surprise, Michael."

"Do you mind if I come along?"

"Do I have the lead?" she teased, as he pulled away from the curb. Technically, vehicles were not allowed to wait in front of the building, but the PC on duty had managed to hover at the far end of the perimeter, so as not to officially notice that a DCI was breaking the rules.

"You do, Detective Sergeant." He gave her his half-smile, but she was not fooled, and wondered what had prompted this sudden desire to join her. Perhaps Savoie had told him that she'd called him, although this seemed unlikely; Savoie was not what one would call a gabbler.

But she was soon to find out Acton's reason, as he glanced at her, and lifted a shoulder in an apologetic gesture. "I believe Trenton has been twigged."

She smiled to show there were no hard feelings. "He wouldn't have been, Michael, but you were a little over-concerned about Williams, and so I put two and two together."

Acton's brows drew together. "Williams should not browbeat you."

"Well, *you* won't browbeat me," she pointed out fairly. "He fills in whenever it is necessary that I be browbeaten."

He reached to put a conciliatory hand on her leg "I am sorry I didn't tell you about Trenton."

Covering his hand with her own, she assured him, "No; I'm sorry I was such a baby about Mathis that you felt you couldn't tell me."

"It is only temporary," he soothed. "So I don't go mad."

"Well, we can't have that," she replied, and carefully did not meet his eye.

Apparently satisfied that she wasn't going to start throwing things at him, her husband then moved on to the next topic. "I've taken a look at Dr. Harding's mobile phone records, and there were two calls that originated in the cell tower area near Trestles. Originating accounts are unknown, so it was probably two disposable mobiles."

"Saints," she exclaimed, although she really wasn't very surprised. "Someone over at Trestles convinced the good doctor to warn me off, then?"

"So it would seem."

She shrugged in mock-resignation. "Could be any one of a hundred."

He smiled in grim acknowledgement. "I imagine the field is a bit narrower."

This was, of course, true because it went without saying that Dr. Harding was not going to do such a thing without plenty of filthy lucre crossing his palm, and Doyle would bet her eyeteeth that it was either Acton's mother, or his nasty heir. Or a combination of both, as it was hard to image the dowager knowing what a disposable mobile was, let alone deigning to go somewhere, and purchase one.

Aloud, she offered, "Perhaps it's just Grady, tryin' to save you from eternal damnation." Grady was the stableman at the estate, an Irishman from Ulster, who was none too happy that the new baroness was Roman Catholic, and thus the next thing to Satan himself.

"I may have to make a visit."

"All right, Michael; do I come along, to do a little listenin'?" She was pleased with herself for sounding as though this plan of action was amenable to her. Not only was his estate a nest of vipers, it was inhabited by ghostly ancestors who made a habit of plaguing her, since she was the only one who could see them. She'd never want to admit it to Acton, but the incumbent baroness didn't particularly enjoy visiting Trestles, which was a drawback, all and all.

"Let me think it over. Since the psychiatrist's plot came to naught, it is not a pressing priority, just now."

"How are those more pressin' priorities, by the way? Is Zao na-min' names?" When one player cracked, usually the others were ea-ger to tell their own tales in exchange for a more lenient sentence; it was a classic police technique, being as the prosecutors were never as interested in the foot soldiers as they were in the higher-ups.

"We're keeping it very quiet, but Zao got his marching orders from the prison's medical examiner."

She raised her brows at this. "The medical examiner at the prison morgue? I suppose that's handy; he can say whatever he wants about a prisoner's death, and no one's goin' to be very interested, in the first place. How does the matron fit in, then—she's his accomplice?"

"Her role remains unclear; she worked on the women's side, and so may have been a go-between."

They'd stopped in front of the office building, and as Acton came round to open her car door, Doyle asked, "Did they find anythin' at the rubbish site—any of the SOCO's photographic equipment?"

"Yes, but unfortunately, no photographs or negatives."

She raised her face, thinking about this. "She may have been an annoyance, Michael, but she was a good SOCO. If there were incrimi-natin' photographs, she'd have a duplicate set, hidden away some-where. The EO has gone through all her things, right?"

He nodded. "He's found nothing of interest. Unless there is a blind security box somewhere, but then we'd be looking for an unaccounted-for key, and we haven't found one."

"No," said Doyle, thinking of the SOCO's cluttered flat. "She wasn't the type to be that organized; I doubt she had a security box."

Any further speculation was cut off by their arrival at the account-ing offices, where they were escorted into a well-appointed confer-ence room. In a short time, Mrs. Moran entered and was shown to be an attractive woman nearing sixty; brisk and businesslike, and wear-ing an expensive scarf arrayed over her shoulders. As they shook hands over introductions, the woman said, "Chief Inspector, I am honored. This must be a matter of importance."

Actón bowed his head. "More a matter of delicacy, I'm afraid."

The woman nodded as though she'd expected this. "Sebastian, I suppose. The chickens have finally come home to roost. Will you be seated?"

A bit taken aback, Doyle remembered that she was supposed to take the lead, and asked, "Which chickens are those, ma'am?"

The woman regarded them for a moment, as she clasped her hands before her on the table. Faith, thought Doyle; she's a nasty mixture of bitterness and—and satisfaction, or something; as though she's rather pleased we're here.

"My husband was unfaithful, and what was worse, he was indiscreet. But God forbid that his reputation suffer for it, so I believe he was being manipulated by the other—here she twisted her mouth in distaste—the other libertines, at the Crown Court."

As Acton was listening without comment, Doyle took a guess at what "libertines" meant, and ventured, "Do you believe your husband was bein' blackmailed, then?"

"Oh, I wouldn't necessarily call it blackmail; he was a willing participant, after all." She paused. "He was in over his head, though, and he knew it—he drank himself to death as a result." This said without a flicker of remorse.

A bit daunted by the woman's serene coldness, Doyle asked, "Can you tell us what sort of manipulation was involved—what was the purpose?"

"They'd let the female suspects go free—for a price." She paused, pressing her lips into a thin line. "Disgusting—to parlay such an advantage."

Resisting the urge to ask why the woman herself hadn't come forward, if the practice was so disgusting, Doyle instead asked, "D'you know who was involved, on the judicial side?"

"No," the woman responded immediately.

This was not true, and Doyle brushed her hair off her forehead, in a signal to Acton. She's a wily one, thought Doyle; she doesn't want to be a witness after the fact, or be charged with obstruction of justice, depending on how much she knows. "Can you remember any particular case, or any particular suspect Mr. Moran may have mentioned? Anythin' to help us get a startin' point on this?"

It appeared that this was something the witness was willing to disclose, which she did with ill-concealed relish. "There was the trollop at his chambers—it all turned out very well for her."

Oh-oh, thought Doyle in dismay. "And which trollop was that, ma'am?"

"Percy, his junior." She paused for a moment, and then could not contain her bitterness. "There is no fool like an old fool."

# 27

While she processed this disquieting piece of information, Doyle was aware, for reasons that she could not explain, that this was not news to Acton. "So his junior was given the job after—after offerin' sexual favors?"

The woman looked at her in surprise. "No, the criminal charges against her were dismissed in exchange for sexual favors. Then I suppose she was offered the job, in exchange for more of the same." She paused. "She's still at it, I understand. Judge Whitteside is the latest name I've heard."

Poor Thomas, thought Doyle in acute dismay, but then rallied, as she reminded herself that DI Williams needn't ever hear this sordid piece of news.

Acton, who'd remained silent thus far, interrupted to ask in a mild tone, "Were you worried—because your husband was drinking so much—that this scandal might come to light?"

But the witness could see where this was headed, and only smiled thinly. "Did I kill him, you mean? No. I was going to divorce him, instead. I was not going to be a laughingstock, as a result of this tawdry scheme. I'd already consulted with a solicitor."

Doyle could feel Acton's gaze rest on her for a moment, to ascertain that the woman was telling the truth, which she was. Doggedly, Doyle tried to gain the woman's cooperation by appealing to her sense of justice. "Are you certain you can't remember any other cases your late husband may have mentioned? This type of thing may still be ongoin', and we must put a stop to it."

"I wish I could help," the woman replied in an even tone, and Doyle lowered her head, whilst brushing her hair off her forehead.

Acton then spoke. "A woman from the CID—a forensic photographer—had your mobile number on a notepad in her flat. Do you know why this was?"

A bit surprised by the change in topic, the witness answered readily, "Yes. I'd hired her to follow Sebastian around and take some snaps—the solicitor said it would helpful with the divorce."

Acton said bluntly, "She's been murdered."

For the first time, the woman's cool assurance seemed shaken, and she looked from one to the other in surprised alarm. "Murdered? How?"

"I'm afraid I'm not at liberty to say. You were unaware of this?"

"I'd no idea. Why—that poor girl."

Again, Acton glanced at Doyle but again, the witness told the truth. Doyle continued, "Had she given you any photographs, ma'am?"

"No; no, in fact, I've been trying to ring her up, because I hadn't heard from her, lately."

Doyle then checked her notes, and was reminded to ask, "Was there anything unusual about your husband's death?"

Still distracted by the news of the SOCO's murder, the woman frowned at her. "I'm not certain what you mean."

Doyle paused, but Acton made no comment, so she explained, "Are you certain he died of natural causes? Was there anythin' that raised a question in your mind?"

Again, the woman looked from one to the other in surprise. "He suffered from cirrhosis, and a variety of other ailments, due to his drinking. I had no indication there was any foul play. Why? Is there some question?"

Acton said, "Not at present." He then rose, indicating the interview was at an end. "If you remember anything of consequence, please contact us immediately. In the meantime, it would probably be best to speak of this to no one. Indeed, it may be dangerous to do so."

"Not a word," she assured him. "I shouldn't admit it to you, but his death was an enormous relief to me, and I've closed that book."

As Doyle accompanied Acton back to the car, she thought over the interview, and what the witness had revealed. "I think—all in all—that I prefer my witness from this morning, Michael; the one who just straight-out took a fire jack to her husband."

"Mrs. Moran was a bit cold."

"As a stone," Doyle agreed.

As they settled into the car, he observed, "Did you notice that it did not occur to her to link the SOCO's death to the corruption ring?"

"I did. I don't think she knows anythin', Michael, but at least now we know why the SOCO had Mrs. Moran's mobile number. She must have been takin' snaps of Moran, and accidentally caught somethin' incriminatin' on camera—somethin' that exposed the Wexton Prison corruption case. So she abandoned her assignment from Mrs. Moran, and started pursuin' the other project, thinkin' she'd gather more evidence, and then blow the whistle."

"So it would seem," he agreed thoughtfully.

She glanced over at him as they pulled out into the street. "D'you think Moran was murdered?"

"There is no indication. I am reluctant to do an exhumation, without more."

She eyed him with suspicion, because there was a nuance in his tone that made her think he was not telling her something that he knew. Speaking of which, she remembered how he'd deftly changed the subject when the witness wanted to cast further aspersions on Percy-the-trollop. "Tell me what you know about Morgan Percy, Michael. Did you find out why she was lyin' to me and Williams?"

She could see that he was debating whether to tell her, and so she crossed her arms and looked out her window in annoyance. "You never tell me *anythin'*, Michael."

"Only because I met with her off-the-record. I told her I knew she hadn't been completely forthcoming about her involvement in the corruption scheme."

This was of interest, and unable to maintain her sulks, Doyle turned back to him and prompted, "Mrs. Moran said Percy was charged in a criminal case, but I didn't see anythin' about that in her record."

"She was arrested when a protest got out of hand while she was attending university. She had ambitions to become a judge, and was terrified she had jeopardized all hope of such a career." He paused. "She was offered an opportunity to have her record expunged."

"Mother a' *mercy*," Doyle breathed.

He tilted his head. "I imagine in light of the lifestyle she was living at school, it didn't seem such a hard bargain."

But Doyle, who'd been living a completely different lifestyle at St. Brigid's School for Girls, could not fathom it. "Faith, Michael; is anyone *not* havin' sex with everyone else, willy-nilly?"

"I wasn't, for one. When we were first working together, sex never even crossed your mind."

She laughed, and tucked a fond hand under his arm. "I'm sorry; it was not somethin' that immediately leapt to mind—I was so in awe of you. But if it's any consolation, now I think about it all the time."

"Let's go home, then. I can spare an hour." He gave her a look with which she was well-familiar.

Smiling, she shook her head. "You'll have to hold that thought, my friend; I'm bein' interviewed by Gabriel's little sister for school, and so it's back to the wretched Met I must go."

But now that the idea had been planted, Acton was reluctant to forfeit the proposed tryst. "I'll call him, and render your excuses."

Unfortunately, Doyle also had her own tryst with Savoie to think of, so she leaned over to kiss his neck. "I can't duck it, Michael. I suppose if you pull over, we can always climb into the back seat."

"I may call your bluff."

"Whist; not a bluff a'tall—I'd best look lively, to keep you away from the Morgan Percys of the world."

With a smile, he looked across at her. "I've missed working with you."

This seemed a good sign, and she ventured hopefully, "I'm as safe as houses, when I'm in the field with you, Michael. Truly."

"Let me think about it," was all he would say, but she was encouraged; perhaps her cubicle confinement would be lifted—or at least relaxed a bit. She hadn't had the dream in a couple of nights, after all.

"Be careful what you say around Gabriel," he added, as though it was an afterthought. "We're not to know it, but he's at the Met undercover, working on the Drake angle."

"He *is?*" She stared at him in astonishment, and then remembered that Acton didn't necessarily want Drake's sins unearthed, as it would only rain hellfire down upon the justice system. "Oh—oh Michael; I hope I won't forget, and say the wrong thing."

"I have every confidence," he replied, and it was not exactly true.

# 28

Doyle made her way up to the third floor canteen, where Williams, Gabriel and his sister were waiting for her, looking out the windows to the street below.

Gabriel introduced Doyle to Marnie, and they decided to conduct the interview at a table near the windows. With an air of importance, the girl pulled a pink notebook from her school satchel, and Doyle could see that she'd written down prepared questions, presumably with the help of her brother, who hovered behind her.

"Shall I have the detective inspector fetch us somethin' to drink, Marnie? This may be thirsty work."

Marnie giggled, and acquiesced, and so Doyle sent Williams for a soda and a cup of coffee; she was in need of fortification, after such a nerve-wracking day. She was afraid to even look at Gabriel, for fear she'd give the game away.

As Williams went to procure the refreshments, Doyle asked Marnie about her school, and the girl readily described her teacher, and the general injustice of not being allowed to play field hockey until next year, even though she was just as good as the older girls. Being in the presence of so much exuberance was a bit exhausting for Doyle, although it was clear that Marnie's brother had cautioned her to be on her best behavior. Privately, Doyle thought it would be slow going if Marnie continued to giggle every time Doyle said anything—there were not a lot of working-class Irish in her school, apparently.

After Williams returned with the drinks, Doyle took a fortifying sip, and prompted, "Now then, Marnie, let's have at it."

Marnie considered her notes. "Where were you born?"

"Dublin, Ireland."

Giggling, the girl repeated, "Dublynn Ayerlund."

Doyle pretended surprise. "Why Marnie; I'd no idea you were Irish, yourself."

The girl giggled with delight, while her embarrassed brother cautioned her not to be rude.

"How old are you?"

Doyle tried not to bristle. "Almost twenty-five."

Marnie appreciated this. "I'm almost eleven," she confided.

"That is excellent," said Doyle gravely.

"How long have you been a police officer?"

"Almost five years. In Ireland, a female police officer is called a banner." She thought she'd throw that in, for interest.

"Do you like it?"

"Yes," Doyle said promptly. "I like it very much."

"What's the best part?"

Doyle thought about it. "I have met many fine people, like your brother, who care more about helpin' people in trouble than they care about their own safety." This was true, she thought, struck. And it's why I hate sitting at my desk because I am supposedly in danger; it is not in my nature.

"And the worst part?"

"The worst part is when you have to give bad news to nice people." Doyle realized belatedly that she probably shouldn't specify the kind of bad news she had to give to the aforementioned nice people. Fortunately, Marnie stuck to her script, and did not follow up.

"Did you get a medal for being brave?"

"I did."

"Can you please tell me what happened?"

"Well, another police officer was hurt, and I was afraid she was goin' to drown. I jumped off a bridge into the Thames to save her."

Marnie went off-script, and lifted her gaze, fascinated. "Weren't you afraid?"

"I was very much afraid, but there was nothin' for it."

Marnie thought about this, her delicate brow furrowed. "What if you died? Your mother would be so sad."

"My mother is never sad; she is abidin' in heaven."

Marnie stared at her blankly, and Gabriel indicated she should get back to the script. A non-believer, thought Doyle, and so she explained gently, "My mother died, two years ago."

"Oh," said Marnie. "What was her name?"

Gabriel looked embarrassed, and bent to say something, but Doyle only smiled and replied, "Mary."

"Mary," Marnie corrected her. "Not 'Meeary.'"

"Mary," said Doyle dutifully, broadening the vowel.

Marnie was pleased. "You see? You can speak normally, if you try."

"It's truly very hard," admitted Doyle, and she could hear Williams laughing behind her.

"Do you have a sister? I have a sister." The manner in which this was said indicated this was not necessarily a fact to be celebrated.

"I do not," Doyle replied, and wondered why her scalp prickled. No question that she didn't have a sister—who did have a sister?

"May I see your medal?"

"Oh—I'm sorry, it's at home." She actually wasn't certain where it was; Acton had put it somewhere.

Gabriel indicated it was time to wrap it up, so Marnie stood, and solemnly shook Doyle's hand, as she had obviously been rehearsed to do. "Thank you for your time, Officer Doyle."

"The pleasure was mine, Marnie," replied Doyle in an equally solemn tone.

Gabriel expressed his appreciation, and the two left. Williams was leaning against the windows with his arms crossed. "Well, that was entertaining."

"And you sniggerin' at me, all the while."

"I couldn't help it; it was just so funny."

"I'm not used to children," Doyle confessed as she hoisted her rucksack. "It's good practice, I suppose."

"You are a natural," he assured her. "Are you heading home? I can give you a lift."

"I have a couple of loose ends I need to tie up, first." These consisted mainly of figuring out how to shake Acton's shadow, so as to get to her clandestine meeting with Savoie, but best not give Williams the particulars; she'd already led him on a ragged day.

He fell into step beside her. "Should I stick around?"

"You may suit yourself." I shouldn't chafe at his concern, she reminded herself; I'm lucky I have an excess of men who want to protect me—a lot of the women we see in this business wind up in the morgue as a result of the tender mercies of their men folk.

As they approached the lift, she asked thoughtfully, "Who has a sister, Thomas?"

"A sister?"

"It was somethin' Marnie said—it made me think that I'm missin' somethin'."

As always, Williams was willing to humor her, despite this rather disjointed explanation. "Zao has a sister, remember? We had to pick her up, to make sure she was kept safe."

But Doyle knit her brow. "I don't think that's it. Does the matron have a sister?"

"Unknown; Munoz did some legwork, and found out her references were all fake—she's a blank slate, and we have no known associates."

Doyle gave him a look. "So; how interestin' that no one at the prison bothered to check out a matron's references."

"I think we can assume the prison higher-ups knew exactly who she was."

To see whether he knew whatever it was that Acton knew, she threw out, "Munoz has a sister who's workin' at the council; it seems to me there are some dicey goin's-on, over there."

Williams, as usual, gave nothing away, and replied in an even tone, "Considering the people who are on the council, we can't just go digging around, Kath."

"That's what the pedophile who was sittin' on the council counted on, remember? That no one would dare to dig around, despite the rumors."

"Then Maguire did everyone a favor when he killed him."

Doyle's scalp prickled again, but she ignored it, because there was no use in getting signals, if you had no idea what they meant— honestly, it was enough to drive a lass to drink. "Murder is murder, Thomas, and there's no excusin' it." Ironic, it was; Doyle was well- aware Acton had helped Williams with his own vigilante murder, and Williams had returned the favor many times over. It was very much like the Wild West, only with Doyle playing the part of the annoying schoolmarm, who goes about lecturing everyone.

Williams took a casual glance over his shoulder, and lowered his voice. "Speaking of which, have we come any closer to figuring out why Drake was targeted by Maguire?"

"Now, there's another situation where it's not easy to do a bit of diggin' around." She paused, thinking about it. "Does Drake have a sister?"

They'd come to the lift, and Williams pressed the button. "I've no idea. Want me to check?"

"I'll do it, Thomas." Quirking her mouth, she looked up at him. "I appreciate how you humor me; never doubt it."

"Every day's a treat, Kath."

She gave him a mock-salute, as the doors slid closed.

# 29

Doyle knew a moment's qualm as she entered the bookstore through the side door; she'd given her shadow the slip the same way she'd done it once before, by taking a circuitous route through the Met's parking garage. Hopefully he wouldn't confess this failing to Acton, she'd hate to have him get the sack, poor man.

She wandered into the religious books aisle, which was where she'd met Savoie in the past, and as usual she arrived first—Savoie was a cautious man, which was no doubt why he'd survived this long, in his questionable business. She pretended an interest in a book of saints, and was not surprised when she felt him sidle up beside her. "Hallo again," she said, smiling up at him. "Thank you for comin'."

His hardened expression did not change, but she was aware he was very pleased to see her. A wonder, it was; he was not one to pursue relationships, was Philippe Savoie, and she could only conclude he was fond of her because she was so completely different from any girl he'd ever known. Of course, she could return this sentiment, in spades.

"Next time we will meet at my flat, yes?" His pale eyes gleamed. "I will buy the *tortes*."

She frowned at him. "The torts?"

He made a gesture that generally conveyed the act of eating something messy. "In the paper—yes?"

"Oh—the fruit pies. Well, Philippe, as delightful as that sounds, I must remind you that I am married, and cannot go about eatin' pies at your flat." She paused, and gathered up her courage. "Instead I like to think that we are friends, and that's why I wanted to meet with you."

"We are chalk and cheese." Very pleased, he was, that he'd remembered the idiom.

"Well—yes; yes, indeed we are. But nevertheless we are friends, and I need to ask you somethin' about your brother Gerry—"

"He tells me you are *l'héroïne*; that you jumped off the bridge." Placing a finger on the tip of her nose, he chided, "This is something you did not tell me, little bird."

"It was made up to be much more than it truly was," she replied a bit crossly, as she brushed his finger away. "*Please*, Philippe; I don't have much time, and you *have* to listen to me."

"I listen, then." He leaned a shoulder against the bookcase. "Speak."

"I would—well, I suppose I would like to know what your brother Gerry is about."

"Ah," he said, and regarded her thoughtfully.

As he made no further comment, she ventured, "I'm in a sticky wicket, here; he's hangin' about with a minister's secretary, and I'm worried he's up to no good, and that maybe you are involved, too. I can't look the other way, but I thought I'd give you a warnin', on account of our friendship." She paused in surprise, because he was very much amused, was Philippe Savoie, even he gave no outward indication.

He bowed his head gravely. "*Bien sûr*; you are the good friend."

Despite his unalarmed attitude, she persevered, "And Gerry's doin' a line with DS Munoz, which—in light of everythin'—makes me very uneasy."

Savoie cocked his head in puzzlement. "What is this, 'doin a line'?"

"Oh—they're datin', I suppose you could say, and I can't think it a good thing."

But his reaction was immediate and unmistakable, as his brows came down in angry incredulity. "*L'Espagnol?*" He stared at her for a moment in shocked disapproval. "*Non.*"

Oh-oh, thought Doyle; I hope I haven't put my foot in it, here. "Well, I think they may be spendin' some time together, but I'm not altogether certain—"

He ducked his head, and said some words in French that were probably not meant for polite company, whilst she stared at him in dismay, thinking the situation appeared to be along the lines of Romeo and Juliet, with Doyle and Savoie playing the role of the disapproving parents. "I didn't realize you didn't know.  I was worried he was workin' with you and tryin—" here she paused, "— tryin' to pull some trick on Munoz."

He assured her a bit grimly, "No, I did not know of this. I do not pull the trick on Munoz, it is my brother who pulls the trick on me."

With a sinking sensation in her midsection, Doyle thought she may as well ask. "Do you pull the trick on Acton?"

Savoie unbent enough to render his thin smile. "*Non.* It is Acton who pulls the tricks."

This was true, and an enormous relief—although if there was anyone who could outfox Savoie, it was Acton. Thinking of this, she persisted, "Are you certain—" here she paused delicately "—that Acton isn't pullin' a trick on you?"

His amusement returned. "Ah—you will save me from your husband, yes?"

Having her dilemma put in those terms made her instantly cross, and so she retorted, "I don't want to be put in that position, Philippe, and there is no point in tryin' to warn you, if you think it's all so very amusin'."

Apparently he'd recognized that she was fast losing her temper, because he bent his head to her, and explained in a soothing tone, "Acton, he has the wicket that sticks. He asks for my help, and I am like the Saint Bernard; I help him." With a shrugged shoulder, he tilted his head in a very European gesture. "He is doing a line, and I help him do this line."

She stared at him, because this was true; as incredible as it seemed, somehow Acton had enlisted Savoie to help him with the Wexton Prison corruption case. "Oh. Oh, I see."

"I can say no more. You are *très ingénue*, and if your husband has not told you of this, you must be as quiet as a mouse at the church."

"Not a problem, my friend; *believe* me."

"I will speak to my brother about this Munoz."

"Thank you; I appreciate it. Do you happen to have a sister?"

He arched a brow in surprise. "*Non.* I have only Gerry, and the brother who was killed by the English policeman." He gave her a significant look.

Doyle blinked, as the dead brother was in fact killed by the fair Doyle, but as this was unbeknownst to Savoie, it seemed best to move on from the subject. "I'm thinkin' there is a sister in this, somewhere. *Cherkay la femme.*"

"Ah," he agreed with a gleam. "*Cherkay la femme.*"

She smiled and shook her head at him. "You should correct me when I get it wrong; else I'll never learn. You're as bad as Acton."

"*Non*—if I was as bad as Acton, I would find a way to bring you to my flat, for *tortes.* Perhaps *you* have a sister?"

"I do not, but I'm sure you'll find a nice girl, who appreciates you." This said a bit dubiously, as it seemed unlikely Savoie would be interested in a nice girl, or a nice girl in him.

He bowed his head. "*Sans doute.*" He continued very amused—a laugh a minute, she was.

Trying to sound casual, she cautioned, "I'd rather Acton didn't know about—about how we know each other, if you don't mind."

"*Oui,*" he concurred. "Me, I do not want Acton trying to take my goat."

"Definitely not," she agreed fervently.

# 30

D oyle tried without much success to stifle a yawn; she'd forgotten that Timothy and Nanda were coming over for dinner, and so she was forced to muster up some energy—she was tired, after her very busy day. At least she was able to participate in the meal without being sick, thanks to the blessed peanut butter, and the absence of any fish products.

Reynolds was in his element, formally serving up the Cornish game hens in a manner more suited to Kensington Palace, with Timothy waxing enthusiastic as he asked for another.

Dr. Timothy McGonigal was a genial, rather shy man who'd gone to university with Acton, and Doyle often wondered at the friendship, as the two men were nothing alike. After the tragic death of Timothy's sister Caroline—at Acton's hands, unbeknownst to Timothy—the man's life had undergone a dramatic change. Doyle had asked him to offer a position at the medical clinic to Nanda, a Rwandan widow of her acquaintance, and Nanda had conveyed her gratitude by becoming his lover. Timothy appeared to be blissfully happy as a result; Caroline, the dead sister, had kept him on a tight leash.

Nanda had a baby who was just beginning to walk, and they explained that they felt they should leave him at home. "A shame," Doyle had said to Acton, when they were in the kitchen. "I should be practicin', I suppose."

"In a few months, you may wish to consider interviewing a nanny, madam," Reynolds suggested, as he carefully arranged the convenience store fruit pies on a silver tray.

"Oh," said Doyle, who was still trying to get used to having friends in her life, let alone strangers. "Do we need a nanny?"

"I would supervise the nanny, madam; you needn't worry."

He'll be wanting to run a staff, one way or the other, Doyle thought in resignation, as she watched the servant carry the tray over to the table. He has his eye on Trestles, and good luck to him, what with that cast of characters over there.

Timothy looked upon the dessert with enthusiasm, and offered, "We miss you at the clinic, Kathleen. Very busy there, lately."

"I did enjoy volunteerin' there, Tim; I met the most interestin' people." Best not mention that two of the aforementioned people were an aspiring rapist, and the notorious Philippe Savoie.

In turn, Timothy took Nanda's hand and smiled at her. "As did I."

Doyle enjoyed Timothy's company because her husband did—and Acton was not one to tolerate anyone—and because Timothy was genuinely kind, and didn't think Acton's marriage was a mismatch of epic proportions. Nanda could cast no stones, of course, having recently gone from impoverished Rwandan refugee to dining with the English aristocracy.

"I saw your mother, Acton," said Timothy, between bites. "She visited my office just the other week, when she was in town." Somewhat abashed, he added, "I'm afraid I mentioned the blessed event—I assumed she would know already."

Doyle assured him, "It's not a problem, Timothy. We were keepin' it quiet, but now it's common knowledge." Privately, she wished she'd been a fly on the wall; the dowager would not have been happy to hear that the Irish upstart was pregnant with the heir to the House of Acton.

Nanda turned to smile upon Doyle. "I was most happy to hear that you are going to have a baby."

"Thank you, Nanda; I'm that happy, myself."

"I will try to speak with Aiki, he will tell me whether the child is a boy or a girl." She nodded. "He knows such things."

After a moment's hesitation, Doyle decided she may as well ask. "Oh—oh, do you still speak with your late husband, Nanda?"

"From time to time," the young woman said placidly, as she cautiously tasted the pie.

To smooth over this strange pronouncement, Timothy asked with bluff heartiness, "Should I be worried? Wouldn't want him unhappy with me, after all."

"Oh, no," the widow said, and bestowed her gleaming smile upon him. "He does not mind; some are dead, and some are not."

"Why, that's exactly what Maguire said," Doyle exclaimed in surprise.

"Who?" asked Timothy.

"He's one of the dead," Doyle explained.

"An old friend," Acton interjected smoothly. "How is your caseload at the clinic, Tim?"

Whilst Doyle sat, and waited for her scalp to stop prickling, Timothy replied with pride, "Nanda has been very helpful in convincing some of the young mothers to trust the clinic; we have a persistent problem, trying to persuade them that their folk remedies are actually more dangerous than our treatment."

"They are afraid their babies will be stolen," Nanda agreed. "Or that they will be arrested." Her dark eyes slid for a wary moment in Acton's direction.

There was a moment's silence, whilst Doyle could feel Acton's sharp interest, which aligned with her own. "Oh? Who arrests them, Nanda?"

A bit flustered, Timothy made an attempt to divert the subject. "It's just a misunderstanding—a problem with the language, I think. Nanda was worried that Acton would try to arrest her, if we came over." He covered the woman's hand and gave her a reassuring smile. "It is a common fear among the immigrant community; that the police will arrest them for no particular reason."

Nanda's gaze dropped to her lap, but Acton leaned forward and said something to her in French—it sounded to Doyle as though he was asking her something, and reassuring her.

But Timothy was embarrassed, and it was clear he'd already cautioned his sweetheart not to raise this controversial subject. "No, no need at all; it's only a misunderstanding—born of ignorance, of course. Thank you, Acton, but I'm certain there is nothing to it."

To change the subject, they began to discuss Timothy's recent purchase of a piano, and Doyle feigned interest, even though her mind was preoccupied with the startling things one learned during dinner parties—perhaps entertaining wasn't such a terrible chore, after all. Although Reynolds was going to drive her mad, with all of his that's-not-the-correct-fork-madam. What difference did it make, for the love o' Mike? She should stab him with one, just to prove the point.

"Do you play, Kathleen?" Timothy asked Doyle kindly.

Privately amused that he would think she grew up in a household that could afford piano lessons, let alone a piano, Doyle shook her head. "I do not; I'm not very musical, I'm afraid."

"Not true; you have a very clear soprano," Acton said.

Doyle hid her surprise; the only time she sang was at church—and Acton never sang. He also never listened to music, which wasn't very Holmesian, when you thought about it. She remembered an uncomfortable conversation at Trestles—one of the many—when the others had mentioned that Acton's late father was musically gifted. Of course, one couldn't be certain the man was dead, being as he'd gone missing many years ago—although apparently, there were rumors that the dowager did away with him. All in all, not as unbelievable as it sounded; perhaps that kind of thing ran in the family.

They made an early night of it, and as soon as Reynolds departed, Doyle retreated to the sofa, dying to discuss the remarks Nanda had made. Acton had shared an after-dinner scotch with Timothy, and

Doyle noted that he now poured himself another, before he joined her. Upset about something, he was; he'd been quiet, after the piano discussion.

He settled in beside her, seated on the edge of the sofa, and cradled the glass between his knees so that he could watch her face. "Tell me."

"Someone that we think is dead is not truly dead—I'm certain of it, Michael. And I think it's important."

"Any guesses?"

"Solonik," Doyle said promptly.

"No; Solonik is definitely dead."

But Doyle could not let it go. "Are you *certain*, Michael? He died in Wexton Prison, after all, and there are some smoky goings-on with the medical examiner, over there."

"I am certain. I verified that it was his body in the prison morgue."

"Oh—oh, I see."  With Solonik eliminated, she tried to think of other players from the turf war, and mused, "No question that Barayev is dead." The man was Solonik's brother-in-law, and apparently a shady character in his own right, although he'd worked in the guise of a well-to-do businessman.

"Unequivocally," said Acton with a trace of satisfaction.

Doyle was reminded that Acton had killed Barayev himself, and so as to gloss over this unfortunate fact, she hastily continued, "How about the Irish contingent from the turf war—the Rourke brothers, from the Laughin' Cat pub?"

"Both dead," Acton verified, as he reached to pour another half-glass.

"Ironic, is what it is," Doyle noted a bit crossly. "I've had my fill of laughin' cats, lately; the SOCO's stupid cat is probably lordin' it over that poor buildin' manager, and feastin' on sardines every day."

Acton looked up. "Would you like a cat, Kathleen?"

With gentle exasperation, she lifted his hand, and kissed it. "No, my friend; I do not want a cat. Or a horse. Or lapis earrings."

She caught a flare of chagrin from him, and had to laugh aloud. "Oh, Michael; did you buy me the earrings, already? Let me see them, then—although they'll probably clash with my hair."

"Tomorrow," he said with a small smile, taking her hand. "Tonight, let's concentrate on the undead."

Recalled to this topic, she wished she had a better grip on what this was all about—there were too many variables. "Mayhap it's not related to the turf wars, Michael; mayhap it's more personal. Perhaps Marta your evil housekeeper is not truly dead—oh," she exclaimed, startled. "There's a sister, somewhere in all this, and Marta's sister is Greta, at Trestles."

Acton lifted his head, trying to keep up, despite having made impressive inroads into the scotch. "A sister?"

She looked over in apology. "I know I'm not makin' a lot of sense."

"Nonsense; you are charming."

Hiding a smile at this gallantry, she persevered, "I think the woman in question—the foreign woman—is someone's sister."

"Then not Greta, as she is not foreign."

"Oh. Oh, I suppose not, then—although are you certain Greta's English? Remember, it's someone who everyone *thinks* is English, but she's not."

Acton was idly playing with her hands, his head bent, but she suddenly had a swift impression of something; a leap of excitement— quickly suppressed, but not quickly enough. "What?" she demanded, bending her head to look up into his face. "What is it?"

"It's just an idea that may go nowhere. Let me check on it, first."

Frustrated, she tried to contain her annoyance. He didn't want to tell her whatever it was he'd just thought of, because—as Savoie would say—she was trays-in-june. But I've got to figure it out, she thought; that's why Maguire keeps poking at me—it's all tangled up together, somehow, and I am needed, even though no one trusts me enough to tell me what's going on.

So as to turn the subject, she observed, "To think that Nanda was afraid of you—even though she was comin' over for dinner. Those poor women, to be livin' in such fear."

"Immigrant women are the most vulnerable, and are least likely to grass on the perpetrators." He paused, then added, "And it was probably standard procedure, in many of their home countries."

"It's so *wrong*," Doyle pronounced with some heat. "To be takin' advantage of the helpless, in such a way."

"Yes. They are forced to negotiate at the most expedient level."

When Acton drank too much, his language reverted to House of Lords loftiness, and so Doyle decided little more would be gleaned this night from her better half, who was fighting off some sort of dark emotion, poor man. She leaned over to wrap her arms around his neck and nuzzle it. "Enough debriefin', husband; should we go climb into the back seat of the Range Rover?"

"Insufficient space." He set down his glass with a click. "Let's to bed, instead."

She bit his ear gently, and teased, "What should *I* be negotiatin'?"

He put an arm up to press it against hers, around his neck. "No more drinking, tonight."

She blushed at being so easily caught out. "Bring the bottle if you'd like, Michael; I truly won't mind."

"No," he said, rising to steer her toward the bedroom. "I want to concentrate."

Later, he lay in bed with his hands behind his head, watching her. She was sitting up, gazing at the bedroom fire, and congratulating herself for diverting him from a black mood—the cure for the dismals always seemed to be a healthy bout of uninhibited sex. While the nuns at St. Brigid's always advised fervent prayer as a cure, fervent sex appeared to be just as useful. The nuns wouldn't know, of course, and therefore couldn't be faulted.

"What are you thinking?" he asked quietly.

She looked over at him. "Do we have amazin' sex?"

"Yes," he answered immediately. It was the truth.

"I thought so." Small wonder Munoz didn't want to give up Lestrade, despite his dubious connections. "Is Timothy still seekin' advice?" Early in his relationship, the good doctor had sought Acton's counsel about matters sexual.

"Not as much; he's getting the hang of it."

She giggled, and rested her chin on her knees. "It's hard to imagine, Michael."

"Apparently she is very comfortable on the subject. They do a lot of role-playing."

Bemused, Doyle thought about this. "I can't think of anythin' I'd like more, than me bein' me, and you bein' you."

"Precisely," he said, and pulled her down beside him.

# 31

Once again, Doyle was watching Edward barricade the door. Poor boyo, she thought; he must be as tired of this as I am.

"You'll be needed," said Maguire.

"You again," said Doyle crossly. "You're precious little help, and now I'm wearin' a vest."

"There's gratitude, for you."

But she continued irritated, watching her son perform his seemingly endless task. "Tell it to Williams; he's the one who thinks you did everyone a favor."

The newspaper man shrugged. "Except for the one, of course. For a detective, you don't always pay attention."

Startled, she looked over at him in apology. "I'm that sorry; I didn't see it at the time. I was distracted by the Masterson mess."

"You do tend to get distracted. *Cherchez la femme.*"

She was instantly cross again. "Everyone speaks French but me."

"That's just as well; you'd be more worried than you are."

Making a monumental effort to focus, she frowned at him. "I need to ask you somethin', and I've forgotten what it is."

"It's not a person, its people."

"Oh, I see." This, even though she didn't truly see at all. "And the cat?"

"The cat is not a person," he explained patiently. "Or he'd be dead, too."

"I suppose that goes without sayin'," she mused, and found that instead of Maguire, she was now standing beside Marnie, who looked up at her with a pale little face. "Tell me about heaven, but try to speak normally."

Doyle found she could say nothing to the girl, normally or not. With a start, she awoke to stare into the darkness of her bedroom, forcing herself to lie quietly, until her heart stopped pounding. Acton hadn't awakened this time, and she decided she'd let him sleep. She had a lot to think about.

The next morning, Acton paused to drop a kiss on her head. "Ready for the doctor tomorrow?"

"Do you think he'll need to draw blood?" She had no problem mucking about with corpses, who were lying in congealing puddles of blood and brain matter, but having a doctor wave a needle in her direction was another thing altogether.

"If he tries, I will take him down with a chokehold."

With sincere gratitude, she pulled him down by the necktie for another kiss. "I'd appreciate it, my friend."

As Reynolds helped him into his coat, Acton remarked, "I believe Dr. Easton will be pleased; you have put on some weight."

"Thanks be to God," she said. "And to Morgan Percy, and her blessed peanut butter."

"Amen," said Reynolds primly, making her laugh.

After packing up his electronics, Acton headed out the door, reminding her to check in with him. "Don't go anywhere without telling me, if you please."

"And Trenton," she added.

"And Trenton." The door closed behind him.

Reynolds came over to clear her plate. "Am I acquainted with Trenton, madam?"

"He's security, Reynolds. I'm truly not acquainted with him, myself."

"If you ever need an escort, madam, I stand at your service."

Reynolds was being territorial again, and so to change the subject, Doyle stretched her arms over her head, and announced. "The baby's a boy, Reynolds, his name is Edward." This said rather firmly, so that she'd get used to saying it aloud.

The servant paused in his movements, and straightened up, as excited as he allowed himself to be. "An heir, then. My congratulations, madam—that is wonderful news."

"Not for Sir Stephen, it isn't." No need to explain who Sir Stephen was; Reynolds probably knew more about Acton's lineage than Acton did.

But Reynolds lifted his lip with a touch of scorn. "Sir Stephen is merely a second cousin, madam; and there is the cloud over his claim, in any event."

This was news, and Doyle stared at him in surprise. "What cloud is that?"

The servant paused at the sink. "I shouldn't gossip, madam."

"Recall, if you will, that the last time that you didn't want to tell me somethin', I ended up savin' your life."

"Very true," the man conceded as he absently polished the stovetop with the tail of his tea towel. "There is some question about the paternal line, from that branch."

With a knit brow, Doyle tried to puzzle out what was meant. "The grandfather who was mechanical—the one who helped repair the airplanes in the war—Sir Stephen's grandfather was his brother, correct?"

"It is unclear," said Reynolds carefully, "whether Sir Stephen is legitimate."

"Oh. Oh—I suppose that *is* a cloud, Reynolds; small wonder he's such a crackin' blackheart. Well, thanks to Edward, it doesn't matter anymore."

"Certainly not, madam."

Doyle looked at the clock, and decided there was no time like the present; hopefully Williams was not hip-deep in whatever skullduggery

Acton and Savoie were hatching up—he certainly didn't seem to be aware that Savoie had signed up on team Acton, and she was not going to be the one to tell him. She rang him up. "Hey."

"Hey, yourself."

"Are you free this mornin' to go to the deli? I need to ask a monumental favor."

"All right, but in exchange I need a monumental favor."

"Done." She was willing; she never got a chance to do a favor for Williams, and she owed him a million times over.

"Contraband?"

"Please; meet you there."

"I'm going to push back a meeting, but I'll get there as soon as I can."

"No rush; I'm still at home."

He was instantly wary. "You'll let Acton know you're coming to meet me?"

"You are *such* a baby, Thomas. Yes, I'll let Acton know; I'll come to no harm at the flippin' deli, for the love o' Mike."

"I'm not going to put myself in that situation again."

"You didn't; it was all my wretched fault, and I've repented fastin' to all concerned. I swear on all the holy relics that I will tell Acton we are meetin' at the deli, but I will draw the line at confessin' about the contraband."

"Right then; see you there."

When she arrived, Williams was already waiting at a table, a small cup of coffee at the ready. She slung down her rucksack, and was sipping from the cup before she even sat down. "Bless you; I am countin' the days till I'm swillin' down lattes again."

"Ladies first," he said. "Name your favor."

But now that the moment was upon her, she hesitated, and fingered the cardboard cup. "You must promise you won't think me mad."

"Can't promise," he said easily, "but I'm intrigued."

She took a breath. "I think somethin' is wrong with Marnie."

There was a pause, while he regarded her. "Marnie Gabriel?"

"Yes. I think she is sick, or has a disease, or somethin'."

"And why is that?"

"I'd rather not say."

He had a good guess. "You know, you're a little spooky."

She ignored the comment, and continued, "So I need to enlist your help. I can't just call Gabriel, and tell him this fantastic tale."

"So I should?"

"No, I was wonderin' if you could tell him you are diabetic, and thought you recognized some symptoms; you could use that as an excuse to urge her to see a doctor."

He thought about it for a moment. "All right."

She reached across to touch his hand. "Thank you, Thomas. I know you hate to speak of it."

"No, it's important. I hope she has nothing serious."

Doyle said only, "Don't let up, until a doctor has seen her."

Soberly assessing her, he nodded. "I won't; don't worry."

Having gotten over that rough ground, she leaned back in relief, and cradled her cup between her hands. "Now then; name your favor."

"Tell me what Morgan Percy told Acton."

Dismayed, Doyle slowly sat upright again. "Oh—oh, I don't know if I should, Thomas."

"Acton made no record."

She was incredulous. "You hacked into Acton's laptop? Thomas, you're the one who is mad." Not to mention the last person to do such a thing was dead.

"I'd like to know," he insisted, his gaze unwavering.

A bargain is a bargain, she thought with resignation, and so she told him.

He listened, and tried to control his reaction, but she knew he was very upset. "So, she is a whore."

"You will watch your language, my friend. She was young and stupid—I'll give you that." Best not mention that the wages of sin seemed to have turned up a trump for Miss Percy.

"You'd never have done such a thing."

She drew a long breath, wishing everything weren't so complicated. "Recall that I was raised by nuns, and a mother who'd learned a very hard lesson. It's different for most girls, nowadays."

"Then it shouldn't be. It's not so hard to make the right choices."

Doyle thought about her adventure with Savoie, and how he'd offered his help in exchange for sex. It was true; she couldn't do it, but she said slowly, "Listen, Thomas, if that was the only way to save Acton, or this baby—or even your fine self, I wouldn't hesitate."

"But you wouldn't to save yourself from a just punishment; don't even pretend you would."

She had no response. "I'm sorry," she said gently.

He contemplated his hands on the table for a moment. "Right. I'll go ring up Gabriel."

"Not just yet; I know who Drake's second murder was—why Maguire decided to come after him."

Fortunately, this turned his thoughts away from Percy-the-jezebel, and his gaze flew to hers. "You do? Who?"

Leaning forward, she said in a low voice, "One of the vigilante murders was a young woman named Bennet—the murder at the Heath, remember?"

"An outlier." Williams nodded slowly. "Different from the others, because she was a female victim, and not killed in a park. Why didn't that occur to us?"

She didn't mention that Maguire was also surprised that this hadn't occurred to them, but then again, it was true that she'd been distracted at the time, worried that Acton was having an affair with Cassie Masterson. "I don't know—it seems obvious now, with hindsight." Doyle refrained from mentioning what they were both probably thinking—that she'd be very much surprised if it *hadn't* occurred to Acton. Instead, she said, "Drake saw the main chance, and committed a shadow murder, whilst we were investigatin' Maguire. I imagine it was a containment murder of his own; the victim's mother said she was the violently jealous type, and unable to control herself. He couldn't take the chance that she'd grass on him."

"So now what?" Williams's gaze rested on her, wary. If Acton wanted to let this particular sleeping dog lie, DI Williams was not going to countermand him.

"I'll mention it to Acton, and see what he says. I can't just do nothin', Thomas, and look the other way."

Williams chose his words carefully. "Murder isn't always murder, Kath. There may be a greater good at work, here."

But Doyle was not having it, as she gathered up her rucksack. "There's no such thing as an honorable murder, my friend."

Williams didn't bother to make an argument, being as they did not share the same philosophy on this subject. That her husband tended to side with Williams was a bit daunting, but nevertheless, Doyle felt she had to make a push to uphold law and order, like they were all supposedly sworn to do.

Williams fell into step beside her, and asked with some constraint, "Did Acton say anything about our little problem in the car yesterday?"

Poor man; he wasn't one to like coming off looking so badly. "As a matter of fact, he did. Acton was amazed you didn't give me the back o' your hand, bein' as I was so very deservin' of it."

But Williams was not amused. "Not a laughing matter, Kath."

Reminded, she stopped short. "I do have a laughin' matter to attend to; I have to go visit the SOCO's stupid cat."

Williams glanced at her in surprise. "I'm sure he's doing fine."

"Yes, he's lucky he's not a person, else he'd be dead, instead of just laughin' at me. Can you drive me, or should I enlist my shadow to take me over there?"

Quickly, Williams checked his messages. "I'll go, but it's got to be fast."

This was nothing more than what she'd expected; Williams was as territorial as Reynolds, in his own way. "That's grand, Thomas. Let me text Acton, so there are no further misunderstandin's; I wouldn't want to be caught in the crossfire."

"Not funny, Kath," he repeated heavily, and pulled out his keys.

# 32

The building manager had been warned they were coming, and so when Doyle and Williams arrived at his door he ushered them in, and asked in his slightly nervous manner, "Have you arrested the murderer yet?  The tenants are still a bit on end."

"Small blame to them," Doyle replied. "It's like someone opened the fourth seal, around here."

"Has anyone shown an unusual interest in the crimes, or asked about the woman from the council?"  Williams was on a deadline, and didn't want to make small talk.

The manager thought about this carefully. "The tenants have been asking about it—and Mrs. Addersley's nephew, of course."

"I meant, anyone who seemed out-of-the-ordinary; who was *unusually* interested," said Williams, who was truly a patient man.

"No, sir." The manager shook his head.  "And no one else has died, since you came last." He seemed rather pleased to make this report.

"And how is the cat?" asked Doyle. "Do you still have him?"

Oh, yes," the young man nodded.  "He likes to sleep in his cat tower—I put it in my bedroom." He smiled, and indicated the closed door. "Sometimes he jumps on me, when I come into the room, just to give me a fright."

"Of course he does," said Doyle, who had taken her measure of the wretched beast. "Would you mind if I looked in on him?"

With a touch of alarm, the man asked, "You'll not be wanting to have him back, now?"

"Definitely not. But I just wanted to have a look-in, for old time's sake."

After apologizing for the unkempt state of his bedroom, the manager opened the door to reveal the cat tower, taking up a great deal of the available space in the small room. Nestled within one of the carpeted caves near the top, the SOCO's cat stared at them with an unblinking golden gaze.

Tentatively, so as to stay well out-of-reach, Doyle ran a finger along the edge of the platform closest to her, her antennae quivering like a tuning fork. "I think we need to search this tower, sir."

Williams pointed out, "I'm sure the EO has already gone over it, Sergeant."

"Not for forensics; I meant we should search it for a hidin' place." Keeping a wary eye on the cat, she began to press along the underside of one of the platforms with more and more confidence. "I think—I think that the SOCO may have hidden somethin' in this cat tower."

On request, the manager coaxed the cat out of its nest, and then stroked it against his thin chest, as Doyle and Williams carefully probed the carpeting that lined the cat tower.

"Here," said Williams suddenly. "Here's something."

He worked his fingers under a seam in the carpet that lined the cat's cave, and carefully extracted a small plastic sleeve.

"That's it," breathed Doyle in excitement. "The SOCO's photographs."

They retreated to the kitchen, where Doyle waited in a fever of impatience whilst Williams donned latex gloves, and carefully pulled out the contents of the sleeve, laying out three photographic prints along the counter. Oddly enough, they appeared to have been taken in a cloisters somewhere—the type of columned walkway that lined a church's inner courtyard. Framed within the slim columns were depictions of people meeting in a shadowed corner—each print a different group, with the time and date automatically stamped on the prints. The photos appeared to have been taken from a distance, and so the darkened figures were a bit undefined. Judging from their posture and bent heads, it was apparent the participants did not wish to be observed, and the photos were only snapped when one or more were briefly visible between the columns.

"There's Moran," said Williams, indicating the first photo with a finger. "The dates must be wrong, though; the second man is the Minister of Immigration—the one who killed himself."

Craning her neck, Doyle peered over his shoulder. "Who's the third man?" There were four men, who appeared to be in close conversation.

"Barayev." With a gloved finger, Williams indicated Solonik's former brother-in-law, now dead by Acton's hand.

Doyle moved around him to lean closer. "Oh; I didn't recognize him without his face blown off. Who's the fourth man?"

"I don't know."

They moved to the second photo. "Look—there's the matron, d'you see? And the same unknown fourth man, again."

"It's a month later, if the date can be believed," Williams observed, noting the date stamp. "Barayev and Moran would have died in the meantime."

"Why, there's Mrs. Addersley's nephew," said the building manager. He stepped forward to point to a figure in the third photo. "Fancy that."

There was a moment of silence. The third photo featured the same unknown man, the matron, and Mrs. Addersley's erstwhile nephew, who appeared to be handing an envelope over to the matron. Only it wasn't her nephew at all, it was DCI Drake. And worse yet, the matron appeared to be looking directly at the SOCO's camera, with an arrested expression.

Grimly, Williams pulled out his mobile. "I'll get DCI Acton over here."

"No, wait." Doyle put a hand on his arm. "The SOCO didn't put any of this on an electronic device, so let's assume she had good reason. "Let me ring him instead, and I'll ask if he can meet me for lunch."

Williams saw the wisdom of this, and as he was emphatically instructing the manager to stay silent about their find, Doyle rang up Acton. "Hallo, Michael, are you free for lunch?"

"I am booked, I'm afraid. We've brought in the prison's medical examiner for questioning."

As the unknown man in the photos could very well be the selfsame medical examiner, she hurriedly improvised, "Well that's a shame. I was hopin' to share a bowl of cereal, with you and Williams."

As "cereal" was their code word for sex, this pronouncement was met with a moment's silence. "I can spare you a half-hour, if you're willing to meet me here, but I can't hold the detainee much longer."

"Done. See you in twenty minutes."

As she and Williams drove over to the Met, Doyle tried to make sense of it. "The matron must have twigged the SOCO, tracked her down to her building, copied a key, and laid in wait to kill her. Then she disposed of the darkroom—and any prints that were there—and then was forced to commit a couple of containment murders, because Mrs. Addersley and Mr. Huse knew too much."

But Williams pointed out the flaw in this reasoning. "That doesn't make a lot of sense, Kath. If the matron wanted to scotch any investigation, why didn't she dispose of the SOCO's body? Presumably she disposed of Mrs. Addersleys' body, after all."

Doyle frowned out the window, stymied. "Faith—that's exactly what Acton said, too. Maybe she couldn't carry the corpse out at the time?"

"I doubt it; it looks as though she had a lot of help to draw from," he observed in a grim tone. He glanced over at her. "Your friend Savoie came to London in this same time frame, and I'll bet anything he's involved in this too, Kath."

Rapidly sorting through what she should and should not tell Williams, she finally gave it up, and simply said, "Savoie is helpin' Acton on this, Thomas, but Acton doesn't want me to know. Unless you know that, already, and I'm the only one who supposedly doesn't know."

He thought about this, and she had the impression that he truly hadn't known of Savoie's involvement. "How do you know this?"

Nothin' for it. "Savoie told me, himself."

But DI Williams had apparently learned his lesson, and showed remarkable restraint in not commencing to beat her about the head and shoulders. "I see. And you trust him?" This said with an edge of incredulity.

"No. But recall—recall that I know it's the truth."

Thus reminded, he ran a distracted hand through his hair. "Don't tell *anyone* about that, Kath—you shouldn't have told even me."

A bit stung, Doyle retorted, "I had to let you know about Percy, Thomas. And we still don't know exactly how *she's* involved in all this."

"She's cooperating."

Doyle decided she'd rather not know exactly how matters were progressing betwixt the two; Williams certainly wasn't in need of advice, and she wasn't exactly sure what she wanted to say to him, anyways. She rather liked Percy, but didn't want to add her to the growing list of friends-who-complicate-the-fair-Doyle's-life.

On the way upstairs, they grabbed some prepackaged sandwiches, so as to support their story, and then met in Acton's office, where he firmly closed the door behind them.

"We found the photos in the SOCO's cat tower," Doyle announced without preamble. "We didn't want to say over the phone." Unlikely that he thought she was truly suggesting a threesome with Williams, but she wanted to make it clear, straightaway, that such was not the case.

Williams was already carefully taking the photos out of the sleeve, and holding them by the edges, but Acton casually reached to take them. "No need to worry about forensics; the only prints will be hers, after all."

Doyle watched her husband carefully review the photos, one at a time, and although his expression did not change, she could sense that he was immensely surprised. She ventured, "We recognized Moran, and Barayev, and the immigration minister—and Drake, of course, but we didn't know who the other man was."

Acton dropped the photos onto his desk. "The other man is Judge Colcombe."

"Judge Colcombe?" Doyle paused in confusion. "Williams was right, then; the time-stamp dates must be wrong, because Judge Colcombe died, years ago. And the immigration minister killed himself last year."

But Acton only leaned back against the desk, crossing his arms, as he contemplated the floor for a moment. "I think it more likely the dates are correct."

# 33

Acton's remark was met with silence, until Williams ventured, "Colcombe's death was a hoax? Is that what you are thinking, sir?"

With a tilt of his head, Acton indicated the photos. "There is nothing of interest, otherwise; nothing incriminating—it could be friends meeting after church, after all. Instead, the SOCO was careful to date-stamp, and to keep the evidence away from the internet, or even a professional developer; she thought it was that white-hot." He paused. "It seems the only explanation."

With a growing sense of wonderment, Doyle quoted Maguire. "Some are dead, and some are not."

"So it would seem," said Acton.

But Williams did not have the benefit of Maguire's pronouncements, and was lost. "I don't understand; how can such a thing happen? Surely their deaths were verified?"

Acton met his eyes. "By whom?"

"The coroner," breathed Doyle. "Holy Mother of God, Dr. Hsu must be involved in the corruption scheme." It was something that was drilled into them at the Crime Academy; once a person died, the remains were under the jurisdiction of the coroner, and only the coroner could release a body to the family, or determine whether further investigation was needed. The coroner's position was a powerful one, and he could countermand even the DCS, if he wished.

Thoughtfully, Acton checked his watch, then gathered up the photos, to slide them into his inner breast pocket. "I imagine this solves the puzzle of why the SOCO's body was left to be discovered; it was a warning to the coroner. The SOCO may have already approached Dr. Hsu with her suspicions."

"Are we certain *she's* dead?" Williams asked.

"Yes—Acton and I both saw her in the morgue." Doyle frowned slightly, still trying to come to grips with such an audacious scheme. "Faith, he's a cool customer, is our coroner. Not a flicker of awareness."

"I imagine he is not a willing participant, if the SOCO's body was meant as a warning," Acton pointed out. "He is no doubt being threatened in some way, as his cooperation is crucial to the scheme."

"So, when it comes right down to it, they're launderin' people, in the same way that money is laundered," Doyle concluded. "Signin' off on death certificates, so that the dead could re-emerge with a new identity."

Acton nodded. "And I imagine it was something similar when it came to the immigrants who were drawn in; no doubt they were promised new identities."

"Now what, sir?" asked Williams. This was a good question, and Doyle waited to hear how Acton planned to go forward; it was as yet unclear how far up the scheme reached.

But her husband only checked his watch again, and stood. "At present, I have an interview. Kathleen, I would appreciate it if you would accompany me to observe from the gallery."

"Right, then," said Doyle with as much wifely supportiveness as she could muster.

Acton turned to Williams. "And I would like you to—quietly—research everything you can find about Barayev's late wife, and get it to me in two hours."

Although Williams simply nodded, Doyle was not following, and looked from one to the other in confusion. "Barayev's dead wife? I don't understand, Michael; wasn't Barayev married to Solonik's sister, before she died?"

"Yes, although she may not actually be dead."

Williams spoke into the charged silence. "The prison matron is Solonik's sister?"

"I shouldn't be surprised," said Acton, and indicated to Doyle that they should go.

As they walked down the hallway, Doyle tried to match his strides, and was silent for a moment, trying to take it all in—it seemed so incredible. "I suppose this would explain why I kept thinkin' that Solonik was still involved in all this."

"Yes," he agreed. "I imagine Solonik's sister has been working behind the scenes at the prison, and then stepped into a larger role, when her husband and her brother were both killed."

"Chershay the fem." That wasn't right, but it was close enough. "Indeed."

Doyle tried to tamp down a feeling of grave alarm. "Saints, Michael, you killed her menfolk; she can't be very happy with you."

"Nor I with her," he replied.

He subsided into deep thought, and so she respected his mood, and stayed quiet—no easy feat, as she always tended to gabble when she was worried. If the matron was actually Solonik's sister, this would explain why Doyle had the impression that the fake Mrs. Addersley knew who she was, and heartily disliked her——the woman would be no fan of the House of Acton.

Just before they parted in the hallway, Acton caught her elbow, and bent his head. "I needn't remind you to say nothing of this—to anyone."

"I won't, Michael. I'll text you, if he says anythin' of interest."

"Thank you," he said, and walked away, still preoccupied.

Doyle entered the gallery to see that Munoz was already there, watching through the glass, and so she made an attempt at unconcerned breeziness. "Ho, Munoz; what brings you here?"

"Drake wants me to listen in."

This was not welcome news, and Doyle's breeziness disappeared. "Well, I don't know why it's so very necessary, Munoz—it's all bein' recorded, after all."

"Why are you here, then?"

Very much on her dignity, Doyle settled into her chair. "I'm on this case."

Munoz's sharp dark eyes slid to hers. "No, you're not."

This was, of course, a fair point, and so Doyle retreated to being cross. "Acton wanted me to lend a hand."

"Oh—did he really?"

The words were heavy with irony, and the girl's speculative gaze continued to rest on Doyle, who was suddenly aware that Munoz was in a foul mood. "And what's that supposed to mean, if I may be askin'?"

The girl shrugged, and with a flip of her hair, turned back to observe the figures seated at the interview table. "Only that I've heard some rumors."

If I strangled her, Doyle thought, there's not a jury in the world who would convict me. "What sort of rumors? That Acton doesn't work here anymore?"

The other girl slid her another glance. "Only that's he's none too pleased with you, right now."

This was so unexpected, that Doyle could only stare; the words were true, which meant there was indeed such a rumor floating around. "Faith, Munoz; who'd be sayin' such a thing?"

But Munoz only lifted a shoulder, as they watched the prison's medical examiner come in with his solicitor.

Perplexed, Doyle continued, "And how is it you're not makin' a smart remark about stealin' Acton away from me? Are you not feelin' well?"

"You're welcome to him. I've given up on men."

Reminded of the girl's star-crossed situation, Doyle felt a twinge of guilt—Munoz was so very unhappy. "Oh; oh I see—things did not work out with Gerry, then?"

"I'm not going to discuss it."

"Discuss what?" Gabriel pulled up a chair behind them.

"Poor Munoz needs a bit of cheerin' up," Doyle suggested brightly, hoping that Gabriel's live-in girlfriend was just a rumor—there were untrue rumors flying about, apparently.

"I'm sorry to hear it," he offered, resting his arms on his knees, so that his head was bent close to Munoz's. "Be happy to go for a pint, if you'd like to talk about it."

Doyle stared at him, as it was not true—he wouldn't be happy to share a pint with Munoz—and she was reminded that Gabriel was here undercover, to investigate Drake. If he wanted to prime Munoz for information, it did not bode well for the other girl's career— Munoz had done some favors for Drake, on the quiet. In a panic, Doyle chirped, "That's grand; I should come along, too."

"Avoiding Acton?" asked Munoz with a knowing look.

"There is *nothin'* wrong with my marriage," Doyle retorted hotly.

Gabriel looked from one to the other in confusion. "Sorry—did I misstep?"

"Shh," both girls responded, as Acton came into the interview. Doyle, however, was having problems settling down to concentrate; Munoz had been sent by Drake to listen in—because he was obviously worried about what would be revealed—and Gabriel could only be here because he was aware that Drake was involved in this mess. But Acton wanted to keep Drake out of it because—as unlikely as it seemed—the other DCI was secretly passing envelopes of money to the villains by mistake, or something.

Doyle closed her eyes for a moment, and took a deep breath. Faith, she needed to calm herself down; it was not as though Acton was going to start waving the incriminating photographs around, for heaven's sake.

Acton took the SOCO's photographs out of his breast pocket, and laid them down on the table before the detainee.

Doyle closed her eyes again, and recalled her job at the fish market with a great deal of fondness.

"May I see these?" asked the solicitor, lifting out of his chair, and craning to see.

But Acton's gaze rested on the prison medical examiner, who was reviewing the photos with undisguised horror. "Where is she?" Acton asked softly. "Either I get to her first, or you will be the next containment murder."

"I say; you can't threaten my client," blustered the solicitor.

"She's—she's staying somewhere to the north of here—" The witness held his head in his hands for a moment, desperate to remember. "I heard them say, once."

"Stop," commanded the solicitor, holding up an alarmed hand to his client. "Don't tell him anything, not until we've been given immunity—"

"There's not enough time," Acton interrupted, his gaze never leaving the detainee. "We are now in the process of rounding up everyone. It would be a shame if you were all in the same holding cell."

"Meryton," the man blurted, raising his head. "I think that's the place."

"Mother a' *mercy*," breathed Doyle, watching with acute dismay.

"What is it?" asked Gabriel, like a hound to the point.

"Nothin'," she managed, but it wasn't nothing; Meryton was the nearest town to Trestles, and if the matron had gone to ground at Trestles, matters were about to get very dicey indeed.

# 34

cton began issuing orders to the CID staff—to keep the prison Medical Examiner in protective custody, and to put out an All Ports Warning for the former Judge Colcombe. Doyle couldn't help but notice that Drake and the coroner were both missing from the list of suspects to be hauled in, but kept her lip buttoned, because Gabriel and Munoz were still hanging about, and she didn't want to interfere with her husband's plan, whatever that plan might be. Knowing her husband, it was no doubt something that would turn her red hair grey.

Acton then paused to check his messages, and looked up. "DS Munoz, please pick up a parolee living in Earl's Court; we already have her statement, but we'll need a recorded interview—DI Williams has the particulars. She will also require protective custody."

"Yes, sir," said Munoz, turning to go.

"I'd like to have a look at the pertinent autopsy records. DS Doyle, would you accompany me, please?"

Doyle nodded; this seemed to be an excuse to go and confront the coroner, which was probably why Acton wanted the truth-detector to come along, but Gabriel moved toward them, and spoke up in a deferential manner. "May I come along, sir?"

No, no, *no*, thought Doyle, just as Acton replied, "Certainly."

Following Acton, Doyle and Gabriel marched down the stairs to the morgue, their footsteps echoing off the walls, and Acton swiped his security card so as to enter the restricted area.

Dr. Hsu was bent over a corpse, dictating a report, and straightened up in surprise, on seeing his unexpected visitors.

"Tell me about DI Chiu," Acton demanded, as he approached to stand on the other side of the autopsy table. "Quickly."

Doyle tried not to look as confused as the coroner, which was no small feat.

"I—I don't understand," the man faltered, his gloved hands still poised above the corpse. "What do you mean?"

Acton moved his head in an impatient gesture. "The CID is moving in on Judge Colcombe and the others; if you are cooperating under a threat of some sort, I should like to hear the particulars."

The man's immediate reaction was to make a panicked lunge across at Acton with his scalpel, causing Acton to jump back, narrowly avoiding the arc of the blade. The man then attempted a desperate dash toward the emergency door, but Acton came around to block him, his hands held out to either side in a placating gesture.

With wary steps, the coroner circled away from Acton to the other side of the autopsy table, still brandishing the scalpel. After an astonished moment, Doyle crouched to retrieve her weapon from her ankle holster, but Acton ordered, "Stand down," and held out a cautioning hand to Doyle and Gabriel. With a glance, Doyle noted that Gabriel had already drawn a weapon, and was aiming it squarely at the coroner's head.

The usually unflappable coroner was sweating, and emanating waves of despair, and Doyle could sense he was on the verge of turning the knife on himself. "No; no, *please*," she blurted out.

Acton slowly began to approach the doctor, his hands still held out to either side. "It is Chiu, isn't it?" he asked, as though there was nothing unusual taking place. "They've already abused her once; it was why she was AWOL, a month ago."

The coroner licked his lips, and continued to back away from Acton, circling around the autopsy table, whilst Doyle and Gabriel stood frozen, awaiting an order.

"I can have her brought in, but we've got to move quickly. She can no longer work here, but at least she will be safe."

The coroner paused at this, and Doyle held her breath. After a silent moment, the man lowered the scalpel slightly. "No one can know."

"They won't," Acton agreed. "I will see to it."

With a frown, Hsu added, "And she must keep her pension."

For the *love* of Mike, thought Doyle; just give over, for heaven's sake. Poor Acton—God only knows where that scalpel's been.

"She will."

The coroner took a faltering breath, and gestured with the scalpel. "Call her, now."

Everyone stood in place, while Acton made the call to DI Chiu, asking her to immediately return to headquarters, and await him in his office. She was not to leave for any reason without his say-so, and she was not to report her whereabouts.

As he sheathed his mobile, Acton addressed the coroner in a brisk tone. "You must put down the scalpel, doctor. Assaulting an officer is a felony, and I'm only willing to overlook the first one." He then took a firm step toward the man, but the ccoroner raised the blade in warning, and stepped back in turn.

The fluorescent lights glinted off the sheen of perspiration on the Chinese man's forehead as he faltered, "For what I have done—I do not deserve to live; but I have your promise—I have your promise you will protect DI Chiu."

Aware that the distraught man was working up the nerve to do himself in, Doyle pleaded, "Please; *please* don't do this, Dr. Hsu."

"I—I do not deserve to live," the man repeated, and focused, for a moment, on the blade.

"Nonsense," said Acton. "You were instrumental in bringing the scheme to light. You took information from the SOCO, and then reported it to me."

Miserable, the man raised his eyes again. "No. That is not true; I let that poor woman die, because I am a coward."

If it were possible, Acton's voice became several degrees more stern. "But no one is ever going to know about that, because now you owe me a favor."

Good one, thought Doyle, as the man stilled for a moment, thinking this over. Turn it into something he understands; a debt of honor.

Acton continued, "You will continue doing your work, say nothing, and refer all inquiries on this matter to me."

Slowly, the other man lowered the scalpel in wonder. "You would do this for me?"

"No," said Acton bluntly. "But I cannot afford to allow the particulars of this scandal—and the people involved in it—become public knowledge." For the slightest moment, his gaze rested on Gabriel, who still held his weapon at the ready. "Now, come with me, and we will record your statement."

As though sleepwalking, the man carefully placed the scalpel on the stainless steel tray with a small clink, and then covered the corpse with a sheet. "What will I say, in a statement?"

"I will tell you on the way over," said Acton. "Come along; we've no time to lose." He looked up at Doyle and Gabriel, as he ushered the doctor toward the door. "If you both would stay close to hand, I would appreciate it."

"Never a dull moment," Gabriel remarked in an aside to Doyle, as he sheathed his weapon.

But for once, Doyle could not come up with an equally flippant reply. She could not be easy with Gabriel's being a witness to what had just transpired, and as they ascended the stairs and made their way toward the interview rooms, she waited with some trepidation for the young man to ask a few pointed questions. None, however, were forthcoming; instead, Acton took Gabriel aside, and spoke to him in a quiet tone for a few moments, as the technicians readied Hsu for his statement, and then Gabriel left, saying nothing further to anyone.

Doyle knew without being told that Acton would want her to stay within arm's length of him until all the villains were rounded up—their m.o. was to threaten women, after all—and so she sat in the interview room and pretended to take notes, while the coroner's statement was recorded.  Without a blink, he testified that the SOCO had come to him with information that death certificates had been falsified without his knowledge, and that when she'd been murdered, he immediately contacted DCI Acton with what he'd learned.

Once the statement was locked down, Doyle then went upstairs to sit for an uncomfortable twenty minutes with Acton's assistant, while her husband spoke privately with DI Chiu in his office.

"Congratulations," said the assistant, eying Doyle in a speculative way.

"I didn't do much," Doyle confessed. "The SOCO broke the case, really."

"I meant, on your pregnancy."

"Oh—oh, yes; thank you."

"Rather a surprise, I understand."  There was an innuendo underlying the words that Doyle could not like; almost as though—almost as though she'd heard the same rumors as Munoz; that Acton was unhappy with her.

Reining in her temper, Doyle instead smiled benignly. "Here's hopin' that you'll start your own family, someday."

"Not yet, DCI Acton keeps me too busy," the girl replied with her own benign smile. "It's rather a shame; he spends more time with me, than with you."

I'd push her out of her chair, but her skirt is so short she'd be exposed to the elements, and probably catch cold, Doyle thought crossly.  I've got to remember not to engage with her type; I rise to the bait *every* time and I *never* learn.  With a monumental effort, she offered with all sincerity, "He appreciates you, he does. He says you do excellent work."

"I just try to keep up," the other replied, losing interest, and turning back to her typing.

To fill the awkward silence, Doyle pretended to be texting messages until Acton opened the door to his office, and said to his assistant. "DI Williams will be here shortly. He will escort DI Chiu to HR."

As he quietly closed the door behind him, Doyle caught a glimpse of Chiu, seated within and unmoving, her head bent forward; emanating a strange mixture of sadness and relief.

Acton's assistant stood. "Yes, sir. Shall I fetch coffee?"

"I'd rather you didn't disturb DI Chiu until DI Williams arrives. Allow no one else to enter."

"Yes, sir."

Acton then took Doyle's elbow. "If anyone inquires, we will be in the canteen."

Doyle blinked. Acton never went to the canteen, being as he was the next thing to a hillside hermit. "We will? Why is that?"

"I am hungry," he offered in a mild tone. It was not true, but Doyle did not demur when, with a nod to his assistant, he led her away.

# 35

Acton barely waited to be out of earshot before he asked, "What did my assistant say to you?"

Doyle tried not to look self-conscious, but knew she fell short. "Nothin' much. Why?"

"You look a bit pulled about."

Trust him to read her like the back of his hand; it was a shame that his wife had all the self-restraint of a three year old. "It's nothin', Michael. Truly."

But he wouldn't let it go, and she could hear the displeasure in his voice. "She shouldn't disrespect you. You are my wife."

She eyed him sidelong, as they approached the lift. "Would you fire her, if I asked?"

"In an instant." It was the truth.

She shook her head in gentle censure. "Knocker; its back to Dr. Harding with you."

With a grim gesture, he pressed the button for the lift. "Dr. Harding is lucky he still has his license."

Because she sensed that he was in a mood—and Acton in a mood was a fearsome sight to behold—she teased, "I'll admit I was impressed by your restraint with respect to Dr. Harding, my friend. If you don't watch out, you'll become a kind and generous man."

Success—his mood lightened a bit. "No chance of that."

Agog with curiosity, she ventured, "Can you tell me what is between Hsu and Chiu? Are they related? Or sweethearts?"

"There is nothing between them."

This seemed implausible, and she stared at him. "But how can that be, Michael? They were threatenin' him with her."

He leaned in so as to speak quietly. "They told him that she'd been forced into the sex ring, and that they would continue to abuse her unless he did as they asked. Remember that she has a royal attribute; such a thing is important to the Chinese."

"Poor Chiu," Doyle breathed, profoundly shocked. "And poor Hsu, thinkin' he was the only thing between her and—and degratation." At his barely-perceptible reaction, she glanced up with a wry smile. "That wasn't right, was it?"

"Degradation. But I knew what you meant."

"You always do," she said fondly, and took his arm to squeeze it. "But then why is it necessary that Chiu resign from the force? She's no longer under threat, now that the case has been broken."

Acton paused as he opened the canteen door for her, and she could sense he was debating whether to tell her. In the end, he said slowly, "She wasn't being forced into it; she was a willing participant."

Doyle stopped dead in her tracks in the entryway, and stared at him for a moment. "Mother a' *mercy*," she breathed. "Truly?"

"Indeed," he affirmed, and then urged her forward, because others in the area were covertly or not-so-covertly watching them. "She emigrated from Canton, and apparently has been involved in high-level prostitution since childhood."

Thinking over this unexpected revelation, Doyle had a sudden memory of Chiu, carefully checking her appearance before her meeting with Acton, and decided that the tale was not as implausible as it seemed. Acton must have known all along, of course, and that was why he'd kept Chiu close at hand, these last few days. He'd done the same thing with raving-lunatic Owens; kept the trainee close by so as to monitor him, all unknowing. Her husband was a wily one; mental note for the thousandth time.

Having purchased her fruit pie, Doyle seated herself across the table from him. "I still feel that sorry for Chiu; she may not have had much choice."

Acton, however, was short on sympathy, as he unwrapped the cellophane from his sandwich. "She may well be a co-conspirator, planted in the CID to discover who had vulnerable relatives to exploit."

"Oh." This hadn't even occurred to Doyle, and it gave her pause. "That's *despicable*, Michael; will you be chargin' her, if that's the case?"

"No. I promised Hsu I would not."

Doyle subsided, but was conflicted about this outcome; Acton obviously thought it was more useful, for his purposes, to have the coroner in his pocket than to prosecute a suspect. Again, he was making decisions that should best be left to a judge and jury, and she could not be easy with his causal assumption of such power. It was very wearing, always having to be the annoying schoolmarm.

Along those lines, she was reminded to ask, "And what about Gabriel? Won't he report what he witnessed, so that all your fine maneuverin' is for naught?"

But her husband seemed unconcerned, as he took another bite of his sandwich—he wasn't enjoying it, she saw, he was just going through the motions. "I told Gabriel that it would be best if these developments were kept quiet. I also told him DCI Drake was working only to infiltrate, off the books, because he was concerned that higher-ups at the CID may be involved."

Doyle gave him a skeptical look. "Did he believe you?"

"No. But he'll maintain the fiction."

This pronouncement created a flare of anxiety in Doyle's breast. "Can you trust him?"

"We shall see." Seeing her concern, he leaned in to remind her, "Officer Gabriel is from counter-terrorism. Their stock-in-trade is keeping information away from the public."

"Oh. I suppose you're right."

Acton handed her a napkin, as she'd dropped some cherry filling on her sleeve. "Not to mention he will be content to have something to hold over me, if necessary."

This seemed a bit alarming, and made her pause in wiping up the stain. "And that's a good thing?"

"Certainly. I have something to hold over him, after all."

Doyle could only shake her head in abject disapproval as she re-addressed her fruit pie. "I canno' like it, Michael. You shouldn't take such decisions on to yourselves—neither of you. It undermines the system."

"I will take that under advisement."

She gave up; no point in hashing out the subject yet again in the CID canteen, but then his mobile pinged, and he listened to the call with an expression of satisfaction. "Take him to Detention; I'll be down shortly." He rang off. "They've caught Judge Colcombe."

Doyle was duly impressed. "Faith; that quickly?"

But Acton was unsurprised. "It was a simple catch; he hadn't caught wind that we knew his new identity, and the prison medical examiner had his mobile number. Whitteside is also being brought in, before he catches wind."

"Their brand-new judge? He'll be unhappy, poor man; having to go to prison along with the rest, even though he's not had a chance to reap the benefits."

"Perhaps he'll turn on everyone; we shall see."

"It's quite the reunion; all that's missin' is our matron." Doyle eyed her husband, well-aware that he'd not mentioned her, or her vicinity to Trestles. And despite having an obvious opportunity, he'd made no attempt to set up a trap and seizure for the matron. Instead, he'd moved in on everyone else, and with lightning speed. No doubt he didn't want anyone putting two and two together, when it came to the matron's nearness to the Acton ancestral estate.

Considering the news he'd just received, Acton seemed remark-ably uninterested in facing down the villains, and so she offered, "If you want to go down to Detention, I'll go to my desk and not stir a step, I promise. Unless you'd like me to stick to you like a burr." She was a bit weary, but knew Acton would not want her to be left vulnerable, even with Trenton on the job.

"We'll wait here a bit," was all he said, as he watched her eat the last bite of her pie.

Thoughtfully, she raised her gaze to his for a moment. "Are we here because we're showin' everyone that all's right with Lord and Lady Acton?"

A look of annoyance crossed his face. "I wish you hadn't heard."

She reached to take his hand. "Faith, Michael; it doesn't matter a pin. There're always rumors; and we're an odd couplin', after all."

"Nonsense; I find that we are very well-suited."

"We're the only ones who seem to think so," she pointed out.

"We're the only ones who matter," he replied. "May I offer you coffee?"

# 36

Doyle walked with Nellie, pew by pew, restacking the missals after mass. St. Michael's was the not-very-affluent parish church she'd attended before Acton turned her life upside-down, so in a way, it was the one constant she could cling to. Acton was taking instruction from Father John, and his routine was to meet in Father John's office after the late morning service. Acton was to be confirmed at Easter, so now the meetings between the two were on a more-or-less weekly basis, depending on Acton's caseload.

The Wexton Prison case seemed to be entering its final throes; the minister of immigration's secretary had resigned, along with half the Prison Board, but the coverage in the papers had been upstaged by the latest royal mishap, so it did seem that the corruption scandal would die a quiet death—thanks to the SOCO, and the laughing cat that had managed to land on its feet.

"Which of the churches around here have cloisters, Nellie?" The question had been niggling at Doyle ever since the SOCO's photos had come to light, and usually when something niggled at her, it was for a good reason.

"Cloisters?" Nellie moved on to the next pew as she considered the question. "Westminster Abbey."

"No, not the Abbey. Smaller cloisters; and the stone is light in color."

"Holy Trinity?" Nellie offered. "They have cloisters—Holy Trinity's very fancy." This said in tones of disapproval; Holy Trinity was technically Doyle's new parish, since it served Acton's upscale neighborhood, but Doyle hadn't any desire to darken its fancy doors with the likes of her unfancy self.

"I bet they never have to stoop to hostin' bingo games in the hall," Doyle teased. Nellie was a Filipino immigrant who helped manage the parish. In truth, it had been an enormous challenge, pre-Acton, since the church building was old and in need of repair, and the parish was poor and in need of cash. Post-Acton, things had improved greatly; he had paid for a new roof, and it seemed he was soon to pay for a new heating system, if Doyle was any judge.

Nellie moved to the next pew and shook her head. "The bingo's not much of a money-maker, in itself. I think I will suggest that a raffle be arranged, with door prizes—or maybe a half-and-half drawing."

"Nellie, Acton will gladly pay for the new heatin' system, I promise you."

But Nellie sighed with resignation. "No—he has been so generous already; we cannot continue begging from him, for every hardship."

Doyle knelt to pick up a pencil from the floor. "Oh, I don't know, Nellie; he may be offended if you don't ask him. The aristocracy feels obligated about helpin' out. It's that—that nobles oblige thing." Doyle wasn't sure she got the words right, but Nellie would know what she meant. Nellie, like many immigrants, was fascinated by the aristocracy, and was hugely disappointed when Doyle was forced to confess that she didn't own a tiara.

"Oh, I see," said Nellie thoughtfully. "Well, I wouldn't want to offer him insult."

"Let me talk to him, then." Doyle could sense Nellie's satisfaction, and smiled to herself; there had been no doubt about the eventual outcome, but the proprieties had to be observed. A wily one, was Nellie.

To add to her general relief about the tying-up of the Wexton Prison case, Doyle was feeling better every day. She was doggedly eating the various peanut butter dishes Reynolds dreamed up, and their visit to the doctor had gone well. Dr. Easton, usually rather brusque, had been very kind to her, and no needles were flourished. Acton has spoken to him, she thought, and for once she was not exasperated with her over-protective husband.

She made her way up the side aisle, illuminated by the weak sunshine that was streaming in through the stained-glass windows along the wall. This window was her favorite; St. Michael was slaying the serpent, the blues and greens rich and vibrant, the dark serpent writhing in frustrated agony.

Suddenly, there was a horrendous crash, and as she watched, the window shattered and collapsed. The force of it propelled her against the end of the pew, and then threw her down to the floor, as shards of colored glass showered all around her. Instinctively, she tried to leap up to see if Nellie was all right, but found that her body did not want to respond to command. Instead, she could hear Nellie scream, as the older woman dropped to her knees beside Doyle, her shaking hands held up in horror.

"Get up, take cover," Doyle tried to say, but only a croaking sound emerged. I can't breathe, she thought in surprise, and fought panic.

The floor beneath her began to vibrate with pounding footsteps, as she stared up at Nellie's sobbing face, which was cut and bleeding. The deacon's face then came into view, an older man, who'd been straightening up the altar. "Now then, you're all right, lassie," he said in his calm voice, but he was shocked, Doyle could tell. He pulled a weeping Nellie away by the shoulders as Doyle fought for breath; odd, rasping sounds emerging from her mouth.

Holy Mother of God, she thought; where is Acton? Groping, she raised an arm to pull herself up by the pew, and then stared in surprise to see that her hand was covered with blood. Then Acton's face—strangely pale—appeared above her, as he handed his mobile to the deacon. "Stay on the line if they need further direction. An ambulance is on the way."

Doyle made a croaking sound, and Acton seemed to understand that she needed to sit up. He pulled her up to a sitting position, and draped her against his chest, while he indicated that the deacon should help him take off her coat. "Shallow breaths," he directed. "Don't panic."

Easier said than done, thought Doyle. Saints and holy angels, what's happened?

The deacon said, "I've a handkerchief; should we bind up her hand?" At Acton's nod, the deacon handed the mobile to Nellie, who held it stupidly, her face bloody, and her eyes wide and frightened.

"Rise up, Nellie," the deacon admonished, as he grasped Doyle's right hand and held it up over her head, pressing tightly. "Not a time for the faint o' heart."

Thus prompted, Nellie began speaking to the emergency personnel, as Acton carefully worked Doyle's shirt over her head, assisted by Father John, who now crouched down beside Acton, his lips moving in silent prayer. With quick fingers, Acton unfastened Doyle's Kevlar vest, and pulled it carefully away; she saw that a disc-shaped metal object was embedded in the center front.

"Glory be to God," breathed the deacon in amazement. "Another miracle, for the blessed lassie."

Acton quickly examined her, running his hands carefully over her torso. "Only the one," he pronounced with relief, "and it was caught."

"I was *shot*?" Doyle rasped out, gasping to catch her breath.

"Don't talk, sweetheart."

Doyle was bemused; Acton had never called her "sweetheart" before, and it sounded very strange.

Acton pulled her against him, and said into her ear. "Try to breathe; you've had the breath knocked out of you."

"I love you," she whispered, clinging to him. "I don't tell you near enough."

"You don't have to say; not to me."

They waited, listening as the sirens approached, the deacon firmly holding Doyle's hand above her head, and Father John crouching silently beside them. Doyle looked over Acton's shoulder at Nellie, and at the shattered glass, scattered on the pews and on the floor, the colors glinting in the light that was streaming in through the open window. "We were lucky, Nellie. Lucky the heater's not workin', and that we were wearin' our coats."

Nellie bent her head, and began to sob again, so the deacon awkwardly put his free arm around her, until Father John could come around, and help with the comforting.

When they arrived, the EMT personnel didn't blink when informed that a woman wearing a Kevlar vest had been shot through a stained glass window. They're rather like the CID, thought Doyle; they've seen it all, and nothing surprises them.

As they examined her hand, Acton explained it was a through and through—the bullet had passed through the webbing between her thumb and index finger, and no bones were broken.

"Lucky it's only my right hand," Doyle offered. She was left-handed.

"I like that hand," Acton protested, and she blushed.

Once in the ambulance, Acton was immediately on his mobile—despite the fact the medic told him it was not allowed—and Doyle had the impression he was speaking to Williams. "I want you there with a crack SOCO team; go over everything, and check for CCTV. Get Mathis to come in, and start processing immediately. I'll get ballistics, I've got the bullet." He paused, listening, and then held the mobile to Doyle's ear. "Tell him you are all right."

"I am all right," she announced dutifully, and the mobile was taken away.

"I'll keep you posted." Acton finished. "Get on it."

He then rang off, and scrolled for another number. Again, he explained briefly what had happened, and added, "You find him, you name your price."

He must be speaking to Savoie, Doyle realized.

"But I sign the report."

Doyle closed her eyes, and hoped no one else recognized Acton-speak as well as she did, but he was already ringing up someone else, this time his tone quite different. "Previ? This is Lord Acton, and I must I beg your pardon—I'm always disturbing you on a Sunday, it seems. My wife was injured when a stained glass window was shot out at St. Michaels's church—vandals, I imagine. I would appreciate it if you could run something on the news and in the papers as soon as you can, to find out if anyone saw anything; it's a sorry state of affairs if she can't be safe in a church, after jumping from Greyfriars Bridge."

Doyle could hear the publisher speak with great excitement about such a follow-up to the original story, and so Acton gave him the particulars, and then rang off.

"Good one," said Doyle. "Nicely done."

"Sir, I must ask that you refrain from using your mobile," ventured the medic.

"Police business," said Acton briefly, not even bothering to look at the man. He then leaned into Doyle, looking into her eyes, as the vehicle swayed. "How are you?"

"I am all right, Michael; truly." The young medic was lucky Acton hadn't taken a swing at him; he was that angry.

"If you know anything at all about this, Kathleen, you must tell me."

Acton was asking if her perceptive ability was giving her any clues and for the first time, it occurred to Doyle that this was what the dreams were all about—faith, she owed Maguire an apology, for giving him so much sauce. "I don't know, Michael. Truly, I don't."

She reached for his hand, and they said nothing further for the rest of the journey.

# 37

"I think," said Doyle, "that there is not enough scotch in London, for this one."

"No," Acton agreed.

They'd arrived at the hospital, and had been whisked up to a private suite, a team of very efficient doctors at the ready. There is nothing like having money and a title, thought Doyle; mental note.

On being informed that Doyle was pregnant, x-rays were scotched, and one of the doctors carefully palpitated Doyle's ribcage whilst she bit her lip—she was beginning to feel the effects of being flung about like a rag doll.

"None broken," he pronounced. "And even if one or two were, there's little we could do, anyway. Take it easy for a few days."

Not a problem, thought Doyle gloomily; Acton will never allow me out of the flat again.

After her hand was treated for the bullet wound, Dr. Easton arrived, accompanied by a radiologist with a portable ultrasound machine.

"The baby's been moving," Doyle offered. Indeed, Edward had been very active since the attack, almost as though he was protesting such ill-treatment.

The doctor nodded. "Good; the baby's still very small and well-insulated, so I am certain there was no harm done. I'd like to have a look to see if the placenta has been impacted, though."

He and the radiologist sat and viewed the screen, moving a small wand over her abdomen. Doyle couldn't make out anything, until the screen froze as a photo was taken.

"Ah," said Acton.

Doyle could see spindly arms and legs; skinny, and alien. In wonder, she compared what she saw on the screen with the young man from her dreams, and began to cry. Acton stroked her forehead, and asked the doctors in his cool, authoritative voice to finish it up, please.

"No harm done, Lady Acton." Easton touched her arm gently. "I'd like you to stay overnight for observation, however."

Acton responded for her. "We appreciate your concern, but we are going home."

Nellie came by to see her, and to say that she'd only needed a stitch or two on her hand; the others would heal. She was leaving with her husband, and Acton asked if Doyle could borrow her coat, being as her own had a ragged bullet hole in the center of her chest, and he wanted to discard it.

Small wonder Nellie and the deacon had been horrified, Doyle thought. While she made herself ready, there was a knock at the door, and Trenton announced that he'd arrived.

Doyle saw that he was carrying another Kevlar vest, and she suppressed a groan; Acton would take no chances. After indicating that Trenton should wait in the hall, he gently fastened it over her torso. "Ready?" he asked.

"I should ring up Williams," she ventured. "If you don't mind."

"I don't, but quickly, please."

Williams answered immediately. "Are you really all right?"

"Yes, we're goin' home, in fact, with no harm done."

"There's an awful lot of blood here for no harm done."

"Thomas, don't make me unwell."

"Sorry. May I come by?"

"Tomorrow," she offered. "I'll ring you when I'm up and about. Please don't worry."

She rang off, and then was quietly loaded into Trenton's sedan at the service entrance, in the basement of the hospital. Both men remained vigilant and on edge during the drive home, and Acton called the concierge at their building to ask that they be extra alert with respect to anyone seeking access. Once at the flat, Acton remained with her by the door, while Trenton carefully searched the rooms, gun drawn, before calling out an all clear. After exchanging a significant look with Acton, Trenton then left. Acton locked the door, and with no further ado, lifted Doyle off her feet, and carried her to the bed.

"This is familiar," she said into his neck.

"No more getting shot," he replied firmly.

"I promise." She kissed his throat; he was in a state, was her poor husband.

He set her on the bed, and examined the bandages on her hand. "Let me get some ice."

"Put it in your scotch instead—I'm all right. I'd like you to come sit with me, is all." Mainly she wanted to keep him close; the last time they'd encountered this type of situation, he'd gone off half-cocked, and she needed to cling to his coat tails, so as to prevent more mayhem.

An hour later, she was pretending to sleep so that Acton could drink in peace—which he'd been ably doing, like a dockman on strike. Despite the near-empty scotch bottle, however, she could sense that her husband was deeply abstracted; trying, no doubt, to figure out who would attempt such a bold murder, in broad daylight. Doyle hadn't had a chance to think this over herself, but now that she did, it was truly a crackin' puzzler. Someone had attempted to murder a peeress-turned-famous-bridge-jumper in spectacular fashion; but it seemed so—so much *overkill*, if one could pardon the pun. If someone truly wanted her dead, there were much easier ways to get the job done.

Hard to believe it was the matron, who was playing least-in-sight, and hard to believe it was anyone connected with the Wexton Prison case, since they were falling all over themselves trying to grass on the others. Stymied, she decided that she wasn't up to putting on her thinking-cap, just yet. In any event, Acton was still emanating so much rage that she didn't think she could concentrate, even if she wanted to—hopefully he'd go to sleep soon, and the black mood that hovered would dissipate. The usual cure for the black mood was a hearty helping of rough sex, but while her spirit was willing, her flesh felt like a beaten mule, and so regrettably, sex was out of the question.

"Can't you sleep?" he asked quietly.

So much for pretending. "I'd give a year's salary for a pint o' your scotch."

He ran a sympathetic hand over her hip. "The pregnancy book says you can take an over-the-counter acetaminophen."

"I'd rather not." She'd already given this poor child a fright; no need to drug him as well.

"Hot shower?" he suggested.

She thought about it for a moment. Ironically, the force of the shot had pushed her away from much of the falling glass, but what cuts she had on her hands and face would no doubt sting in the shower. Also, she was worried that Acton may be unsteady on his feet. "Not just yet."

Very carefully, he pulled her against him, and even though the movement hurt her back, she didn't protest. He smelt of scotch, and began gently stroking her arms. "Don't die; I couldn't bear it."

"All right then; I won't."

"Christ, it was such a noise. . ."

"Michael," she said firmly. "I don't want to talk about it, just now."

"Sorry. I am afraid I am drunk."

He was truly in a sorry state, if he was willing to admit as much. She took one of his hands, and lifted it to her mouth, kissing the palm. "Knocker."

His hands continued their circuit and he was quiet for a moment. "So extraordinary, to see Edward. He'll be the fifteenth baron."

"He looks better in my dreams."

"Thank God for your dreams."

"Thank God for you and your vest."

"It worked." He was sounding sleepy, and his hands slowed.

"Good to know."

"Yes." The stroking stopped, and then his arms tightened slightly around her. "Love you," he murmured.

Ouch, ouch, ouch, she thought, but said gently, "Go to sleep, Michael."

She must have gotten comfortable enough to fall asleep, because she was once again having the dream, only this time Edward was not present. Instead, Doyle stood beside Maguire, as they regarded the closed door.

Maguire said, "That's the problem with this vengeance business; it never ends."

She looked over at him in surprise. "That sounds more like somethin' I'd say, not you."

"It's all very symmetrical, when you think about it."

Doyle frowned, battling to pay attention. "What is symmetrical?"

With a shrug, he turned toward the locked door, and quoted her. "Some people are looking to get murdered, and some people are not."

"I'm lost," she offered apologetically. "Can you speak a bit more plainly?"

He laughed. "You are one to talk."

After a moment, she turned to consider the closed door. "Who would want to kill someone in a church? A despicable act, for the love o' Mike."

"Depends on the church," said Maguire.

"I'm going to see." With a monumental effort, she forced herself to step forward.

"You are one of the bravest people I know."

She opened the door to behold a man in his late forties, staring at her with an expression of unabated fury.

With a gasp, she sat upright in the bed, the sudden movement making her groan aloud. Acton began fumbling for the light, trying to focus.

"*Máthir naofa*, Michael; 'tis him; I saw who was behind the door." She paused, recovering her wits, and trying to decide how best to break it to him. But she'd been shot, and he was drunk, and there was no time like the present. "It's your father."

Propped up on an elbow, he rested his unfocused gaze on hers, and said nothing, his expression unreadable.

She repeated, "Your missin' father; he's tied up in this, somehow."

He lifted a hand, and brushed a tendril of hair away from her face. "No, my father is quite dead."

She frowned at him, trying to sort out what she could remember of the dream. "But Michael, I saw him—he may be alive, still."

Acton held her gaze, his own eyes dark and opaque. "You are mistaken, Kathleen; I killed him myself."

It was the pure truth, and she was speechless for a moment, staring at him. "Oh," she said, striving for a normal tone. "I see. Well, then; I'm sorry for it."

"I am not."

This was also the pure truth, and she wasn't certain how to respond.

He lay back down, and turned to switch off the light. "I would appreciate it if you did not mention it to anyone."

"Yes—well, I think that's probably a good strategy, all in all." She hovered on the edge of asking him more about it—that he was willing to say even this much was surprising—but the black mood threatened, and she didn't want to trigger it.

He gently closed ran a hand along her arm. "You should go back to sleep, Kathleen."

This seemed an indication that he wasn't going to tell her any more about his father's death, and truth to tell, she was relieved; there were too many crises in the present, to try to dissect one from the past, and besides, she wasn't completely sure she wanted to hear about it. Contrary to what Maguire seemed to think, she was a coward about most things. "All right," she said, and laid her aching body back down next to Acton's.

# 38

Acton's mobile began vibrating as soon as the sun came up, and Doyle, who'd precious little sleep, was forced to awaken, also. She lay for a while, assessing herself, and then crept out to sit at the kitchen table, whilst Acton made and returned calls.

He looked up as she came in, covering the speaker to his mobile. "Sorry. I tried to be quiet."

"Whist; I'll take a nap later." She'd have plenty of time; she knew she was going nowhere until this was resolved.

"How are you?"

"Better," she lied—the aching was worse today than it was yesterday. On the other hand, she was actually in a fairly good frame of mind, all things considered; they'd dodged yet another catastrophe, and she was safe at home with a husband who was bent, as only Acton could be bent, on finding the attacker. He did not seem to be suffering any ill effects from drinking too much, and the black mood had disappeared to be replaced by the sharp and efficient DCI that the public knew and loved.

Doyle's scalp prickled, and she paused in surprise; wondering what it was she was trying to understand. Acton was himself again—thanks be to God—and how he would have been if the killer had succeeded, almost didn't bear thinking about. What he'd said last night was true, he couldn't have borne it if she'd died; he'd have run amok—as he'd done once before—or simply shot himself, to put an end to his misery. Her scalp prickled again, and she was suddenly aware that she was on the wrong track. What? She thought in surprise. Of course Acton would be devastated; the man was a Section Seven stalker, after all—contrary to the occasional pretend-affair with a newspaper reporter, or the occasional rumor of marital strife, making the rounds at the Met.

Her thoughts were interrupted when Acton walked to stand beside her chair. As he listened to his mobile, he pulled her robe aside to look at her chest, and winced when he saw her bruise.

"Hideous," she whispered. "Black as the third horseman."

"Put a trace on it," he said into the phone. "Well done."

He rang off, and then scrolled for another number. "Williams is going to climb the walls until he sees you."

She was embarrassed, and could feel herself blushing. "If you don't want him over, Michael, that is perfectly all right with me. He should learn his limits."

"This afternoon, perhaps," he replied. "I confess I can sympathize with him."

He then walked into the bedroom to engage in the next low-voiced phone conversation, out of earshot. It must be Savoie, Doyle surmised. That, or he was speaking about something he thought might upset her. I do believe I'm past being upset, though; must be a symptom of being shot in the chest.

When Acton came back, he was emanating satisfaction. "What do we have?" she asked hopefully.

"A partial plate and a footprint. A casing."

This was a surprise, and she stated the obvious. "He's an amateur, then." Someone who was proficient at this type of thing would never have left such a wealth of evidence, lying about.

She caught a flare of exasperation from him. "Unfortunately, the church has no security cameras."

"No. And they'll be needin' a new heatin' system, and a stained glass window, too."

Amused, he ran a fond hand over her head. "You are catching me at a weak moment."

"My mother didn't raise a fool."

He bent to kiss her, and examine the bandage on her hand. "Does it hurt?"

"What hurts the most is my back, of all things. You didn't cancel Reynolds, did you? I am *starvin'* for bacon and eggs."

He paused to look at her in surprise. "Are you indeed?"

She teased, "Indeed."

Smiling, he leaned over to kiss her again. "A silver lining, then."

"I prefer the old cure, myself."

His mobile pinged, and he was back at it. Despite his seemingly benign mood, she was not fooled; this amateur attacker would never see the inside of a holding cell, because Acton would kill him, and not kindly. Father John would be disappointed, but the Seven Spiritual Acts of Mercy were no match for the crackin' bruise on her breastbone. Again, her scalp prickled and she ignored it, exasperated.

Reynolds arrived, and was equal parts dismayed by her scratched-up appearance and delighted to hear that Doyle was hungry. "Bacon and eggs, please," she requested. "And toast with strawberry jam."

Acton hung up, and came to sit with her, indicating to Reynolds that he'd have what his wife was having. "No prints on the casing," he reported to her. "A shame, but not unexpected. If it was an amateur, he probably panicked in vacating the scene, and didn't realize the casing was still on the ground."

While Reynolds bustled around the kitchen, Doyle indicated the servant with her eyes, and lowered her voice. "Do we need to get our story straight?"

Acton said merely, "The paper will report that vandals shot out the window, and that you were injured by the glass."

She nodded. "What caliber was the bullet?"

".243; so presumably, a bolt-action hunting rifle."

"A hunting rifle?" This was in keeping with the theory that the shooter was an amateur, and would therefore get himself caught by making amateur mistakes. On the other hand, if he was not a habitual criminal, it meant they'd have no likely suspects, and nothing on file to compare any prints to.

While the aroma of frying bacon filled the flat, she watched Acton scroll through the messages on his mobile, and was cautiously optimistic; he seemed confident, which meant that she'd probably be allowed to see the light of day in a few short years.

"Maguire was in my dream, again." Acton had not inquired about her dream, no doubt because he didn't want to discuss how he'd murdered his father, and small blame to him. Nevertheless, the dream could be important; it had been important before, and she regretted that she hadn't thanked Maguire for saving their lives when she'd had the chance—it was such a struggle to have a normal conversation. "When I asked how someone could kill someone in a church, he said that it depended on the church."

Acton looked up at this, thinking, and she ventured, "D'you think he was referring to Grady? There must be hunting rifles at Trestles." Grady was the Irish stableman who was from Ulster, which meant he was Protestant, and not a fan of Doyle-the-mackerel-snapper.

"I will make some inquires. Did Maguire say anything else?"

"He said somethin' that didn't make a lot of sense, when you consider that it was him, sayin' it. He said, 'The problem with vengeance is that it never ends.'"

Acton looked out the windows for a moment, whilst Reynolds served up the hot plates, and with one eye on her husband, Doyle tucked into her breakfast with a gusto that had been lacking for several months.

"You said you ran into Cassie Masterson when you were with Williams the other day."

She paused, mid-forkful, because it did seem that the disgraced reporter was a prime candidate for vengeance-taking. "Yes, when we were at the Metro animal shelter."

Slowly, he asked, "Can you be absolutely certain that the meeting wasn't contrived? Perhaps she's been monitoring your movements."

Doyle considered this, then shook her head. "I don't think so, Michael; she was truly surprised to see me." No question that Acton would believe this; sometimes it seemed that he trusted her perceptive abilities more than she did.

He nodded. "Nevertheless, I'll have a look. Anything else?"

She thought about it, and shook her head again. Other than Maguire telling her that she was brave, she couldn't remember anything else. She didn't want to tell Acton about this last little detail, however, since she had the feeling that Maguire had said it because more bravery would soon be needed, and the last thing she wanted was to be fitted out in Kevlar from head to toe.

# 39

Doyle spent the rest of the morning bored and lying on the sofa, hoping this was not to be her foreseeable future. "Any chance we can have bangers and mash?" she asked Reynolds hopefully, as she positioned her pillow. "The kind with the hard skin?"

"Certainly, madam," he replied without a flicker, and Doyle sighed in happy anticipation—nothin' like getting your appetite back, with a vengeance. She hoped Reynolds knew enough to fry the bangers in oil, rather than steam them, like the stupid English did, but decided she'd best mention it, just in case.

After lunch, she dozed for a bit on the sofa, and then woke to see that Acton and Williams were seated at the table, conferring quietly. With an effort to appear cheerful, she sat herself up. "I'm awake; hallo, Williams."

"Hey, Doyle: I brought you something." With a gesture, he indicated a latte, sitting on the counter, and then met her eyes. "Don't worry, it's decaffeinated."

This was a lie, and hiding a delighted smile, she replied, "That is so good of you, Williams. Heat it up, Reynolds, I'll drink it down."

Ruthlessly pulling her wayward hair into a pony tail, she joined them at the table, as Reynolds brought over the coffee drink. It was too hot to drink right away, and so she blew on it impatiently.

"How are you feeling?" Williams asked. He was tired and upset, poor man, and trying to hide it.

"As well as can be expected, I suppose. I told Acton that my hand doesn't hurt so much, it's my back that hurts the most."

"How'd you hurt your back?"

"The force of the shot threw me into the end of the pew." She paused, as he'd lowered his gaze, and was struggling. Knocker, she thought; you're making Williams miserable. She changed the subject, "Is there an ID on the plate yet?"

Williams glanced at Acton. "Yes—rental car, and we've traced it to Kympton."

"And where is that?" Geography wasn't Doyle's strong suit.

"It's up by Meryton," Acton explained into the silence.

"Oh." Doyle tried to hide her alarm, since she was aware—as Williams was not—that the disposable cell call to Dr. Harding was also from the Meryton area. All in all, it was beginning to look like someone from Trestles had conspired with the missing matron to do away with the fair Doyle—Grady the stableman was not the criminal mastermind type, after all—and Doyle eyed Acton with some misgiving. If the dowager or Sir Stephen were involved, she didn't know what he'd do—he'd killed his father, after all. She knew without a doubt that Acton would want to keep it quiet; she knew that Trestles, with its long and storied history, was very important to him—almost as important as she was. Her scalp prickled.

Acton rose. "I'll make a call to Hudson, to see if he's aware of anything unusual going forward."

Doyle was going to comment that it would be difficult to distinguish the unusual from the usual in that household, but refrained in front of Williams, who didn't need to hear of family matters.

After Acton retreated to the bedroom to make the call, Williams leaned forward, and indicted her hands. "No stitches?"

"Not a one." She offered them up for inspection. "Nellie needed stitches for one cut, but overall, we were lucky."

He was going to argue, then bit it back.

"I think I'll have a permanent bruise on my poor chest," she teased. "You know me."

"Stop; I don't want to even think about it." He paused, absently holding her hands in his. "Don't make a habit of this, please."

"No argument here. At least I volunteered for the bridge jump."

"Another medal?" he teased, the blue eyes glinting up at her.

"I don't think they give you a medal for bein' shot in church, Thomas."

Reynolds abruptly appeared, and set a plate of biscuits before them. He then lingered and asked Williams about his participation in the bridge-jumping incident, whilst Doyle hid a smile; the servant had apparently decided that a chaperone was needful. During the conversation, Williams met her eye with a quick gleam of amusement, and made no further attempt to touch her.

Once Reynolds had exhausted the subject, and retreated to the kitchen again, Williams switched to a less objectionable topic. "I wanted to report success about the Marnie situation."

Saints, she'd almost forgotten about the Marnie situation. Doyle sat up, despite the effort it cost her. "Good work, Thomas; what's happened?"

"I rang up Gabriel, and spoke to him. He was concerned, of course, and I emphasized that she needed to see a good internist, not just her regular pediatrician."

"Because her regular doctor hadn't noticed. Very good, Thomas."

"She'll go in tomorrow."

"I'm that relieved." She'd done all that she could; perhaps it was nothing, after all.

In an overly-casual manner, Williams drew a finger along the table edge. "Remember when you called me, and asked if I needed help, or if I thought that someone would want to kill me?"

She could see where this was going, and hurried to reassure him. "No, I've had no crazed premonitions about you, Thomas. I was just misunderstandin' somethin'."

"All right. Thought I'd check."

Acton returned to the room, and announced, "I will leave for Trestles tomorrow morning. If you would, Williams, please help Trenton keep an eye on my wife; I will try to be home before nightfall."

"Yes, sir. Would it be possible to pull DI Chiu over to the stolen fetus case? We haven't had any leads, and we'll need more personnel."

"I regret to say that DI Chiu has withdrawn from the force," Acton replied, and offered no further explanation. "Instead, I will double-assign DI Habib."

Poor Habib, thought Doyle; his sweet side won't be likin' that case.

Nodding, Williams moved to stand by the windows, as he and Acton discussed what needed to be done on some of Acton's more pressing cases. Doyle could feel her pulse quicken, and her palms sweat, as she struggled to stay calm. "Williams," she finally said, "D'you think you could step away from the window?"

Glancing up in surprise, Williams stepped back, and then Acton came over to stand behind her, his reassuring hands on her shoulders.

"Sorry," she said, embarrassed. "Not over it yet, I guess."

Acton asked gently, "Would you like to rest for a bit? We'll go for a walk, and leave you in peace."

"I would," she replied readily, trying to make light of it. "I'll go off to bed, and pull the covers over my head."

She watched them go with interest; the only reason her husband would leave her side, just now, was because he didn't want her to hear whatever it was he had to say to Williams. She was not surprised; no doubt they were coordinating what was to be done, depending on who the Trestles-shooter was, and it wouldn't do to have the disapproving schoolmarm listening in to plans for yet another vigilante murder.

Reynolds came over to wipe the already-wiped tabletop with his tea towel, and bestow a sharp look from the corner of his eye. "A dedicated fellow, the detective inspector."

"That he is," she replied in an absent tone. "I'm tryin' to find him a girl, Reynolds; let me know if you come across one."

Doyle's mobile pinged, and when she saw that it was Munoz, she picked up. "Hallo, Munoz."

"Who is supposed to be covering your desk?"

"Don't fret yourself, there's nothin' to cover. I've no field assignments, so I'll do research from home." Doyle was touched; Munoz was worried about her, and being obnoxious was her way of showing it.

"I almost forgot; you don't have to work, you're having Acton's baby."

Doyle smiled. "I'm all right, Izzy. Truly."

"Williams is not telling me *anything*."

"There's not much to tell; some scratches and cuts. A through-and-through near my thumb, but no real harm done. I went to the hospital so they could check me out, but I was fine."

"I went to the hospital, but you'd already gone," the other girl admitted.

"Thank you Munoz, that was kind."

"It was only fair; you visited me after the bridge jump. While I was there, I met your pediatrician, but I can't say I was impressed. He made a run at me, which seemed poor form, under the circumstances."

Doyle knit her brow in puzzlement. "I don't have a pediatrician."

"That'll be news to him. He seemed to know a lot about what happened."

Doyle froze. "Faith, Munoz, what did he look like?"

"Like a pediatrician," she replied. "Why, what is it?"

Doyle sat up, alert. Obviously it wasn't Grady, since the stableman was unmistakably Irish. "Can you come here, to my flat? I need you to make a sketch of him—it's very important."

"All right; let me check with Habib."

"No—no; don't mention it to anyone, Izzy, *please*."

Munoz was no fool, and immediately became briskly business-like. "Give me your address, and I'll be right over."

Doyle rang off, and debated whether or not to call Acton, then decided there was nothing to tell, as yet. Twenty minutes later, Munoz was at the door. "DS Munoz is an artist," Doyle explained to Reynolds, as she escorted the other girl over to the table.

Munoz, however, was too distracted to notice the servant's polite greeting. "Look at this place," she said bitterly. "Oh my God."

The last needful thing was to have Munoz vent about letting Acton slip through her fingers in front of Reynolds, so Doyle prompted, "Please Munoz, try to sketch the man. And make notes so you remember exactly what he said—Acton will want to know."

Munoz sat at the table and sketched, occasionally stopping to think. Her hand moved deftly, and the outline of a man's face soon appeared.

We can send it out to all the local station houses, thought Doyle as she watched her work. We might be able to make a visual ID, even if he hasn't got a record, and his prints aren't in the index. The other girl began to fill in the details: eyebrows, eyes, hairline. As she watched, Doyle's scalp began to prickle. "Saints and holy angels," she breathed.

"Who is it, madam?" asked Reynolds, leaning over in fascination.

"Why, it's Dr. Harding," said Doyle, astonished.

# 40

*H*e could still remember his reaction when he got the call. He was worried, nonsensically, that Acton wasn't telling him the truth; that she was dead. Not the case, but indicative of the unfamiliar panic that had enveloped him.

He tried to focus on evidence recovery; he bullied the best crew to come in, even though it was Sunday. He supervised the site, and painstakingly pieced together the results, all the while fighting an urge to leave it all and go to her. Ridiculous; she was not his to go to.

The blood on the site had shaken him; if the vest had caught the bullet, why was there so much blood? Perhaps there was another bullet, one that had gone unnoticed. The panic rose again, and he shook his head to clear it; Acton would have made sure. An older Scottish man gave his account; he'd been a witness. The blessed lassie and another woman had been cut by the falling glass. Her hand had been shot through; she must have been holding it in front of her.

"How was she when the ambulance took her?"

"Good," the man said. "She's a braw lass—a policewoman, you know, and wasn't it a miracle that she was wearing her bullet proof vest? Saints be praised." He left to help the priest board up the window.

There was enough evidence to be very optimistic. They would soon know who'd done this; he had complete faith in Acton. He decided that as soon as he finished up, he would go to the hospital, just to check in for a moment—just to see. She didn't like doctors, and he may be needed to cheer her along. He wondered if she would have surgery on her hand, and debated calling Acton again. Then she called to reassure him, because she knew, even with her crisis, that he needed reassurance. She knew him better than anyone, except his mother, who would ask him if he had met any nice girls with a knowing concern in her eyes.

He put his mind to following the leads, and putting together a report for Acton. He'd see her tomorrow, and she'd need some coffee.

When he came to the flat in the morning, Acton anticipated him, and opened the door, indicating that she was asleep on the sofa. He looked her over as he walked by; she was on her side with her hands curled level with her chin, one heavily bandaged. There were cuts on her face and her hands. He had to fight the urge to lift the blanket and climb in; to stay beside her for a few days, just holding her safe. He was being ridiculous again, and this was neither the time nor the place—there was a shooter to be apprehended, and work to do. Despite his best efforts, however, he felt a bit bleak; it had never been clearer that he was on the outside, looking in.

And then she was up, and laughing, and giving him a sly glance about the contraband coffee, and he thought: I am a lucky man. It's only that Acton is luckier, and that can't be helped, it's just fate.

When Acton took him out for a walk, he knew what was coming; they hadn't discussed it in a while, and the circumstances on the ground had definitely changed.

"I hope you are not too disappointed," Acton said, half-humorously. "The contingency plan is on hold."

He smiled in return. "Of course I'm not disappointed; this is the best of all possible outcomes—an uncontested heir. My own claim would have been equivocal, at best."

They were silent for a moment, as they waited for a pedestrian to pass by, and then Acton continued, "On the contrary, I made certain that your claim would ultimately prevail. There are documents in the archives at Trestles that support you, and Hudson, my steward, would have testified about your supposed branch of the family tree."

*He nodded, unsurprised that Acton would go to such lengths. "Good to know, sir, but fortunately it is all moot, now."*

*"It may not be. It is entirely possible that the succession was the reason for the attack."*

*In fact, this had already occurred to him, as the attack had happened just after Kath's pregnancy was made public. "Someone wanted to destroy your heir, and then in due course, destroy you, knowing you are unlikely to remarry."*

*"Yes. If that was indeed the motivation, it may be helpful to make your own claim public. On the other hand, your claim relies on the element of surprise—and having the matter set before the right committee judge. If you bring it too early, there is a chance your story may be discredited."*

*He nodded, thinking about this. "I'll do whatever is most likely to keep Lady Acton safe."*

*"Good; I would ask that you step down from the CID."*

*He'd not been expecting this, and looked over at Acton in surprise. "Step down, sir? I don't understand; how would that help?"*

*They walked a few paces before Acton answered. "Another theory would be that the attack was to prevent any further investigation into the corruption scandal. I know too much for certain people to be comfortable."*

*"Have you been warned-off?"*

*"Not as yet. But the detective chief superintendent is involved; he used me to try to frame a Home Office official, who'd caught wind of the scandal. Now that I've backed off that arrest, the DCS must be aware that I am suspicious."*

*Here was another unpleasant surprise, and he ran his hand through his hair in disbelief. "Christ, the DCS himself is implicated? Are you certain, sir?"*

*"I am."*

*There was a pause, while he considered this daunting problem. "Is the situation salvageable? Or will he need to be eliminated?"*

*"We shall see. And you should be aware that Philippe Savoie has infiltrated the ring at my request; he'll be given immunity, once the dust settles."*

*This was unwelcome news, and he asked cautiously, "Can you trust Savoie?" He distrusted the Frenchman with good reason; Acton did not know that Savoie had a thing for Kath.*

"In this, yes. He has his own interests in the matter."

This probably meant that Savoie would be allowed to continue the smuggling rig that Solonik had tried to cut in on. It was none of his business, but he hoped that Acton knew what he was doing; it seemed like a volatile mixture of allegiances, to him.

They walked a few moments in silence, and he ventured, "I'm not clear on why I should step down; I thought the long-term plan was to establish me in a policy-making position."

Acton put his hands in his coat pockets, and raised his gaze to the trees for a moment. "Ours is a dangerous job, and we are making some powerful enemies. I would not be surprised—" here he paused for a moment. "I would not be surprised if someone was attempting to take a vengeance, against me."

But this seemed implausible, and he allowed his skepticism to show. "Vengeance? Do you really think so, sir? This shooter's such an amateur, leaving evidence everywhere. And shooting your wife through a stained glass window in broad daylight—it can't be a career criminal, and who else would be seeking vengeance? The succession theory makes more sense to me."

"All true. Under either theory, however, I am the ultimate target, and so we must create a protocol in the event he achieves his aim."

He waited, not certain what was meant. A protocol in the event Acton was murdered?

"If I am killed, you must marry Kathleen." He said it matter-of-factly, as though they were discussing the weather.

Floored yet again, he struggled with a response. "I will help her in any way I can, of course, but you must know that she's not one to be talked into such a thing."

This remark seemed to amuse Acton for some reason, but he continued, "Then you may have to be persistent; it would be the best for her child, after all. You will make known your own claim to the estate, and—if it comes to a court battle over the guardianship of the child—the court would look with favor on such a symmetrical solution." He paused. "There is a great deal of money at stake."

He made a movement of protest, but Acton ignored it. "You must see that I have no other solution. My wife. . . despite all appearances, my wife is a timid creature, and I fear she would not be willing to fight the battles that would need to be fought. I would appreciate it if you would set my mind at ease."

He felt he should state the obvious. "I hope I never have to console her for such a loss, sir." He meant it sincerely; she would be in agony, and wouldn't be over it quickly.

"Nevertheless, I would like to have a protocol in place, in the event of such a contingency." He gave him a glance. "You must keep her away from Savoie."

So much for having to warn him. "So you want me to step down from the CID, so as to protect me."

Acton glanced at him in sympathy. "Yes. I know it would not be your choice, but I hate to think what would become of her—and the child—if we were both taken out."

But he couldn't like this idea. "My work is important—our work is important; and not just to me. And Kath—Lady Acton will not willingly quit the Met; you must know that as well as I do. I think we should continue with the original plan."

Acton considered this, as they walked for a few paces. "All right, then. But at the very least, you must pull off the Wexton Prison case, and keep well-away from any fallout."

"Agreed." He had a sneaking suspicion that this was Acton's original goal, and that he'd been manipulated to readily agree, where he'd have put up a strong argument. It didn't matter; he had a lot to think about. Definitely no longer on the outside looking in; that was for certain.

"Thank you," said Acton, having apparently settled the matter to his satisfaction.

# 41

As Munoz and Doyle waited for Acton's return, Reynolds served up finger sandwiches. Doyle fell upon them like a jackdaw, but Munoz was distracted, texting someone who was apparently not answering. Doyle hoped it wasn't Lestrade, and tried to think of something to talk about, as she munched on cucumber filling. "Have you seen Drake lately?"

This was apparently a touchy subject, because the girl's mouth turned mulish. "No. I'm not dating him, if that's what you mean."

"I was just wonderin', Munoz; no need to be so defensive." Reminded of her suspicions, Doyle decided to take a cast. "Speakin' of which, were you ever workin' on the Bennet case for him—the girl who was murdered on the Heath? I remember he wanted you to check on somethin' on the quiet, and I wondered if that was it."

Munoz checked her mobile again. "I'm not supposed to talk about it." Unable to resist, she gave Doyle a sidelong glance. "But I think it was an old girlfriend, and when she was murdered, he was worried the EO might find something connecting him to her."

"I shouldn't be surprised, I suppose," said Doyle in a casual tone, her suspicions confirmed. "Men; honestly."

Munoz made a face that indicated her general agreement with this sentiment. "He's going to get himself into trouble, someday."

Mainly, thought Doyle, Drake's lucky that Acton is willing to pull his coals out of the fire—and that Gabriel is apparently willing, too. Assuming a light tone, she teased, "That's not him you're hopin' for a call-back from, is it?"

Munoz dropped her mobile on the table in frustration. "Good God, no. I'm trying to get through to Elena."

Relieved that the other girl wasn't reporting back to Drake, Doyle nonetheless felt a small stab of envy. "It must be nice to be Elena, and have your big sister watchin' over you."

Munoz gave her a look. "She borrowed my designer purse, and I need it tonight."

"Ah. I stand corrected."

"So who is Dr. Harding?"

Doyle regretted mentioning the man's name in front of Munoz and Reynolds, being as she couldn't very well explain that Acton had been seeing a psychiatrist because he was a supposedly-recovering Section Seven stalker. Instead, she improvised, "The doctor was a suspect in an assault, but there wasn't enough to hold him."

Munoz's gaze was sharp upon her. "So, do you think he's the shooter?"

Doyle's scalp prickled in the affirmative, but she said to Munoz, "I don't know." Nothin' for it; if they arrested Harding, there was no way to prevent Acton's treatment from being made public. God only knew what revelations were in store, if that particular can of worms were wrest open; she had no idea how much Harding knew.

Fortunately, at this juncture Acton returned with Williams, and Doyle willingly laid the whole at his feet.

"Harding," said Acton thoughtfully, as he crossed his arms, but Doyle could sense that he was very surprised.

"Shall I bring him in?" asked Williams, who seemed eager to do so. Probably wants to sock him again, thought Doyle.

But Acton shook his head with regret. "We need to place him at the scene, first."

Doyle kept her gaze on the table, as this statement was not true. Presumably, Acton did not want to discuss the protocol in front of Munoz, being as the protocol would feature Acton-style vengeance-taking.

Acton addressed Williams. "Let's show a snap of the suspect at the car rental place in Kympton, to see if they remember him—that would be a link." Turning to Munoz, he nodded. "Good work, Sergeant."

Munoz, who recognized a dismissal when she heard it, rose to her feet. "Happy to help, sir."

In response to Acton's glance, Williams rose also, and offered to walk out with Munoz. The other girl, however, did not appear to appreciate this unlooked-for boon, as she checked her mobile yet again, a small crease between her brows.

Reynolds also recognized his cue, and as soon as the servant shut the door behind him, Doyle apologized to her husband. "I'm wretchedly sorry, Michael; I shouldn't have said anythin' in front of the others, but I was that gobsmacked. Blessed saints and holy angels— Harding, of *all* people."

But as always, Acton wouldn't hear of her foolishness. "No, it is I who am sorry; I found him believable when I questioned him—I should have had you listen in."

Doyle offered, "Well, you can hardly be blamed; he's a psychiatrist, after all."

Absently, Acton took hold of her pony tail, and wound it round his hand. "Yes; and not someone who would leave a crime scene cluttered with evidence. There is something here that we are missing."

"You truly don't mean to bring him in?"

"No, not as yet—he doesn't know we've twigged him, and I'll have Williams shadow him, to see where he goes, and with whom he meets." He released her hair, to watch it spill, and then wound it up again. "Since he spoke with Munoz at the hospital, he knows the attempt was not successful, and will have to make this unhappy report to whomever he is working with. We shall see who he contacts."

Doyle's scalp prickled. "Remember the SOCO's snaps? Holy Trinity Church has cloisters. And Maguire said whether or not someone would commit murder at a church would depend on the church."

Acton's hand paused. "Holy Trinity Church also has a permanent seat on the Health Professions Council."

She considered this interesting little fact in the silence it deserved. "It seems the dots are all gettin' themselves connected."

Acton unsheathed his mobile, and texted a message. "It does indeed. Nonetheless, I must go to Trestles."

This was a bit surprising—that he still wanted to make the trip— and it indicated to Doyle that her unhappy husband wanted to find out whether his assorted relatives were involved in this plot—probably to cover for them in the event they were conniving to murder the incumbent Lady Acton, who had proved inconveniently fertile. That, or Acton was planning to murder them all outright, and stage it as a boating accident, or something.

This unwelcome thought gave her pause, and she offered with false brightness, "Shall I come with you? I could hide on the floorboards of the car, out of sight, or wear a false mustache."

But he was in no mood, and met her eyes very seriously. "I would ask that instead you stay here, away from the windows, and wearing a vest at all times. Harding is still at large."

"Aye then," she sighed with regret. Locked in her tower, she was. Still worried about what he intended to do, she toyed with asking him outright about Harding's potential accomplices, but lost her nerve, and decided to take a different tack. "Have you thought at all about your father's appearance in my dream?"

He took a breath, and answered slowly. "I am not discounting it, but I cannot see how it fits in. Even if the attack was about the succession, he no longer has a role."

She persisted, "It seemed odd that he was there, in the dream. Is there some—I don't know—some *reason* that he'd be involved in all this?"

But Acton shook his head. "Successions based on primogeniture are very straightforward."

Doyle wasn't certain what the word meant, and so she left it alone, although she knew it was important, for some reason. At present, however, she was too worried about her husband's unexpected desire to venture off to stupid Trestles, when it truly did not seem necessary. "You will be very careful, Michael? Do you solemnly promise me?"

He must have known that she was worried about his state of mind, because he pulled her over onto his lap, and carefully closed his arms around her. "I do solemnly promise. But I will do whatever is necessary to resolve this matter, so that you may walk the streets again as a free woman."

She decided to take the bull by the horns, since being tactful never seemed to work out, anyway. "Remember that you mustn't go about killin' people."

"I will keep it to mind."

She leaned back into his chest as he began the rhythmic stroking that was part of his compulsion, and hoped for the best. "I'll miss you." She slipped two fingers between his shirt buttons, fingering his skin. She was feeling well enough for a bout of goodbye sex, and it would be an easy way to redirect her husband's volatile thoughts.

"And I will miss you. Do you remember about the fungible assets?"

She stilled her fingers. "Michael, you are scarin' me; have done." The fungible assets were cash, gold and jewelry he kept in an anonymous safe deposit box. He'd instructed her to access it in the event of his death, so that if his mother and Sir Stephen attempted to tie up the estate, she'd have immediate access to funds.

He gently lifted her bandaged hand to inspect it. "We have a protocol, is all, and I would rest easier if I knew you would follow it."

"Then rest away; I'll not forget the stupid protocol." Impatiently, she slid her fingers between the buttons on his shirt again.

"Let Williams help you."

"Michael, you give Williams an inch, and he'll take a mile, believe me."

It seemed he was going to say something, then thought the better of it. "All right."

She decided on the direct approach, and unbuttoned a button to kiss the skin beneath. "Let's go to bed, husband."

He tightened his arms. "Are you feeling well enough?"

"As long as you don't squeeze too hard, my back is still achin'."

"Then perhaps I should sleep on the sofa," he teased, as she impatiently unbuttoned more buttons. "To spare your poor back."

"No, instead it's your back that can bear the brunt of it, for a change." After she pulled his head down to kiss him open-mouthed, he needed no further encouragement, and swung her up to carry her off to the bedroom.

A very satisfying hour later, Doyle lay on her side with her back to his chest, sleepy but aware that he was wide awake and thinking— still simmering, he was. She thought about Dr. Harding, and Acton's neurosis, and reflected that it didn't seem to be getting any better— perhaps it never would, poor man. Small wonder, with such a set of parents. We are a symmetrical pairing, she thought; I had all hardship and a loving mother, while he had no hardship but unloving parents. It's easy to see which one was the better; he wanted to name the baby after my unknown mother, and his own parents didn't warrant a passing thought.

"Do you want to feel Edward?" she asked.

"I do," he replied, and did.

# 42

The next morning, Doyle saw Acton off, and then decided she'd best do some work, or the time would hang heavy on her hands. Remembering her conversation with Munoz about Drake's involvement in the Bennet investigation, she decided to take another look at the long-ago pawn broker shooting, knowing what she now knew.

After running an archives search for female suspects, acquitted or dismissed in Colcombe's court where Drake was involved in the prosecution, she came up with three names, none of them Bennet. One, however, fit the murdered girl's general age and description, and so Doyle leaned in to study the case sheet. The female suspect was arrested for shoplifting, and held without bail—which was a little strange, unless it was a repeat offense, but there was no such indication. The arraignment was delayed, and after the suspect had been held in gaol for a week, the charges were dismissed without comment.

Doyle then pulled up the report about Drake's shooting of the pawn broker. The dead man was survived by a wife. Doyle noted that Drake had killed the pawn broker during the same time period that the female shoplifting suspect had been held in custody, and it wasn't a hardship to draw the conclusion that needed to be drawn; the imprisoned wife was Bennet—they must have used an alias, so as to obscure her connection to the slain pawn broker. It appeared that the woman had been tucked away in gaol, while her extraneous husband was set up to be murdered.

Doyle raised her head to stare into space for a moment, because she couldn't see how Acton's theory that Drake was an unwitting participant could possibly be true—certainly Maguire thought the worst. When Acton had said it, however, she knew that he'd *believed* it to be true. With a small frown, she closed the files, and wished she had a bit more information. Unfortunately, she couldn't very well ring up Drake and ask him outright, and now both the husband and the wife in this sordid little scenario were conveniently dead.

Her fingers stilled, as she entertained an idea. If Muhammad couldn't go to the mountain, she decided, the mountain would have to be invited over. She dialed Morgan Percy's number.

The girl answered, and Doyle affected a casual air. "I was wonderin' if you would mind comin' over to my flat for lunch. I'm stuck at home, and starvin' for company."

Percy was not buying it. "If its information you want, I'd like some information in return."

Doyle thought it over. "Done. But I reserve the right to hold back state secrets."

After ringing off, she blandly informed Reynolds that she was to have a guest for lunch.

He eyed her with misgiving, but didn't demur. "What shall I serve, madam?"

"I'll be happy to eat anythin'. She'll have some sort of fancy salad; she's that type." Doyle then called the concierge and Trenton to inform them of the coming guest, and wandered off to make herself presentable.

Upon her entrance to the flat, Percy paused on the threshold, and had the same reaction everyone always did. "Wow, what a view. No wonder you chose Acton."

"I love my husband," Doyle protested mildly, and decided not to add that she hadn't seen where he lived until after they'd been married almost a week. Too much information, and it would only confuse the issue.

Percy looked her over. "What happened to you?"

"A window fell on me." This was more or less the truth.

"Bad luck," the other girl commented dryly, obviously aware there was more to the story.

I'd forgotten that she's very sharp, thought Doyle; best watch myself.

Reynolds served them lunch, and at its conclusion, Doyle met his eyes, and he willingly retreated to the far corner of the kitchen.

"So," said Percy.

"I think you killed Mr. Moran, to save him," said Doyle.

If she was surprised by this accusation, Percy hid it well; instead, she merely regarded Doyle with an amused expression. "I'd never admit to such a thing."

"It's loyalty to the extreme. I can't approve, but I can understand."

The other girl's delicately arched brows drew together, as she absently turned her gaze to the windows. "He was such a great man—such an amazing legal intellect. But he was drinking too much, and he couldn't stop talking about the sex ring."

"Guilt, d'you think?"

Percy shrugged. "Perhaps. It would have killed his wife, had she ever found out."

Not true, thought Doyle; Mrs. Moran had taken matters into her own hands, had hired the SOCO, and in doing so, had triggered this whole sequence of events. "What do you know about a woman named Bennet, who was arrested on a made-up charge of shopliftin'?"

Percy eyed her shrewdly. "My turn, first."

"Ask away," said Doyle with an air of resignation. She'd a very good guess as to the topic of inquiry.

"Have you slept with Officer Williams?"

"No."

"Do you plan to?"

"No." Doyle was a bit shocked. "Recall that I am a married woman."

Percy gave her the same look Acton gave her, when he teased her about being a Puritan. "He behaves as though there is something between you."

"There is; he is my dearest friend, and I'll never find another like him."

The other girl's eyes narrowed. "You seem to have a great deal of influence."

But Doyle shook her head. "No, you are mistakin' the matter. He is his own man—faith, we're always comin' to cuffs." Best not to mention the subject of those arguments.

Percy regarded her silently for a moment. "Does he speak of me?"

Doyle was not fooled; this was the important question. "Yes," she answered carefully. "He has mentioned you, and more than once."

Percy digested this. "And?"

"I'm afraid I'd rather not say; it would be betrayin' a confidence."

The other girl lowered her eyes and said nothing for a moment. When she spoke again, Doyle knew that she was being completely honest, for once. "Do you think it's hopeless, then?"

Doyle thought about it. "No," she said. "I don't." Otherwise Williams wouldn't be so bothered about her.

Percy apparently felt that Doyle had upheld her end of the deal, and so clasped her hands on the table in a businesslike gesture. "Aboudihaj was before my time, but I heard Mr. Moran speak of it— speak of how it was a miracle they'd pulled it off."

Doyle sat up; Aboudihaj was the dead pawn broker. "What happened?"

"A detective on the police force was having an affair with the wife, but the husband found out. The husband was Muslim; the penalty for adultery is stoning, and he was furious—he was going to drag her back to his home country, to seek the death penalty. The detective arranged with Colcombe to set up a fake prosecution, and hold her in custody until they could take out the husband."

"Saints," breathed Doyle. She'd guessed as much, but nonetheless was taken aback by the audacity of such a scheme.

Percy shrugged a shoulder. "It was wrong, of course, but the object was to stop something that would have been far worse."

"There's no such thing as an honorable murder," Doyle retorted. "And that's somethin' both sides in this cautionary tale should have remembered."

But Percy—who had, after all, decided that her old lover had to die to protect his reputation—was not the type to wax philosophical. "What's done is done. And word spread like wildfire amongst the immigrant population; if you were willing to sleep with the right men, you wouldn't go to jail. The next thing you knew, there were people taking advantage of it, and then other people setting up a blackmail ring against the men who'd indulged."

Focusing carefully on the other girl's reaction, Doyle offered diffidently, "Judge Whitteside, for one."

The other girl emanated a flare of hostility and chagrin, but calmly replied, "I would not be surprised."

"I was wonderin'—I was wonderin' if perhaps there was somethin' between the two of you."

The girl pressed her lips together. "Not anymore. After he was appointed to the bench, he was full of himself—started acting like a skiver, so I broke it off."

Now, there's a good word, thought Doyle; I'll have to file it away for future use, once I figure out what it means. "Probably just as well, if he's involved in this mess." And this would explain why Percy was not at all sorry that she'd twigged them out; she must have been having an affair with Whitteside, and he'd thrown her over for the next dewy-eyed junior barrister. That, and I believe—although I may be too optimistic, here—I believe that she's rather sick of all the debauchery.

The girl leaned back, trying to disguise her intense interest behind an offhand manner. "I understand that Whitteside's already been called in for questioning."

You don't know the half of it, thought Doyle; so has the long-dead Judge Colcombe. Aloud, she replied, "I'm afraid I can't be discussin' a pendin' investigation."

Percy conceded with a shrug. "Fair enough—I understand the need for discretion. And speaking of which, I owe your husband a huge debt of gratitude; he's not at all what I expected. What's it like, being married to him?"

Doyle gave her stock answer. "He's very private, I'm afraid."

# 43

After Percy left, Doyle sat and stared at nothing in particular, thinking over what she'd learned. Her mobile pinged, and she saw that it was Williams—speak o' the devil and up he pops. She answered, "Hey."

"Hey, yourself. How are you feeling?"

"Come visit; I've discovered somethin' of interest, and I'll be needin' your excellent input."

"Can't you tell me now?"

"Well, all right, if you're so very busy."

"It's not that I'm busy, it's that your servant wants to shoot me."

"His name is Reynolds, and don't say 'your servant'; it makes me very uncomfortable."

"Reynolds wants to shoot me."

"He knows you're nothin' but trouble, Thomas Williams."

"All right, tell him to lock and load—I'm on my way."

She giggled, and after ringing off, approached Reynolds. "DI Williams will be visitin', and I'd be grateful if you didn't glower at him."

Reynolds was slightly taken aback, as she'd never reprimanded him before. "Did I glower?"

"Yes, you did. Acton will do the glowerin', if glowerin' is called for."

Reynolds was immediately contrite, and bowed his head. "I beg your pardon, madam. I misunderstood the situation."

"That's all right, Reynolds, I don't truly understand the situation, myself. But Williams is a good man, and Acton trusts him completely, as do I."

He bowed. "Very good, madam."

When Williams arrived, Reynolds took his coat very respectfully, served them pound cake, and then retreated out of earshot. Williams shot her a look, as he picked up a slice, and she admitted, "I did say somethin'. He shouldn't be offerin' you insult."

"I'm impressed; that is not your style at all."

"No one mistreats you on my watch, DI Williams."

He smiled at her with such a warm light in his eyes that she decided she'd best change the topic, or she'd be sorry she'd snubbed Reynolds. "I've discovered what Maguire knew about Drake."

She recited the story that Percy had told her, and he listened without comment. At its conclusion, she reflected, "So now we know Drake's original motive, and how the corruption ring started, and I think Acton knows how far up it reaches, but he doesn't want me to know, which is a bit alarmin'."

"I would not be surprised," Williams offered in a neutral tone, "if he is hoping to contain the fallout."

Hearing the nuance, she eyed him with suspicion. "Do *you* know somethin'? Who else is involved—never say it's anyone at CID?"

"Can't say," he replied, and left it at that.

"All right, then," she returned a bit crossly. Faith, you'd think he'd toss her a bone, just once in a while; he was as bad as Acton.

Affecting a negligent air, he picked up another slice. "So—you spoke to Percy at some length?"

"I did. I wanted some more information, so I invited her over for lunch. She's a bit of a puzzle." Doyle waited for the inevitable question, and felt a little sorry for him as he tried to resist asking, but couldn't.

"Did I come up as a subject of conversation?"

"Indeed, you did."

He gave her a look which indicated he did not appreciate having to prod her. "And?"

"And why don't you ask her yourself—I'd rather not be tellin' tales."

He was annoyed, both at her and at himself for betraying his interest, and lifted his coffee cup to drink. "Never mind, then."

Annoyed in turn, she retorted, "I forgot; she's a jezebel, and unworthy of Saint Thomas."

But this touched a sore point, apparently, and he lowered his cup to the table with a click. "I'd rather not be number one hundred in a long list. You wouldn't understand."

"I'm thinkin' I'm more understandin' than some, if you don't mind my sayin'."

"You have *no* frame of reference, and have *no* idea what you are talking about." He was very cross with her, was DI Williams.

"I do *so* have a frame of reference; I know that if I was number one hundred in Acton's long list, it wouldn't matter a *pin* to me."

He said stiffly, "It's different for a man."

She made a sound indicating extreme impatience, and against her better judgment, retorted, "You are *such* a flippin' hypocrite."

He replied with grim dignity, "I'm not a hypocrite; I have standards, and I'm amazed that you of *all* people don't understand this."

From the corner of her eye, Doyle noted that Reynolds, hearing the raised voices, opened the laundry room door and then, seeing the combatants glaring at each other, quietly retreated. Lowering her voice, she nevertheless persisted, "You *are* a hypocrite; if I wanted to have an affair with you, I can't imagine you'd put up much of a resistance, even though it would be wrong on at least ten different levels. So do not preach to me of your standards."

Their gazes remained locked for an intense moment, and then he stood abruptly. "I should go." With an angry gesture, he pushed in his chair.

She sprang to her feet, aghast, and instantly remorseful. "Thomas—oh, Thomas, I am *wretchedly* sorry; please forgive my *miserable* tongue."

He bent his head and braced his arms against the chair back for a moment, as he teetered on the edge of storming out.

"*Please,*" she pleaded; "I shouldn't have goaded you about her, after I told you I wouldn't. And I broke my own rule about not talkin' to you about sex. I am the hypocrite here, truly."

He lifted his eyes to hers—they were very blue. "You have a rule?"

"Of course I do," she admitted crossly. "You have a crackin' fine body, and I'm only flesh and blood."

He suddenly started to laugh, and she couldn't resist joining in. After their mutual amusement was spent, he pulled the chair out, and sat down again. "I'm sorry, too, Kath. I don't know why she bothers me so much."

"Don't listen to me, I was bein' vicious. For what it's worth, I agree that she is not your type, even though I rather like her."

But he was unwilling to let her off the hook so easily. "I remember your lashing out at me, once, for trying to run your life."

"I was wrong, wrong, wrong. The worst friend *ever.*"

He smiled his lopsided smile. "Maybe not the worst."

"I'm just hatin' bein' under lock and key, Thomas, and I kept pushin' your buttons. Tell me what I should do to gain your forgiveness, except for that which must not be spoken of."

"There is nothing to forgive," he said generously. You were right; you almost always are."

"Almost?" she teased.

"You were right about Marnie."

She met his eyes, which were suddenly serious. "Is she going to be all right?"

"Gabriel called, very shaken up. He explained it wasn't diabetes, but a rare type of leukemia. Too early to know, but at least she has a fighting chance."

So, the dream was true. "Holy Mother, Thomas."

"Good catch," he said somberly.

"I'm only glad I could help—poor Marnie." They sat in silence for a moment, and yet again, she was grateful that he didn't ask any questions about her intuitive abilities, even though he must have had many. To change the subject, she asked, "What do you know about him—about Gabriel?"

He looked up. "Not a lot, why?"

This was true, and indicated that Williams was not privy to the fallout from the showdown at the morgue, and that the fair Doyle had best be careful what she said. "He seems a good sort, is all." She certainly hoped that Gabriel was a good sort, if Acton was willing to trust him. Although she was fast coming to the conclusion that Acton trusted no one, except perhaps her fair self. Her scalp prickled, and she wondered why this was important.

"I should go. Are we all right?"

"Of course we are, Thomas. Never better."

He grinned. "Except for the occasional fisticuffs."

"Faith, Thomas; it's clear you've never lived amongst the Irish." She walked him to the door. "Now be gone with you, before I start in again."

"I will keep you posted."

"That's a lie, my friend; no one *ever* keeps me posted."

"I will do my best to keep you fully informed, then."

Interestingly enough, this was not true, which probably meant Williams knew a thing or two about whatever Acton was up to. After closing the door behind him, she decided that it was a wonder she didn't start shooting out a few windows, herself.

# 44

After her visit with Williams, Doyle decided she needed to call Acton, who *never* got into shouting matches with her.

He picked up, but said, "Is it an emergency, or may I ring you back?"

"Just checkin' in," she replied easily, and rang off. She contemplated her mobile, trying to decide if it was a good thing or a bad thing that he was involved in something that was more important than easing her boredom. With a small sigh, she decided to reapply ointment to her cuts, and was engaged in this mundane task when Reynolds cleared his throat to get her attention. With a smile, she glanced up. "Hallo, Reynolds; you were so quiet, I forgot you were here."

The servant bowed slightly. "I wanted you to know, madam, that if assistance is ever needed, I stand at the ready."

Poor man, thought Doyle, hiding a smile. All he can figure is Williams is trouble, one way or another. "Thank you, Reynolds. You are a trump."

As she watched the servant begin to inventory the pantry—he must be as bored as she was—she decided she should actually be a bit insulted by his offer. She was a trained police officer, after all, and Reynolds was not a large man. On the other hand, she shouldn't be resentful that she had a surfeit of champions.

Her mobile pinged and she pounced on it. "Michael," she asked in a low voice, "who do you think would do better in a fight; me or Reynolds?"

To his credit, he did not hesitate. "You."

"Yes," she agreed, feeling vindicated. "That's what I thought, too."

There was a pause. "Is there anything I should know?"

"No. I was just thinkin' about it."

"Ah."

She giggled. "How goes it?"

"Dr. Harding rented the vehicle, using a false ID."

"Oh? Well, how's this: Percy killed Moran."

"You win."

She smiled. "Did you already know?"

"I did not," he said, and it was the truth.

"She was savin' his reputation."

"And her own," he reminded her.

"Yes; she's grateful to you for that."

"A little too grateful," he said, with a great deal of meaning.

"Well, you can't be surprised; that's the way she does business, and you're such a handsome thing. And she covets your flat now, too."

"Fortunately, I'm unassailable. How are you feeling?"

"I'm well. How is your mother?"

"She thought that I'd come alone, because I'd left you."

"Oh—how disappointin' for her, Michael."

"You'd best her in a fight, too."

"Anytime, anywhere," she teased.

"It would be a forfeit; she's terrified of you."

"That's because she thinks I'm a barbarian, and half-expects me to paint my face blue, and come after her with a pike. Cheer up; when Edward marries, it will be my turn to be the dowager, and she'll finally have to descamp."

"Decamp; but good attempt."

"Next you'll be tellin' me what 'unassailable' means."

She could feel him smile. "It means I love you."

Smiling in turn, she was touched; her husband was not one to wax romantic on the phone. Or at any time, come to think of it. "Have you discovered anythin' of interest?"

"Some pieces are falling into place." Wily, he was; he didn't want her to know, and knew better than to lie to her.

"Well, that is excellent news," she said with irony, so he'd know she didn't appreciate being treated like a child.

He didn't budge, however. "Please rest; perhaps no more visitors, today."

"Now there's a shame, I was thinkin' of postin' up a sign, downstairs."

"I'm afraid I'll have your promise, Kathleen; you both need your rest."

Instantly contrite, she assured him, "I promise. Please don't worry, Michael, I am eatin' like a cow, and bored to flinders."

"That's my girl," he said, and rang off.

So as to give Reynolds a little breathing room, she retreated into the bedroom to have a lie-down, and whilst she dozed, she had another dream. Maguire was standing beside her with his hands in his pockets. He was alone this time; no Marnie, or Edward, or Acton's father. "Look alive; you'll be needed."

"Needed for what, exactly?" Doyle asked.

"Pack your bag."

"Acton won't let me leave," she explained. "I'm a princess, locked away in a tower."

He shook his head. "You're no princess; you're the bridge-jumper."

"Exactly. Visit Acton's dream and tell him, if you please."

"It's all very symmetrical. What he doesn't know could hurt him."

Frowning, she regarded him, trying to make sense of it. "What doesn't he know?"

"Look alive, you'll be needed," he repeated, and the next thing she knew she was gazing up at Reynolds, who was leaning over to speak to her in a soft tone.

"Madam, I am sorry to wake you, but the concierge has called to say that there is a visiting nurse, downstairs."

Propping up on her elbows, she looked at him through her tousled hair. "A visiting nurse?"

"Yes, madam."

They looked at each other for a moment. "Do you know anythin' about this?"

"No madam. Shall I make a further inquiry?"

With the dream still fresh in her mind, Doyle's scalp prickled. "No—allow me, Reynolds."

Running her fingers through her hair, she padded over to the intercom, and asked the concierge to put the nurse on the phone.

The man on the other end introduced himself rather impatiently as a visiting nurse from the Metropolitan Service. "I have an order from Dr. Easton, who wants a follow-up visit after your injury. Since you cannot leave your house, I was sent."

Doyle listened carefully, but what the man said was true. However, it was also true that Dr. Easton would be unlikely to send anyone other than himself to attend to such an illustrious patient. Assuming a neutral tone, she asked, "Are you affiliated with the Health Professions Council?"

"No, ours is a private service." This was true.

"Are you affiliated with Dr. Easton?"

"No, I'm with the Metropolitan visiting nurse service," the man repeated as though she were a simpleton. "Dr. Easton will come by after office hours, but asked that I take care of the preliminary screening—vital signs, vitamins, that sort of thing. It will save him a lot of time, and I will let him know if there are any areas for concern."

Every word rang true. Frowning, Doyle tried to think of another question. "And you are a registered nurse?"

"Yes. I can show the concierge my credentials, if necessary." This was also true, but Doyle found it hard to believe that—given the circumstances—this fellow would just show up and demand entrance without *someone* letting them know that he was coming. And on top of that, there was something that Acton did not know that might hurt him.

Coming to a decision, she said, "Give me the concierge, and I'll have them send you up, then."

After she rang off, she warned Reynolds, "I'm not sure if this is on the up-and-up, Reynolds. I will take you up on your offer, and ask that you stand at the ready."

The servant was duly alarmed by this assessment, and stared at her. "Is that so, madam? Perhaps it would be wisest to contact Lord Acton, and await instruction."

"No," said Doyle slowly. "Instead, I'm to pack my bag, and look alive. Let's find out what this is all about."

# 45

When the visiting nurse came to the door, he introduced himself as Mr. Rooke. Doyle beheld a harried-looking middle-aged man, carrying a black medical bag which would have been thoroughly screened, downstairs. She didn't have the impression that he was anything other than what he said he was, and she let out a breath, not aware she'd been holding it. "Come in." With a gesture, she indicated where he could set up at the table. "Do you do this type of thing often?"

"Oh, yes, all the time. Pregnant housebound are a large percentage of our cases." He paused, and then said with dawning recognition, "Say; aren't you that policewoman who jumped off the bridge?"

"I am," she confessed, and pinned on a smile.

"I would never have done it," he pronounced with certainty, as he dug into the bag. "I'm not one to take risks."

"I see," she said, not certain what type of response was called for.

"It's good for people like me that there are people like you."

"I suppose that's true."

"It's the way of the world. Open up." He took her temperature, recorded her blood pressure, and examined the cuts on her hands and face. "Untempered glass; a real hazard. Had any other problems?"

"No. Mornin' sickness," she amended.

"Your first?"

"Well—yes, I suppose. I did have a miscarriage, earlier this year."

"You'll do just fine," he assured her. "Everything's in order."

"That's just grand." She smiled upon him, grateful that apparently there was to be no further physical examination; she was not one who liked to be poked and prodded about.

"Let me give you your injection, and we'll be finished here."

"Injection?" asked Doyle in surprise. "What injection?"

He lifted an instruction card and read from it. "Prenatal vitamin injection." With a deft movement, he pulled out a pre-filled syringe, and snapped off the cap. "Doctor's orders; hold still."

*Danger,* Doyle's instinct warned, and she reached out to clasp his wrist. "Hold on. Who gave you this?"

Rooke looked at her in surprise. "Dr. Easton." It was the truth. "I went by his office to pick up my orders, and he said your husband had called to say that an injection would be necessary, since you've been so sick."

"My husband?" Doyle stared at the syringe, and suddenly remembered the two Mrs. Addersleys. "What did Dr. Easton look like?" She turned to Reynolds. "Where's Munoz's drawing?"

"Why? Is there a problem, here?" Rooke was a little annoyed as he lowered the syringe. "If you want to refuse your shot, that is your prerogative; take it up with your doctor."

But Reynolds had produced Munoz's drawing of Dr. Harding, and Rooke stared at it in surprise. "Why, yes; that's him. That's Dr. Easton."

"Holy Mother of God," Doyle breathed. "*That's* what Acton doesn't know. She's framin' him—the matron is framin' him for my murder, and this is Plan B."

While both men stared at her in confusion, Reynolds ventured, "I beg your pardon, madam?"

For the love o' Mike, one fine day she'd quit blurting out things in front of people. Thinking furiously, Doyle asked the nurse, "Are you to report back to Dr. Easton, after this visit?"

"Of course. Particularly if there are any concerns."

"I would like you to call him and report that I seem to be doin' fine, and that you gave me my shot."

Rooke drew himself up in outrage. "I will not tell him you had the injection of vitamins when you refused; that would be very unprofessional."

Doyle pulled her gun from her ankle holster, rose, and aimed it at his forehead. "Do it anyway."

The man gaped at her for several long moments, and Doyle could feel Reynolds emanating waves of alarm behind her.

"My stars," Rooke said weakly, holding out his hands. "Let's all stay calm."

"I'm calmer than a ferryman. Make your call."

Doyle watched Rooke cast a panicked glance of appeal at Reynolds, who rallied to announce, "She's a very good shot, you know. And she's a police officer. I would do as she says."

Rooke pulled out his mobile and, with hands that trembled slightly, began to scroll for the number.

"Take a breath," Doyle instructed him. "Try to sound normal."

Rooke did as she asked, and if he sounded a bit reedy, Doyle decided no one would know anything was amiss; he was the reedy sort to begin with. He rang off.

"Shall I phone Lord Acton, madam?" asked Reynolds.

"Not yet. Mr. Rooke is going to be locked in the laundry room. Be very careful when you take the syringe—put on the cleaning gloves, first."

"Very good, madam."

Still holding him at gunpoint, Doyle directed the visiting nurse into the laundry room, and asked Reynolds to take the man's mobile, and search him for any other items of interest. Rooke did not resist, but protested that he had other patients awaiting him.

"This is police business," Doyle announced, which was sort of the truth, if you didn't count the illegal weapons, and the ongoing personal vendettas.

"Then I have rights," Rooke insisted.

"Good one; I'll get back to you." Doyle locked the door on him, and turned over various protocols in her mind. It's all very symmetrical, Maguire had said, and now she knew what he meant; it was another Solonik trap, only this time with his sister-the-matron pulling the levers.

She had the advantage; the villains didn't know she'd twigged them. She could have Harding arrested as soon as she knew what was in the syringe; together with Rooke's testimony, he'd be a gone goose. But Acton was being framed for her murder—she was certain of it— and this meant she had to be very careful about how she went about this. There'd been the attempt at the church, with evidence left like a bread-crumb trail; evidence that the phone calls, the rental car—and no doubt the hunting rifle—had originated from the Trestles area. Now this second attempt on her life would be shown to be at the request of her husband, and the current rumor going around the Met was that he was regretting his impetuous marriage. It was only luck that Munoz had mentioned meeting Harding, and the deception had come to light. Her scalp prickled, and she knew she was on the right track.

"Would you like me to ring up Lord Acton, madam?" Reynolds asked for the third time. The poor man was on pins and needles, and small blame to him.

"No," she said slowly. She should assume all communications were being monitored, just to be safe. Her priority should be to set up a trap at this end, and then get to Acton before she was supposedly dead, to show him that she truly wasn't. Look alive, Maguire had said, and now she knew what he meant.

With a knit brow, she thought about the set-up for her trap and seizure—no doubt Harding would be lurking about, waiting for her lifeless corpse to be removed from the flat, so as to verify that the plan had worked. He would then report to the matron, who was waiting like a spider to set some sort of frame-up for poor Acton, who wouldn't handle the news of his wife's death very well—understatement of the century; they had no idea what they were dealing with.

She paused with that thought. Perhaps they did indeed know what they were dealing with; there would be scorched earth for miles, which would only add validity to the theory that Acton had murdered his wife. Dr. Harding was no doubt counting on Acton's extreme reaction, since he'd analyzed him, and knew what to expect. Then, once he was in the witness box, Harding wouldn't hesitate to testify against Acton; the psychotherapy privilege didn't exist, where a crime was involved.

Tamping down panic, Doyle chewed on her thumbnail. First things first; she needed to know what was in the syringe, so that she knew if they had a case against Harding, and also how much time she would have to fake her own death, and hotfoot it over to Trestles. Unfortunately, both Reynolds and Trenton were under strict orders from Acton not to allow her to set foot outside the flat. Pack your bags, Maguire had urged—you'll be needed. Apparently, it was time for the princess to break out of her tower.

She turned to Reynolds. "First, I'll need to have Trenton come up here, but the call has to come from you." She thought about it for a moment. "Please text him on your mobile and tell him his lunch is ready." Reynolds never made Trenton lunch; with any luck he would come straight up to investigate this strange message.

While he was texting, she pulled her hooded jacket out of the hall closet, and carefully wrapped the syringe in plastic wrap before stuffing it into a pocket. "If anyone asks, say I'm sleepin'. I'll switch mobiles with you; don't let Mr. Rooke out, but don't tell anyone he's here." She frowned, thinking. "That's all; if anyone asks, I'm sleepin', and you'd rather not disturb me. I'm goin' to call you, once I find out how much time we have, and give further instructions."

"Very good, madam." The servant's tone changed slightly. "Am I to understand you are departing?"

She looked at him apologetically. "Yes. It's very important, Reynolds, that you don't call Acton—I must have your solemn word of honor. I want to set up a trap and seizure at this end, and I have to be very careful, in the meantime, to make sure I don't make things worse for Acton. If you like, I can tell him that I held a gun to you, and you'd no choice."

"I would rather," the servant suggested delicately, "that Lord Acton believe I was hoodwinked."

"Done," she agreed. Best not mention to Reynolds that he was going to have to stage a heart attack before the day was done; one step at a time.

# 46

Trenton's voice could be heard from outside the front door. "Ma'am?"

She opened the door, and saw he stood to one side, weapon drawn, and on edge. "It's all right, Trenton, we're clear. I just needed to speak to you without usin' the phone."

He holstered his gun. "Quickly, please; I should be downstairs."

Not a chit-chatter, was our Trenton. "There's been another attempt on me. The visitin' nurse was goin' to give me an injection, and I'll swear on all the holy relics that it's somethin' toxic. They don't know we've twigged them, and we're to set up a trap and seizure. After an appropriate time, Reynolds will send for an ambulance, so as to draw in the suspect. The suspect—" she handed him the drawing of Harding "—will be lurkin' about, probably waitin' to take a snap. Hold him, and await instruction."

"Right," he said, and took the drawing.

"They may be monitorin' the calls, so don't call Acton, and don't call here."

"Understood."

"Thanks, that's all for now."

Having been given the impression that he was following Acton's orders, Trenton turned down the hallway to approach the lift, studying the drawing as he did so. Behind his back, Doyle sped, soft-footed, over to the emergency stairwell, and quietly slipped through the door. Whilst Trenton was reestablishing his position, she'd slip out through the parking garage, with him none the wiser.

A short time later, she shut the door quietly behind her at the Met's forensics lab, and was relieved to see Lizzie Mathis, seated at a counter, and measuring DNA suspensions into test tubes. Doyle approached, and leaned in to speak to her. "Mathis, I'm sorry to be interruptin', but I need a huge favor from you."

Mathis paused, and turned to look up at her, making no comment as her gaze took in the cuts and scratches on Doyle's face.

"Please call DI Williams, and ask him to come down—here's his mobile number. Tell him—tell him the contraband person is here, and needs to speak with him. Please don't use my name."

The girl's eyes narrowed suspiciously, and Doyle hastened to explain, "It's not what you think, Mathis; I need him to drive me somewhere—I can't drive myself." Carefully, she drew the wrapped syringe out of her pocket. "And while we're waitin',' I need to know what's in this syringe, please."

"Right." Mathis held out a gloved hand.

"Be very careful," Doyle cautioned. "I think it may be deadly."

The girl paused, emanating wariness. "Which case is this? I should log it in."

Doyle swallowed. "This one's off the books, I'm afraid."

Mathis scrutinized Doyle as though she were a specimen under a microscope. "I see. Does DCI Acton know of this?"

Here was a tangle patch—Acton trusted Mathis, but Mathis did not necessarily trust the fair Doyle. "Not yet, but I promise he will; I think he may be in danger." Doyle paused, struggling with what to say so as to enlist the other's help, but still keep the particulars a secret. "I'm afraid to call him, because it may be the wrong thing to do under the circumstances, and I don't know enough, as yet."

Apparently satisfied with this rather disjointed explanation, Mathis rang up Williams, and then rolled her chair over to the spectrophotometer, carefully positioning the syringe so as to inject some of the contents into the machine. Very quickly, the screen displayed varying calibrated columns, with a designating label beneath each.

"Pancuronium bromide," the girl announced, and looked at Doyle.

Resisting an impulse to shake her, Doyle instead asked, "And what is that, Mathis? I haven't a clue."

"At this dosage, it would induce a progressive coma."

Doyle was expecting this, but she was shaken, nevertheless. "And death?"

"Yes. And death."

Doyle blew out a breath. "How long would it take?"

"How heavy is the target?"

Doyle swallowed again. "About eight stone."

Mathis eyed her. "Perhaps two hours. Less than three."

At this juncture, the door opened to admit Williams, who was looking remarkably grim as he shut the door behind him. "Start talking, and this had better be good."

"No need to take that tone," Mathis informed him coldly. "This is a very serious matter."

Williams ignored the other girl, and addressed Doyle. "Are you *insane*? No need to ask if Acton knows you're here."

But Mathis was not to be ignored, and before Doyle could attempt an explanation, she interjected, "Lady Acton has come to me because she believes Lord Acton is in danger, and must be warned."

Williams turned to the other girl in irritation. "She goes by 'Doyle,' here at work."

"Thomas," Doyle cautioned, "Not important, just now."

"This is a very serious matter," Mathis said again, with just a hint of rebuke. "You should listen to her."

Williams frowned at Doyle. "All right; tell me whatever it is, and I'll report to Acton, but meanwhile, I'm taking you directly home."

"No; I'm needed—and I don't have time to discuss this with you," Doyle replied impatiently, mainly because she wasn't clear on why she was needed, herself. "You must drive me to Trestles so that I can warn Acton. And I have to call Reynolds on the land line, but I don't remember the number."

Williams reached for Mathis's desk phone, but Mathis got to it first, and entered the number for Doyle. Doyle then rang up Reynolds, and instructed him to wait three hours before calling an ambulance. "Pretend you're havin' a heart attack, or somethin'. Try to cover your face when they wheel you out; we have to draw the suspect in, so that Trenton can collar im."

"Who is being collared?" demanded Williams in the background.

"Never you mind," said Doyle, mindful of Mathis listening, and then hung up on Reynolds, who was in the midst of expressing his deep apprehension about this turn of events. "Now, let's go to Trestles, and track Acton down."

"I'll drive," announced Mathis, rising to her feet.

"No," Williams and Doyle protested at the same time.

After a small pause, Doyle continued in a more amicable tone, "Thank you, but not at all necessary, Mathis."

"I'm driving," the other girl repeated, pulling on her coat. "Neither one of you is familiar with that area, and I can call my great-uncle, to see if I can discover anything of interest."

This did seem a helpful point, and Doyle nodded her acquiescence, mainly because she was worried that Mathis would squeak to Acton as soon as they left, anyway. "Mathis's great-uncle is the steward at Trestles," she explained to Williams.

"Hudson?" he asked.

"Yes, Hudson." Surprising that Williams would know his name, but then again, Williams was Williams.

"Keep your hood up, and your head down," Williams instructed Doyle as they made for the door. "I'll put my arm around you, and you can lean into my shoulder."

At this instruction, Doyle had to laugh. "Faith, Thomas; if you have your arm around someone, it would draw even more attention than if you didn't. Tanya at the front desk would probably start weepin' into her hands."

"Let's switch coats, then," Mathis suggested.

But Doyle could not like this plan, either. "No thank you; I've bad memories from the last time I switched coats. Instead let's just walk out to the garage like we're all goin' on a break, and there's nothin' to be ashamed of."

Having reached the utility garage without incident, Lizzie's car was revealed to be a Mini Cooper.

"I should drive," said Williams, holding a hand out for the keys.

"Why should you drive?" demanded Mathis, ignoring his hand.

"You'll need to make your call."

"I am capable of multitasking, Officer Williams." The girl gave him a withering look as she unlocked the car with the remote. "Perhaps you can take notes—have you a pen?"

"Have you a pen, *sir*," he prompted with suppressed fury.

"I'm a civilian, *sir*," she returned with the merest thread of sarcasm, and deposited herself in the driver's seat.

It's a shame I can't crack their heads together, Doyle reflected as she slouched down in the back seat. I *truly* must learn how to drive myself about; mental note.

# 47

After they were underway, Williams asked Doyle, "What's happened?"

"It's a long story, Thomas." They had time for a long story, but Doyle didn't want to tell it in front of Mathis. She didn't mention the syringe, and neither did the other girl. It was almost funny; Williams and Mathis each knew parts of the story, but neither knew the whole, and each would jealously prevent the other from knowing what it was that they knew.

"Who is threatening Lord Acton?" asked Mathis.

"I'm truly not certain," Doyle lied.

But apparently she wasn't very convincing, and as Mathis drove, she offered in an even tone, "If you need to tell Officer Williams, I will keep whatever you say confidential."

"It's not that I don't trust you, Mathis, but Acton would want to keep it a private matter." This was diplomatic; Doyle had experience with women who were devoted to Acton, and she didn't trust them an inch. She hadn't yet decided if Mathis fit into that category, and so caution was advised—after all, Mathis may not be one to mourn the fair Doyle's demise.

Williams was apparently still smarting about his misguided attempt to pull rank, and said with a bit more venom than was necessary, "It's not your concern, and the less you know, the better."

The other girl glanced at him in rebuke. "If I can help Lord Acton, I will do as I'm told; you needn't be so nasty."

Before blows could be exchanged, Doyle relented, and hastily explained, "There's been another attempt on my life, Thomas, and I think someone's tryin' to frame Acton for my murder." It had suddenly occurred to her that she should probably tell them, just in case the matron managed to pull it off.

Williams turned in his seat to stare back at her. "Christ, are you sure?"

With an exasperated breath, Doyle blew a tendril of hair off her face. "You mustn't blaspheme, Thomas Williams."

But he was alarmed, and beyond worrying about the niceties. "Why can't we ring him up, Kath? He should be warned."

"I worry that his mobile is bein' monitored, and I don't want the suspects to know they've been twigged. We've got to time it just right; I've set up a crackin' good trap and seizure at the flat to catch the killer, but I also want to show Acton that I'm alive so he doesn't—so he doesn't do anythin' rash. I imagine they are countin' on him to react a certain way, as part of the set-up." Hopefully, she needn't say more, and Williams would know what she meant. No question that Acton would not react well, which would only lend credence to the whole illustrious-chief-inspector-has-gone-bad storyline. It wasn't that much of a stretch in the first place.

Williams ran his hand through his hair, and said with heavy emphasis. "Acton will slay me for bringing you into danger, Kath. Let me call for a car, and we can send you back home."

"That might leave her vulnerable," Mathis pointed out. "I think now that she's here, she's better off with us."

"Thank you for your input, Miss Mathis," said Williams with icy politeness, "but I think we've little choice—we can't take her straight into danger." He paused, and then said with some meaning, "And he'll not appreciate it if we interfere with his protocol."

This was of interest, and Doyle raised her brows. "*Is* there a protocol?"

"Yes," said Williams. "There is." He offered nothing more.

"Oh." Doyle thought about this for a moment, but shook her head. "He doesn't know about the frame-up—I'm sure of it—and what he doesn't know might hurt him. And—" here she paused for a moment, trying to decide how best to put it "—and I've been told that I'll be needed.  It's—it's similar to the Marnie situation."

Williams glanced over the seat at her, thinking this over. "Oh. Well, I guess I can't argue, then."

Frowning in thought, Doyle peered out the windscreen at the road ahead. "You're right, though; we can't go crashin' in like the cavalry, and ruin whatever plan he's got on his end."

Her voice must have betrayed her concern, because Williams put his arm over the back of his seat, holding out a hand to her, and she willingly placed her hand in his.

"Hey." He squeezed her hand. "Not to worry."

She took a steadying breath. "No; it's counterproductive. But even though the attempts have been made on me, Acton needs to know that he is the target, here—he's being framed, and I'm only the collateral." She could feel Mathis's eyes slide over to watch her in the rear view mirror.

Williams slowly replied, "He's already aware of that possibility, Kath.  We've discussed it."

She raised her brows. "You have? I suppose I shouldn't be surprised; trust Acton to outfox everyone."

Mathis added, "He's taken precautions; he is wearing a vest."

Doyle blinked. "He is?" She thought back to their last embrace. "He wasn't when he left."

"He came by to get one, and to check on some mobile phone records."

Doyle felt an irrational twinge of jealousy that Mathis knew more about this than she did, and craned her head to look at the girl. "Whose mobile records?"

"How do *you* have access to mobile records?" demanded Williams.

"I don't have access to mobile records," Mathis replied calmly, and didn't elaborate.

ANNE CLEELAND

But Gabriel does, guessed Doyle, and had to admire her husband's ability to recruit his henchmen. "Whose records?" she repeated.

Mathis hesitated for the barest moment, and then said, "I'm afraid I can't say."

"So you want us to tell you what we know, but you don't have to tell us what you know," Williams summed up in an angry tone. "Wonderful."

"I must honor Lord Acton's requests."

"But Lady Acton is in danger," Williams reminded her with a full measure of scorn. "Where's your loyalty to her?"

Mathis made as if to say something, then pressed her lips together, two faint spots of color appearing on her cheeks.

In a manner very uncharacteristic for him, Williams lost his temper, and leaned over to berate the other girl. "Oh, please—it's obvious that you're mooning after him; don't think we both can't see it. You're only embarrassing yourself; he's madly in love with his wife."

Emphasis on the "mad," thought Doyle, and watched with interest as Williams and Mathis went at it, hammer and tongs.

Mathis glared back at him, her color high. "You are mistaken, *sir;* I admire the chief inspector for his intellect, which is more than I can say for *your* crush."

"Now, that's just *mean*," declared Doyle, stung, but the combatants were paying no attention to her.

"So you are in no position to make accusations," Mathis concluded with some heat, and turned away from him to watch the road again. "Pot, meet kettle."

Williams threw his head back in derision. "Don't make me laugh; if Acton paid the slightest attention to anything other than your intellect, you wouldn't hesitate."

Outraged, she turned to face him again. "How *dare* you."

Pointing an angry finger at her, Williams emphasized, "You wouldn't hesitate, and it would be wrong on at least ten different levels."

Doyle slouched down in her seat, and stared in amazement at the back of Williams' head. Truly, this entire experience was bordering on the fantastic; if she weren't so worried, she'd be hard-pressed not to laugh out loud.

"I will not dignify that remark with an answer," Mathis retorted.

"Fine," said Williams.

"Fine," said Mathis.

Silence reigned, and Doyle slid her eyes from one to the other. I'm no expert on sexual tension, she thought; but if I keep watching, I will be.

After a few silent moments, Mathis offered in a stilted tone, "I beg your pardon, Lady Acton."

Doyle smiled into the rear view mirror. "Just Doyle, Lizzie. And please don't mention it; I've a temper that could saw wood, myself."

Williams had regained his composure, and was looking for a way to ease the tension. "My fault; I shouldn't be goading the driver. I'm sorry, Miss Mathis."

"Lizzie, please," the girl said, but Doyle could see that she was embarrassed and uncomfortable—neither one of them was used to pitching a fit, being as they were both English in the stiffest tradition.

With a mighty effort to pretend the donnybrook had never happened, Williams suggested, "I think there's no reason I can't make a call to Acton, just to report in. It would be a way to feel the situation out."

"Your position could be triangulated," Mathis noted, trying her best to maintain a level tone. "An interceptor would know you were on the way."

"A very good point," Williams conceded with a fine show of cooperation.

Doyle was tired of trying to out-think everyone—truly, Mathis was right, and she was not the brightest of bulbs—and wished that Maguire had given her some detailed instructions, or a written list, or something. "I wish I knew what was best to do. If Acton has a protocol in place, I don't want to muck it up."

Williams turned to take her hand again. "Trust Acton, Kath, and try not to worry. How does Edward?"

"Edward is excellent. Never finer."

"Edward is the baby," Williams offered in an aside to Mathis, eager to show he had more knowledge than she did.

"After Lord Acton's grandfather," the other girl agreed.

Touché, thought Doyle.

But Williams was not to be outdone. "That's where the current heir's claim got a bit muddled, I understand."

Surprised that he'd studied up on the House of Acton's lineage, Doyle was about to disclaim any knowledge of the situation, but saw that he looked to Mathis for a response, almost as though he was testing what she knew.

There was a small silence, and since Doyle was never one to pour oil on troubled waters, she offered, "I think Sir Stephen knows that there's a problem with his claim."

"Its water under the bridge, now," was all the girl replied. "Although I probably shouldn't use that idiom around you, Lady Acton, since you don't have fond memories of the water under a bridge."

"Good one," said Doyle, who appreciated this attempt at humor, such as it was.

"She asked you to call her 'Doyle'," Williams was quick to remind Mathis.

# 48

They were about twenty minutes away from Trestles, and Mathis was on her mobile with Hudson. "I thought I'd ring you; I was in the area to visit Gram, and if you're free, I'll come by."

She listened for a moment, then said, "Well, that's the way of it, I suppose—do you need any help at table?"

After listening again, she assured him, "No, don't worry; it was just a thought, and I'll see you soon."

Slowly, she pressed off her mobile, and reported, "Lord Acton has brought unexpected guests, and so Hudson's at sixes and sevens, having the new cook pull together a decent dinner." She paused. "He's worried they'll only have three courses, and he has nothing appropriate for children."

This information was digested in the surprised silence it deserved. "Makes no sense a'tall," Doyle finally decided. "We need to know more. It does sound as though Acton's got some plan underway." For a moment, she debated whether to proceed, but remembered Maguire's warning, and knew her presence was important, for some reason. With this in mind, she fell back on her training. "There are too many unknowns, so we need to reconnoiter, and assess the situation."

"I don't know how we can reconnoiter," Mathis pointed out. "There's a very good security system."

"I don't doubt it," said Doyle, who knew her husband very well. "I suppose I could just go up to the door, and hope for the best; it's not as though they can refuse me entry."

"You wouldn't arouse suspicion, Lizzie," Williams suggested. "Why don't you say you decided to come by to help Hudson, and then leave the kitchen door unlocked behind you? Doyle and I can enter on the quiet, and take an assessment. If it looks like Acton has the situation well in hand, we can retreat, and wait for you in the car."

Doyle was all admiration. "Faith, Thomas; that is an *excellent* plan."

They proceeded up the long, tree-flanked drive, and Mathis parked the car by the kitchen door. "Give me a minute or two. If it's safe to come in, I'll open the curtain on the door."

The girl entered the house, and as they waited in car, Williams asked, "Do we trust her?"

"I don't think we've much choice, Thomas. I know Acton trusts her, and I suppose that's enough for me. Faith, I hope we're doin' the right thing—if I queer his pitch, Acton will be fit to murder me."

"No, he won't murder you; you're carrying his heir. He'll have to be satisfied with murdering me twice, for bringing you here."

"I had to come, Thomas; it's important that I show up in person, for some reason."

He glanced at her, but asked no questions. "All right. We'll just have to make it up as we go."

She quirked her mouth. "Fortunately, that's my usual protocol. Faith, I wonder who the guests are? It's a shame we can't peek into the drawin' room windows from here—that's where everyone gathers before dinner."

The curtain on the kitchen door twitched aside, and they had a quick glimpse of Mathis' profile before she turned away. "There it is—let's go."

Crouching, they ran across the yard, and Williams carefully pushed open the door, with Doyle close behind him. As they moved through the kitchen, they could hear voices approaching from the corridor, and Doyle frantically gestured toward the stairwell that led up to the dining room. After scrambling up the stairs, they paused on the landing to flatten themselves against the wall, listening as two footmen walked past below them.

". . . push dinner back, so hold off on serving drinks. Her ladyship's not happy that there was no word sent ahead of time; she may not come down."

"Not a surprise; he likes to pull her tail."

"I'll put together a tray, in the meantime. It may be a long night. . . "

The voices trailed off, as the men continued into the servant's hall. Doyle let out a relieved breath, and resisted the urge to make a smart remark to the ancestral ghosts, who were fluttering around like doves, overhead. Excited, they were; and jockeying for position.

Quickly, Doyle led Williams into the entry foyer, and then around the majestic main staircase toward the drawing room's far door, which would suit their spying purposes, and hopefully allow them to avoid the servants. With soft feet, they skirted around to the door, and then, with Williams hovering behind her, Doyle very slowly turned the knob, hoping it wouldn't creak, and opened the door just enough to peer through.

An extraordinary tableau was presented to her gaze: Acton was seated in a wing chair with his back to them, casually leaning back, and watching the woman who sat on the edge of her chair across from him. Doyle was astonished to behold the matron—sitting in the drawing room at Trestles, cool as glass. She sat regally, with her hands crossed—much as she'd done the time Doyle had interviewed her at the SOCO's building. Off to one side of them sat Philippe Savoie, an arm thrown negligently across the back of the settee as he smoked a cigarette. At his feet, a small boy played on the floor with a wooden set of Noah's ark animals. Doyle wasn't very good with children's ages, but she guessed that the boy was about six.

It was evident what had happened, what had made her husband depart from her side to come to Trestles, where the vile plotters were doing their vile plotting. Whilst Doyle was running around on the periphery, so very proud of her trap and seizure, Acton had gone straight for the jugular. The little boy was undoubtedly Solonik's son, the matron's nephew, and perhaps her only surviving relative, after the bloodbath of the past few months. The boy played at the feet of Savoie, the implied threat evident to everyone but the boy, as the adults no doubt discussed the matron's terms of surrender; it wasn't clear what they were discussing, as the conversation was in French.

Although—although it didn't seem to Doyle that the matron was unsettled by any of this. Acton addressed her, and she answered him in a composed voice, her gaze never resting for a moment on the child. She's confident, and listening for something, Doyle realized. The matron was waiting for an interruption—perhaps the announcement of the fair Doyle's death.

Behind her, Williams gently touched her arm. He wants to withdraw, she realized, since it was clear that Acton had the situation well in hand. But she ignored the signal and stayed where she was, because Maguire had said she'd be needed, and what Acton didn't know could hurt him.

Suddenly, there was a commotion in the entry foyer outside the drawing room's main doors, and Hudson's voice could be heard, raised slightly in dignified protest.

The room's occupants paused in their conversation to turn their heads toward the sound, and Doyle could hear Williams' quick intake of breath as the Met's detective chief superintendent strode into the room, a PC flanking him on either side.

Even more astonishing, close behind them came Dr. Harding, and Doyle felt a pang of bitter disappointment that her clever trap and seizure was doomed to come up empty. But at least Harding had been apprehended—although it seemed a little strange that they'd brought him here, and that he wasn't in cuffs.

The DCS stopped before Acton, to address him in a grim tone. "I have the unfortunate charge of placing you under arrest, Michael."

It was Doyle's turn to gasp, as Acton rose to his feet, unruffled. "Do you, Edwin? And what is the charge?

"Your wife's murder. Come along, now—I think there is no need to read you the caution."

Doyle's mouth dropped open and she stared in abject horror. The DCS—the highest ranking officer at the Met—knew that the charge was not true. And Williams—Williams who stood behind her, was not at all surprised by the accusation. Holy Mother of God; the DCS was in on Acton's frame-up, and Williams already knew that he was bent.

But she had no time to reflect on the cataclysmic events unfolding before her, because her poor husband had gone quite still at this news. "What do you mean, my wife's murder?"

His tone woke her out of her frozen horror, and even from across the room she could feel the gathering of a terrible, terrible fury. Step up, Doyle; it was time to look alive.

Pushing through the door, she entered the room, and announced, "Here I am—definitely not dead." Hesitating, she looked to the DCS and added, "Sir."

# 49

For a long, silent pause, everyone stared at Doyle with varying degrees of surprise and chagrin—except for the ghostly ancestors, who were agitating overhead. Faith, it's like an Agatha Christie novel, thought Doyle, with everyone gathered in the drawing room for the deynoo—for the deynoo-something. She resisted an almost overwhelming urge to bite her nails.

"Kathleen." Acton walked forward, emanating waves of relief, but the matron stepped into his path, her pale face fixed on Doyle, and her wrath so palpable that Doyle took a step back.

"You," she breathed incredulously, the syllable released with a hiss. "*Nyet; eto ne mozhet byt.*" She then turned her furious, accusing gaze to Harding. "She lives!"

"Silence, everyone," ordered the DCS, who was understandably concerned that the situation might take a very bad turn for him, if any more revelations were to be thrown about.

But Doyle was feeling a fair bout of fury, herself, and clenched her fists. "Sir, I have evidence that this man—Dr. Harding—posed as my doctor, and tried to kill me."

There was a moment of charged silence. "Is that so?" asked Acton, and turned to regard the man.

"Yes," Doyle continued. "Mathis is here, and she has the evidence—there's a syringe filled with—with pancreas bromide, or somethin'.

Whatever it is, it's deadly." There, she thought with grim satisfaction; that should tie the DCS's hands, so that he had no choice but to make an immediate arrest.

"No—no, that's not true," Harding protested, his face reddening. "I'm the one that uncovered Lord Acton's scheme, and the murder of the visiting nurse only seals it. I called the police as soon as I suspected—"

Doyle listened to this last bit in surprise, then realized that it only made sense; Mr. Rooke could not be allowed to live, being as he was the one witness who could implicate Harding in the attempt on her life. Fortunately, Rooke was safe and sound, kicking his heels in her laundry room.

For a moment, no one moved, and it seemed to Doyle that Acton was waiting for the DCS to break the silence. For his part, the DCS appeared to be thinking rapidly—trying to find a way to salvage the situation, no doubt. After frowning for a moment, he apparently came to the conclusion that they could go forward with the plot, despite the annoying wife's unexpected appearance. "I'm sorry, Michael, but Dr. Harding is a credible witness, and he has sworn out an affidavit that would establish—at the very least—a charge of attempted murder. I'm afraid I must discharge my duty."

Outraged, Doyle took a step toward him. "Well, I will swear out my own affidavit—"

Savoie interrupted by leaning casually toward the boy, who'd been watching the adults with wide eyes. "Come; sit closer to me, if you please."

But despite this reminder, the matron would not buckle, and instead pointed an accusing finger at Acton. "It is him—do not believe the wife; it is the husband who wants her dead."

With a full measure of scorn, Doyle played her trump. "That is *not* true and the visitin' nurse is *not* dead, but he will testify against Dr. Harding, also."

The matron stared at her, white-faced and furious, while Harding blustered, "I have no idea what this woman is talking about . . . it appears that I am being unjustly accused."

Acton, who'd been listening to these charges and countercharges without comment, now pulled the bell rope, and offered, "Perhaps we should step back for a moment, and reassess the situation before any further accusations are made."

Thoroughly astonished, Doyle eyed her husband with extreme misgiving; he was taking a conciliatory tone, which was very unlike him. All things considered, the massacre she'd feared should be commencing right about now, but instead of releasing the hounds, her volatile husband was calling for Mathis to serve coffee. Faith, she thought in surprise; you marry someone, and you think you know him.

Into this highly-charged scene, the dowager Lady Acton stepped through the open doors, and stood for a moment on the threshold, her autocratic gaze traveling over the assorted persons in her drawing room. "And what, may I ask, is the meaning of this?"

"We have guests, Mother," Acton replied in an even tone. "And my wife has joined us."

The dowager's gaze rested for a moment on Doyle. "You may not remember, my dear, that at Trestles, we dress for dinner."

The DCS took this opportunity to bow his head toward the dowager with all appearance of regret. "Lady Acton, I must apologize for the disturbance, but I have come on police business, and there have been some serious accusations made. I'm afraid I must interrupt your evening for a small time, so that I can question these witnesses."

He then stretched out a placating hand toward Acton. "Let me separate these two, Michael, and take statements—here and now—and I'll get to the bottom of this alleged attempt on your wife. I must beg your pardon—" here he looked toward Doyle "—and yours too, DS Doyle. It is entirely possible that I was misled."

"No—" began Harding in alarm, but he was silenced by a glance from the other man.

"An excellent plan, Edwin," said Acton. "I am certain we can resolve this misunderstanding in short order."

This last comment was surprisingly true, and again, Doyle eyed her husband with misgiving. It went without saying that Acton would not allow Harding and the matron to disappear into the night with the treacherous DCS—pigs would fly before Acton would allow these people to get away with this.

Briefly, her husband met her eyes with a message of reassurance. I'm to stay quiet, she thought; fine with me, it's exhausting, always having to save the day. Sinking down into the settee, she deliberately turned a shoulder to the agitated knight overhead, who was extremely upset that someone had allowed a Frenchman into the house.

The DCS began to direct the others. "Let's take Mrs. Barayev to the foyer, and put Dr. Harding in the dining room—no one is to leave. We'll start with Harding." He made an apologetic gesture toward Acton. "I don't think I can allow you to be present for the questioning, Michael."

Acton bowed his head in understanding. "I will keep company with my wife, then."

The matron was escorted into the foyer to await her turn, while the others left for the dining room, Harding emanating an incredulous sort of fury, as the door was closed behind him.

Mathis and one of the footmen came around to serve out the coffee, and with a mighty resolve, Doyle refused a cup, even though it smelt wonderful, and she was in dire need—and coffee was a rarity at Trestles; usually they served only tea, since the dowager considered coffee a vulgar, new-world contrivance. To take her mind off it, she asked her husband in an undertone, "Do you have time to hear the tale?"

"Not as yet," he replied. With an unhurried step, he walked over to the back doorway, and signaled to the footman with the coffee tray, as he passed by.

Doyle decided that she should ring up Reynolds, so as to scrub the mission, so to speak. As she pulled out his mobile, she felt a stab of exasperation. Obviously, Harding had not been monitoring their communications, so it would have been miles easier simply to call Acton, and tell him not to believe any reports of her death. Maguire was wrong; she hadn't been needed, after all—her husband had the situation well in hand, and was behaving with commendable restraint, to boot. It all made little sense.

Fortunately, Reynolds answered the call, which meant she'd caught him before he staged his heart attack. "Madam."

Very much put-upon, he was. "I wanted to tell you that you needn't call an ambulance, Reynolds. Just stay there, and don't allow anyone in." Cautiously, she inquired, "How's our Mr. Rooke?"

"He remains in the laundry room, madam. He is complaining that he has missed his other appointments."

She thought about it for a moment, then instructed, "Tell him he was slated to be murdered today, and we are keepin' him safe. Find out if the fake Dr. Easton had other appointments for him, and ring up Trenton to tell him about them—someone was goin' to kill Rooke along the way. And don't touch anythin' in his medical bag, Reynolds; somethin' else may have been poisoned."

"Very good, madam."

She smiled into the phone; trust Reynolds to handle a crisis without turning a hair. "I'll consult with Acton, and get back to you."

"I quite look forward to it, madam."

After ringing off, Doyle saw that the boy was watching her from his position on the floor, then he quickly dropped his gaze back to the animals. Kneeling down, she tried to decide what one said to comfort small children. "What lovely animals." She reached for a well-worn zebra, but the boy quickly moved it beyond her grasp, his dark eyes regarding her warily.

Savoie, who'd been watching these events without comment, instructed the boy to give her the zebra, and with poor grace, the boy relinquished the animal.

Diplomatically, Doyle left the zebra to graze on the thick Aubusson rug where the child could easily reclaim it, and turned her head to

Savoie. "I'm that surprised to find you here, my friend. Promise me you'll keep your hands out of the silver drawer."

Savoie's impassive gaze scrutinized her scratches. "Your poor face."

"I need only break my nose, and no one could choose between us."

In response to this sally, he offered up his thin smile, but he was coldly angry, was Philippe Savoie. "He will pay for this."

This was no doubt true; between Acton and Savoie, Harding stood little chance of coming out of this with a whole skin—not to mention the matron looked as though she'd like to strangle him with her bare hands, for bungling the plan. Nevertheless, Doyle warned Savoie in a low voice, "Best behave yourself; the DCS is dyin' to arrest someone, and you're a prime candidate. Perhaps you should slip out the back, before someone decides to run a background check."

In response to this sound advice, Savoie drew on his cigarette. "You will slip out the back with me, yes?"

"Can't." She shook her head with mock-regret. "Its havin' a baby, I am."

"Ah—yes?" His eyes glinted for a moment, and he shrugged. "Ah—this baby, it could have been my baby."

"I believe, all things considered, that it is just as well it is my husband's, Philippe."

He chuckled in his rusty way—she'd forgotten how much she amused him. She glanced at the dining room door, and reiterated, "You truly should leave, I think; I'd rather not have to be breakin' you out of prison."

Idly, he picked up a tiger, which earned him a wary glance from their small companion. "I do not doubt that you could; you can make everyone believe you—it is a useful trick."

Doyle made a face. "I think you are confusin' me with the matron. She could teach the devil himself a few tricks."

Savoie manipulated the tiger so that it wandered across Doyle's lower leg. "*D'accord.* That one, she learned from her cracking brother. He is the wolf wearing the clothes from the lambs."

Doyle could only nod in agreement; she didn't have fond memories of Solonik. "He was killed in prison; I suppose you heard?"

Her companion nodded solemnly, his gaze on the tiger. "Yes."

"A good riddance—the world is well-rid of him."

Savoie cocked his head in disapproval. "Now, now, little bird; remember that he sought your prayers."

She answered grimly, "He'll be needin' them, where he is."

"You are harsh," Savoie pronounced, gently chiding. The tiger wandered over to investigate her hand, where it was spread on the floor.

"That's a stunner, comin' from you."

The dowager, who'd been watching the trio sprawled on the floor with rigid disapproval, called out, "Who are these people, my dear? I don't believe we've been introduced."

Savoie promptly rose to his feet, and approached the older woman, holding out his hand and speaking in rapid French. Doyle didn't know what he said, but whatever it was, every word was a lie.

The dowager answered in kind, and looked upon him with wary approval, then asked several questions and listened with interest to the answers. Doyle guessed he was turning her up sweet with some tale of aristocratic heritage, and hoped he wasn't setting the stage to make off with her mother-in-law's jewel case. While the others spoke, the boy took the opportunity to reach over and retrieve the wooden tiger, an eye on Doyle, to make sure she wasn't going to report him.

"And what is your name?" she asked kindly, working hard to control her accent.

"Jonathon," he whispered, ducking his head and staring fixedly at the animals.

This didn't seem very Russian to Doyle, but as she was winding up to ask another question, Savoie turned to call out something to the boy, and held out a casual hand to him. The dowager directed them down the hallway, and the two ducked out the door.

"What has happened to your face, my dear?" The dowager's tone made it clear that she fully expected Doyle to confess that she'd been brawling in the streets.

"A window fell on me, ma'am." Doyle picked up the zebra again, running her finger along its smooth neck. She knew, without asking, that the toy set had belonged to Acton, and she began packing the animals into the ark; they were destined for Acton's son, not Solonik's, thank you very much.

"You must be more careful," the older woman advised. "You seem very accident-prone."

Doyle was spared having to come up with a response when a shot suddenly rang out, from the direction of the dining room.

# 50

Doyle sprang to her feet, but before she could decide whether it would be poor form to leave the dowager undefended, Acton strode over. "Stay, please," her husband instructed her, a hand held out as he swiftly crossed toward the dining room.

Before he arrived, the door swung open to reveal the DCS, looking a bit shaken, as he stood framed in the doorway.

Acton halted before him. "Was that a shot, Edwin? What's happened?"

The DCS took a long breath. "We'll need the coroner. Dr. Harding has taken his own life."

"Acton," the dowager remonstrated in disapproval, "You mustn't bring your work home."

After a moment's astonishment, Doyle brushed her hair off her forehead; when the DCS said that Harding had taken his own life, it wasn't true. The DCS must have wanted to make certain that Harding would make no further revelations, and so had committed a containment murder of his own.

But to Doyle's surprise, Acton casually picked up Savoie's discarded cigarette, and entered the adjoining room to view Harding's body, lying beneath the massive mahogany table. Crouching down beside the still form, her husband drew on the cigarette for a moment, then applied it to the decedent's leg. The doctor lay still for few seconds, then jerked and gasped in pain.

"Not quite dead," Acton pronounced, rising again. "Cuff him, if you would."

"Why—why, I don't understand." The DCS blustered as he turned to the attending PC. "How could you not have known that he was feigning?"

Acton spared the PC from having to come up with an explanation. "It would do him little good; the coroner's office is no longer in the recycling business."

There was a moment of dismayed, charged silence. "I don't know what you mean, Michael," said the DCS, and Doyle brushed her hair off her forehead, although it hardly seemed necessary.

Acton said only, "I believe you will soon receive a full report. Shall we proceed with the interviews?"

Doyle almost felt sorry for the DCS, who seemed to be having trouble gathering his wits, in the face of this onslaught of unwelcome news. It was apparent that Acton knew more than he was saying, Doyle was producing clouds of witnesses to foil his frame-up, and between the two of them, his goose was well and thoroughly cooked.

As Harding was hauled to his feet, he gave the DCS a meaningful glance, his voice a bit high. "I demand to see a solicitor."

Faith, the solicitor's dead too, thought Doyle; these people aren't up to speed at *all*.

"Take him out to the response car, and await my instruction," the DCS told one of the PCs, and then turned to speak in a low tone to Acton. "Perhaps—perhaps we should indeed take a step back, and discuss these matters, Michael. I confess I'm inclined to think that this witness is no longer credible, but if he wants a solicitor, I'll have to provide one. It may be better to keep this matter quiet; obviously the doctor is in need of some therapy, himself."

Acton's unwavering gaze rested on Harding's retreating form, but he spoke in a benign tone. "Yes, I think it best. My wife would not like to be the focus of such a story."

Oh-oh, thought Doyle.

"You are very forgiving," the DCS offered. "I confess I don't think I could do the same, in your place."

"Nonsense; he is clearly unbalanced, and I'm not one to seek retribution."

Oh-oh, thought Doyle again, in acute dismay.

Unaware of the mayhem to come, the DCS continued in a conciliatory manner, "Let me take him in, then, and he can sweat it out a bit. I'm sure he'll be reasonable, and if he isn't, I'll bring in the psychs to do an evaluation, and we'll get it done it the hard way."

"Right, then," Acton agreed, never for a moment believing that this would actually happen.

"And Mrs. Barayev?" The DCS lifted his gaze toward the foyer, and shrugged his shoulders. "What of her? Unless Harding implicates her, we've no charges to bring."

"We have obstruction of justice, sir," Doyle interrupted firmly. "She gave false information to the police in connection with the SOCO's murder—I'm a witness to it."

With a flare of annoyance, the DCS thought about this, and then had no choice but to nod his head. "Right. Let's caution her on that, and let her sweat it out, too. She'll have to be wondering whether Harding will turn on her, and maybe we'll get a confession before she demands a solicitor."

Having taken her measure of the matron, Doyle was doubtful that the woman would falter under pressure, but it seemed evident that the DCS was stalling as best he could, and small blame to him; he'd crossed swords with Acton, had come up spectacularly short, and now faced almost certain ruination.

"Acton, shall I have Hudson put back dinner?" called out the dowager, in disapproving tones.

Acton took Doyle's arm to lead her back to the settee. "If you would, Mother; I'm afraid we've more police business to complete."

This seemed a gross understatement, given the situation. As the DCS had a quiet conversation with the remaining PC, Acton pulled his mobile from its sheath, and began scrolling for a number. Leaning forward, Doyle took a wary glance through the drawing room doors at the matron, who was seated on one of the Chippendale chairs in the foyer. She no longer seemed confident, but instead rubbed her temples with her fingers, as though her head hurt. The footman who was positioned against the wall had a wooden expression, but Doyle knew that he was secretly pleased about something, which seemed a bit odd, considering the circumstances. He reminded her of someone, somewhere else, and Doyle's scalp prickled. But before she could grasp at the elusive memory, Acton interrupted her thoughts.

"How did you twig Harding?" He glanced at her, as he held his mobile to his ear.

"It was a crackin' red flag, Michael. A visitin' nurse came to say that my husband insisted I have a vitamin shot."

"Clumsy," observed Acton, who was, after all, an expert on unclumsy murders. Doyle's scalp prickled, but before she could think about why this was, someone answered his call, and he spoke quietly into his mobile. "Howard, I am sorry to interrupt your dinner, but I believe it is time to move." He paused. "If you would ring up Previ, I'd appreciate it."

As he rang off, Doyle remembered that Howard was the Home Office official—the one who was investigating the corruption ring— and the one that the villains had tried to frame by using Acton. But she couldn't quite place the other name. "Who's Previ?" she leaned in to whisper. "I forget."

"He's the publisher of the *London World News*." Acton sheathed his mobile. "They've an exposé of the corruption scandal, ready to go. There will be no containing the scandal after publication, and therefore—we can only hope—no more containment murders."

Doyle, however, shook her head, because she was still having trouble grasping the breadth of it. "Mother a' mercy, Michael; the DCS, of *all* people." She eyed him for a moment. "You don't seem very surprised."

He brought his chin to his chest, his absent gaze resting for a moment on the matron's form in the next room. "I had my suspicions. The scheme could only work if there were well-placed players in the judiciary, at the prison, and at the Met."

"There'll be no coverin' this up, my friend—instead, we'll be lucky if there's anyone left to prosecute all the blacklegs."

"Unavoidable," he agreed, with palpable regret.

"Will they have enough to go after the DCS? Would anyone believe him, if he claimed ignorance?"

"I very much doubt that he will avoid a lengthy prison term," her husband replied, and it was true.

At this juncture, the dowager called out to Doyle, "My dear, what has happened to the *comte*, and his son?"

"Oh; oh—I'm not certain, ma'am." As Savoie's failure to return seemed an ominous development, Doyle turned to Acton. "What has happened to the *comte*, and his son?"

Acton seemed unalarmed. "He had a pressing engagement, I'm afraid."

Oh-oh, thought Doyle, for the third time.

"A charming man," the dowager pronounced, sipping her aperitif. "His mother is a d'Amberre, of the Normandy d'Amberres."

Doyle warned in a low voice, "Michael, neither one of you is going to hurt that little boy."

The dowager mused, "I must write her; the *comte* mentioned that she suffers from ill health."

Acton took Doyle's hand in reassurance. "No, the boy will not be harmed; there's little point, since it is clear that his aunt wouldn't care, one way or the other."

"Faith, I could have told you that—she's cold to the core." Her scalp prickled, and she resisted a mighty urge to lean over again, and stare at the woman through the open doors. Have done, Doyle, she thought. Its imagining things, you are.

Instead, Doyle focused her attention on her husband, who—unlike Maguire—had no trouble whatsoever living with himself after committing dark deeds. It seemed clear he was ready to commit a few more, if she were any judge of the tell-tale signs, and so it was time for the fair Doyle to make yet another stab at redemption—after all, Acton's confirmation was fast approaching, and she didn't want St. Michael's to be struck by lightning for the event. She asked him gently, "Is Dr. Harding goin' to make it as far as the end of the driveway, my friend?"

He bent his head to finger her hands. "I'd rather not say, I'm afraid."

His tone discouraged any further discussion of the subject, and so she subsided, a bit ashamed that she was willing to give it up so easily. Acton and Savoie would probably have a fistfight over who got to murder Harding, and the matron would presumably fare little better—Doyle's husband was going to mete out his own version of justice, yet again.

She sighed, and contemplated the floor, because she didn't want to look toward the entry foyer again. It was always a bone between the two of them; she knew that the justice system was imperfect, but it was miles better than letting everyone—including Acton—decide that they were better qualified to act as their own judge and jury. Faith, centuries of civilization were at stake—and if they got it wrong on occasion, so be it; that was the price of peace, the price of everyone's having agreed to respect the process, for the greater good.

But the annoying schoolmarm found that she could dredge up little conviction, this time. Could anyone *truly* say that Acton was wrong to take the law into his hands, considering the situation? They knew without a doubt that Harding had tried to murder her—twice—and besides that, the psychiatrist knew too much about Acton; God only knew what would come to light, if he attempted a plea negotiation. I should make a push to talk my renegade husband out of yet another vigilante murder, she acknowledged to herself; but my heart's not in it, and besides, the ancestors huddling in the rafters are all rooting for bloodshed, and lots of it.

Unable to help it, Doyle's gaze was drawn once again to the foyer. The matron was now resting her head against the chair back, with the footman standing attendance, and the DCS pacing the floor in his preoccupation. The elegant tea table held the remains of the coffee service, and a portrait of one of Acton's ancestors looked down upon all of them, his expression faintly disdainful.

No, she firmly instructed herself, quickly looking away. You're just being fanciful, my girl; have done.

But Doyle closed her eyes, trying to remember the scene at the lab, when Mathis had injected some of the syringe's contents into the machine. The girl had kept the syringe, of course—it was off the books, and the stuff was dangerous. How much of the drug had been left in the syringe? And then Acton had asked Mathis to bring in coffee. . . .

Beside her, Acton reached to cover her hand with his own. "I am sorry, Kathleen; I did not mean to be so short with you."

The black mood hovered, but he was trying to control it, worried about her, sitting here stewing, with her eyes closed. She opened them, and mustered up as sincere a smile as she could manage. "Don't worry, Michael. I'm all right."

Only she wasn't. You'll be needed, Maguire had said. Stubbornly, Doyle closed her eyes again, and refused to look toward the foyer. After all, she couldn't be certain that Mathis had used the drug on the matron—it was a wild guess. And even if the wretched woman died, it was nothing more than she deserved, and it meant there would be no further vengeance-takings on Acton—it would be the *good* kind of containment murder, for a change. Maguire was right; this revenge business never seemed to end, and if Solonik's evil sister was shuffled off this mortal coil it would bring this whole chapter to a fitting end, with the added bonus that all the other villains in greater

London would think twice before coming after Acton and his family. Faith, it was only by the grace of God that she—and Edward—had managed to survive this latest go-round.

By the grace of God. By the most holy grace of God.

With a sigh, Doyle reluctantly rose to her feet. "Somethin's wrong," she announced, as she approached the woman in the next room. "I think Mrs. Barayev has taken some sort of drug."

# 51

In the general confusion following Doyle's announcement, she became aware that—if the reactions were any indication—there were more suspects in the matron's attempted murder than not. Acton stood to one side, unmoved, and asked Hudson to call for an ambulance, whilst the DCS crouched to flip back one of the unconscious woman's eyelids and suggest—without any real urgency—that Harding be brought back in, as he was a medical doctor.

Whilst Harding was being fetched from the response car, Doyle looked around at the impassive faces and urged, "I think we are supposed to induce vomitin'—although I imagine it depends on the drug. Perhaps Mathis will know." This said diplomatically, because she probably shouldn't implicate Mathis in the attempted murder, at least not without Acton's say-so.

Mathis was duly summoned to give her opinion, and the PC who'd been guarding the matron rushed back into the room to announce that Harding had disappeared from custody, and that the other PC who'd been guarding him had been coshed.

On hearing this, Doyle had the immediate suspicion that the DCS had arranged for Harding's escape, but then she caught a flare of genuine surprise and dismay from the man—he was not happy about this news. By contrast, Acton was not surprised by Harding's disappearance, and Doyle quickly concluded that the good doctor was now making the dubious acquaintance of Philippe Savoie.

The footman who'd been stationed in the foyer was dispatched to direct the EMT personnel when they arrived, but as he passed her by, Doyle knew he was hiding his satisfaction. Her scalp prickling, she suddenly realized why his attitude had seemed so familiar, and the memory from her visit to Wexton Prison came rushing back. Solonik had arranged for her to visit the prison in an attempt to frame her for murder, and the only reason she'd figured it out was because the prison guard had been in on the scheme, and she could sense his secret gloating. Now, she had that same sense from the footman—that he was secretly gloating.

Whilst Doyle stood very still, trying to make sense of it, Mathis announced from her position on the floor, "It doesn't appear to be a caustic substance, so we should induce vomiting. Help me roll her over—careful, now."

"My nerves are quite shot," the dowager complained from the drawing room. "If you would call for tea, Hudson."

"Yes, madam," said Hudson, who was up to his elbows helping Mathis with the unconscious matron. "I'll have it brought out straightaway."

Tea, Doyle realized in frozen shock; holy Mother of God—tea. Tea was what was served here, not coffee. But coffee would mask the drug better than tea would, which meant—which meant that the gleeful footman was conniving with the DCS to frame Acton for the matron's murder.

Forcing herself to move, she leaned forward to put a hand on her husband's shoulder, as he crouched down beside Mathis. "Sir," she whispered through stiff lips. "Sir, if I could have a word—it's about Caroline."

Acton turned to look up at her in surprise, which was not unexpected; he'd killed Caroline, and staged her death to look like a suicide—which was whatever the opposite of 'symmetrical' was, but she hadn't time to think about vocabulary, just now. Doyle met Acton's eyes, an urgent message contained in her own. "It will just take a moment."

Acton rose and drew her aside, his gaze assessing her face. "What is it? Are you unwell?"

Trying to control her surge of panic, she spoke in an undertone. "It's a set-up, Michael—they're framin' you for the matron's murder, and I'm not sure how many are in on it. The footman—the footman who brought the coffee is in on it." She paused, remembering the conversation she and Williams had overheard from the stairwell. "Another footman, I think, and perhaps Mathis, too—she's the one who had the syringe."

Acton regarded her gravely for a moment, and made no reply.

Her throat dry, Doyle urged, "Shouldn't we ask some questions, so that I can listen to the answers? And we have to warn Williams—where is he? Holy mother, Michael; what if they've taken him out, already?"

"Please don't worry, Kathleen," Acton replied. "It's not about Caroline. Instead, it's about Barayev."

Staring at him, she had to think about what was meant by this cryptic comment. Barayev was the matron's dead husband—and a blackleg in his own right; the SOCO's photos showed that he was also involved in Solonik's corruption ring. He'd died because Acton had killed him, and had framed Solonik to take the blame—

The penny dropped. "Michael," she breathed, "That is *diabolical.*"

"I would ask that you sit quietly, please."

Nodding in bemusement, she allowed him to seat her in one of the elegant Chippendale chairs behind Mathis, who was ministering to the matron with no real urgency. *I had it backwards,* she realized in wonder; *it is a conspiracy, but it's Acton's conspiracy. I'd forgotten, for a moment, that he's the grand master at turning the tables. Instead of Acton's being framed for my murder, the DCS is being framed for the matron's murder. The gloating footman is Acton's man, and he will gladly testify that the matron implicated the DCS in the corruption ring, and that the DCS was striving mightily to keep* her from making any further revelations during the course of this evening. Faith, it was brilliant—Acton came to Trestles to set a trap, and the DCS had walked right in, with the added bonus that Harding had served himself up on the vengeance platter, too. Small wonder Maguire had said that it was all very symmetrical.

The ancestor in the portrait above her was a very unpleasant fellow—small blame to him, as he'd died of the pox—and she threw him a scornful look. "Snabble it, you; it doesn't matter to me a'tall. Save your tattlin' for someone who cares."

"Madam?" Mathis turned to ask in surprise, but at this juncture, Hudson opened the massive front doors to allow entry to the medical personnel, and they began to pepper Mathis with questions—most of which she answered dishonestly. As they prepared the matron for transport, the DCS observed from a small distance, standing with his arms crossed, and unaware that evidence was no doubt being gathered to show that he'd administered the fatal dose.

But—but something was wrong, and between the still-fluttering ghosts and her prickling scalp, Doyle was mightily confused. Maguire had said she'd be needed, and that what Acton didn't know might hurt him, but it seemed that the only contribution the fair Doyle had made to this little morality play was to try to save the matron from her fate—which ran counter to Acton's plan. There must be something else—something else that she was missing.

As if on cue, Williams appeared before her, quietly picking up the coffee tray from the tea table before her. "Hey," he said, glancing up at her.

Doyle quirked her mouth. "Hey, yourself. Don't get your prints on anythin', else you'll be the one windin' up in the nick."

He didn't deign to respond to this little attempt at manipulation–of-evidence humor, and instead informed her softly, "Acton's going to go back with them tonight; the matron will be booked into the prison infirmary."

"And he'll be wantin' to meet with the Home Secretary." This went without saying; one couldn't just arrest the DCS without going through the proper channels; her poor husband was in for a long night.

"You're to stay here, with me, and you're not to go outside."

"Grand," Doyle groused. "It's lucky that Acton has a castle keep at hand, ready-made for lockin' away his free-range wife."

Williams gave her a look as he turned away with the tray. "Mathis will stay with you, also."

"Even grander."

He gave her another look over his shoulder—this one amused—and carried away the evidence that would bring down the head of the CID.

"Madam?" Mathis approached, and Doyle heaved an inward sigh, as the girl folded her hands. "I'm to escort you to your rooms."

"In a minute," Doyle replied, just to be contrary. "Let me see Acton off, first."

"As you wish." Mathis bowed her head, but Doyle could see that she was impatient; Acton must want Doyle upstairs, and safely locked away—although there was no one left to cause any trouble, one would think. Hard on this thought, there was a generalized excited flurry in the rafters, far above her head.

Exasperated, Doyle lifted her face, and warned the ghosts, "Everyone needs to calm *way* down."

"I am perfectly calm, madam." Beneath her serene exterior, Mathis bristled a bit.

Doyle drew a deep breath, in an attempt to settle her frayed nerves. "Of course you are, Mathis; you've done exigent work tonight—"

"—I believe you mean exemplary, madam."

"Yes; yes, I did," Doyle agreed heavily, holding on to her temper with both hands. "I've been unforgivably rude, and I keep sayin' things I shouldn't. Shame on me."

Mathis unbent enough to commiserate, "Then shame on me, too. I shouldn't have lost my temper with Officer Williams."

"He's too masterful, or somethin'." Doyle scowled crossly. "It drives you crazy."

"Exactly," her companion agreed with some heat.

"May I interrupt?" The remaining PC approached, and bestowed a charming smile upon Mathis. "I just wanted you to know that we'll be leaving—may I take your mobile number, Miss Mathis, in the event any further information is needed?"

"Of course," Mathis replied, but Doyle knew the man was mainly interested in the fair Mathis, which just went to show you that it took all kinds. Doyle had the impression that the officer was something of a boyo, thinking he was irresistible to the ladies, and good luck to him, since Mathis would be one tough nut to crack.

The PC turned his smile upon Doyle, whilst Mathis entered her number into his phone. "And at last I meet the bridge-jumper."

Friendly, he was. Almost too friendly, considering she was his senior officer, and her husband was his much-senior officer.

"That's me," Doyle agreed, pinning on her smile.

As Mathis returned his mobile, the PC confessed, "I can't say as I would have jumped, myself; I'm something of a skiver."

Skiver, thought Doyle in surprise. There's that word—

"We are all very proud of Lady Acton," Mathis said, and it was not exactly true.

But Doyle wasn't thinking about that, instead, she was listening to the roar of movement overhead, as swords were drawn from their scabbards, and her scalp prickled like a live thing. With a conspiratorial air, she smiled up at the PC. "Would you like to see my medal?"

She could feel Mathis's incredulous gaze slide toward her, but the PC seemed more amused than anything. "I would indeed."

Doyle met his gaze in what she hoped was a flirtatious manner—channeling Munoz, she was. "It's in the archives. Quick-like, before anyone sees."

The man radiated pleased anticipation, almost unable to believe his good fortune. "Lead the way."

Soft-footed, Doyle hurried down the hall to the stone-lined archives room, which had been part of the original keep, whilst a host of ancestral beings raced along the high ceiling behind her. Opening the heavy door, she took a guilty glance over her shoulder, and then signaled to the PC that he should enter. He slipped past her, and she immediately slammed the door after him, turning the huge brass key in the lock with a decisive twist of her wrist. He's lucky they're only ghosts, she thought grimly; otherwise he'd be hacked to death within the minute.

She turned to call to Mathis, but then froze on beholding Grady, the Irish stableman, approaching rapidly as he brandished a shotgun.

"What's afoot?" he asked urgently, as a faint pounding could be heard on the other side of the archives door.

Swallowing, she managed, "I've—I've got to speak to Acton."

"I can't go fetch im, I'm to stay w' ye," the man explained. "Let me call to Mathis, and she'll fetch im."

And so they waited together, Grady shielding Doyle against the stone wall, his shotgun at the ready. *"Go raibh maith agat,"* she offered, a bit abashed by her initial reaction.

"Don't mention it, my lady."

In a blessedly short time, Acton could be heard approaching with Mathis. "What's happened?"

"The PC is actually Judge Whitteside," Doyle explained in a rush. "He was going to ride with you to the Met, and you were going to be the next death in custody—I don't know the exact plan, but you were not going to survive."

After the barest pause, her husband sent Mathis for Hudson, and took Grady aside to issue a few quiet orders.

Spent, Doyle closed her eyes, and leaned against the ancient door, listening to the muted pounding from the frustrated villain on the other side, and the muted murmuring of frustrated warriors overhead, who'd been hoping for a pitched battle. I thank You for Maguire's warning, she thought; if I may say so, perhaps You might have been a little clearer, but all's well that ends well, and I've no grounds to quibble.

# 52

Doyle sat with Acton at the long table in the servant's hall as they ate a whole cooked chicken with their hands. Acton had been reluctant to leave her side, and so all villains were now locked up with the local constable, and the Home Secretary had been informed that he should clear his calendar for the next morning, and have the crisis control team brought in.

It was well past midnight, but she'd confessed to her husband that she was starving, crisis or no, and if she didn't eat soon, she'd be gnawing on the bell ropes. Therefore, they'd descended to the kitchen and roused the poor cook, who'd already had her dinner ruined this night, and who was now hovering in the doorway to serve this makeshift meal in her nightgown, emanating equal parts nervousness and wonder.

Doyle bit into a chicken leg with relish. "I'm sleeping with you; none of this separate chambers nonsense."

"No argument here."

She took a swig of cider, straight out of the bottle. "I imagine this is the most excitement the local station house has seen in a while." The local police were still searching for Harding, who'd disappeared without a trace, and although the matron had been arrested and charged, it was as yet unclear whether she would survive the night. Mathis had left, wanting to go straight to the lab to examine a suspicious coffee cup, and no one seemed to remember that Savoie had been a visitor, and so he was not mentioned in the police reports.

Doyle wiped her chin with the back of her hand. "Who's left to charge the DCS with murder? You?"

"We don't have a murder, as the matron has not yet died," Acton pointed out reasonably.

"Oh. Well, I suppose that's to the good," Doyle observed, and tried to mean it. "Murder is murder, Michael, even when it seems like a fine solution to all outstandin' problems." She paused, trying to decide how much to berate him over this—it was nothing that she hadn't said before, a million times. "You can't go about decidin' that there are good containment murders, as opposed to bad ones. They are *all* bad—there's no such thing as an honorable murder."

"I will take it under advisement." He tapped his bottle to hers in a toast, and drank.

Thinking over the evening's events, she twisted off the other chicken leg from the carcass. "Maguire needs to improve on his warnin's, I barely sorted it out in the nick of time."

"I disagree; he warned me very clearly."

This was of interest, and she paused in gnawing on the bone. "Maguire warned *you?*"

"Yes. He'd discovered the Wexton Prison corruption ring, and sent his research to me, knowing that I'd put a stop to it, one way or the other."

Frowning in surprise, Doyle considered this—it did explain why her husband had been troubled about this for months, and so secretive. "Why wouldn't Maguire just post an article in the newspaper, like you will, and expose them?"

"I imagine he was afraid."

Thoughtfully mopping up the juices with a piece of bread, she could only agree. "Yes; he said as much to me, once—said he was a coward, who ran away from the all the problems he'd caused."

"He's atoned, certainly."

Licking her fingers, she could only agree. "In spades; this was a nasty bunch."

"Indeed."

She shook her head in wonder. "And they were so brassy; faith, it's still hard to believe."

"Not such a risk, actually. Remember, they had an easy solution if any investigation was launched—they'd stage their own deaths. And the DCS could always work to neutralize any exigent threat."

"I got 'exigent' wrong," Doyle confessed. "And in front of stupid Mathis, no less."

He leaned in to kiss her. "You got everything else right." He raised his empty bottle to the cook, indicating that he wanted another, and the woman hurried over, her forehead shiny with nervous perspiration.

"Do you think there are any more to be nicked?" She eyed him; watching his reaction. After all, the no-account matron had gone to ground near here, and it seemed evident that someone from Trestles had been conspiring with the evildoers. Sir Stephen, Acton's heir, was mysteriously absent, and no one had offered an explanation as to his whereabouts. It only made sense that someone was lurking about in London to make sure the fair Doyle was well and truly dead—Doyle had assumed it was Harding, but Harding had been needed here, to testify against Acton. And then there was the little matter of Holy Trinity Church, and the Health Professions Council, which seemed to serve as operational command for all the dark doings in greater London.

"I shouldn't wonder."

She wiped her fingers in resignation, knowing this was the best answer she'd get, and then leaned to give him a slightly greasy kiss. "I'm that pleased that reports of my death were extravabated."

He leaned to kiss her back. "I couldn't put it better, myself."

Thus reminded, Doyle looked at the tall clock in the corner. "I forgot to ring up poor Reynolds; the visitin' nurse is no doubt still locked in the laundry room."

"I'll phone Trenton. How did you manage to get by him, this time?"

The words were casual, but Doyle could sense the underlying displeasure, and she rested her wrists on the table's edge. "Can we not tell him I got past him again, Michael? The poor man's going to need a psychiatrist, himself."

Acton paused for a moment, swirling the liquid in his bottle. "I can't seem to keep you in check, can I?"

She ventured, "Best that you don't try, Michael. Truly."

He leaned his shoulder against hers, and again tapped her bottle with his. "All right."

Doyle felt relief flood over her—no longer a princess in a tower, thank all the saints and holy angels; she wasn't cut out to be a princess. She wasn't cut out to be a baroness, either, but Acton had given her little choice.

They ate in silence for a few moments, and as she plucked at the remnants on her chicken leg, she mused, "Maguire was right; it was all very symmetrical. Solonik was plottin' to frame me for murder, and then his sister took up the mantle, and plotted to frame you."

"Solonik was framing you for murder?" asked Acton in a mild tone.

She paused, having forgotten that he didn't know about this troubling little detail. "Oh; oh—I suspected as much," she stammered. "It only makes sense."

"Ah," he said.

Hurriedly, she changed the subject. "You should have seen Williams and Mathis in the car together, Michael; they were brawlin' like Sailortown shants."

This caught his attention, and he paused in lifting his drink. "Is that so? What about?"

She giggled. "They were arguin' about who had the more hopeless devotion."

He stared at her. "Good *God*."

Laughing with delight, she threw her arms around his neck, and clung—so, so happy that they could look back on all this, and laugh. Acton kissed her like he meant it, and the makeshift meal was instantly abandoned so they could retreat to the master's chambers, Doyle beyond caring that the cook would no doubt make a full report of such goings-on to the staff.

Later, they lay entwined in the huge canopied bed, watching the firelight flicker on the wood wainscoting. "Your bed is better," she declared running her fingers along the mattress. "Mine's too soft."

"Then you will have to stay here, for the interim."

"Do you want some scotch, my friend? It's deservin' of it, you are."

"Not yet; I cannot move."

"Good one. My work here is done."

"No it's not; give me a few minutes."

She giggled, and rolled over to place a kiss in the hollow of his throat. "Do your worst; I'll still be the last one standin'."

"We shall see."

She giggled again, and decided to take advantage of his compliant mood. "When can I return to field work, then?"

He was amused, and propped an arm behind his head. "You've caught me in a weak moment, again. Do you know how much the church's new heating system is going to cost?"

"Is it ridiculously expensive? We could break into the fungible assets—we won't be needin' them."

"I'd prefer to leave them alone."

She traced a finger on his chest. "Should Nellie run a raffle, then?"

"I was teasing you; I will pay for the heating system."

Thoughtfully, she watched the moonlight spill through the diamond-leaded window panes—they hadn't bothered to shut the drapes. "If it's all the same to you, I'd like to bury the SOCO in the grave site next to my mother, since I'm to be buried here, with you."

Gently, he closed his hand around hers, on his chest. "We can bring them all here to Trestles, if you'd like."

She thought about this, and absently pulled on the hairs of his chest. "What if you marry again? Wife number two would just kick the lot of us back to London again."

"I would never marry again." It was true.

She smiled and kissed the back of his hand. "Whist, man—that's crazy talk. A good way to get your pregnant wife shot at."

"I won't mention it to anyone else, then."

She rolled onto her back, and nestled into his side. "You know, Michael, that if I was gone, I would be very unhappy to see you drink yourself to death. If I knew about it, that is."

"I know. Let's not test it." He placed his hand on the small mound of her abdomen. His hands were so long that he could span her pelvis between his thumb and small finger.

"He's quiet, tonight," she said.

"What color were your mother's eyes?"

"A pale sort of green." Emotion closed her throat for a silent moment. "He'll be tall, but not as tall as you. My fault."

He was silent for a moment, and she could sense he'd been distracted by something she'd said—what? That Edward would have green eyes? That he wouldn't be as tall?

"Tell me if you see him again."

"I will." Reminded, she added, "Harding's bullet is lodged in one of the—whatever it's called—the wood-carved decorations in the corners of the dinin' room ceilin'." She paused. "There's a woodworker who's very unhappy about it."

Acton didn't miss a beat. "I'll have it removed, forthwith."

She smiled. Well, then; as long as it's 'forthwith,' and not 'interim.' I'd best get back to the vocabulary manual, else I'll have no idea what you and Edward are talkin' about."

"Don't change anything on my account."

She hesitated, then decided she may as well bring it up, because she was not very good at keeping things from her husband—just look at the slip-up she'd just made about Solonik's plot, as an excellent case in point. "Here's the thing, Michael; there's a portrait, hangin' in the foyer. Some sort of ancestor, wearin' lacy cuffs, and with a feather in his hat."

Tracing her fingers with his own, Doyle's husband accepted this rather disjointed change of topic. "Yes, I know the one."

She swallowed. "Well, the man in the portrait seems to think you are some sort of imposter."

There was a small pause. "I am not surprised," he agreed in an even tone.

"Right then; I just wasn't certain that you knew." She waited a beat, then asked, "D'you want to tell me?"

"No."

"Aye, then. You know it doesn't matter a pin to me—faith, I'm the one who would never marry again; no one could hold a candle to you, my friend."

He pulled her against him. "You say that now, but what if Williams is promoted to DCI?"

She laughed, which is what he'd intended, and the tension was broken. "Williams is hip deep in your doin's, husband, and has his own alarmin' moral philosophy."

"Good man."

"You'd best look lively, or you'll lose Mathis to him."

He rolled atop her, pinning her down. "Mathis is not mine to lose."

Whilst he began to kiss her neck, she smiled and addressed the ceiling. "Let's drive somewhere, now that the crisis has passed—we can tour about, like an ordinary mister and missus."

"Brighton?"

"Brighton," she agreed.

41009352R10202

Made in the USA
San Bernardino, CA
03 November 2016